R. GEORGE CLARK

SOUTHBOUND TERROR

This story is a work of fiction. Names, characters, businesses, places, events and incidents are either the products of the author's imagination or used in a fictitious manner. Any resemblance to actual persons, living or dead, or actual events is purely coincidental.

PROLOGUE

The Previous September

In the rolling hills not far from the capital city of Salem, Oregon, a farmer and his two sons are busy harvesting a crop of beans. The area's Mediterranean climate provides a long growing season, perfect for a wide range of agricultural possibilities, including vegetables, sedges, assorted grasses, cherries, Christmas trees, hops, and more recently, wine grapes, especially the vaunted Pinot Noir. The soils of the Willamette Valley are thick with fertile sediments left from the last ice age.

But the crop being harvested today on Sam Park's farm is a fairly new one for the valley; in fact, he is the first farmer in the U.S. to grow and harvest this new variety of beans, the seeds of which were shipped to him from his cousin living in the Hainan Island province of China. To evade the U.S. Department of Agriculture's Animal and Plant Health Inspection Service, the seeds were shipped in a box marked "Electrical Components." The seed, originally from the plant *ricinus communis*, or Castor Bean Plant, had been carefully hybridized in a secluded laboratory to enrich the plant's triglycerides, specifically to boost its ricin levels to over triple its natural output.

Sam and his sons are unaware of the plant's genetic composition, they know only that they are being paid a generous premium for the production and delivery of the beans to a laboratory in New Jersey, where they ostensibly are to be used as a key ingredient in a new weight control remedy.

Sam's two teenage sons both do well in school and although he can get by growing a variety of crops on his two-hundred acre farm, like many farmers he struggles to make ends meet and certainly cannot afford to send them to a good west coast college like Stanford, or Santa Clara University, or even the University of California at Berkeley. But Sam hopes that will soon change. By growing and harvesting these special beans, Sam Park will be able to provide the quality education for his sons that they deserve. And so, for him, plucking the beans from their pods that rest atop the six-foot stalks of the bright red-leafed plants has become a labor of love. He has been warned, however, to always wear protective clothing and breathing equipment during the harvest, lest he and his sons could become sick if the beans, (even a single one), somehow crack open. What his cousin neglected to tell Sam is that ingesting a minute particle of the residue from a damaged bean would not just make him sick, but could result in a most horrific death.

Chapter One

"Come on Archie, what's taking so long?" Marc LaRose muttered to himself as he waited for his target to appear.

Seated in the rear of his Civic, surrounded by fifty other cars parked in the Elizabethtown County offices' parking lot, the clock on his dash read 1:00 p.m. The mid-day August sun was hovering overhead in a blue cloudless sky, and the bank thermometer across the street registered a sweltering ninety-five degrees. To get some relief, Marc slid the Civic's tinted windows down a crack, which did little more than let in more hot summer air. He was tempted to start the car's engine and turn on the air conditioning, but he knew that doing so could attract undue attention from passers-by. Workers' compensation fraud surveillance can have its exciting moments, but this was not one of them.

Marc LaRose, a licensed private investigator, had recently accepted a workers' compensation surveillance assignment of a former town of Moira employee, one Archibald Dermody.

According to the risk management firm, Dermody had been employed at the Moira Highway Department, when four months earlier he claimed a back injury while loading hand tools into a town truck. Not surprisingly, there were no witnesses to the incident that took him over a week to report.

Dermody located a family physician in Plattsburgh who, after examination, concluded his pain symptoms were so severe he should remain out of work and refrain from physical activity. Marc noted that the X-rays failed to show any signs of injury. According to the doctor, however, sitting at a desk was also out of the question as it would cause more pain. He also felt Dermody should be placed on full disability pending the outcome of a lengthy therapy regimen.

Sources reported that since he began collecting his monthly disability checks, Dermody's injuries had not prevented him from filling his idle hours with a home construction project. From previous surveillances, Marc had noticed the size and shape of this new venture situated adjacent to Dermody's present abode, a dilapidated hunting camp he and his live-in lady call home, appeared suspiciously suited to hold the frame of a double-wide mobile home. To this end, Marc noted that Mr. Dermody seemed to find renewed strength and stamina, providing his own labor, much of it by hand, all the while insisting his back pain was too severe to return to his employment with the town highway department.

Marc has spent much of the past month in his camouflaged ghillie suit, lying on his belly suffering the stings and bites of Adirondack black flies and mosquitoes while surreptitiously surveilling his target from a nearby wood lot, as Demody poured sweat equity into the construction of this new foundation. He patiently watched as Dermody scrubbed the area of offending pine, maple, and spruce trees, cutting them to ground level with a powerful chain saw, which led Marc to wonder when the Moira Highway Department last took inventory of their hand tools.

Armed with his video camera, Marc returned each day to the secluded position to observe Dermody, as he cut the downed trees into neat face cord length logs perfect for a wood stove. After the lot was sufficiently cleared, Dermody meticulously measured and staked the outline of the foundation that would support his dream manse, then carefully measured, cut, and assembled the forms meant to hold the concrete in place. Marc watched as Dermody mixed yards of concrete using an electric mixer, curiously painted the same orange color as the Moriah Town Highway trucks. Then, he repeatedly loaded the mixed cement into an orange wheelbarrow and maneuvered it up and over a temporary scaffold, filling the forms with the concrete that would hold his future manufactured palace well up off the ground.

At the moment however, Marc's concern for the whereabouts of Mr. Dermody was assuaged as he caught sight of the main door to the Essex County Social Services office opening, and held there by a passing Good Samaritan, assisting this seemingly pathetic cripple.

Of course the 'cripple' is Archibald Dermody, and as Marc activated his video camera, Dermody shuffled along the sidewalk behind his shiny new walker. Marc continued to video as his target padded onto the hot tarmac, the two cut out tennis balls attached to the back legs of the walker scuffing along as he slowly propelled himself toward his waiting pickup truck conveniently parked in the handicapped parking zone.

Marc documented Dermody's exaggerated anguish as he continued his ruse, all the while holding a large manila envelope under his arm that contained his approved food stamp application as well as a spanking new benefits card. Through the Honda's tinted windows, Marc watched, as Archibald reached his Chevy truck and carefully folded the walker, then, let it drop into the open back of the pick-up. Leaning against the side of his truck for support, Dermody slid his way toward the driver's door, opened it, tossed the folder on the passenger seat, and finally fell inside the truck, slamming the door shut behind him.

"And the envelope please," Marc whispered to himself, silently congratulating Dermody on another stellar performance, as his camera continued to catch the action.

Dermody started his engine and pointed its nose toward the parking lot exit. After watching the pick-up pass a row of cars, Marc slid into the front seat, turned the Civic's ignition key, and started after the Chevy.

"Come on air conditioning," he whispered.

Although Elizabethtown, N.Y. is the Essex County seat, it is nonetheless a small town and Marc was aware many of the "locals" know each other by sight, and the vehicles they drive, so tailing someone without arousing suspicion in a rural village can be a challenge. Marc kept a discreet distance between him and his target.

As Dermody turned north out of the parking lot onto State Route 9, Marc already suspected where old Archie might be heading this hot afternoon. Although Dermody maintained his residence of record at the shack next to his foundation project, today he was heading in the opposite direction toward the hamlet of Lewis, a five-minute drive to the north.

Over the past few weeks, Marc discovered Dermody has an apparent ongoing relationship with another woman he visits when her husband, also an employee of the Moriah Town Highway Department, is at work, keeping the town roads in safe repair.

Sure enough, as Archie's pickup approached Lewis, the truck made a left turn onto the long dirt driveway. The red and white doublewide trailer, perched on a knoll at the end of the driveway was easily visible from the road. A clothes-line connected to a light pole at one end and an 80's style satellite dish at the other end was heavy with sheets, towels and a few colorful undergarments that hung dead still in the hot afternoon sun.

Marc continued a short distance past the driveway, then whipped the Civic into the parking lot of the Lewis Post Office. Quickly he slid to the passenger seat and focused his high definition video camera with its 30 X optical zoom.

The camera's record button chimed as it caught Archibald Dermody alighting from his pickup, then, at full gallop running past the line of pink undies, dangling black bra straps and stained white tube socks toward the side door of the double-wide. Marc smiled as he recorded every hop, skip, and apparent pain-free jump that Archey took before he climbed the stack of cinder block steps and disappeared inside the trailer.

"The lure of those workers comp benefits will do it every time," Marc muttered with a grin, knowing this case was pretty much a wrap.

He packed his camera away, backed out of the post office parking lot, and turned the Civic north onto Route 9, toward the City of Plattsburgh, some forty miles distant.

Chapter Two

Marc arrived at his favorite parking spot on Margaret Street in downtown Plattsburgh, then made the walk to his office located on the second floor of a three story converted apartment building. The bottom floor storefront of Marc's building is presently occupied by Mia's Beauty Salon; last year it was a Chinese take-out.

He climbed the interior stairwell to his office that he shares with an old police buddy, Norm Prendergast. The office door was locked; Norm is probably out somewhere serving summonses, he surmised.

'Back in the day,' they'd worked together as New York State Police investigators. After retiring from the force, Marc started his own private detective firm. Norm, not a big "people" person, went into the process serving business. It wasn't long before the two decided to share an office space to cut down on expenses. Notwithstanding the friendly jabs that had become routine, each has amassed a bounty of local knowledge and occasionally assist each other as the need arises.

As he unlocked the office door, Marc was greeted by the cool pleasantness from the air conditioner humming from its perch above the room's single window. Inside the one room office were two metal desks, butted together, each with the empty square of a darkened computer screen. There is one floor lamp, a coat rack, an apartment size fridge and three desk chairs, one for each desk and an extra that Norm uses as a foot rest.

Marc noticed that Norm had been in the office earlier in the day as evidenced by the littering of cookie crumbs and a half-filled coffee cup on his desk. Or maybe it's from yesterday he thought, after eyeing the coagulated blotch of yellow cream floating in the dregs of Norm's mug.

"I pity that boy's momma," Marc muttered to the empty room.

The red light on Marc's answering machine blinked '5', indicating there were voice messages to be retrieved.

"They'll have to wait," Marc muttered as his computer screen lit up and he began the process of filing his report for the risk management company.

Although Marc has a basic cell phone, he doesn't rely on it for all his calls due the nature of his business and the fact that coverage in the Adirondacks is spotty at best. Smart phones, blogs, and twitter are not a part of his lexicon.

Referring to his daily log sheets, Marc's report outlined the investigative actions including the still photos, video, interviews conducted, a listing of his mileage and expenses, complete with a final tabulation of his bill for services rendered.

Marc's report will show no judgments or conclusions regarding the appropriateness of Mr. Dermody's actions, only what he observed and heard. Conclusions are the sole purview of the Workers' Compensation Board Referee who will make a determination after a hearing is conducted, probably long after Mr. Dermody is comfortably ensconced inside his shiny new manufactured home.

An hour later, Marc's report is sealed inside a Priority Mail envelope ready for shipment to the Risk Management firm in Albany.

After mailing his report, Marc made the short drive to Shirley's Flower Shop.

Shirley, the local florist is also Marc's ex, and although the two had been divorced for over five years, they stay in touch, calling one another every few days. A set of metal chimes fastened to the door announced his entrance.

"Hi, Dad." A petite lass with a blond pony tail, dressed in blue jeans and flip-flops with a green flower shop smock welcomed Marc. Marc smiled at Ann Marie, the sole product of Marc and Shirley's union. Besides attending the local State University, she still helped her mom in the flower shop.

"I thought you had classes today. Summer session's not over already, is it?" Marc asked.

"Dad, it's well past noon. You know I only do morning classes. Besides, I need the work. I've got expenses too, you know."

"Saving up for a new car?"

"Yeah, right! You know mom won't let me buy a car until I graduate. I need some new clothes for fall and besides, I can always use extra spending money."

"New clothes? Oh, that's right. You've finally graduated out of that grunge phase you were taken up with. So, what's it now? A post-retro-outdoorsy thing with red and black checkered trousers and woolen scarves?"

"Look who's talking? I've seen your old school photos."

"I give up, you win. Is Mom around?"

"Uh, she left about a half hour ago to make a few flower deliveries. Should be back around five or so. Don't imagine you'll want to hang that long," Ann Marie said with a hint of angst.

Marc hesitated. "Something wrong?"

"Nope," she answered a little too quickly. Then recovered, "Why? What could be wrong?" she added.

"Nothing, you just seem a little nervous about something."

"Sorry, maybe I'm more tired than I thought," she said.

"That's OK sweetie. Tell mom I stopped by," he said as he turned back to the front door.

"Will do, Daddy."

"Tell her I'll make it up to her. Love you."

"Love you too, Dad."

Marc left the flower shop feeling kind of funny about the exchange with his daughter. He'd been aware of Ann Marie's becoming her own woman and knew it wouldn't be long before she would be out on her own. Since he and Shirley had been apart, he regretted missing some of Ann Marie's best years, he thought wistfully.

By the time he reached his car, he realized he'd forgotten to retrieve the messages from his answering machine. Rather than return to the office however, he figured he'd get them from his condo.

Marc's cats, Brandy and Rye, greeted him as he opened his front door. Both weaved around his ankles as he made his way inside, meowing and purring at the same time.

"You guys missed me that much, or is it because your kibble bowls are cleaned out?" Marc asked, to which the cats replied by continuing their dance as he made his way to the kitchen. He refilled their bowls, then took a peek inside the refrigerator, grabbed the last can of beer and peeled the tab back.

With cold beer in hand, he slid a blank sheet of paper from the copy machine tray located in his office/living room, and dialed his office number. When it answered, he entered the code to access his messages.

The first was from a housewife asking for his domestic investigation's rate. Although he disliked 'domestics,' he'd make a point to return her call and if need be, steer her toward another PI, or offer some free counseling to assuage her anxiety. The second was an old state police chum, Tim Golden, looking to play golf at the Bluff Point Country Club.

Sorry Tim, too hot, even for golf.

Marc made a mental note to return Tim's call.

The third and fourth were hang-ups, "Pain in the ass telemarketers," he informed the cats, who were lying at his feet, licking whatever it is that cats enjoy licking. The last message was from a woman. At first Marc assumed it was another domestic inquiry, but as he continued to listen, he learned otherwise.

Her voice was accented and, apparently unaccustomed to talking to a machine, she spoke haltingly, half expecting the device to respond. Marc noted her voice didn't have the anxious tenor of a jilted lover, but was rather matter-of-fact, simply stating that she needed to speak with Mr. LaRose regarding her missing husband, followed by her phone number.

"Well boys, what do you think? Shall we see what Annika's got to say?" Brandy made for the kitchen, while Rye continued licking.

"Some help you are." Marc said as he dialed the number.

After the first eight rings, Marc figured he'd be calling back at another time, when a voice answered with a simple, "Hello".

Marc recognized it as the woman who left the message.

"Is this Annika?"

"Yes," she said, skeptically.

"My name is Marc LaRose. I believe you left a message to return your call. Something about your husband missing?"

There was a pause, "Yes, Mr. LaRose. You're the detective I tried to reach earlier today. I didn't hear back and presumed you might not call."

"I just got in. How can I help you?"

Another pause, then, “I’d rather not discuss this over the phone. Is it possible to meet someplace?” she asked.

“I have an office downtown on Margaret Street. Are you familiar with Mia’s Beauty Salon?”

Another pause.

By now, Marc figured if this woman was calling from a cell phone, she must have unlimited minutes because she was short on information and long on dead air.

“What if you came to my house instead?” Annika finally offered.

Before Marc could reply, the woman gave Marc the address. He immediately recognized the street. It was located on the Old Plattsburgh Air Force Base officer’s quarters.

“OK, when’s a good time?” Marc asked.

“How about half an hour, around five thirty, if that would be acceptable to you, Mr. LaRose.”

Now it was Marc’s turn to pause, as he mentally checked his schedule.

“Mr. LaRose?”

“Yes, sorry. I was just thinking. That’s not far from where I live.”

“I know Mr. LaRose, thank you.”

Before Marc could respond, he heard a click, then the dial tone.

Mark set the handset back into its cradle. As he finished the can of beer, he replayed the conversation in his mind, then, glanced at the wall clock.

“OK boys, out of my way, I’ve just enough time for a quick shower,” he said, sending the cats scurrying.

Thirty minutes later Marc arrived at the address Annika had given him. It was one of several imposing brick structures that previously housed the base’s senior military staff overlooking the old parade grounds.

As Marc climbed the front steps he vaguely remembered this particular residence once housed the former deputy commander and his family when the base was a thriving Strategic Air Force command some twenty years before.

As he was about to ring the doorbell, a rather dignified looking woman opened the door.

"Good afternoon, Mr. LaRose. Thank you for coming on such short notice. Please come inside where it's cool."

"You must be Annika," Marc stated as he followed her into a darkened parlor, shaded by heavy curtains covering eight-foot high windows.

"Oh, yes. Please forgive me. With all that's happened I've forgotten my manners."

Marc noticed his prospective client was as tall as he and appeared to be in her mid fifties. Her pleasant face was accentuated with blond hair with threads of gray, worn in a bun. Despite the warm weather outside, Annika seemed comfortable in her long-sleeved wool jacket. Her form-fitting green slacks went well with her toned physique.

"Please, Mr. LaRose, have a seat," she said, gesturing toward an ornate *chaise* that Marc suspected was an original Louis XV Fauteuil Armchair.

"Can I offer you something to drink? Coffee, tea, a soft drink perhaps?"

"No thank you Ms."… Marc said, fishing for her family name.

"It's Karlsson, Annika Karlsson, that's with two n's in Annika and two s's in Karlsson.

"Swedish?" Marc asked, immediately regretting this foray into guessing one's nationality.

"Close, but no. My husband and I are from Finland."

"Sorry!"

"It's a common mistake. We immigrated to Canada ten years ago, but, you see, we're stuck with our native accents for life."

"So, your husband is missing?" Marc asked, crossing his legs while pulling his note pad from his breast pocket.

"Yes. Hugo, that's his name, of course. Hugo Karlsson."

"What makes you think Hugo's missing?" Marc asked.

She paused, gazing at one of the curtained windows before answering. "Wednesday, he left for the home office in Brossard, Quebec. That was around 7:30 in the morning. He travels there once or twice a month for company meetings. He said he'd return later in the afternoon. He rarely stays overnight and when he does, he calls to let me know. I've tried him on his cell phone numerous times, and left messages. No answer."

He left Wednesday, so she hasn't heard from him in two days, Marc thought.

"Who does your husband work for?"

"Barbeau Transport. As you're probably aware, they have an assembly plant here in Plattsburgh, but the headquarters is in Brossard."

"Have you talked to anyone at Barbeau?"

"Yes, the plant manager, Mr. St. Onge. He said they missed Hugo at the meeting, but assumed he was ill."

"Have you notified the police?"

Marc noticed Annika's eyes water as she dabbed them with a tissue.

"Yesterday. A nice young officer came and I told him what I've told you. He asked for Hugo's information. You know, name, date of birth, height, weight, and so on. He said they would enter the information into the national missing person's database. He was very polite, but I got the impression 'missing males' aren't very high on their priority. When he left he said to be sure to call when Hugo returned. Mr. LaRose, I've known Hugo for over thirty years. I'm afraid something bad has happened to him," she said, and quietly wept into the now fragmented tissue she held in both hands. Marc gave her a moment to compose herself.

"I'm sorry, Mr. LaRose. This has never happened before. I know what you're thinking, but Hugo has been a faithful husband for thirty-two years. Besides, Hugo and I have a special bond. We have no family in either the U.S. or Canada and very few friends. We rely on each other for practically everything. I would know if Hugo had found someone else."

Marc handed her his fresh handkerchief, which she immediately took. This was not going to be the short interview he had envisioned as he waited for her to again regain her composure.

"I understand how difficult this must be for you, Ms. Karlsson, but I'm afraid I have to ask you some of the same questions the police did, such as your husband's physical description, clothing, make of car and license plate number, that sort of thing. If you prefer, we could continue this later."

"No, please don't go, Mr. LaRose. I only need a moment."

As Marc waited, he glanced around the room and noticed a framed eight by ten photograph of Annika and a man about the same age as her propped on an end table.

Reaching over to pick up the photo, Marc hesitated, "May I?"

Annika glanced up from the handkerchief, snuffed away tears, and nodded her assent.

"It was taken this past winter, mid February. You probably recognize the Valcour Island lighthouse. Hugo and I were cross-country skiing on Lake Champlain and we thought the lighthouse would make a lovely background. The ice on the lake must have been over a foot thick. It was such a beautiful day.

Judging from the photo, Hugo was six inches taller than Annika, which put him at about six-four, probably around two hundred pounds. He didn't appear to be your typical computer nerd, rather a dignified middle-aged gentleman with a thick mane of white hair who seemed to have taken good care of himself. Marc recognized the lighthouse sitting above the rocky cliffs of the Island behind them.

"Do you have any other recent photos of Hugo I could take? I'll make a copy and return the original."

"I don't think so. Why don't you take the one you're holding, but I would like it back, please."

"Certainly," Marc said as he set the photo on a coffee table and retrieved his notepad. Annika appeared to have collected herself sufficiently.

"What is the make of the car he uses?" Marc asked.

"It's a company car. A Lexus, I think. But I'm not sure."

Marc made a note to check with Barbeau Transport for its description.

"Do you know who Hugo worked with at Barbeau Transport, or perhaps the name of his supervisor?"

Annika thought for a moment, "Originally he was with research and development, but recently he was made the project manager for one of Barbeau's new trains, but I don't recall him mentioning who he worked with. The local plant manager is Jean Pierre St. Onge, but Hugo told me he reported directly to the president of Barbeau in Brossard, Quebec.

"You mentioned that you called St. Onge when Hugo hadn't returned home; did you talk to him about your husband's disappearance?"

"Disappearance?" Annika said, turning her head toward the curtained window again. "Forgive me, Mr. LaRose, I hadn't thought about Hugo not coming home from work as a 'disappearance'. It sounds so final."

Marc regretted using the word, given Annika's sensitive mental state and decided to change the line of questioning.

"Have you noticed any changes in Hugo's behavior lately?"

"I don't understand, Mr. LaRose."

"You said he is a project manager. Was there any indication that something at work was bothering Hugo?"

"No, nothing I can think of. He seemed to be concerned with the upcoming meeting in Brossard, but that's not unusual. He takes his work seriously."

Marc closed his notebook. "I think I have enough to get started. Let me make a few inquiries. In the meantime, if you hear anything, please let me know," Marc said as he stood.

"What about your fee?" Annika asked as she too rose from her chair.

"Ordinarily, I get a $500 retainer, but let me make those inquiries first. We'll discuss my fee later," Marc said as he made his way toward the door.

"As you wish, Mr. LaRose, and thank you for seeing me on such short notice. I'm sorry about your handkerchief; I'll get you a new one," she said as she opened the front door.

"Not to worry. I'll report back to you in a day or so, but let's hope we hear something before then," he said, and made his way to his car.

As Marc drove to his office, he mentally reviewed what Annika had told him. The first thing he wanted to do was to have a chat with Hugo's boss, Mr. St. Onge.

When he got to his office, Norm Prendergast was sitting at his desk working on a daily racing form.

"Got your winners picked out?" Marc asked, knowing Norm's penchant for off track betting, but also aware that his betting history was below the 'break even' point.

"Ever heard of a horse named Palace Malice?" he asked.

Marc thought a moment. "Name's kind of familiar. Where's she running?

"She's a he, and he's not running anywhere."

"So why are you asking?"

"He's supposed to have sired a horse running next week in Saratoga's Travers Stakes. I'm thinking about putting a few dollars down on him."

Marc rolled his eyes, "Good luck with that. But look, I've got something a little more meaningful to ask you."

Norm paused and looked up from the racing form, "Your breaking my concentration here, it better be important."

"You still have any contacts at the Brossard PD?"

"Of course, doesn't everybody?" he asked with a tinge of sarcasm.

"Think you could hook me up? I might need some help with something I'm working on across the border," Marc said.

"Gonna cost you."

"I imagined as much. So what's his name?

"He's a she, and her name is Sylvie, Sylvie Champagne. Hold on a minute, I've got her number here someplace," Norm said as he scrolled through his smart phone, then, scribbled a number on a note pad, tore off the page and handed it to Marc.

"Thanks," Marc said as he glanced at the number, then stuffed the note in his pocket before heading for the door.

"Aren't you forgetting something?" Norm said.

"Yeah, I know; Mickey D's egg and tater special. Think you can hold out until tomorrow?"

Chapter Three

It was after eight-thirty the following morning when Marc dropped the grease-stained bag with Norm's breakfast special on his desk, then proceeded to charge up the coffee machine. As the aging Mr. Coffee started to wheeze, a quick Google search revealed the main phone number for the Barbeau Transport offices. Marc placed a call.

"Barbeau Transport, how may I direct your call?" the nasally receptionist answered.

"I'd like to speak to Jean Pierre St. Onge please."

"Is Mr. St. Onge expecting your call, sir?"

"Probably not. My name is Marc LaRose. I'm a private investigator and I need to speak with Mr. St. Onge regarding one of his employees."

There was a short pause. "Mr. St. Onge is in a meeting. Is there a number where you can be reached?"

Marc gave the receptionist his cell number.

"I'll make sure he gets your message, sir. Thank you." The click left Marc holding a dead phone.

As Marc replaced the handset in its cradle, the office door opened with a bang. He looked up to see Norm balancing a half-eaten sugar donut atop a lidded Styrofoam coffee cup with one hand and clutching a stack of legal folders in the other.

Closing the door with his foot, Norm spotted the take-out breakfast bag sitting on his desk.

"Damn, I didn't think you'd remember," he said, dropping the files on the desk and shoving the remnants of the donut in his mouth.

"I'm sure you can handle both," Marc retorted.

"Have you talked to Detective Champagne yet?" Norm asked in a muffled voice, sending a plume of powdered sugar in Marc's direction.

"Not yet. I'm waiting on another call. I'd like to find out a little more of what I'm dealing with first."

Dave Brubeck's *Take Five* chimed on his cell. The caller ID indicated 'Barbeau Transport.'

"Marc LaRose."

"Mister LaRose, this is Jean Pierre St. Onge. I have a message to call you. Something about one of my employees?"

"Thank you for getting back to me. Any chance we could talk about this in person rather than on the phone?"

"I think I know what this is about. Unfortunately, I'm booked this morning, but could we get together for lunch?"

"Sure. Anyplace in particular?"

"How about Antoine's at noon? I'll be driving a silver BMW."

"Antoine's it is," Marc said, and ended the call.

"Hope he's buying. I don't think Antoine's does two-fers," Norm said, already half-way through his sack of the "Big Breakfast" special.

"That's what's nice about sharing an office with a penny-pinching eavesdropper. I get free advice about restaurants he's too cheap to eat at."

"Anytime I can help, Marky," Norm said, as he stabbed a soggy Tater Tot with his plastic fork.

"Norm, what do you know about Barbeau Transport, other than they assemble passenger train cars?"

"Well, they're one of Plattsburgh's biggest employers, about six hundred full-time. Produce around a hundred and twenty rail cars a year at $1.5 mil a copy. Pay pretty good, but most of the managers are Canadian. Overall, I'd say the Plattsburgh economy would be up the creek without Barbeau."

"How do you know so much about this stuff?"

"When you work for as many attorneys as I do, serving subpoenas, running errands, and being their all around butt-boy, you assimilate a lot of local trivia."

"So, who is Barbeau's competition?" Marc asked.

"Locally? Nobody. Worldwide? There's an emerging stable of contenders. Why?"

"Nothing. Just building some background for this missing person case I'm working on."

"I'd be surprised if you get much from St. Onge. He's strictly a numbers guy—cost per unit, productivity, down time, that sort of shit."

“Maybe so, but I have to start someplace,” Marc said as he grabbed his car keys and started for the door.

“Go get’em tiger,” Marc heard Norm call out between bites as the door closed.

With a little time to kill before meeting St. Onge, Marc drove to the Plattsburgh Police station in the hopes of talking with the officer who had interviewed Annika Karlsson. When he arrived, he was greeted by the desk sergeant, Dave Rabideau, who Marc remembered from his state police days.

“Hey, Marc, long time no see.”

“How’re you doing, Dave?”

“Getting older, fatter, and not much wiser. What brings you to the house of Plattsburgh’s finest this warm July morning?”

“You guys answered a complaint a couple days ago on the Old Base. Annika Karlsson. She reported her husband, Hugo, as missing. Just wanted to know what you’ve got on this so far.”

“Sounds like someone’s got a new client.”

“It’s a living,” Marc said with a shrug.

“Let me check the log,” Dave said as he wiggled the mouse to light up his computer screen, then scrolled down a few pages.

“Yep, here she is. Thursday afternoon. Ms. Annika Karlsson. She said her husband failed to return home Wednesday evening after a business trip to Brossard. You probably have this already.”

“Is there anything else?”

Rabideau continued to scan the computerized police blotter entry. “A patrol was dispatched to interview the complainant, Ms. Karlsson, at her home on the Old Plattsburgh Air Base Oval. She gave the patrol a physical description of her husband, Hugo, but no vehicle data. Stated he was using a company car.”

Rabideau turned toward Marc, “If we don’t hear anything in another day or so, we’ll put Mr. Karlsson’s name in the National Crime Information Center’s data base. But you remember how these things usually work out, Marc. The old man goes off alone, finds a honey, and decides to extend the business meeting a couple extra nights. When he finally gets home, he throws himself at the mercy of the old lady and begs for forgiveness.”

“You may be right Dave, but could you do me another favor?”

"Shoot."

"The U.S. Customs and Border Protection keep records of everyone entering the U.S. Would you mind calling their Champlain office and ask if they have a record of Hugo re-entering since Wednesday? I'd do it myself, but being a civilian, they'd probably tell me to go pound salt."

"Can't hurt to ask," Dave said as he penciled a note on a pad. He turned from the computer back to Marc. "Look, I just put on a fresh pot. Got a few minutes?"

"Sure, why not," Marc said, not one to pass up an opportunity to cultivate relationships with the police.

As Marc accepted the mug of fresh coffee, he asked, "So what's up in town, anything new?"

"Just the usual. The annual Mayor's cup sailboat race out on the lake went off without much trouble. A boat from Burlington won again. The Fourth of July celebration with the big fireworks display by the monument drew the usual crowds, but of course, we had to arrest three or four local mutts for disorderly. There's another bass fishing tournament coming up in August. That should keep the marinas hopping. Then, of course, there's the preparations for Amtrak's inaugural run of their new passenger train next week."

"New passenger train? What's that about?" Marc asked with a puzzled look.

"Where've you been? Amtrak's showcasing its newest passenger train. They call it the 'Laser.' The inaugural run will take it from Montreal through Plattsburgh, on to Albany, then down to New York City. Supposedly, this new train will cut the travel time in half, and the best part is 'The Laser' is built right here in Plattsburgh by Barbeau Transport."

"I knew Barbeau made subway cars for big city metro systems, but this is the first I've heard about anything called 'The Laser.'"

"Until recently, Barbeau's been pretty tight-lipped about it. It's being touted as 'The Next Generation of Rail Travel,' whatever the hell that means. Anyway, it supposedly has an enhanced propulsion system and the ability to take corners at higher speeds. As you know, the tracks that run along the lake have plenty of twists and turns."

"I'll say. Last time we took the train from Plattsburgh, it took four hours to get to Albany. I can get there in less than three by car," Marc said.

"According to the press release, the Laser will get you to Albany in two hours and all the way to New York City in three."

"Whoa, that's fast. So, whose idea was this?"

"Like I said, Barbeau's building the engines and the cars. I understand they have a contract with Amtrak to build forty of them."

"Barbeau Transport, huh? Sounds promising," Marc said thinking about his latest case.

"Yep. Rumor has it that the Premier of Quebec and the Mayors of both Montreal and Plattsburgh will be on-board, picking up the governor in Albany. Then, they're going to have a big shindig when it arrives at Penn Station, with the governor, a bunch of Senators, maybe even the Vice President, right there at the end of the line. And guess who else?"

"I can't wait," Marc scoffed.

"The Plattsburgh High School Band will also be on board to perform when they get to Albany and New York. That should help put our little burg on the map."

"I'm sure every news camera in the North Country will be on this," Marc said as he took a swallow of his coffee.

Both men, veterans of staged political photo-ops, chuckled knowingly.

"Yeah, and the city has allocated an extra five thousand for overtime, but we'll probably use that up pretty quick."

"Good time to start padding your retirement," Marc said with a chuckle.

"So Marc, you look good; retirement's obviously treating you well."

"Working for myself has its benefits. The best one is I don't have some crotchety supervisor to answer to," Marc said, thinking back to last winter's case in Lake Placid.

"But it must be nice to set your own hours, and pick and choose your cases. Sounds good to me," Dave said.

"If that were only true," Marc said, shaking his head.

Just then, a patrolmen with the face of a teenager stuck his head in the door, “Sarge, we got a woman out here, wants to make a complaint. She got a speeding ticket. Says the officer was rude.”

“Tell her ‘tough shit. If she’d slow down, the officer wouldn’t have been so rude.’”

The young officer’s gaze froze for a second.

“Just kidding. I’ll be right there,” Dave said, shaking his head.

As the officer left, Dave turned toward Marc, “Fucking rookies, don’t know how to take a joke.”

“You had me convinced,” Marc added, “Looks like you’ve got some ‘politicking’ of your own to do.”

When they stood, Marc glanced at his watch, “I should be going anyway. Thanks for the coffee and bringing me up to speed about the deal with the Laser.”

“My pleasure. If anything comes up on your missing person, I’ll let you know.”

“Thanks, Dave. I’ll do the same.”

Chapter Four

When Marc got to his Civic, the dash clock read eleven thirty.

Just as well get over to Antoine's and wait for St. Onge.

When Marc arrived at Antoine's parking lot, it was still early and the lot was only about half full. He found a spot with a view to anyone entering the lot. A few minutes later he saw a silver BMW pull in a few spaces away. Marc watched the male driver get out of the car and survey the parking lot.

St. Onge was tall, a little over six feet, about forty-five, Marc figured, fit, black hair graying at the temples.

When Marc exited his Civic, St. Onge eyed him over the roofs of the cars parked between them. Marc gave a short wave as St. Onge removed his Ray-Ban Aviators, and started in Marc's direction.

"You must be Marc LaRose," he said. Marc noted a hint of Quebecois accent.

"And you're Mr. St. Onge?" Marc replied as the two shook hands.

"Jean Pierre, or JP, please."

"Thank you for taking time to meet me on such short notice. Let's get out of this heat," Marc said, motioning toward the restaurant entrance.

Once inside, they were seated in a booth with a window overlooking an herb garden. Two ice waters were quickly delivered along with menus.

"I'll return for your orders, gentlemen," the waitress said, and retreated toward the kitchen.

"So, apparently no word yet on Hugo's whereabouts?" St. Onge asked.

"Nothing so far."

"How can I help?" St. Onge asked with a concerned look.

"We'll get to that. First, I have a few questions."

"Sure," St. Onge said taking a sip of water.

"How long have you known Mr. Karlsson?"

"Hugo's been with Barbeau for over five years. Solid employee."

"What's his position with Barbeau?"

"Besides heading our R&D team, he was, is, the overall systems components coordinator for the Laser project."

"Systems component coordinator? Sounds pretty technical," Marc said.

"Fancy way of saying he is the project manager. Without getting too specific, the Laser is built around several proprietary operating systems that work together as a totally self-contained unit. The on-board systems communicate with each other to make millions of split second decisions. Karlsson put this system together for Barbeau, practically single handed."

Just then, the waitress returned.

"So gentlemen, have we decided?"

St. Onge motioned to Marc to order first while he continued to scan the menu.

"Rueben with fries and a Diet Coke."

"Sounds good. Same for me; and just one tab please," St. Onge said.

"I'll get this right in, gentlemen," the waitress said as she left.

"So Mrs. Karlsson told me Hugo was going to Brossard for a company meeting. What was the meeting about, if you don't mind my asking?" Marc said.

"I'm not sure of the specifics, only that Hugo had a concern he wanted to talk with the head office about. Unfortunately, he missed the meeting, so we have no idea what he was concerned about."

"So Hugo never showed up?" Marc asked.

"No, the meeting was scheduled to start at nine, Wednesday morning. At first we thought he was probably held up at the border crossing. Even though he has a Nexus Card allowing him to bypass tie-ups, the crossing is always busy this time of year. Around 10:00 a.m. I called his cell. No answer, so I left a message. We had other business to conduct, so we continued with the meeting thinking he'd still show. When he hadn't arrived for lunch, we called his home, but again there was no response. We didn't realize he was missing until the following morning when his wife called and said he didn't return home Wednesday evening."

"Do you know if he actually crossed the border into Canada?" Marc asked.

"No. We only know he didn't show up for the meeting. His wife said he left Wednesday morning and was expected to return later that evening. That's about it."

"Does Hugo's disappearance have any effect on the Laser's inaugural trip next week?" Marc asked.

"I see you've done your homework. I like that," St. Onge said, sipping his water, apparently collecting his thoughts. "But to answer your question, no, it shouldn't have any major effect. All systems have been tested and retested. Despite Hugo's latest concern, everything checks out and is on schedule. We're still a go for next week."

"Outside of his wife, you were probably closer to him than anybody else in Plattsburgh. Any ideas as to what may have caused him to miss the meeting?" Marc asked.

St. Onge paused, "If you're thinking he has a girlfriend, or something like that, I'd be very surprised. He's not like that. I can only say his disappearance, besides being highly unusual, is a bit troubling."

"How's that?" Marc asked.

"Hugo is not only a valued employee and the best in the business; he's dependable, good natured and gets along with everyone, which in this industry is not easy to do. Building a system as complicated as the Laser takes a team of highly trained people working together and Hugo made it happen."

"Did Hugo have any history of tardiness, taking unscheduled days off, anything like that?" Marc asked.

"You could set your watch by him. Another reason this is so troubling."

Marc hesitated as he thought how to frame his next question.

Just then, the waitress appeared with their lunch orders and set their plates on the table.

"Anything else I can get you, gentlemen?"

"A little vinegar, perhaps?" St. Onge asked.

"Certainly, sir."

Within a moment she retrieved a small cruet from a nearby pantry and placed it alongside St. Onge's plate. "Will there be anything else?"

"No thanks, this is perfect," he exclaimed, gingerly sprinkling the vinegar on his fries. Then, after the waitress left, he returned his attention to Marc, "Now where were we?"

"I understand he was using a company vehicle. Could I get its description and plate number?" Marc asked.

"Sure. I'll get that for you when I get back to the office."

The two ate in silence for a few moments.

"If it turns out that an affair is the cause of his sudden disappearance, I would truly be shocked," Jean Pierre said, before taking a fork full of his vinegar scented fries.

"So," Marc summed up, "What I'm hearing is that Hugo's work ethic is solid. He always shows up on time. He isn't prone to stray. He's devoted to his wife, and the pressures of the job don't seem to be an issue. Does Hugo have any close friends? A co-worker or perhaps someone he knew outside of work, or shared lunch with?"

Jean Pierre slowly dabbed the corners of his mouth with his napkin, then, seemed to study the remains of his lunch on his plate. "As big as this project is, Hugo had a pretty tight management contingent, only himself and three engineers plus a couple of techs. They work pretty closely, but I don't know if he had any favorites." He finally said.

"Is there anything else I can get for you, gentlemen?" The waitress asked, as she was passing by.

"Just the check," St. Onge said, still somewhat detached.

After the waitress left, Marc asked, "Any chance I could speak to Karlsson's co-workers?"

"Let me see what I can do. As you know, the schedule's pretty tight right now with the rollout coming up. I'll get back to you on that," St. Onge said.

The waitress returned a moment later with a leather folder and laid it on the table.

St. Onge picked it up and quickly glanced over as a couple sat down at a nearby table. "If you don't mind, let's continue this in my car."

The BMW chirped as St. Onge unlocked its doors. Once they were seated, he started the engine, lowered the windows a crack to allow the hot air inside to escape, and turned the AC to maximum.

"It'll just take a moment to cool things down a bit," he said.

After a few seconds, Marc could feel the icy coolness from the air conditioner rushing through the vents and St. Onge slid the windows shut again.

"Have you ever heard of a company called Canton Jade Holdings?" St. Onge asked.

"Sounds like a web address for an on-line discount jewelry store," Marc quipped.

"Not quite," St. Onge said without grinning. "They're a rail systems developer. Chinese. Over the past few years, they've started to branch out, mostly in developing countries in South East Asia, South America, and Africa. Recently, they've opened offices in Toronto and Montreal. Testing the waters, we suspect."

"What does Canton Jade Holdings have to do with Hugo Karlsson?" Marc asked.

"I don't know. Maybe it's just a coincidence, but we received a confidential company bulletin about a month ago. I can't go into details, but basically it was a heads up to the fact that Canton Jade may be going up against us in bidding on another project we've been working on."

"OK, but I still don't see how this has anything to do with Hugo's disappearance, unless…" Marc let the sentence hang.

"He could have been abducted — or worse," St. Onge said.

A car pulled into the space next to them, giving Marc a moment to ponder this revelation.

"Hugo's expertise is so valuable that someone would try to kidnap him?"

"That's one scenario. Another could be that someone thinks his employment with Barbeau Transport poses too big a threat, and that he should be eliminated."

"Seems like a lot of trouble. I mean, Hugo's apparently a pretty smart guy, but China's full of smart guys. Couldn't they just find one of their own without eliminating someone?" Marc asked.

"Hugo's not just any smart guy. He's gifted. His thinking is a generation beyond even the brightest engineers in the business."

"Well, let's not get ahead of ourselves. There could be a less tragic explanation for Hugo's disappearance—an unknown girlfriend or a gambling problem or whatever. From what I've heard so far, it sounds like he's been under a lot of stress lately. Maybe he just needed some time away to decompress."

"I understand your skepticism, Mr. LaRose. But you don't know Hugo like I do."

"I see," Marc said, thinking. "Tell you what. I've got a few things to check on. If you could get me the description of the vehicle he was using, along with the address of your company's home office in Brossard, that would be helpful," Marc said, handing St. Onge his card.

"Besides my phone numbers, my fax and email are included at the bottom of the card," Marc said, opening his door.

"You'll have the information by this afternoon, Mr. LaRose, and please, if you find something, anything, please let me know."

"Sure thing, and you do the same," Marc said as he shut the door to St. Onge's 'Beamer' and headed to his Civic.

As Marc drove down Cornelia Street toward his office, Dave Brubeck's *Take Five* tune signaled another incoming call. He saw "Plattsburgh PD," on the cell's screen.

"Marc LaRose," he announced.

"Marc, Dave Rabideau. I talked with my contact at the CBP, Customs and Border Protection in Champlain. She checked their computer for our guy, Hugo Karlsson. They show numerous crossings for him coming into the U.S. from Canada, the last one about a month ago, but nothing for the past week. They haven't conducted any out-bound checks lately, so they don't have anything for him leaving the U.S. To get that, you'd have to check with the Canadian Customs."

"Good job, Dave. Thanks," Marc said and ended the call.

Hugo is still someplace in Canada, or maybe, he never left the U.S.

Back at his office, Marc noticed the empty foam container from Norm's breakfast special on his desktop, along with a fax from Jean-

Pierre St. Onge with Hugo Karlsson's vehicle data along with Barbeau's address in Brossard, Quebec.

He studied the fax—New Lexus sedan, tan, New York tags.

Marc retrieved the note with the phone number for the Brossard detective Norm had given him earlier from his shirt pocket and dialed.

"*Bonjour, le détective Sylvie Champagne à votre service.*"

"Hello detective. My name is Marc LaRose. Norm Prendergast gave me your name."

"*Ah oui.* You must be the private detective that Norman talks about. How is Monsieur Prendergast?" she asked.

Marc noticed she spoke clear English with the familiar Canadian accent he was used to hearing while listening to hockey games on CBC.

"Norm? Same as always," Marc replied, stifling an urge to say something derogatory.

"*Bon.* What can I do for you, Monsieur?" she asked.

"I'm looking into the recent disappearance of an employee of Barbeau Transport."

"*Oui*, I'm familiar with Barbeau Transport. Their office is nearby on Boulevard Leduc. But why are you looking for a missing person from Canada?"

"The guy I'm looking for lives in the States. He works for Barbeau in their Plattsburgh plant."

"I see."

"His name is Hugo Karlsson. He left Plattsburgh Wednesday morning to attend a business meeting at Barbeau's Brossard office but never arrived. His wife has reported him missing."

"OK." she replied, cautiously.

"Would you mind checking your records? I need to find out if he's been involved in an auto accident, or anything else."

"That's kind of, eh, how do you say, irregular? Ordinarily, we only do such things for the police."

"I understand…" Marc started, but Detective Champagne cut him off.

"However, since you're a friend of Norman's, I believe we can make an exception. Give me the particulars."

What did Norm do to impress this chick?

Marc smiled to himself as he related Hugo Karlsson's vitals, along with the vehicle details supplied by St. Onge, followed with his own cell number.

"I'm presently busy with another matter. Give me a day or so and I'll see what I can find," she said.

"That would be helpful," he said, then after a pause, continued, "There's one more favor I need to ask."

"Yes?" she asked, her voice hesitant.

"Could you check with the Canadian Customs to see if Mr. Karlsson crossed into Quebec this past Wednesday? U.S. Customs has no record of him re-entering the U.S."

The line was silent for a long moment.

"Hello, Detective? You still there?" Marc asked.

"That might be tricky. I'll let you know on that as well."

"Thank you," Marc started to say, when he heard a click and the line went dead.

No goodbye, farewell, get lost? Just hang up? Must be a French Canadian thing.

Chapter Five

Marc spent the afternoon at the computer conducting background research on Barbeau Transport.

About an hour in, he heard Norm stomping up the stairwell.

"Christ's sake, it's hotter than a camel's nut sack out there," Norm announced, as he slammed the office door shut and threw a manila folder on his desk.

Marc noticed damp sweat rings around the armpits of Norm's shirt, and when Norm turned to get a drink of water from the office cooler, Marc could see a salt line had formed along his waistband.

"Tough day?" Marc asked.

"Went to serve a summons on some dick-head in Wiggletown and had to pepper spray the owner's pit bull that doubled as his welcoming committee," he said, wiping his face with a handkerchief.

"Sounds like fun," Marc said with a grin.

"Then the prick wouldn't answer the door. Dumb fuck kept yelling from somewhere inside the house that he didn't live there anymore, so I shoved the document through a hole in the window screen."

After Norm had settled down, Marc asked, "I called your friend at the Brossard PD. She sounded like she might be helpful."

"She's had it tough, but she's good people."

"How do you mean, 'she's had it tough?'"

"Remember the kid on the motorcycle that was blown up in the parking lot in Champlain, back when we were both on the job?" Norm asked.

Marc nodded. "Vaguely. It had something to do with a Montreal biker gang connection. Wasn't that the one where someone hooked a bomb to the ignition on his motorcycle?"

"That's him. He was my informant. We were grooming him to testify against the biker gang for transporting drugs across the border. Poor shit never knew what hit him."

"So, how does Sylvie Champagne fit into this?"

"The kid was Sylvie's older brother. We eventually learned who planted the bomb, but couldn't prove it. Sylvie was pretty busted up about the whole thing."

"And for that, she's willing to help you out?"

"A year later, the bomber was killed in a fight with a rival gang member. Someone started a rumor that he was looking to expand his territory. Biker gangs are pretty parochial."

"So, you wouldn't know how a rumor like that got started, would you?" Marc asked with a wry smile.

"Sylvie eventually joined up with the Brossard PD, and she's been a friend ever since," Norm said, ignoring Marc's question.

"I see."

"Anything new on your missing person?" Norm asked, apparently anxious to change the subject.

"Not much. Detective Champagne is checking for any record of him crossing into Canada. Said she'd let me know."

"Don't worry, she will. Anything else?"

Marc hesitated, "Just something that St. Onge said."

"What was that?" Norm asked.

"He seemed concerned. Even inferred that Karlsson may have been kidnapped–or worse."

"Kidnapped? What gave him that idea?"

"Corporate rivalry, it seems."

"And they haven't called the police?"

"Right now it's just speculation. There's a rumor going around about some Chinese firm moving into the area."

"Be careful, Marc. Remember Sylvie's brother. Territorial squabbles can be deadly."

"That was a biker gang rivalry. This is different," Marc said without conviction.

"OK, but don't say I didn't warn you."

As Marc thought about Norm's warning, the familiar sounds of *Take Five* sounded on his phone.

"Marc LaRose."

"Mr. LaRose, this is JP St. Onge. If you're free, I'd like to speak with you, again. My office."

"Sure. Fifteen minutes?"

"I'll be waiting," St. Onge ended the call.

"Speak of the devil. That was St. Onge. Sounded kind of urgent."

"Think you'll need my pepper spray?" Norm asked.

"I don't expect there'll be any pit bulls."

"That's what I thought."

Marc grabbed his notebook and headed to his car for the ten minute ride to the offices of Barbeau Transport, which he knew were located adjacent to the flight line of the old Plattsburgh Air Force Base. The base had been closed in '95, and since, it had been converted to civilian use. Marc remembered Barbeau had snapped up a few parcels and converted an old hanger situated near the railroad siding to build its rail car manufacturing plant.

At the security gate, Marc was waved through to the main office. St. Onge was waiting in the lobby as he was buzzed in.

"Thanks for coming by so quickly. Follow me," he said leading the way.

Heading down a long hallway that Marc figured led to the rear of the building, St. Onge pulled a couple of disposable head and shoe covers from a box next to a rack of lab coats and handed a set to Marc. "These are required while we are in the lab." After donning the protective gear, St. Onge led the way past a series of offices until they arrived at a door with a "Restricted Access" sign. St. Onge waved what appeared to be a proximity card near a reader. A soft click indicated the locking bolt had released and he pulled the door open.

"After speaking with you today, I thought it might be helpful if you met Hugo's co-workers as soon as possible," St. Onge said.

They entered a cavernous room, ablaze with powerful overhead lighting. Marc observed that one side of the room was taken up with what appeared to be a long slender mechanism. Its dizzying display of components, clusters of multi-colored wires, connecting rods, electronic panels, switches, and batteries, along with an untold number of odd-shaped gizmos strung together in some sort of an organized structure, reminded him of an exposed fuselage of a jetliner.

St. Onge pointed to it and said, "That's the Laser. It's actually a prototype we use for testing. Without the skin, it allows us to observe its individual components as we put it through its paces."

Marc could sense a low humming noise coming from somewhere. Although the noise wasn't particularly loud, it seemed deep and intense.

Toward the left side of the room, there were several individual glassed-in spaces, like large cubicles, except these reminded Marc of his high school chemistry labs. Inside one of them, he observed three people dressed in their white frocks and hair coverings. They appeared to be working on individual projects.

As St. Onge led Marc toward a door at the center of the cubicle, Marc paused and observed several electronic panels lit with hundreds of flashing colored lights. He watched as the techs busied themselves, taking various readings as they peered up at the panels, then back down at their clipboards, making notes.

St. Onge waived the proximity card over the door's locking mechanism, and as the two entered the glassed-in room, Marc felt the humming, as it seemed to penetrate through him.

As if reading Marc's concern, St. Onge said, "It's harmless, Just takes a few minutes to acclimate, then you'll hardly notice it."

St. Onge asked Marc to remain near the door as he proceeded to where the techs, two men and a woman, were working. After briefly conferring with them, he motioned for Marc to join them.

"People, I'd like you to meet Marc LaRose. Mr. LaRose has been hired by Hugo's wife, Annika, to determine what, if anything, happened to Hugo, or where he might be."

Three sets of protective eyewear turned toward Marc in unison.

"Mr. LaRose, these are Hugo's closest co-workers. St. Onge motioned to the first of them, "The big guy here is Stan Benjamin."

Stan, who Marc estimated to be about six foot four and in his early forties, reached over and shook Marc's extended hand with a single pump. "Nice meeting you, I guess," he said.

Marc thought he detected a mid-western accent.

"Likewise," Marc replied.

"This is Jimmy Lee," St. Onge said, motioning toward a man of apparent Asian descent and the shortest of the three. Marc could see a pair of horn-rimmed glasses behind Lee's protective eye wear.

"Pleasure," he said, with a slight bow and a vigorous shake of Marc's hand.

"And this young lady is Giselle Montclair," St. Onge said, motioning to the last of the coated mannequins.

"Hello," she said, timidly shaking Marc's proffered hand.

Through her head covering, Marc could see her red hair had been pulled back. Her eye protectors hid most of her face, but what he did see looked pleasant enough, despite a serious expression.

"Mr. LaRose would like to speak to each of you regarding Hugo's apparent disappearance. Although your cooperation is not mandatory, I would consider it a personal favor if you would."

"Mr. St. Onge, if it's not too much trouble, I'd like to speak to each individually. Preferably, somewhere private," Marc said.

"I can arrange that. Who wants to be first?"

"I was ready for a break anyway," Stan Benjamin said.

"Great. Why don't you show Mr. LaRose to the clinic. It's empty today so you should have plenty of privacy. Is that acceptable to you, Mr. LaRose?"

"The clinic sounds fine."

"Right this way, Mr. LaRose," Benjamin said, as he held the door open.

Exiting the cubicle, then the prototype room, Stan removed his eye protectors and stuffed them in his coat pocket. He slid his head covering off and deposited it in a waste bin that already contained a few others. Marc followed Stan's lead.

At six foot four, Stan set a good pace, even in his scruffy cowboy boots that were half hidden under a pair of faded denims. Marc figured Stan to be in good shape at about two hundred pounds. His dirty-blond hair hung over his ears and a deep five o'clock shadow that seemed to have become the rage among the younger set covered his face.

"First, how about we grab a cup of coffee? There's usually a fresh pot in the break room. It's just down the hall from the clinic."

"Sounds good," Marc replied, now at a half run.

After filling their Styrofoam cups, Marc followed Stan around the corner to a door with a 'Clinic' sign. Stan passed his key card over the reader allowing them to enter. As the door opened, Marc was hit with the smell of antiseptics. Inside, there was just enough room for the nurse's desk and chair, plus another chair that appeared quite comfortable, except for its pair of raised armrests. Marc assumed the chair was used for blood drawing. A weight scale was positioned next to the door.

Stan dragged the blood drawing chair to a position in front of the desk, placed his cup on one of the padded arm rests, sat down, and motioned toward the chair behind the desk.

"Just as well get comfortable, Mr. LaRose."

Marc set his cup on the desktop and sat down. He pulled a note pad from his shirt pocket and clicked his pen.

"Let's start with your name and address," Marc said.

"Stanley S. Benjamin, Adirondack Lane, Plattsburgh. But please, everyone calls me Stan."

"Age?"

"Thirty-five, as of June fifth."

"How long have you worked at Barbeau Transport?"

"Just short of three years."

"How long have you known Mr. Karlsson?"

"He was here when I hired on."

"How closely did you work with him?"

"We confer just about every day. As the project manager, Hugo oversees the Laser's overall functionality, whereas I deal specifically with the power train."

"How do you like working with Hugo?"

"Good. He's a no-nonsense kind of guy. Takes his work very seriously."

"When's the last time you saw him?"

"Last Saturday. We were preparing for Wednesday's meeting in Brossard to bring the main office up to speed on our latest findings, but I understand he didn't show up. Haven't seen or heard from him since."

"Do you know of any reason why he wouldn't show up at the Brossard meeting?"

"No, except…" Stan didn't finish.

"Except what?" Marc asked.

"I don't know. Can't put my finger on it. He seemed sort of distracted. Like maybe something was bothering him, but I didn't ask. Hugo's a private kind of guy.

"You said Hugo was supposed to bring the main office up to speed on the latest findings. What's that about?"

"It's kind of confidential."

"I assure you, whatever you say, stay's here." Marc said.

"Stan exhaled and looked around the room, as if he were looking for guidance among the colorful anatomy charts that decorated the walls."

"As you may have heard, the Laser is having its premier roll-out next week, but there still could be a few issues. That's not uncommon with any new product, especially one this complex."

"What kind of issues?" Marc asked, looking up from his note pad.

"I'm certain it's not with the power train, or I'd have heard about it. I doubt it's anything major, but it could be any number of things. This baby's pretty complicated."

"I see," Marc said, and took a slow sip of his coffee.

"How did Hugo get along with his other co-workers?"

"OK, I guess. Like I said, we all have different specialties. But overall, I haven't noticed anything but good team cooperation."

Marc thought for a moment as he set his coffee cup down, then drummed his pen on his note pad.

Finally, he said, "OK, that's about all I have. Thanks for your candor, Stan. Would you mind asking Mr. Lee or Miss Montclair to come on back, whoever's available?"

"Will do, and good luck, Mr. LaRose," Stan said as he left the room. The door plunger quietly hissed as it closed."

As Marc considered his interview with Stan, he glanced around the room at the various anatomy charts that earlier helped Stan make a decision to divulge something he thought was confidential. There were several, many with different views of human organs; some with 'before and after' disease depictions.

So that's where the duodenum is located.

Chapter Six

There was a soft tap on the door. When it remained shut, Marc called out, "Hello," and Giselle Montclair partially opened the door and peeked around.

"Come on in, I won't bite," Marc said, sporting his natural grin.

"Sorry, Stan said you were waiting, but I hadn't seen Jimmy Lee and wasn't sure if he was with you or not. I didn't want to intrude."

As she spoke, Marc noted the Quebecois accent typically found along the northern border of New York.

"Well, I haven't seen Mr. Lee yet, so I guess you're not intruding."

Giselle timidly ventured a little further into the room.

"Have a seat," Marc said, gesturing toward the blood drawing chair. "I just have a few questions."

Without her head covering, Giselle's red hair laid naturally across her shoulders. Marc guessed she was taller than average, five eight or so. With her lab coat opened in front, Marc could see she was wearing a smart looking tan blouse and brown slacks. She leaned forward slightly in the chair, her hands holding her knees like a paratrooper preparing for her first jump.

"Just to make sure I got this right, your name is Giselle Montclair, correct?"

"*Oui*, I mean, yes, that is correct."

Marc scribbled in his notepad, then glanced back up at Giselle,

"Address, please."

"1212 Avenue Duchastel. That's in the Outremont section of Montreal."

"Hate to ask, but what's your age?"

Giselle eye's cast downward and hesitated. Marc noted a slight reddening in her cheeks.

"Thirty-one," she said, haltingly.

"Thanks. The hard part's over," Marc said with a smile, attempting to put her at ease.

She gave an almost imperceptive nod and the beginnings of a grin.

"How long have you known Hugo Karlsson?"

"Since I started working here, just over two years ago."

"How often do you work with him?"

"Practically every day, depending on the project, of course."

"You must know Hugo pretty well then?"

"I'm not sure what you mean, Mr. LaRose."

"If something was bothering Hugo, would you have noticed?"

"Probably. We deal with problems all the time and share our concerns."

"No, I meant would you know if something was bothering Hugo at home, or somewhere outside of work?"

She hesitated. "I don't know. Mr. Karlsson rarely talked about his family. I know he is from Finland, and he is married, of course. I met his wife, Annika, at one of the office Christmas parties. But that's about all."

"Regarding the meeting he was scheduled to attend in Brossard, did he mention any concerns he may have had?"

Giselle looked away and chewed her lower lip as she seemed to think about the question. "Nothing comes to mind," she said.

"Do you think he was concerned about the Laser's rollout?"

"He could have been, I suppose. It's a pretty big project and the Laser is a complicated piece of engineering."

Curiously, Marc sensed a trace of animosity in her voice. Had she been passed over for a promotion, perhaps? He made a mental note to check into that later.

"How did Hugo get along with your co-workers, Jimmy Lee and Stan Benjamin?"

"Same as me, I guess. As I mentioned, the Laser is as complicated as any hybrid engine can be. We each have specific areas of responsibility. Mr. Karlsson coordinated our research."

"Hybrid engine? What do you mean?" Marc asked out of curiosity.

"Most locomotives are diesel-fueled or run on electricity powered by a turbine, or both. The Laser utilizes jet engine technology to operate an electromagnetic turbine."

"What's your area of expertise?"

"Mechanical engineering. I specialize in railway traction."

"Railway traction?" Marc asked.

"Kind of technical, but simply put, it deals with reducing overall EC, or energy cost per passenger to maximize efficiencies, with the added benefit of reduced energy consumption," she said matter-of-factly.

Marc stared blankly at her for a moment, "OK, I'll take your word for that. What about Stan and Jimmy? What do they do?"

"Stan's strictly power train. You know, the engine and the turbine and everything in between. Jimmy deals with overall design functionality and its affect on air flow and resistance."

"Besides providing a more modern appearance, what does air flow and resistance have to do with trains?" Marc asked, more to satisfy his own curiosity.

"It's pretty important. You see, reducing resistance or drag enhances overall efficiencies producing greater performance with less fuel," she said in the voice of a second grade teacher explaining to a child how to cross the street.

"To get back to where we started, you felt there may have been something bothering Hugo before the meeting in Brossard?"

"Like I said, I'm not sure. It was just a feeling I had I guess like a woman's intuition, or something like that," she said as she again glanced around the room, apparently anxious for this interview to end.

Marc's gaze wandered toward the height chart, then back to his note pad as he thought about what Giselle and Stan had said. Finally, he handed Giselle his card, "Thank you for your time, Ms. Montclair. If you think of anything that would be helpful, please call me, anytime," Marc said as he stood.

Giselle took the card, glanced at it briefly, and placed it in her jacket pocket as she rose.

"Is that all, Mr. LaRose?" she said, apparently surprised the meeting ended so quickly.

"Unless you can remember anything else?"

Giselle hesitated, "No, but if I do, I'll be sure to call."

"If you find Mr. Lee, would you please ask him to come on back?" Marc said as he opened the door for her to leave.

“*Bien sur,* eh, of course, Mister LaRose,” Giselle said as she quietly left the room.

Ten minutes later, Marc got out of the chair and was about to go looking for Jimmy Lee when the door suddenly opened. Lee entered the room.

“Sorry I took so long, Mr. LaRose. Ms. Monclair just located me.”

“Thought maybe you’d hopped the southbound train,” Marc said, jokingly, then motioned toward the blood drawing chair.

Lee looked stunned at first, then, slowly, the corners of his mouth turned up as he apparently realized the quip was an attempt at humor. “No, no southbound train, Mr. LaRose,” he said as he slowly sat with his hands gripping the ends of the padded chair arms.

Marc flipped to a fresh page on his notepad.

“Is it Jimmy Lee, or James?”

“Jimmy, please.”

“Where do you live?” Marc asked.

“South Shore, St. Hubert,” he said, referring to a bedroom community near the St. Lawrence River, south of Montreal.

“I’m familiar with Saint Hubert. Any particular street?” Marc asked, a little firmer than he meant.

“Sorry, 6670 Rue Racine, apartment 73.”

“How long have you been with Barbeau Transport?”

“Two years, I guess,” he said, hesitantly.

“Now, I understand your work with the Laser was focused on the train’s overall design?”

“That’s right, but what does my work here have to do with Mr. Karlsson’s disappearance?” Lee said with a touch of irritation.

“How did you get along with Mr. Karlsson?” Marc asked, ignoring Lee’s question.

“Fine, I guess.”

“You guess?”

“I mean good. We got along well,” he said, touching the frame of his horn-rimmed glasses, then crossing his legs. Marc noticed his lime-colored shoe laces matched the florescent green of the soles of his Adidas running shoes.

"I see," Marc said. "Have you noticed any change in Mr. Karlsson's behavior lately? You know, coming in late for work, irritated more than usual, anything like that?"

"No, uh, nothing that I recall," he replied, hesitantly.

"Did he seem concerned about the meeting in Brossard that he was scheduled to attend? Did he say anything to you about it?"

"Uh, no. Nothing comes to mind," Lee said, again adjusting his glasses.

"Are you looking forward to the Laser's inaugural trip next week?"

Lee appeared surprised by the question. "What, oh, of course. We're all excited about this trip. This will be a new day in train travel."

Lee's pronouncement sounded more like a sound bite from a travel and leisure commercial.

"I assume, along with political dignitaries, there will be people from Barbeau Transport on the train. Will you be on it?"

"Me? No, I, I have other things to do," Lee said as he looked away, and with a flurry of fluorescent green, recrossed his legs. "Besides, as you know, I'm a simple engineer, not a dignitary."

"Was Hugo Karlsson supposed to be on that train?"

"Mr. Karlsson? Sure, I guess so," Lee said as he glanced toward an anatomical chart of a colorectal polyp taped on the wall next to his chair. "I mean, he is the project manager, so yes, I suppose he will be."

Despite the air conditioning, Marc noticed Lee's pallor had seemed to flush as beads of sweat formed on his forehead.

"You have family in the area?" Marc asked.

Lee hesitated. "Uh, sorry." He finally said, apparently distracted.

"Does your family live in Canada?"

"My family? No, my parents live in Singapore. That's all the family I have. Just my parents."

"So, you live alone?"

"Yes, but what does that have to..."

“Probably nothing, just curious,” Marc added before Lee could finish, then let the statement hang in the air as he studied Lee’s reaction.

Marc sighed and closed his notebook.

“If you should happen to hear anything, I’m sure Mr. St. Onge would appreciate it if you could let him know, or you can call me anytime, day or night,” Marc said as he slid one of his business cards across the table.

“Top number’s the office, my cell’s on the bottom.”

Lee held the card, but rather than putting it in his pocket, he kept staring at it, as it if it were a curious insect.

“I will, Mr. eh, LaRose,” he finally said, standing, then turning to open the door.

“Thanks for your help,” Marc said as he watched him leave.

Something’s bothering him.

Marc picked up his note pad, tossed his Styrofoam cup in the waste basket and left the clinic.

As he headed back toward the main exit, Marc heard St. Onge call to him from the opposite end of the hallway, “Mr. LaRose, wait!”

Marc turned and stopped.

“I wanted to have a word with you before you left.”

“What’s up?” Marc asked, as St. Onge caught up and the two continued toward the front entrance.

“Were you able to learn anything from the interviews with Karlsson’s team?”

“Not much really. The general consensus is that Karlsson kept his personal life mostly to himself, but was apparently troubled by something a day or so before the meeting in Brossard. Not much more than that.”

“Problem solving is what he did best, but if something extraordinary was bothering him, I think he would have come to me,” St. Onge replied.

“Curious,” Marc whispered, almost to himself.

The two men continued in silence. When they reached the building’s main entrance, St. Onge held the door open.

As the two shook hands, Marc said, “Thank you for your cooperation. If I hear something, I’ll let you know.”

“Thank you, Mr. LaRose. I look forward to hearing from you.” St. Onge said.

Marc walked to his car parked in the visitors’ parking area.

Inside the Civic with the AC turned on high, he took out his note pad and reviewed what he’d written from his interviews with the three Barbeau engineers.

The big guy, Stan Benjamin seemed pretty solid, but I think Lee and Montclair know more than they’re letting on. Wonder what it could be?

As the air conditioner kicked in, he exhaled deeply and closed the note pad.

Rabideau’s probably right. Karlsson’s found a strange piece up in Montreal and is no doubt making excuses for missing that meeting and being out of touch for so long. Might as well wait and see what tomorrow brings, I guess.

He picked up his cell and found the number for Tim Golden.

“Tim, you still up for a few holes of golf this afternoon?”

Marc’s work rarely interfered with his golf game, but that afternoon thoughts of the investigation kept niggling at him as he played. At the end of the round, Golden took the match. The first time Tim had won since spring.

Chapter Seven

At 7:30 the following morning, Brandy and Rye circled Marc's feet as he sat at the kitchen table nursing a mug of coffee while studying the day's crossword puzzle. His cell phone came alive with a Montreal area code number on its screen.

"Monsieur LaRose, this is Detective Sylvie Champagne."

"Good morning, Detective. How are things in Brossard?"

"I'm calling about your missing person, Mr. Hugo Karlsson," she said.

And a good morning to you as well.

"OK."

"The CBSA, Canadian Border Services Agency, indicated Mr. Karlsson arrived at the border crossing in Blackpool, Quebec, last Wednesday morning, at five past eight."

"I see," Marc said, thinking back to his interview with Annika Karlsson. "That would corroborate his wife's report of him leaving the house around 7:30 a.m. for the meeting in Brossard."

"There's more."

"Go ahead," Marc said, curious.

"We've located his car. The license plates had been removed, but we've identified it through its Vehicle Identification Number."

"Where was it found?"

"Ile des Soeurs. Do you know where that is?" she asked.

"Nuns' Island, off the Champlain Bridge connecting the South Shore with the city of Montreal."

"You're familiar with the area then, Mr. LaRose."

"Somewhat. Any damage to the vehicle?"

"There doesn't appear to be any. A patrol found it near the entrance to the park. They were going to impound it, but when I learned it was owned by Barbeau Transport, I had it towed here, to our station in Brossard."

"Good work," Marc said. "I don't imagine the keys were left in the car?"

"No, and it was locked. We haven't tried to get in. Figured we'd wait for the owner."

“Good,” Marc said. “I’ll contact Barbeau and get the keys. If you’re going to be around today, maybe we could meet up and look at it together.”

“D'Accord. I have a few things to do this morning, but I’ll be in the office around noon,” she replied.

“I’ll look forward to seeing you then,” Marc said and ended the call.

He looked down at Rye, lying at his feet, his jaw resting on his bedroom slipper.

“Doubt if St. Onge will get to the office much before nine. What’s a four letter word for ‘patience?’”

“Meow,” Rye responded.

“Probably not. Unless I’m wrong it begins with a ‘g,’” Marc whispered, then continued to work the puzzle as he sipped his coffee.

An hour later, he dialed the number for Barbeau. The same receptionist answered, but today he was immediately routed through to Jean Pierre’s office.

“Good morning, Marc. Tell me you have good news.”

“I have news, but I don’t know how good it is.”

“Not sure if I like the sound of that.”

“The police found Hugo’s car, locked and abandoned on Nuns’ Island.”

“Nuns’ Island? I don’t understand. That’s a bit out of the way if he was going to Brossard,” he said, sounding confused.

“My thoughts exactly. Look, I’m heading up there later today to meet with a police detective. Any chance you have a spare key for Hugo’s car? I’d like to look inside.”

“Yes, I’ll leave it at the gate with the security officer.”

“I’ll let you know what I find,” Marc said and signed off.

After a shower, Marc drove downtown, past his office, and stopped in front of Shirley’s Flower Shop.

The set of chimes above the door tinkled as he entered. The air was heavy with the scent of fresh flowers.

“Hey, Dad,” Ann Marie called from behind the front counter. Marc could see his daughter was busy unpacking a box of fresh carnations.

"Mom around?" he asked.

"Haven't seen her," she said, as she continued to busy herself with the flowers. Then, after a pause, "She should be in a little later. Can I give her a message?"

"No. Just passing by and thought I'd stop and say 'hi.'"

Without pausing, she plopped a handful of the colorful flowers into a waiting bucket of water.

Noting his daughter's indifferent attitude, he asked, "Is everything OK?"

"Yeah, I guess so. Why?"

"Nothing. Just it's unusual for your mom not to be here first thing in the morning."

"Yeah well, uh, probably has something to do with her working late last night, maybe," she said, breaking open a box of stargazer lilies.

Marc hesitated. "It's good that you're around to help out."

"I just have one class today, Poly Sci and that isn't until this afternoon," she said, as she gave a handful of the lily stems a fresh cut.

Marc noticed that Ann Marie seemed to avoid eye contact.

"Well, when you see Mom, tell her I stopped by."

"Will do, Dad," she said, continuing to work with the flowers.

Marc left the flower shop with an uneasy feeling.

Something's going on. Shirley's always here first thing in the morning and Ann Marie's not telling me something.

Feeling somewhat perplexed, Marc drove his Civic to the Barbeau Transport plant and picked up the key for Hugo Karlsson's car.

The twenty-five minute trip north to the border went smoothly until he arrived at the Canadian Customs' crossing and found traffic backed up with lines of cars waiting to cross into Canada.

Looks like I should have taken one of the smaller side ports of entry.

Once through customs, it was another forty-five minutes to Brossard, which, due to urban sprawl, was almost indistinguishable from the other twenty-five intermingling municipalities that stretched across the St. Lawrence River from Montreal.

Marc found the Brossard Police station off the main highway, located a parking space, and dialed Detective Champagne's phone number. She picked up on the first ring.

"Hello Detective, this is Marc LaRose."

"Good. Where are you?" she replied.

"I'm parked across the street."

"OK, I'll meet you out front."

Marc crossed the street and waited at the bottom of the building's steps. Several uniformed officers passed by, but paid him little attention. He noted several security cameras fastened to the building's exterior. Someone inside was probably monitoring his presence, he figured.

He was momentarily distracted by a patrol car leaving the police parking lot with its lights and siren activated, when he heard above the fading din of the siren, "Monsieur LaRose?"

Marc turned and observed a woman, neatly dressed in a business pants suit, descending the steps toward him.

"Detective Champagne?" he said.

She extended her hand. "Pleasure to finally meet you," she said, giving Marc's hand a firm shake.

"Right this way," she said, and led Marc around the corner of the building to a fenced-in police parking lot. She punched a code at the pedestrian gate and held it open for Marc, then secured it behind them.

"The car you're looking for is right over here," she said, and led Marc toward the opposite side of the lot, away from the line of parked police cars and a few civilian cars that Marc assumed belonged to police department employees.

Marc noted that Detective Champagne was a bit shorter than he, around five seven, trim, with shoulder length acorn brown hair that framed a pleasant oval-shaped face. Unlike many Quebecois women he'd known in the past, her make-up was barely noticeable. As she walked in quick purposeful strides, her low-heeled wedged shoes clicked and scuffed along the asphalt.

Before she could point it out, Marc spotted the Lexus sitting alone near the fence, minus its tags. He retrieved the car's key fob and pushed the unlock button. There was a mild chirp as the door locks activated. A quick scan of the interior showed nothing had been left on the seats or the floor of the vehicle.

Marc slipped on a pair of surgeon's gloves that he kept in his back pocket, opened the driver's side door, and got in behind the wheel.

As he inserted the key fob into its receiver, Detective Champagne said, "Please be careful, in case this turns into something more serious than just a missing person case."

He looked at the odometer and wrote down the mileage in his notebook. He pushed the trunk release button, which opened with a soft click.

Detective Champagne walked to the back, and using her pen, raised the trunk lid to peek inside.

"Nothing here. Looks clean," she called out.

Marc noted the gas gauge read three quarters full.

"Seems you made the trip for nothing, Mr. LaRose," she said, walking back to the driver's side of the car.

"You said the car was found on Nuns' Island?" Marc asked.

"*Oui*. Yesterday afternoon."

"Would you mind showing me exactly where it was found?" Marc asked.

"I suppose. It's a short drive, about twenty minutes," she said, glancing at her watch. "We'll use my car, in case I get another call."

Marc closed the trunk lid and locked the car doors.

The ride through the city of Brossard, although busy with the crush of traffic, was quiet as Detective Champagne was apparently not given to small talk. As they approached the entrance to the Champlain Bridge, Marc decided to break the ice. "Norm mentioned you joined the police force about five years ago?"

"Five and a half. About the same time you retired from the state police."

"So Norm's been talking about me?"

"No, not really. He only said you were a good detective and that you live alone," she said, maneuvering her car onto the entrance to the bridge, staying in the right lane.

They continued in silence for the next mile when the exit for Nuns' Island, situated near the middle of the St. Lawrence River, came into view.

"Nuns' Island must be outside of the City of Brossard's Police district, is it not?" Marc asked.

"Yes, we are in the city of Verdun, but all the police departments in the Montreal urban community work together as one. We don't share the rivalry between police agencies that you do in the U.S.," she said as she deftly maneuvered the vehicle off the exit and onto the island.

"I see," Marc said.

"This is Nuns' Island Boulevard. The next left is the cul-de-sac where Mr. Karlsson's car was located."

When Sylvie turned down the cul-de-sac, he noticed they were passing through a neighborhood of stately homes separated from each other by thick stands of trees. The driveway to each home was guarded by a heavy wrought iron gate, distinctly designed so as not to look like another.

"This is all part of West Vancouver Park," she said as she stopped the car at the end of the road. "According to the responding officer, the vehicle was located right about here."

"Think it could have been a robbery?"

"Maybe, but why not steal the car as well? As you know, reselling stolen cars is big business in Montreal, especially high-end cars like the Lexus Mr. Karlsson was driving."

"Has anyone checked the area or tried knocking on a few doors of the houses we passed on the way in?"

"No, this came in as a possible abandoned vehicle complaint, so apparently the officers didn't see the need. Or maybe they didn't want to be bothered," she added.

"Do you know who called it in?"

"As I recall, it may have been a jogger who noticed it sitting here the day before, but I'm not sure. I suppose we could check the blotter when we return to the station."

Marc opened his door. "If you don't mind, I'd like to take a look around. Someone may have dropped something."

"OK," Sylvie said doubtfully. "You take this side, and I'll take the other," she said crossing to the opposite side of the street.

Marc shuffled through the tall grass that lined the road. He spotted a trail leading from the woods in the direction of the St. Lawrence River flowing just beyond.

Probably the trail the jogger was using when he spotted Hugo Karlsson's car.

"Mr. LaRose, you'd better take a look at this!" Sylvie called out.

Marc could see she was bent down next to the curb examining something at the side of the road.

As Marc turned toward Sylvie, he stepped on what he thought was a small stone in the grass. He absentmindedly turned the grass over with his foot and saw something shiny. Bending down to get a better look, Marc saw a small chain, but when he retrieved it, he found that it was attached to a fob. Upon examination, he realized it was similar to the one for Hugo's car. Slipping the fob into his pocket, Marc walked to where Sylvie was kneeling. She seemed to be concentrating on a strip of sand that had been pushed toward the curb, probably left there from the previous winter.

"What'cha got?" he asked.

"Look here, in the sand."

Marc studied the area Sylvie was pointing to.

"Looks like some sort of tire track," he said.

"Yes, you see that?" she said, using her pen as a pointer. "A motorcycle tire track, probably a Harley. A motorcycle was parked here, and not long ago. It hasn't rained for about a week, so these tracks were made since then."

"How do you know it was parked? And what makes you think that the motorcycle, or whatever it was, was somehow connected to Hugo's car?"

"I know a few things about motorcycles, Mr. LaRose. I can tell it was parked because the track is close to the curb, besides, see these footprints," she said pointing to a partial print in the sand. "I don't know if these have anything to do with your missing person, but, I know this area. This is not a neighborhood for motorcycles."

Marc studied the tire print. "Why do you think it was a Harley?"

"I've seen this tire pattern before," she said, again pointing to the track in the sand. "You see how the diagonal lines of the tread spread out from the center? That helps to disperse water at high speeds." Pointing to another track, she said, "and this smaller one is the bike's front tire."

Marc held his cell phone over the track and snapped a few photos. He then retrieved the key fob from his pocket and holding it by the chain, dangled it in Sylvie's direction.

"Where'd you fine that?" she asked.

"Right over there," he said, pointing to the spot in the grass. "I stepped on it, thought it was a stone. I think it's Karlsson's car key. He may have suspected something and tossed it there."

"That could help explain why whoever took Karlsson didn't take his car as well," Sylvie said.

"Still, I can't understand what Hugo Karlsson would be doing here. This is at least six miles out of his way," Marc said.

"Possibly, he was lured here by someone. A friend perhaps. Who knows?" Sylvie suggested.

"Maybe," Marc said doubtfully. "If you have time, I'd still like to knock on a few doors. Find out if anybody saw anything."

"We could try, I suppose. But I must tell you, the people who live around here like their privacy."

"Yeah, I saw the iron gates we passed. They were all closed."

Sylvie looked at her watch. "Well, let's start with the closest and work our way back toward the bridge. Most people in this area are Francophones, so let me do the talking, OK?"

"Sure," Marc said, not letting on the fact that he spoke French fluently.

Sylvie turned the car back up the street about a quarter mile and arrived at the first driveway. A black wrought iron gate, decorated with a "Fleur De Lis" adorned its center. She pulled up to a black box mounted on a post, rolled down her window and hit the "call" button located under its key pad.

A scratchy feminine, "*Oui*," responded within a few seconds.

Sylvie held her police ID toward the camera mounted at the side of the gate and explained in French who she was, and asked the woman if she would mind speaking with her regarding a police matter.

Marc heard the whirring of an electric motor as the gate slowly swung open.

Sylvie followed the crushed-stone driveway for about fifty yards through a neatly landscaped area that led to a stately manor house. The driveway ended at the side of the residence near an attached three-car garage. Looking past the house, Marc could see the St. Lawrence River through a maze of birch trees.

As the two exited the car, Marc spotted a pair of running shoes neatly placed on the deck next to the side door.

The door opened and a young woman appeared, holding it open for them to enter.

"Please, right this way, officers," she said with a distinct English accent. "I figured someone from the authorities would be along eventually."

Sylvie introduced herself, then motioned toward Marc. "This is Mr. LaRose from the United States. He is a private investigator."

"A private investigator? How exciting. I don't believe I've ever met one in person," she said, shifting her gaze toward Marc and extending her hand. "My name's Rylee, Rylee Brooks."

"Pleased to meet you, Ms. Brooks," Marc said. "Tell me, what did you mean when you said you figured someone would be along eventually?"

"I assumed this is about the abandoned car, the one left at the end of the cul-de-sac. I called the police about it."

Marc glanced over to Sylvie, "Do you mind?"

"Of course not," she said, and shrugged her shoulders, giving Marc her blessing to continue the interview.

"Ms. Brooks, when did you first notice the car?"

"Let me think. It must have been three days ago. I was returning from my run around the island. There's a path I like to use that follows along the river and ends up at the end of our cul-de-sac. I find it very relaxing. Anyway, as I was returning, I noticed the car parked there, along with another car. There were two men inside."

Marc thought a moment.

"Did you get a look at the men?" he asked.

"Not really, although I remember one, the driver, had grey hair, and looked around fifty, maybe older."

"And the other man?"

"Let me think," she said, then paused. "He might have worn glasses, but I'm not sure. Like I said, I was just jogging by and noticed the car sitting there. It's not unusual to see cars parked there. It's kind of secluded, you know."

"Do you remember what the other car looked like?" Marc asked.

"It was lime green, but I don't know what kind it was, just that it was small, and bright green."

"Anything else?"

"Not really. I mean, the men seemed to be talking, arguing actually. But I couldn't hear what they were saying."

"Who was arguing? Was it the older man?"

"Both, I think. I didn't pay them that much attention. I suspect people use the cul-de-sac as sort of a private rendezvous, if you know what I mean."

"Have you ever seen either of these cars parked there before?"

"I don't think so."

"How often do you pass by there?"

"Every other day or so. I'm visiting my mom who lives here. It's my stepfather's house actually. He's the manager of The Bay store, downtown."

"I see," Marc said, then turning toward Sylvie, "Any further questions, Detective?"

"Do you remember seeing any motorcycles in the cul-de-sac recently?" she asked.

Ms. Brooks appeared to think about the question. "Now that you mention it, I remember hearing a motorcycle engine shortly after I returned from my run the same day I saw those cars parked there."

"Could you tell if there was just one motorcycle, or were there more than one?"

"I'm not sure. I was unlacing my running shoes. Serge doesn't like me to wear them inside the house. That's when I heard the noise, but I couldn't tell. I remember there was a lot of racket, even though we're back off the road. We don't have many loud motorcycles in London the way they do here. Like I said, I didn't think much of it at the time."

"So, you didn't actually see any motorcycles. You just heard them," Marc said.

"The noise seemed to be going that way," she said, motioning with her arm in the direction of the cul-de-sac. "But no, you're right. I didn't actually see them. I just heard the noise."

"Did you hear them leave?"

"No, sorry. I had a drink of water then went upstairs to shower."

Marc and Sylvie glanced at each other. Marc shrugged his shoulders indicating he had no further questions.

"Thank you for your time Ms. Brooks. If you think of anything else, please call Detective Champagne or myself." Marc said, handing her one of his business cards.

"Certainly. Sorry I couldn't be of more help."

As they were driving off, Marc said "I guess that confirms your analysis of the tire tracks. Plus, it sounds like Mr. Karlsson had at least one visitor, someone in a small lime green car."

They tried the next three residences on the street, but either no one was home or they didn't want to get involved. When Sylvie turned the corner to the main road, Marc noticed the gates to these residences seemed to be spaced further apart than in the cul-de-sac.

"What do you think, Mr. LaRose? You want to try knocking on a few more doors?"

"I don't think so. We're getting too far from the where the vehicle was found. I think we'd just be wasting our time."

"So?" Sylvie said, glancing at her watch again.

Am I really that boring?

He retrieved the notes from his interview with the Barbeau employees he had talked with the day before.

"One of Karlsson's coworkers lives on the South Shore. How familiar are you with the City of St. Hubert?"

"I can find my way around. What's the address?"

"6670 Rue Racine, apartment 73.

"Rue Racine." Sylvie repeated the street name. "If memory serves me, that's just off Chemin de Chambly, one the city's main streets."

"I wouldn't know. That's the address he gave me."

Twenty minutes later, Sylvie parked outside an apartment house with the number '73' over the main entrance. The parking area was fairly large, with spaces for around fifty vehicles, about a quarter of them occupied this time of day.

"Do you know what kind of car this co-worker you interviewed has?"

"No, but I'll find out. He should still be at work and probably won't return home until six or so this afternoon." Marc said.

"If you don't mind my asking, how many co-workers did you interview?"

"There were three, not including the plant manager. Why?"

"And you're interested in this particular person, because…"

"Just a feeling. He seemed a little too nervous when I spoke with him. Something just didn't seem right."

"I see. So, is there anything else I can do for you, Mr. LaRose?"

As Marc was about to suggest lunch, he noticed two parked motorcycles, sharing a single parking space.

"Detective, can you tell what kind of bikes those are?" Marc asked, nodding in their direction.

"They're both Harleys. The red one is a Superlow. The other is a 1200 Custom. They both have custom-made handlebars. Not sure, but they could be gang bikes."

"Let's pass by them and take a closer look," Marc suggested.

As Sylvie made a slow pass, Marc used his phone to take a series of photos.

"Did you happen to notice the tire tread on that first one?"

"Yes. Hard to tell without getting closer, but from what I could see, it looked similar to the tread pattern we saw in the sand at the cul-de-sac," she said.

Sylvie turned toward the parking lot exit.

"I think we should leave the area for now, lest we attract undue suspicion with our presence," she said.

Marc thought her voice carried the tenor of renewed interest in his case.

"Good idea," Marc said, flipping through the photos on his cell phone.

As they drove back onto the main street, Marc said, "I think I'd like to take these photos, the ones of the tread marks in the sand, and the motorcycles' tires and download them on a computer where we can examine them for comparison."

"Uh huh," she responded, again glancing at her watch.

"I think it's more than just a coincidence those bikes are in the same parking lot where Jimmy Lee lives."

"Who's Jimmy Lee? The nervous one you interviewed at Barbeau?"

"Yes, I'm thinking that maybe he had a reason to be nervous."

"That's possible. Still, like you just said, it could be just a coincidence," Sylvie said, as she turned the car toward Brossard.

After a couple of blocks, Marc asked, "Do you have someplace else you've got to be, Detective?"

Sylvie hesitated, "I do have a small errand to run. It should only take a moment."

Six blocks and three turns later, Sylvie parked the car in front of a one-story brick building with a large sign above the entrance, Ville de Brossard Ecole des Enfants.

Marc interpreted the sign as the Brossard Children's School.

"I'll just be a moment," Sylvie said and left Marc sitting alone as she hurried into the building. A few minutes later she reappeared, followed by a small boy Marc guessed to be no more than seven years old. He was wearing shorts and a tee shirt, his two small hands clinging to the straps of a backpack almost as big as he was. When they arrived at the vehicle, Sylvie opened the rear door and tossed the backpack on the seat before settling the boy next to it. After clicking the boy's seat belt, she resumed her position behind the wheel.

As she put the car in gear, the boy asked in French, "Who is he?"

Before Sylvie could answer, Marc turned to the boy, and in French, said, "My name is Mr. LaRose, I'm working with your Mom today. What is your name?"

"Simon," the boy said softly, then turning his attention back to Sylvie, asked, "Où est grand-père?"

"Grandpa couldn't come today. He has a doctor's appointment."

After a few moments of silence, Sylvie said, "I have to bring Simon to his grandparents' house. They help with the babysitting."

"No problem," Marc said.

A few blocks later, Sylvie stopped the car in front of a modest four-story apartment building. There was a long green awning over the main entrance to the street with the inscription "2525 Boulevard Simard" in white letters.

"Sorry, Mr. LaRose, this should only take a minute."

"No problem," Marc said.

"OK, Simon, Grandma's waiting," Sylvie said, reaching back to unhook his seatbelt.

"Goodbye, Simon," Marc said, giving the boy a quick wave.

"*Au revoir*," he managed.

Marc watched as Sylvie led Simon into the apartment building, his backpack bouncing off the backs of his knees.

Five minutes later, she returned.

As Sylvie pulled away from the curb, she said, "Sorry about that. Ordinarily, his Grandfather picks him up from school."

"Summer school?" Marc asked.

"Swimming lessons two days a week," Sylvie said.

"Oh," Marc said, glancing at his watch. It was a quarter to one.

"Not much more we can do now anyway. How about a lunch break? My treat."

Sylvie continued on in silence, then said, "I know a place, not far from here. But I cannot accept your offer to pay. I will pay for my own."

"Sure, whatever."

A few more blocks of silence passed between them.

"So, Mr. LaRose, you spoke French to Simon. I didn't realize you could speak the language."

"I get by," Marc said.

"Forgive me, but you're the first American I've met who speaks French."

"French is what we spoke in the house when I was growing up and I attended a Catholic school administered by French nuns until the eighth grade. It was mandatory back then."

"So, have you ever had poutine?" she said, changing the subject.

"Not lately, but if you know a decent place, that sounds good to me."

Chapter Eight

Sylvie turned into the parking lot of a diner adorned by a neon replica of a giant laughing pink pig. Painted across the side of the building were the letters "Le Cochon Fou."

"I've always wanted to eat lunch with a strange lady in a place called 'The Mad Pig,'" Marc said with a grin.

"It's not as bad as it looks. And their poutine is the best on the South Shore."

Inside the brightly lit restaurant, Sylvie led Marc to a booth.

He noted there were several waitresses dressed in bright pink blouses with skintight black shorts. "Le Cochon Fou" was embroidered in pink letters across their backsides.

Marc grabbed a menu that was tucked behind the napkin dispenser and studied the offerings. He discovered there were more than a dozen ways poutine was served…and, the menu claimed this diner served the best to be found in all of Montreal. There was the "Le Cochon Fou Classic," which Marc recognized as basic poutine —French fries and cheese curd covered with gravy. Flipping the menu over he found that poutine could also be served with lobster chunks and gravy, with bacon and gravy, with maple syrup, with a bourbon sauce, and with slaw and barbeque pork, and that only covered the first half of the page. For those adventurous enough to test their cardiac limitations, poutine could be selected as a side dish to a deluxe double cheeseburger, a sixteen-ounce steak, or a rack of baby back ribs.

"I'll have whatever you're having," Marc said, closing his menu.

"I know. It can be a little overwhelming. I'm not starving, so I was thinking a plain hamburger and a coke."

"Make that two," Marc said, replacing the menu behind the napkin dispenser.

"But, Mr. LaRose, you have to try their poutine. I guarantee you won't be disappointed."

Just then, a waitress appeared with pad in hand, ready to take their order. Marc estimated she was somewhere in her mid-twenties, cute face in a Barbie doll sort of way, with extra radiant red hair that

Marc suspected came from a bottle, pulled into a tight pony tail. As she bent over the table to circle the selections Sylvie gave her, including an order of poutine, Marc tried not to stare as the buttons on her pink blouse were losing the battle to contain her natural, or possibly, un-natural assets.

When Sylvie finished her order, the waitress clicked her pen shut and announced, "Très bien merci," and turned to leave.

As Marc's gaze wandered toward 'Le Cochon Fou' bobbing back toward the kitchen, Sylvie broke his reverie, "Mr. LaRose, what's your next move?"

"First off, can we dispense with the 'Mr. LaRose'? I'd much prefer to be called Marc."

"We'll see, Mr. LaRose."

"OK, what can you tell me about Montreal's motorcycle gang network?"

Sylvie paused, "I assume Norman told you what happened to my brother."

"He mentioned it, but didn't go into detail. I got the feeling he felt partially responsible in some way."

"He shouldn't. Paul, my brother, made some bad choices. What happened to him was no one's fault but his own. When he started with the Rock'n Rollers, he didn't realize what the club was all about, just thought that being part of a crew was cool. Then, later, when he wanted out, he became a liability."

"The Rock'n Rollers?" Marc asked.

"Yes, but most people refer to them as just the 'Rollers.' They were one of several motorcycle clubs trying to gain a foothold in the local drug trade back then—pot mostly. They didn't start out that way of course. Originally, the Rollers were just a bunch a guys who liked to ride, mostly on weekends. Over time, a few of the members lost their jobs and began looking for a way to turn their hobby into a moneymaking career. Eventually, they took on a few new members, and the once innocent club morphed into a full blown gang. Now, it's into everything—pot, coke, meth, ecstasy, even gambling and loan sharking."

"How many motorcycle gangs operate in Montreal?"

"Ever since the gang wars of the nineties, it's been pretty much the Rollers and the Rockets. Of course there have been a few 'wannabe's', but they don't seem to last. They get the word pretty fast not to tread on another gang's territory."

"Those bikes we saw at Jimmy Lee's apartment—you thought they may be gang bikes. Any idea which gang?"

"No way of knowing for sure without tailing them, and that could be dangerous. Except for special occasions, like club meetings, they don't wear their 'colors,' vests with the club's name across the back. They're not big into advertising who they are. It's bad for business. Besides, it attracts unnecessary attention."

"What about running the plates to get the registered owner's names, see if we could link them to a gang?" Marc asked.

"Possible, I suppose, providing they have a police record."

Just then, the redhead delivered their drinks. "Your burgers will be up in a moment," she said in French.

Marc busied himself unwrapping his paper-encased straw in a veiled effort to ignore the gyrating 'Le Cochon Fou' as the shorts bobbed off toward another table.

"What are you getting at, Mr. LaRose? Do you suspect Mr. Lee may be tied to a gang?"

Marc took a draw on his soda.

"You identified the tire tracks in the sand where Karlsson's car was parked as those made by a motorcycle. That was verified by Ms. Brooks, who said she heard motorcycles near the car. There are two motorcycles with similar tread patterns in the same parking lot where Jimmy Lee lives. Taken separately, these facts probably don't add up to much, but together…" Marc let the sentence hang.

"So, what do you have in mind?" Sylvie asked.

"I figure Lee should be returning home from Plattsburgh around six this afternoon. I thought I'd take up residence somewhere in his parking lot and see what happens."

"A surveillance?" she asked.

"Why not? It's what I do."

"Using your car?" she asked incredulously.

"What's wrong with my car? It's small, dark green, windows are nicely tinted."

“That’s all well and good, but don’t you think those gaudy blue and gold New York license plates on your front and rear bumpers will attract attention?”

Marc took another pull from his soda. He felt a little embarrassed that he hadn’t thought about his car’s tags, especially seeing that the Quebec plates are white with blue letters and numbers.

“Suppose I could take them off. At least the front one,” he said, meekly.

“You really think that will help?”

The waitress arrived carrying a tray with their lunch orders and set it on the table between them.

"Bon appétit," she announced, dropping the check on the table and leaving, ‘Le Cochon Fou’ jouncing in time with a Quebecois version of ‘Rocket Man’ piped in over the restaurant’s speaker system.

Marc snapped up the check and put it in his shirt pocket. As Sylvie began to protest, Marc raised his index finger, “Look, it’s the least I can do. I’ve only been in Canada for a couple of hours and already, you’ve saved me from blowing a perfectly good surveillance opportunity.”

“This was not our agreement,” she insisted.

“Your agreement, not mine. Now, let’s eat while it’s still hot. I’ve heard there’s nothing worse than eating poutine with cold gravy.”

They ate in silence for a while.

Finally, Sylvie said, “So what are you going to do? About the surveillance I mean.”

“Don’t know for sure, I’ll figure something out.”

Marc took a bite of the burger.

“I may have a suggestion,” she said.

“OK,” he managed, a loaded fork suspended over his plate.

“I have a friend who might be willing to loan you his van. It’s perfect for what you have in mind. I’d have to ask him, of course, but I don’t think it’d be a problem.”

“That would be great, but do you think you could get it for this afternoon?” Marc said as he savored the poutine.

"I don't see why not, but there would be one condition," she said.

"Uh-oh. Why is there always a condition?" he asked light heartedly.

"I'd have to stay with the van."

"But what about your son, Simon?" Marc said looking over his container of soda. "Who would take care of him?"

She hesitated before answering. "Simon is not my son. He was my brother Paul's. Between my parents and me, we're bringing him up together."

"Oh, I see," Marc said, slightly embarrassed. He thought about Sylvie's suggestion regarding the van as he finished his lunch.

Marc glanced at his watch. It was a little after one p.m.

"How long will it take to get the van?" he asked.

"Probably no more than an hour. I just have to fill out some paperwork."

"Paperwork?" Marc asked.

"Yes, my 'friend,' is the Brossard Police Department. The van is a drug surveillance vehicle," she said as she stood, signaling the lunch was over.

"Any friend of yours is a friend of mine," Marc said.

After paying the check, the two left the restaurant. Sylvie drove back to the police station and parked behind Marc's car.

"First thing I have to do is make sure the surveillance vehicle is available. Would it be alright if you waited out here? It shouldn't take more than an hour. If something comes up, I'll text you." Sylvie said.

"Look Detective, I really appreciate your help, but I don't want you to get into trouble doing this for me."

"You don't understand. Norm Prendergast did me an enormous favor a few years back. This is the least I can do for a friend of his. Besides, if I can get something on these guys, it might save some other kid from getting hurt."

"Alright, I just don't want to see you get jammed up because of me."

"Not to worry. I'll contact you in an hour or so," she said.

"Sylvie, one more thing–let me give you Jimmy Lee's date of birth. If you have a chance, run his name through your system. See if anything comes up."

Marc ripped a page out of his notebook that contained Lee's personal info, and handed it to Sylvie. She took the paper, looked at it briefly, and put it in her handbag.

"I'll see what I can do."

"Good–and thanks again," Marc said.

He got out and Sylvie drove her car back through the police parking lot gate.

Marc unlocked his car and retrieved his Yankees' ball cap.

No sense risking a sunburned nose.

He walked a few blocks, found an ATM and withdrew two hundred dollars so he had some Canadian currency to walk around with. He entered a Books-A-Million store, located a thick guide of Montreal, ordered a coffee, and, although he was somewhat familiar with the city, settled in on one of the store's couches to study the area in detail.

An hour later, his cell chimed with the receipt of a text.

It was from Sylvie. "Meet me at 5440 Rue Dufresne. 30 min."

Hmm, small change of plans. Wonder what's up.

Marc located the address across the street from a public parking garage. He pulled into the only available parking space behind a black SUV. Sylvie exited the SUV and walked back to Marc's car.

"I wouldn't advise leaving your car on the street, especially with those New York license tags. It should be safe inside the parking garage," she said, motioning toward the garage entrance. "I'll wait for you here."

After securing his Civic inside the parking garage, Marc returned to the SUV, a GMC Yukon. Sylvie was barely noticeable through the tinted windows, sitting behind the wheel. As Marc got in, she started the engine and pulled away from the curb. He noticed a curtain had been drawn behind their seats.

"I was expecting a cargo van, but this should do fine," Marc said.

Sylvie gave Marc a sideways glance, "We stopped using those way back when. Nowadays, about the only time you'll see a panel van used for surveillance is on a TV cop show, usually with the name of a local utility company painted on its side."

Marc glanced at his watch. "Looks like we still have a couple hours before Jimmy Lee arrives at his apartment. That's a long wait sitting in his parking lot. Any suggestions?"

"I thought we'd take a run by the 'Rock'n Rollers' headquarters. It's on the west island, near St. Laurent."

"They actually have a headquarters?"

"They don't advertise, but if you're in the business, you just know. It's actually a gentlemen's club they use as a front."

The drive took them from the glitzy high-rise office buildings and upscale hotels of Montreal's city center to the four-lane boulevards and tree-shaded avenues of the St. Laurent suburb. After a few turns Marc noticed the surroundings steadily deteriorating. They passed through a maze of narrow streets and shabby two-story houses that seemed to close in on one another. As he checked to make sure his passenger door was locked, Sylvie turned the SUV down a one-way street. 'Rue Pombrio' the corner street sign read. This seedier section of St. Laurent was dotted with vacant storefronts, greasy-looking car repair shops and corner convenience stores with steel bars latticed across their windows.

"The Montreal chapter of the Rock'n Rollers Motorcycle Club is coming up on your right," Sylvie said.

The clubs and bars on Sherbrooke Street in downtown Montreal's center played to tourists with their garish facades of multicolored flashing neon lights, computer-driven and molded to portray an array of gyrating feminine bodies. This club was a drab, windowless, two-story cinder block building with a solid steel door that served as the front entrance.

On the opposite side of the road, a line of motorcycles, mostly Harleys, with a few Hondas and Kawasakis, were backed in and parked perpendicular to the curb. A painted signboard above the building's door read, 'Le Club Erotika,' then underneath, in French, "By Appointment Only."

As Sylvie guided the SUV slowly past the Club, Marc could see several security cameras strategically positioned along the front of the building.

“Did you remember to call ahead for an appointment?” Marc asked with a smirk.

“Slipped my mind,” she said as a corner of her mouth ticked upward.

“It might be helpful if we could get a photo of those bikes, just for reference,” Marc said.

“Consider it done.” Sylvie reached around the steering wheel with her left hand, keeping the wheel steady with her right. Marc heard a rapid succession of clicking sounds. “This thing has several cameras built into the body. I can’t get a photo of their license plates. They’re all facing the wrong way, but this should get you what you need.”

Marc glanced over and saw a panel with an array of buttons and switches located on the lower left half of the dashboard between the steering wheel post and the driver’s door.

“Does this thing have any more toys?”

“A few. Hopefully, I’ll have the opportunity to demonstrate them for you.”

“I’m looking forward to it,” he said.

“The thing is–we’ve made several arrests using this equipment. They, (nodding in the direction of Le Club Erotika) are aware of what we’re capable of. We just keep improvising, hoping to stay a step ahead,” Sylvie said as she continued down the narrow street.

“Just curious, where do these guys live?” Marc asked.

“A few of the old timers, the ‘Patched’ members, live upstairs, over the club. The ‘Prospects,’ you know, the ones that haven’t been fully accepted, are scattered around the area, living with their girlfriends or whoever. Those bikes we saw in the parking lot at Mr. Lee’s apartment could be prospect bikes.

“The cameras along the front of the ‘Club’? I assume that’s to watch for the police,” Marc asked.

“Police, rival gang members, customers, whoever.”

“Have you ever been inside?” Marc asked.

“Le Club Erotika? No, not my style,” she replied with a subtle grin.

“I didn’t mean as a customer,” Marc said.

"The police conducted a raid a few months ago, but I wasn't involved. That was a MUC task force operation."

"MUC?"

"Montreal Urban Community. We have a dedicated team that responds to major incidents and conducts raids."

Sylvie turned left at the corner, then left again at the next side street.

"Although we didn't see anything inside his vehicle, I assume Mr. Karlsson has a cell phone," Sylvie said.

"Yes, his wife has called him repeatedly, but nothing. I figure it's probably been disabled by now."

"We still have a few minutes. I thought we'd sit on the corner up ahead, and see who passes by."

"Fine with me," Marc said.

Sylvie found a parking space between two smaller vehicles on a cross street with a good view of the intersection, just out of sight of the headquarters of the Rock'n Roller's Motorcycle Club.

"Anybody going to Le Club Erotika, or, 'Le Club' as we refer to it, has to pass through this intersection."

The street traffic was fairly steady, which helped camouflage their presence.

"I take it you've used this location before," he said.

"We try not to. Lessens the chance of drawing attention."

After a few minutes of silence, Marc asked, "So tell me, what happened to Simon's mom?"

Sylvie didn't answer right away.

"Wondered how long it would take you to ask." She finally said. "The short answer is we don't know for sure."

Marc studied her face. "Do we have time for the long version?" Marc asked.

"Martine, Paul's wife, disappeared the same day that Paul was killed. Simon was staying with his grandparents, my parents, while Martine was at work. She never came home. We suspect she was picked up by the gang to keep her quiet, but without evidence, there's not much we can do."

"No car?" Marc asked.

"She took the bus to work. We talked to her employer. Only thing he knew was that she received a phone call at work that Simon was sick. She left right after getting the call."

"Did the employer say who called?"

"No, and that's where the 'long part,' comes in. Neither my mom or dad called her, and, Simon wasn't sick."

"Was there any sign that Paul and Martine were having problems before this?"

"Not really. I mean, she wasn't happy with Paul's involvement with the Rollers, but she knew he wanted out."

"Did she know anything about Paul being an informant?"

Sylvie paused again.

"That's something we've asked ourselves. I don't believe she did, but we really don't know."

"Sounds like she either met her fate with the gang, or, maybe was in on it the whole time," Marc said.

Before Sylvie replied, a Harley rolled through the intersection, its four-stroke engine filling the air with the distinctive racket that only Harley fans seem to appreciate, "Ba-ta-toe, Ba-ta-toe," then "pop, pop, pop," when the bike slowed as it approached the 'Club'.

"That looks like the red Superlow we saw parked in front of Jimmy Lee's apartment complex," Sylvie said as she started the SUV's engine. After a short pause, she eased the SUV into the traffic. Reaching the intersection, they saw the brake lights of the Superlow illuminate off to their left. She turned the SUV in the direction of Le Club.

As they slowly approached, they watched the biker back his machine in line with the other bikes, facing outward toward the street. His thick biceps and bulging forearms were almost completely colored with an array of tattoos as he gripped the customized "Ape Hanger" handlebars. Although his face was turned away as he back peddled his bike against the curb, Marc noticed his head was 'protected' by a MC gang version of a German WWII helmet.

'Achtung,' Marc thought, as he heard the Yukon's covert camera click away.

After Sylvie maneuvered the Yukon away from Le Club, Marc accessed his phone's photo archive.

"Can't tell for sure, but I'd say the bike that 'Adolph' back there was operating and the one we saw at Jimmy Lee's are probably one and the same," he said, holding his phone toward Sylvie so she could also see the photo.

"What would those bikes be doing outside of Mr. Lee's apartment?" Sylvie asked, more to herself.

"Is there an echo in here? That's the same question I asked earlier," Marc said.

They rode in silence for a few blocks.

Sylvie glanced at the dashboard clock. It was almost five in the afternoon. "Speaking of which, we should be heading back to St. Hubert, before Mr. Lee gets home from work."

"I'll second that motion, but before we settle in there, I need to make a bathroom stop," Marc said.

"There's a small *privy* in the back," Sylvie said, motioning with her thumb, "We use it on stakeouts." The hint of a smile tilted the corners of her mouth upward.

Marc gave her a look. "It's no emergency, yet. But this is Montreal. There has to be somewhere between here and Lee's apartment where we could stop."

Sylvie's expression became amused.

"We passed a chicken place on the way over. You could use their facilities, and while we're there, pick up something for dinner."

"Fried chicken in a cardboard bucket. Really?" Marc said with a hint of sarcasm.

"Well, I suppose we could take our time and look for something more to your liking, if you think you could hold on for a while longer," she said, her grin widening.

"*Privy* roulette? I don't think so."

Forty minutes later, they arrived at Jimmy Lee's apartment. There were noticeably more cars parked there than before, and although most of the spaces were reserved for tenants, a few were marked 'invité'or guest. Sylvie found an open space and parked the Yukon, facing it away from Lee's apartment, and turned the engine off.

"OK, I guess there must be a reason to be looking toward the highway rather than at Lee's apartment." Marc said.

Sylvie reached behind her seat, retrieved a folded sunshade, and spread it across the inside of the windshield. Marc saw what she was doing, and helped fit the shade on his side, covering the window. A trickle of light eased through the heavily tinted side windows.

Sylvie swiveled her seat 180 degrees and slid the curtain divider open. Marc released his seat lock and did the same, giving him a chance to observe the array of surveillance gadgetry at the back of the SUV.

There were two captain's chairs, facing opposite sides of the vehicle. Where the side windows should be, Marc observed a set of flat video screens. Next to the screens was a stack of compact DVR's and other gadgets fitted onto shelves fastened to the sides of the vehicle. A side panel contained a row of switches and buttons. The arm of each chair was fitted with a joystick.

"You have any of this in your Civic?" Sylvie asked with a smirk.

Marc was still trying to comprehend the array of electronic gear before him.

"All I have is a handheld video camera and a Chi-Chi's salsa bottle."

"Salsa bottle?" she asked, puzzled.

"A PI's portable *privy*," Marc winked.

Sylvie rolled her eyes. "You take that seat, and I'll sit here," she said, motioning toward one of the chairs. She reached to the panel of switches and flipped one up. Marc barely heard the soft puttering of a motor start up from somewhere under the vehicle.

"That's a battery-powered air conditioning unit. It's good for about twelve hours without a charge. That way we'll draw less attention than we would sitting in a parking lot with the engine running."

He immediately felt a cool breeze from an overhead vent.

She flipped another switch and one of the flat screens lit up. Using her joystick, she moved an embedded camera lens in the direction of the parked motorcycles they had observed earlier. She toggled the camera and zoomed in on a lone Harley 1200 Custom motorcycle.

"You could be right about the red Superlow parked there before; it's probably the same one we saw at 'Le Club,'" she said.

She continued panning the area to determine its viewing limits, then switching on another screen, toggled a different camera to the parking lot entrance which showed traffic on the main street.

"It appears we probably have a half hour before Mr. Lee gets home from work. Let me give you a quick lesson on how these things work," Sylvie said, motioning to the bank of screens and switches.

It was 6:40 when they saw a lime green Kia compact pull into the parking lot.

"That's Jimmy Lee behind the wheel," Marc said, staring intently at the screen.

As they watched Lee drive through the parking lot, Sylvie initiated a third camera. Then she flipped another switch, "Might as well record some of this."

They continued to watch as Lee parked his car.

When he exited the Kia, they continued watching the flat screen. Lee was dressed in jeans with a colorful tee shirt and carrying a briefcase. He made his way to the entrance of the apartment building, then disappeared through its main door.

"Well, if nothing else, he's at least corroborated his story that he gets home around this hour. I guess we'll just have to wait and see what else he does."

Sylvie glanced at her watch, "I suppose."

After a few moments, Marc said, "He's probably washing up, or whatever. You up for some chicken?"

"It's all yours," she said, scrunching her nose.

"Watching your figure?"

Sylvie didn't respond as she continued to monitor the screens.

A few minutes later as Marc was finishing a drumstick, Sylvie pointed towards one of the screens, "Here he comes."

Marc looked up and saw Lee exiting the apartment, now wearing a pair of dress slacks and a casual short-sleeved shirt with a floral pattern.

"That was fast. Could be heading out to supper," Marc said as he dropped the remnants of the leg bone in the bucket and grabbed a paper napkin.

Sylvie pulled the curtain separating them from the front seats.

"Dinner's over. Time to find out what he's up to."

After settling back into their seats, they quickly refolded the sunshade. With Jimmy Lee behind them, they watched from the Yukon's rear view mirrors as he approached his car. Just as Sylvie was about to start the engine, Lee turned away from his Kia and pointed what was apparently an entry fob at another car parked nearby. They barely heard the chirp as a red Tesla's taillights blinked on.

"Looks like Jimmy's stepping out in style tonight," Marc said, curious about Lee's choice of transportation.

A moment later, the electric-powered sports car silently slipped past the Yukon toward the parking lot exit. Sylvie let the Tesla get some distance away before she started the SUV's engine. They watched as the Tesla turned left out of the parking lot, toward the Champlain Bridge. Sylvie maneuvered the Yukon behind the Tesla at a discreet following distance. A mile later, the Tesla turned again, this time north onto Autoroute 20.

"Wonder where he's going?" Marc whispered to himself.

Sylvie remained silent as she continued the pursuit, allowing a few cars to get between them and Lee's car.

After a few miles, the Tesla's signal light blinked as he exited the Autoroute.

"He's heading toward the Jacques Cartier Bridge, across the river to Montreal," Sylvie said.

But, as they approached the bridge, the Tesla's signal light illuminated again, signaling an unexpected turn onto St. Helen's Island.

"This is strange. St. Helen's is basically a park, unless…" Sylvie left the thought hang between them as the Tesla turned onto the island. Another three turns and a giant lighted billboard appeared in front of them which read, "Casino de Montreal."

"Look's like Mr. Lee has a taste for the slots," Sylvie said, as they watched Lee's vehicle stop at the entrance gate to the Casino's parking lot.

After Lee cleared the parking gate, Sylvie waited a few moments before bringing the Yukon through the gate as well.

They both spotted the Tesla's brake lights two rows from where Sylvie parked the Yukon.

"We should tail him inside the casino. See who he talks to and what he does," she said.

"I can't follow him in there. He knows what I look like. If he spots me, the game's over."

"Who said anything about you? Stay here and make love to your bucket of chicken," Sylvie said as she grabbed her purse.

"*Bonne Chance*," Marc said, as the door slammed shut.

We're going to need all the luck you can get.

Marc watched as Sylvie took her time crossing the parking lot, keeping some distance between her and Lee, before they both disappeared behind the ornate entrance to the Casino.

Just as well get comfortable, this could be a long wait.

He slid through the curtains into the rear of the SUV, flipped the switch to start the air conditioner, then pushed the buttons activating one of the cameras and a flat screen. He panned in on the red Tesla and copied its license plate number, then, he panned back to the casino's entrance so he could watch for Sylvie and/or Jimmy Lee, whoever appeared first.

As he settled in for what he knew could be long evening, he thought back to when the casino was built, after the world's fair, locally dubbed 'Expo 67,' when the planners combined the France and Quebec pavilions by adding a third connecting building.

Marc switched on a second camera and panned over the casino's unique structure, with its ten floors of steel built in angles shooting off in every direction, the gaps filled in with massive windows. Marc thought it looked like a giant Lego set, put together by a sixth grader who had been forced to read *Popular Mechanics*.

Marc panned the camera over the half-full parking lot, then across the St. Lawrence River and to the city of Montreal's skyline. As time passed and darkness began to set in, a giant cross, illuminated with red neon could be seen atop Mount Royal, the City of Montreal's namesake.

It was just after nine-o'clock when Marc saw Sylvie on the flat screen crossing the parking lot coming toward the Yukon. As she approached the SUV, he could hear the sound of her heals scuffing along the pavement and he slid back into the passenger seat.

She climbed into the Yukon, dropped her purse on the floor next to her seat and started the engine.

"So, did you break the bank?" Marc asked.

"With quarter slots? I don't think so. But I think Mr. Lee must get paid well down at the Barbeau plant."

"He's an engineer, so he probably gets by. What makes you say that?"

"He likes blackjack—a lot. But I don't think the cards liked him, at least not tonight."

"Oh," Marc said, waiting for her to continue.

"He drinks heavy, tips heavy, and loses a lot more than he wins."

"Any idea how much?"

"I saw him make three trips to the cashier's window, then return to the tables with a thousand dollars worth of chips each time," Sylvie said.

"Ouch. Sounds like his Tesla payment may be late this month."

"Also, everyone there seemed to know him. I mean the dealers, the pit boss, the cashier, the waitresses. They all called him by name, like he was a regular."

Marc thought about this latest revelation.

"Was he still gambling when you left?" Marc asked.

"Last I saw him, he was in the dining room ordering dinner, and I got the feeling he was being 'comped.'"

"What do you mean?" Marc asked.

"I heard the waiter say, 'anything you like, Mr. Lee, it's all taken care of.'"

Marc stared across the river at the city lights as he thought about what Sylvie had seen. "If his meals are comped, then he's definitely a steady customer, and a high roller. I can't imagine Barbeau paying him that kind of money."

"So, either he's real lucky, which he wasn't tonight, or he has another source of income, or…" she didn't finish her thought.

"Or he inherited a pile of money, but still doesn't want to give up his day job that he drives over an hour each way to get to and return home from," Marc said with a sly grin.

"Are you serious?" Sylvie asked a confused look on her face.

"No, not really. I think there's something else going on."

The two sat in silence for a few minutes.

"OK, let's think about this a moment," Marc said. "We know that Karlsson went missing, presumably in the Montreal area because his vehicle was recovered on Nuns' Island. A witness spotted his car along with two people, one matching the description of Karlsson, with a lime green compact parked nearby. Lee has a lime green Kia. Motorcycle tracks were located in the sand where Karlsson's car was located. There are motorcycles parked in Jimmy Lee's parking lot that appear to be connected with the Rock'n Rollers' motorcycle gang. Lee acted nervous when we spoke, and, now we find he apparently has a gambling problem."

"So, what's next?" Sylvie finally asked.

"It would appear that Lee is the link to locating Karlsson. Under Canadian law, do you think there is sufficient probable cause to bring him in for questioning?" Sylvie sat in silence, seeming to think about Marc's question.

"According to the Canadian Charter of Rights, we could bring him in, but I seriously doubt a judge would give me a warrant."

"I was afraid you'd say that," Marc said, his voice edged with frustration.

The pair continued to stare at the lights of the Casino in silence.

"It doesn't appear he's leaving any time soon. Tomorrow is Saturday, so he probably has the day off from work, he might be here for the rest of the evening. I'm all for calling it a day," Marc said.

Sylvie seemed to hesitate, "What are you going to do? Go back to Plattsburgh tonight?"

"Not sure. Can we still use this vehicle again tomorrow?"

"Actually, I have it through Monday morning."

"Oh, well maybe I could check into a motel, or something. Save me the round trip to Plattsburgh and back."

Sylvie gave a nervous cough, "Look, Paul's room is available. It's been empty since he was...uh…since the incident."

"Thanks, but no. I don't want to be a bother. I'm sure your parents have enough to deal with. I'll just get a room somewhere."

"What do my parents have to do with this?"

"I assumed Paul lived with your parents, and…"

"You assume too much," Sylvie said as she started the engine and headed out of the Casino's parking lot.

They rode in silence as Sylvie drove off the island and back toward Brossard.

After a few minutes, Marc said, "Sylvie, I was just thinking, it's not quite ten o'clock, and the night's still young. How about I make an 'appointment' for Le Club Erotika."

"And do what? Tell them you're a friend of Jimmy Lee and thought you'd check the place out?"

"I suppose I could start with that," he said half-heartedly.

Sylvie exhaled deeply as she seemed to consider what Marc was suggesting.

"Marc, you don't know what you're getting yourself into. What you're suggesting could be dangerous, more dangerous than you know."

"I understand, but I can't just sit by and wait for something to happen."

The fact that Sylvie had actually called Marc by his given name for the first time since they had met was not lost on him.

Sylvie continued driving toward Brossard in silence. They went about ten blocks before she finally spoke, "OK, but I can't let you go in there alone. If you're determined to go, I'm going with you, no questions."

"You don't think they'll remember you?" Marc asked.

"I just said, 'no questions.' And no, they've never seen me. I've intentionally avoided them and that place."

Sylvie pulled off the road into an empty parking lot, retrieved her cell phone and dialed the number for Le Club Erotika.

Marc listened as she talked to whoever answered the phone. The rhythmic thumping of loud dance music could be heard over the phone even from his side of the vehicle.

"Yes, I'd like to make a reservation for two for tonight," she led off with.

"Madame Sylvie Levesque, and a guest," She said in French, in reply to whoever was taking the reservation as Marc listened to the one-sided conversation.

"No, we're straight," she said, giving Marc a sideways glance.

Marc flashed his eyebrows in mock agreement.

"Strip tease? Of course, anything else?" she asked.

"A lap dance? Possibly, what else," Sylvie asked, sounding as if she were ordering lunch at a drive through.

"Contact dancing and private rooms? Umm, probably not," she said glancing at her watch. "Eleven this evening, then?" She asked, and then listened intently for the answer.

"*Merci beaucoup*," she said, ending the call.

"They're open till 7:00 a.m. There's a $50 cover charge, each. Think your insurance company will go for that?" she asked.

"Depends on how much I have to tip for the lap dance," he said with a smirk.

"I need to stop at my apartment and change into something a little more appropriate," she said.

"If you think it's necessary."

"You don't get out much, do you?" she said with a sideways glance.

"The night life in Plattsburgh may be a little less glamorous than it is in Montreal, but I get around," he said assuredly.

A few minutes later, Sylvie stopped the Yukon in front of the green awning where she had earlier taken her nephew, Simon, to her parents.

"So, do you also live here, with your parents?" Marc asked.

"This will only take a minute. I'll be right out," she said, ignoring Marc's question.

He watched her spring up the short flight of steps and through the glass doors to the front entrance of the building.

Marc waited patiently, observing a few vehicles pull in and leave the parking lot, which had become increasingly busy as the night progressed.

Five minutes later, Marc caught sight of Sylvie making her way down the walkway. She was wearing a black lace cocktail dress, cut just above the knee and topped with an ivory bodice and a modest neckline.

Despite the dress, or maybe because of it, she gracefully slid behind the wheel.

"Now, I feel underdressed." Marc said.

"You're fine, besides, I'll be doing most of the talking and they'll be looking at me."

Sylvie started the engine and pulled out into the street for the trip across town to Le Club Erotika.

"So, how do you think we should handle this?" Marc asked.

"I have a few ideas. First, we just sort of get comfortable with the surroundings; act like we're out on the town and having a good time. Then, after a few drinks, I was thinking we'd let it be known that we're in the market for a business loan. See where that takes us."

"You think anybody there would buy that? Sounds a little out of place, I mean, who goes to a night club looking for a loan?"

Sylvie gave Marc a quick glance.

"I was thinking about a scenario. After we're there for a while, we could start arguing. When someone asks what the problem is, I'd mention you being turned down for a loan, or something like that."

"It's a possibility, I guess," Marc said without conviction.

"Besides drugs, these guys are loan sharks. Believe me, if they're hungry for business, and if we play our cards right, I think it might work."

"OK, say this little plan of yours works and someone falls for it. What's next?"

"I doubt anyone will approach us right off. This is sort of an introduction, you might say. If I'm any judge as to how these guys do business, they'll contact us later, after they've had a chance to check us out."

"Check us out?" Marc asked.

"You know, ask around. See if anyone else has loaned us money in the past, or if you are known by anyone else in the 'business.' I have an extra ID you can use, she said, handing a Quebec driver's license to Marc."

Using the car's interior light, Marc studied the driver's license. It had been issued to Gilles LaFountain who was the same age and general physical description as Marc. Although the license was still valid, the grainy photo showed a male with a droopy moustache and goatee, topped with a mop of dark hair that hung over his ears.

"Nice try, Sylvie. But I look nothing like this guy."

"It's the best I could do on short notice. If someone asks, say the photo was taken before you decided to go into business for yourself. Mr. LaFountain died in a car accident last year, so he won't need it. Commit his particulars to memory and lock your own ID in the glove compartment."

"You really think they'd search me?"

"Like I said, if they take the bait, they'll probably want to check you out."

Reluctantly, he spent a few moments memorizing his new personal information. As they passed over the Champlain Bridge, he removed his driver's license from his wallet, and slid LaFountain's behind the plastic ID holder.

They continued in silence for a few blocks.

"Tell me, have you had much experience with sex clubs?" Marc asked, unintentionally exposing a sly grin.

"Enough. I worked vice for three years before transferring to Robbery-Homicide."

"So, who's manning the desk while you're helping me locate Mr. Karlsson?"

"We've got plenty of good people. Besides, I'm on leave as of one o'clock this afternoon."

"On leave? You took leave to help me with a missing person case?" Marc asked, his eyebrows raised.

"If you wanted my help, that's what I had to do. Besides, my brother was murdered five years ago this week, and I needed some time off."

They passed a rusty street sign indicating they were entering the city of St. Laurent.

"I don't want to leave the SUV near the club. I know a safe place," she said, turning down a dimly lit street two blocks from their destination. She pulled to a stop in the parking lot of an all-night laundromat.

"You call this place 'safe'?" Marc asked, taking in the shabby neighborhood surroundings.

"The owner lives upstairs. I trust him," she said, nodding toward a window above the laundromat.

After securing the Yukon, they made the ten-minute walk to Rue Pombrio, toward Le Club Erotika.

As they approached the Club, Marc noticed, in addition to the increased number of motorcycles parked across the street, a number of cars, double-parked directly in front of the building. Most bore Quebec license plates, but there were also a few from New York, New Jersey, and Connecticut.

"No sex show would be complete without an international audience," Marc said, attempting to lighten the mood and to mollify his own anxiety.

At the club's entrance, a plain black steel door, he noticed there was no doorknob, just a button off to one side. Sylvie pressed the button. Although they heard no sound, a woman immediately opened the door, scantily clad in black short-shorts and a sequined bra. The rhythmic music Marc had heard earlier over Sylvie's cell pushed past her.

"Bienvenue à Club Erotika," she said in a well-practiced provocative tone. "Under what name did you make your reservation?"

"Madame Sylvie Levesque," Sylvie said.

The sensuous sentry referred to a pink plastic-covered notepad.

"*Ah, oui*, here we are, two straights for the strip tease," she said, making a check mark or something on the pad with a black pen that was topped with a large pink feather. Then she turned, and motioning with her plumage, said, "This way, *s'il vous plaît*."

Following the scantily clad greeter through the entrance, they squeezed past a pair of bouncers flanking the doorway. Marc thought they looked more like rejects from the pro wrestling ring, wearing snug fitting triple-X sized black tee shirts with their heavily tattooed arms folded across their chests. Neither man seemed to pay much attention to Marc and Sylvie, who apparently posed no threat. Marc thought he recognized one of the men as the motorcyclist he had observed wearing the Nazi helmet earlier in the day. At the end of the hallway, the 'greeter' pulled a black curtain to one side, and handed Marc and Sylvie off to a tall bottle blonde wearing a red mini skirt and a skimpy white top, accented with mesh nylons and four-inch heels.

"Hello, my name is Nadia. I'll be your hostess for the evening. Would you like a table, or would you prefer to sit near the bar?" She asked in passable French with an accent that Marc couldn't place.

"*Une table, s'il vous plait,*" Marc answered.

As they entered the lounge, Marc noticed there were men, mostly, sitting around a semicircular bar with a close-up view of the raised stage behind. He could see there were about a dozen or so small tables scattered about the dimly lit room, mostly occupied by couples. At the center of the stage were two women, one white, one black, both clad in what Marc could only speculate was something smaller than a g-string, perhaps a mini thong, if such a garment truly exists, taking turns making love to a chrome-plated pole, then to each other, then back to the pole again, all in time with some kind of noise that barely passed for music.

After being seated, Nadia announced, "Zombies are the specialty tonight, twenty dollar; but I can get you whatever you want, alcohol, or otherwise."

"A strawberry daiquiri for the lady and a Molson Export for me," Marc said.

"Is this a special occasion?" Nadia asked, in what Marc figured was her standard sucking-up-for-tips routine.

"Actually, we are celebrating. Gilles closed on a big deal today, didn't you, baby?" Sylvie said with a wink, giving Marc a cue.

"It could be a big deal if the bank goes for it," Marc said with an assured laugh.

Nadia smoothly joined in the laughter. "That sounds like a good reason to celebrate. I'll be right back with your drinks."

They sat in silence as the pair on stage continued massaging each other while curling around the dance pole. The black girl seemed underage, sixteen or so, Marc guessed. The white girl was decorated with multicolored tattoos. Both were sweating profusely, possible due to their physical exertion, or maybe, they were actually enjoying themselves.

Lost in the din of the music, Sylvie said something that Marc couldn't make out, but before he could ask her what she said, the drinks arrived.

"One strawberry daiquiri for madam and a Molson for monsieur," Nadia exclaimed, setting the drinks on the table, the words 'daiquiri' and 'monsieur,' barely recognizable through her accent.

Marc reached for his wallet.

Nadia stayed his hand. "I've started a tab. Besides, I'm up next, so enjoy," she said, running her tongue across her upper lip, already shiny with gloss. She then disappeared around the back of the bar.

As Marc and Sylvie began nursing their drinks, the music/noise stopped.

Thank God for small favors.

The two that had been slinking around the fire pole untwined, and scurried off the stage.

Hope someone scrubs that thing down with antiseptic wipes between acts.

Just then, a man wearing an ill-fitting toupee and a cheesy smile with a polyester suit to match appeared on the stage holding a microphone.

"*Bonsoir, Madames et Monsieurs. Bienvenue à Le Club Erotika.* Tonight we have a very special show for your viewing pleasure. Please join me in welcoming our featured dancer of the evening, direct from Odessa in the Ukraine, 'Naadiaa, The Tangerine Dream,' he announced, extending an arm toward a corner of the stage.

Didn't know they grew tangerines in the Ukraine. Maybe they're introducing a new crop.

The music, actually a sultry trumpet number, started and Nadia appeared from around the curtain wearing a black skirt opened with a long slit down one side, a matching half jacket, and a pair of patent leather stiletto-heeled boots. Moving slowly in time to the lilting notes of a steamy tune, she wrapped one leg around the pole, bent over backwards and blew kisses toward the men sitting at the bar.

There were a few cat calls from the men, along with a smattering of applause from the tables.

After circling the pole a couple of times, she slowly unbuttoned her jacket, then, with a toss, it disappeared. Marc couldn't help but notice that Nadia had apparently forgotten her bra. Another couple of twirls and the skirt was flung in the same direction as the jacket leaving poor Nadia with little protection from the elements—or the salacious stares of the men at the bar, save for her knee-high boots and a sequined tangerine-colored thong, precariously held in place by what Marc figured had to be a small length of monofilament fish line.

As Marc was about to take a sip of beer, he felt a tap on his shoulder. It was the tattooed bouncer that Marc remembered wearing the Nazi motorcycle helmet.

"Got a minute?" He asked in French, while he jerked his thumb toward a door behind them that Marc hadn't previously noticed.

Sylvie started to say something, but Marc raised his palm toward her.

"What's up?" Marc asked.

"Follow me," Nazi helmet growled as he turned and started for the door.

"Gilles, should I come with you?" Sylvie asked.

"I'm fine. This should only take a minute," he replied.

He again held his palm up to her, a sign he wanted her to remain seated, but he could see the concern in her face.

Marc caught up to the big man who had opened the door and held it for Marc to enter. As they made their way down a short darkened corridor, Nazi helmet reached around Marc and opened another door and motioned for him to go through.

Marc entered a small room lit only by a bank of CCTV monitors glowing along a wall facing a metal desk. A quick glance at the monitors showed views of the street in front of the club, a view of the inside of the main entrance, one of the stage and another of the tables where Marc and Sylvie were sitting. Marc could see the darkened outline of Sylvie's shape at the table he had just left.

Sitting behind the desk was an older man. Early sixties, Marc estimated. However, despite his wire-rimmed glasses and a mane of grey hair that was pulled into a tight pony tail, he appeared no less menacing than any of the bouncers Marc had seen since entering the club. He probably weighed in at over two hundred pounds and wasn't showing an ounce of fat. But, unlike the "greeters," he wore a tan suit jacket with a blue turtle-necked shirt. An oversized gold cross pulled on the chain circling his neck.

Wonder if he'll treat the audience to a sermon after the show.

"Forgive me for intruding on your evening, Monsieur Gilles. I don't want to keep you from the show, and I promise, I will have you back with your lovely lady in just a few moments. My name is Maurice Bashaw and I would like to personally welcome you to Le Club Erotika," he said in French as he arose from his chair just enough to give a sense of civility, and stretched his hand toward Marc.

"It's Gilles LaFountain. To what do I owe this honor," Marc asked, as he felt the man's vise like grip envelop his hand.

Bashaw's tone was low, but confident, as he motioned Marc to a chair at the opposite side of the desk.

"I understand 'congratulations' are in order," Bashaw said.

"Congratulations?" Marc asked, feigning surprise.

"Oh, come now, Gilles, don't be so modest. Word has it that you just succeeded in closing some kind of big deal. A deal so big, that you and your lovely lady have taken the time to visit my club to celebrate.

Sylvie was right. The hint of cash is not lost on these people.

"Oh that; yeah, well, actually, I haven't finalized it quite yet, but it looks pretty good," Marc said, matter-of-factly.

"I just wanted to let you know that if there is anything I can do to assist you, I am here to help, in any way I can," Bashaw said with an exaggerated grin.

"Thanks for the offer, but I don't think that will be necessary. There are a few financing issues that still have to be worked out, but other than that, I think I can manage on my own."

"I understand," Bashaw said, undaunted. "I have been involved in a number of big deals, and I know how difficult they can be sometimes, especially when it comes to the intricacies of financing. I just wanted to take this opportunity to introduce myself and let you know that if your project, whatever it is, is ever in need of assistance, financially or otherwise, we have resources. I personally look forward to assisting you any way I can." With that, Bashaw slid a card across the desk.

Marc glanced at the card. 'Bashaw Enterprizes,' was emblazed across the top in raised gold print along with the Club's address and several contact numbers.

"The top one is my personal cell number. Call me anytime."

"Thanks, I'll keep it in mind," Marc said as he nervously tapped the card on the desk a few times.

"Thing is, I'm embarrassed to say, my credit rating isn't what it should be."

Bashaw smiled. "Not to worry. I have several clients whose past has been plagued with similar problems. I make it a business to help people overcome those difficulties to the satisfaction of all parties concerned. In the end, we all profit."

"I see," Marc said, hesitantly, taking another moment to study the card.

"Like I said, I will certainly consider your kind offer, Mr. Bashaw. This is certainly food for thought. I can look at this as a fallback position, a plan B, if you will, in case the banks turn me down."

"Take your time, Mr. LaFountain. Just remember, when the need arises, you have my number." Bashaw glanced at his watch. "*Tabernac*, look at the time. Here I am, going on. I'm sure you want to get back to your lady friend," Bashaw said, rising from his chair and again extending his hand. "Oliver will show you back to your table. Have a good evening and enjoy the rest of the show."

He provided another extra firm handshake.

"Merci, I'm sure I will," Marc said as 'Oliver' opened the door and held it for him to leave.

Oliver? Odd name for a Nazi helmet-wearing ape. And was that a cobra's head I saw peering over his neckline?

When Marc arrived back at the table, Sylvie seemed relieved to see him, but remained quiet until Oliver had strutted off. Nadia was still on stage, making animated love to the dance pole while the crowd clapped and sang to a Montreal party favorite, "*Voulez-vous coucher avec moi, ce soir?*"

"I was beginning to wonder what had happened to you," Sylvie said.

"I'll tell you later. Don't look now, but we're on candid camera. Act like we're into the show," Marc said and started clapping in time with the music.

After another couple of songs, Nadia left the stage, and was replaced by another hostess Marc had noticed waiting tables earlier. A few minutes later, Nadia returned to their table wearing her hostess outfit.

"So, what did you think of my show?" she asked.

"Pretty nice, I guess," Marc said.

"Pretty nice? Nadia pouted, playfully miming her affront.

"I was summoned to the office where I spent part of your show talking with your boss, Mr. Bashaw," Marc replied.

"Oh?" she said, glancing around the room.

"Seems someone informed him of the reason for our celebration here tonight."

"Oh, I don't know, er, I, I mean, I didn't mention it to anyone," she stuttered.

"Actually, I wanted to thank you, or whoever it was, for the invitation. Never know, I might need his help someday."

Nadia seemed relieved as her painted lips turned up in a relaxed smile.

"Well, I'm happy for you both. Is there anything else I can do for you?"

"Maybe. But for now, how about another round of drinks," Marc said.

Nadia resumed her hostess face, "a strawberry daiquiri, and a Molson coming right up," she said as she turned and headed back toward the bar.

Marc leaned in close to Sylvie, "Watch what you say, there may be microphones close by," he whispered.

Sylvie replied with an almost imperceptible nod. The pair continued to make small talk as the show progressed.

A few moments later, Nadia arrived with their drinks.

"She's pretty good, don't you think?" Nadia said, motioning toward the stage as she set their drinks on the table.

"She's not bad, but, we really did enjoy your show," Marc said, careful not to sound too patronizing.

Nadia quickly glanced around the room, leaned in, and rearranged the napkins on their table. With no more than a whisper, she said, "I have to tell you. This is only my second night working here, and I really wasn't sure how I was doing. I mean, I noticed the usual cat calls, but nobody's said anything about my performances."

"Now you know and, believe me, we've seen quite a few." Marc boasted.

"Thank you, she said resuming her normal voice," as she straightened up.

"We'll be leaving right after this set, you can bring our bill anytime," Marc said.

"Oh, so soon? We still have a lot of girls you haven't seen. We're just getting started."

"That's OK, next time perhaps. We have a big day planned for tomorrow, and we'll have to get up early." Marc replied.

"All right, but it's your loss," she said, and left the table.

Nadia retreated toward the back of the bar where Sylvie watched her conferring with one of the bouncers.

"So, you're making friends with foreign striptease dancers, as well as gang leaders now?" Sylvie whispered, teasingly.

"You catch more flies with bullshit than vinegar," Marc whispered, returning the wink she had given him earlier.

"Be careful, these are not mere flies, they're wasps. Their stings can be very nasty." Sylvie said, then noticed the waitress heading toward them again.

Nadia placed a small tray with their tab on the table.

"You're only being billed for your drinks. The cover charge has been taken care of," she said.

"That's very kind, but you really didn't have to," Marc said.

"You can thank Mr. Bashaw next time you see him," she said.

Marc placed a Canadian hundred-dollar note on the tray.

"This should cover it. We enjoyed the show, as well as your service."

Nadia scooped up the tray in a well-practiced move. "My pleasure," she said with what seemed a genuine smile, as she slid off towards another table, she glanced back at Marc.

"Aren't you a regular honey pot, Mr. LaFountain," Sylvie said with a smirk.

Just then a large group of partygoers entered the room raising the noise level to that of a Boeing 747 during takeoff.

"Ready?" Marc shouted over the din.

"Thought you'd never ask."

Back on the street, Marc and Sylvie, aware of the security cameras, mingled in with a few other patrons as they left; then steadily made their way along the sidewalk, back towards the laundromat and the Yukon.

They had just turned the corner, when they heard a Harley engine starting up from the direction of the Club.

"Quick, this way," Sylvie said, leading Marc toward the entrance of an apartment building, then raced down a flight of steel-grated steps toward the darkened entrance of one of the apartments, stopping about half way down. "Keep out of sight," she said, ducking below the level of the street. The motorcycle slowly approached the intersection with its engine idling.

Peeking from behind the wrought iron railing, they observed the Harley come to a stop as the operator balanced the bike with his feet. The rider, wearing the now familiar Nazi helmet, scanned the street toward the laundromat, then, slowly continued away from the intersection. When he was about a block away, Sylvie said, "OK, let's go."

They both scampered up the steel stairs. When they reached the top step, they heard a door open at the bottom of the stairwell.

"Why don't you Anglo sex addicts go do your fucking someplace else?" Marc heard a woman yell in French, followed by the sound of the door slamming shut.

They listened to the receding rumble of the Harley's engine as they quickly made their way toward the laundromat.

Once inside the Yukon, Sylvie started the engine, but rather than head back the way they had come, she pulled onto the street, turned left, and slowly drove away from the club, careful not to attract any undue attention. When they were about five blocks away she made another turn along a back street.

"Just to be sure not to run into that biker, we'll take the long way back to Brossard."

"Do you think they made us?" Marc asked.

"I'd be surprised if they did. I think they're just curious to know who they're dealing with."

"So, you think they bought the story about my 'big deal?'"

"Possibly. They're suspicious of everyone. They have to be to stay in business."

Silence filled the cross-town trip to Brossard. When they arrived at the apartment where Sylvie left her nephew earlier in the day, she parked the Yukon in a parking space marked 'Guest'.

"Why are we going to your parent's condo?" Marc asked.

"I live in a separate unit, one floor up. I figured you'd be better off crashing here for the night, what's left of it."

"Uh, sure."

"Before you get any ideas, you'll be in the spare bedroom."

"Fine, but I left my overnight bag back at the parking garage," Marc said.

"I have a spare toothbrush," she said as they made their way across the parking lot and up the stairs to the second floor.

Sylvie stopped on the landing and unlocked the door to her unit which opened directly into a large living room.

At first glance, Sylvie's condo seemed sparse, but neatly decorated. A three-piece sectional faced a flat screen TV mounted on an inside wall. There were two windows, the larger one overlooking the parking lot they had just crossed. The second, facing the main street, was covered with heavy drapery, probably to deaden the noise of city traffic, Marc guessed. The open floor plan had a small kitchen area, complete with a dinette table in the corner, surrounded by family photos along the wall.

"Cozy," Marc said.

"Your room is this way," Sylvie said, leading Marc down a short hallway. He noticed there were three doors, two on the left and one to the right.

Sylvie opened the first door, "This is the toilet or, as you Americans call it, the bathroom. I'll leave a towel and washcloth on the sink for you, along with the toothbrush I promised."

Closing the door, she proceeded down the short hallway and pointed to the second door. "This will be your room for the night. I hope you find it adequate."

"I take it the other door is probably not to your open bar," Marc said, pointing across the hallway, allowing himself a devilish grin.

She held the door to Marc's room open and said, "If it's all the same to you, I'd like to skip the nightcap. We'll get an early start in the morning."

Marc shrugged. "Pleasant dreams," he said as he entered the bedroom. The door clicked shut behind him.

Marc undressed and laid his clothes on a chair in a corner of the room. Sitting on the edge of the bed, he took in his sparse surroundings. There was a small window covered with a dark curtain. When he pulled back a corner, he saw a narrow paved lane behind the building. Marc's eyes followed the lane off to his right and saw where it emptied back onto the main street. In the shadows there was a large steel box that he figured had to be the community dumpster. On the other side of the lane was a six-foot wooden fence separating Sylvie's condo building from another. Letting the curtain drop, he scanned the room. There was a small maple dresser along the wall next to the bed. On its top were two framed black and white photographs. Both looked to have been taken some years past. One was a family photo of a couple with two children, a boy, a bit taller, and a girl in her early teens. Marc recognized the girl as Sylvie.

The second was of the boy in the first photo, now a young man, taken a few years later.

Probably Sylvie's brother, not long before he was killed.

Marc pulled the covers down, switched off the light and lay on the cool sheets. Pulling the top sheet up to his chest, he thought about what he had learned since arriving in Quebec earlier that day. Jimmy Lee was an ardent gambler. There seemed to be no doubt about that. What he was unsure of was Lee's ties to Maurice Bashaw at Le Club Erotika and the Rock'n Rollers motorcycle gang. Was the gang responsible for Hugo Karlsson's disappearance? If so, why? What would a motorcycle gang have to do with the disappearance of an engineer working for a railcar manufacturer?

Perhaps they could make some sense of all this tomorrow.

As Marc felt himself drift off, he thought of Nadia's little act, swinging around the pole at Le Club Erotika. Strangely, however, it wasn't Nadia's face he envisioned playfully beckoning him to join her on the stage, it was Sylvie's.

Chapter Nine

The following morning, Marc was awakened by the sound of a vehicle backup alarm coming from the rear of the condo complex. He pulled the curtain back and saw a trash hauler hooking onto the dumpster he had noticed the night before. He pulled on his tee shirt and slacks and padded barefoot down the hallway toward the bathroom. The smell of fresh brewed coffee filled the air.

Five minutes later he was fully dressed. As he made his way to the kitchen, he found Sylvie sitting at the dinette table with a cup of coffee, reading the French edition of Montreal's daily newspaper, *La Presse*. A basket of breakfast rolls, plus a second plate and cup waited at the opposite side of the table.

"Bonjour, Monsieur Marc. I trust you slept well?"

"Well enough, thank you," Marc answered.

"What would you like? Mom made breakfast rolls. She still loves to bake. We have coffee, but I can brew a cup of tea, if you'd prefer."

"Coffee, with just a bit of cream would be fine."

Sylvie brought a container of cream from the fridge, along with a sugar bowl from the counter, and sat them next to the empty plate.

Marc added a dollop of cream, and took a roll from the basket.

"So, have you had time to think about our trip to 'Le Club' last night?" Marc asked, as he broke one of the rolls in half.

"For one thing, it confirms the rumor that Bashaw is definitely into loan sharking. I also think it's safe to speculate your Jimmy Lee could be into the mob for some pretty big bucks."

"I agree. What bothers me is his collateral? What is he using? I can't see Bashaw handing out money without some guarantee of a return," Marc said.

Sylvie took a slow sip of her coffee. "I learned a long time ago that you don't mess with men like Maurice Bashaw. He must be certain that Lee will pay, unless…?" She hesitated to take another sip.

"Unless Lee has already given him what he wants," Marc finished.

Sylvie nodded as she folded the newspaper and laid it aside.

"We can agree that Lee may have already given Bashaw something, but what? Outside of a flashy new sports car and gambling lifestyle, it appears he lives alone in that condo, which is not exactly a palace, and he drives to work in a compact. Something's not adding up," Sylvie said.

"I would agree that on the surface it would appear that Lee has little of value—except his position at Barbeau Transport."

"His position? What do you mean? You said he works in research and development and has something to do with the overall design of the Laser. That doesn't sound like anything Bashaw would need.

"Perhaps, but I was thinking about a possible scenario before I dropped off to sleep last night," Marc said.

Without waiting for Sylvie to respond, he continued. "Hugo Karlsson is, or was Lee's boss at Barbeau. Karlsson was upset about something before he went to meet with Barbeau's head management. Ms. Brooks, the girl we interviewed yesterday, said she heard two men arguing in Karlsson's car while it was parked in the cul-de-sac. According to her description, the other car generally matched Lee's, plus Lee seemed pretty nervous when I interviewed him at work. I'm wondering if what they were arguing about had something to do with what Lee sold to Bashaw."

Buttering one of the rolls, Sylvie thought about Marc's theory.

"I'm still a little confused. Lee and Karlsson are both employees of Barbeau Transport. What could either of them have that Bashaw wanted, a thirty-ton train car? I don't think so. I seriously doubt that Bashaw is some kind of train buff."

Marc took a sip of coffee. "Jimmy Lee is the design engineer for the new Laser locomotive that is about to make its inaugural run from Montreal south to New York City, with daily trips to follow.

"I understand. You've already said that. But what's his connection to the mob?"

"I'm beginning to believe Lee's designed something in that locomotive that Bashaw can use."

"I'm sorry, Marc, you're not making any sense. What could Bashaw possibly use a locomotive engine for? He couldn't care less about transportation developments."

Marc took a moment before answering, washing down another bite of roll with his coffee. "Think about it. People are apprehended every day crossing the U.S./Canadian border for smuggling all sorts of things: drugs, money, you name it. Smugglers often conceal their contraband in hidden compartments in cars, trucks, campers, or whatever. But in a train, they are limited to hiding contraband on themselves or in their luggage. Occasionally, the authorities find someone trying to hide something in the train car's bathroom or overhead luggage compartment, taking the chance the officer or drug dog will miss it."

"I'm aware of that," Sylvie said.

"But what if there is a built-in compartment, secreted somewhere in the train, made to look like a critical component. There's no telling what that would be worth to an enterprising businessman such as Bashaw."

Sylvie took a moment to digest Marc's theory. "I think I see what you mean—daily shipments of practically anything crossing the border with little or no chance of discovery. It could mean millions to a trafficker, or anyone else in the smuggling trade."

"And that brings us back to my reason for coming to Canada in the first place. Where the hell is Hugo Karlsson?" Marc asked.

"I think we'll have to ask Jimmy Lee that question," Sylvie said.

"Under Canadian law, based on what we know so far, do you have enough to bring him in for questioning?" Marc asked.

Sylvie finished off the last bit of roll as she considered the evidence.

"Although Karlsson's car was located in Canada, he's officially been reported missing in the States. Outside of the discovery of his car on Ile des Soeurs, the only thing we have linking Mr. Lee and Karlsson is a witness alleging she observed a car that may have looked similar to Lee's parked at the cul-de-sac where the missing man's car was recovered. Bringing Lee in for questioning by the police based on that would be a stretch."

"I understand, but time is of the essence. If Lee designed the Laser with some sort of an embedded secret compartment, and has sold that information to the mob, Karlsson's life is in serious jeopardy. After all, what use is Karlsson to the mob if he knows what Lee's done?"

Marc's cell emitted a low buzz as it danced along the table toward his coffee cup. He picked it up and tapped the screen.

"Marc LaRose."

"Hello, Marc. Jean Pierre St. Onge, from Barbeau Transport."

Marc could detect an edge to St. Onge's voice.

"Good morning, Mr. St. Onge."

"I just received a call from our head office in Brossard. It appears Hugo Karlsson's been kidnapped. He's being held for ten million dollars ransom."

"Do you know if the caller had any terms? Bill denominations? Where to leave the money? Have the police been notified?"

"Nothing about bill denominations, and according to the head office, if we notify the police, he will be killed. I'm getting this second-hand, but I've been told that the kidnappers said we had twenty-four hours to get the money. Then they would contact us with the details. The main office is in frantic mode, but they're trying to round up the cash as we speak."

Marc thought a moment. "Sounds like the ball's in the kidnapper's court for now. That gives us some time to come up with a plan. Tell me, who exactly took the call?"

"I'm not sure, but I believe it was the receptionist on duty at the Brossard office."

"Look, Jean Pierre, I need to talk to whoever took the call. Would you mind calling the head office and let them know that I'm coming down there to speak to them about this?"

"Sure. I'll tell them you're on your way. When you get there, ask for Mr. Claude Benoit, the office manager. But please, they are trying to keep this quiet, at least for now."

"How about Mrs. Karlsson? Has anyone contacted her?"

"No, not yet. We were hoping to have more information before contacting her."

"OK. I'm near Brossard now. I can be at Barbeau's head office in…" Marc looked toward Sylvie. She held up ten fingers. "Do me a favor and let Barbeau know we'll be there in ten minutes."

"Thanks, Marc. Keep me posted."

"Will do," Marc said and ended the call. He then related the substance of the call to Sylvie.

"If we're going to get there in ten minutes, we'll have to get going," Sylvie said as she rose from her chair and started to pick up the breakfast dishes.

"Sylvie, the kidnappers warned not to involve the police."

"You forget, I'm on leave. Today, I'm your assistant. Just put your cup in the sink, I'll get to these later," Sylvie said as she put the cream in the fridge.

Twelve minutes later, Sylvie parked the SUV in the visitor section at Barbeau Transport's main office. Marc noticed a few cars parked in the employee parking lot off to one side. As they reached the glass doors of the entrance, a balding gentleman, dressed in a suit and tie, approached the door from the inside, unlocked it, and held it open for them to enter.

"Mr. LaRose?" He asked.

"Yes. You must be Claude Benoit."

"Mr. St. Onge didn't say you'd be with anyone," Benoit said as he motioned toward Sylvie.

"This is my, assistant, Ms. Sylvie Champagne."

Benoit hesitated a moment, "Right this way, please."

After relocking the door, Benoit lead Marc and Sylvie down the wide hallway past a reception desk staffed by a uniformed female security guard, and through an office door labeled 'Conference Room'. As Marc heard the door close behind them, he took in the long table positioned in the center of the room with an array of leather-padded chairs arranged around it. At the far end of the table two men were seated. One, a little older and rather distinguished looking was also dressed in a suit and tie. The other, about the same age as Marc, was dressed in a tee shirt and jeans.

Benoit said something in rapid French that Marc couldn't catch. As the men both arose from their chairs, the jeans and tee shirt guy made his way around the table to where Marc was standing.

"Mr. LaRose, my name is Jules Barbeau," he said, extending his hand. "I apologize for intruding on your Saturday like this, but given the circumstances, I'm sure you understand." He gave Marc's hand a firm shake.

Marc noticed Barbeau spoke with a refined Canadian English accent.

"Mr. Barbeau, this is Mr. LaRose's assistant, Ms. Sylvie Champagne," Benoit said, motioning toward Sylvie.

"Pleasure," Barbeau said with a nod.

By this time, the second man came to where everyone else was standing.

Motioning toward the suited gentleman, Barbeau said, "Mr. LaRose, this is the president of Barbeau Transport, Mr. Jacques LaFleur." After another round of handshakes, Barbeau motioned for everyone to be seated.

Barbeau glanced at Benoit who had remained standing, "Claude, would you fetch us some coffee, please?"

Benoit turned and left the room.

Barbeau waited for the door to click shut. "That should only take a moment." Returning his attention to Marc, he said, "I understand JP St. Onge has hired you to look into the disappearance of our employee, Mr. Hugo Karlsson."

"Yes, Sylvie and I have traced his…," Marc was suddenly interrupted.

"And now, we learn he is being held for ransom," Barbeau said firmly.

Marc was surprised at Barbeau's sudden outburst, but continued, "We believe he left Plattsburgh for a meeting that was to be held here this past Wednesday, but was somehow lured to Nuns' Island where his vehicle was located. We've been working on leads, but to this point, there's been nothing solid."

"Forgive me for my outburst, Mr. LaRose, but with all that's going on—with the rollout of the Laser, and now this thing with Hugo's disappearance." Barbeau exhaled and ran his hands through his head of curly brown hair. "I suppose I probably should let someone else handle this." Looking at Marc, he said, "So, where should we start?"

At that moment, Benoit opened the door carrying a tray with a pot of coffee and four cups. He placed the tray on the table, poured the coffee and passed the cups around.

"Would you like me to stay, Mr. Barbeau?" He asked.

"No, thank you, Claude. If we need anything else, I'll call."

"Certainly, sir." Benoit said and slipped out the door.

"First, when did the ransom demand come in, and who took the call?" Marc asked as he pulled his notepad from his pocket.

"I took the call. It was just after six a.m. this morning," LaFleur said, speaking for the first time.

Marc noticed that LaFleur, like Barbeau, spoke manicured English with just a trace of Canadian accent.

What is the president of the company doing here at such an early hour?

"Is it customary for the president of the company to be in the office at six o'clock on Saturday morning?" Marc asked.

"There were extenuating circumstances," LaFleur offered, letting his excuse dangle between them as he glanced over to Barbeau.

Marc thought of perusing this, but relented for now. "Male or female?"

"I'm sorry, was that a question?" LaFleur asked with a confused look.

"The caller. Male or female?" Marc asked again.

"Oh, sorry. I believe it was a man, but it was hard to tell. The voice sounded odd, like the caller was talking through a machine. In any event, he didn't leave a name."

"Probably using an electronic voice transformer," Marc said, then continued, "tell me, as best you can, exactly what the caller said."

LaFleur hesitated, then cleared his throat. "He said, 'if you want to see Hugo Karlsson again, it will cost you ten million dollars.' Of course, I was a bit dumbfounded. I'd been up most of the night, so I asked him what he meant. He said, 'you heard me the first time. If you want to see Hugo Karlsson again, it will cost you ten million dollars. You have twenty-four hours.'"

"The caller stated you have twenty-four hours to come up with ten million dollars?"

"Yes."

"What did you say?"

"I asked where Hugo, Mr. Karlsson, was. He said, 'You'll find out when we get the money.'"

"Did the caller say where to bring the money, specify denominations, anything else?"

"No. He said that if we call the police, we will never see Karlsson alive. He also said he would call again with further instructions, then the line went dead."

"That's all he said—that he had Hugo, he wanted ten million dollars within twenty-four hours, and not to call the police?"

"Yes, as best as I can remember."

"Did he say when he'd call again?"

"No."

"Any chance the call was recorded on your end?"

"Unfortunately not. I received the call on my cell."

"How do you think he got your cell phone number?"

"I don't know."

"Do many people have access to your cell number?" Marc asked.

LaFleur seemed to consider Marc's question.

"I use it for business, as well as personal calls."

"How long have you had that number?"

"Oh, probably four or five years, at least."

"Did the caller's phone number show up on your cell?"

"Yes, I wrote it down," LaFleur said, and retrieved a scrap of paper from his shirt pocket and gave it to Marc. "I even tried to call them back, nothing."

Marc looked at the number. It had a 514 Montreal area code. "This is probably registered to a disposable phone, but you never know. I'll check to see where the number was issued. Maybe we'll get lucky."

Marc noticed Sylvie was doing something on her smart phone.

"Mr. LaRose, don't take this the wrong way, but have you had much experience with kidnappings?" Barbeau asked.

"Yes, but to be honest, it's been a while," Marc said thinking back to a case involving a family from South America visiting the Adirondacks, six years before.

Sylvie nudged Marc's arm, "Excuse me, Mr. LaRose. The cell number the caller used is in a batch that was leased to the Verizon network, so it's probably a Track Phone."

"Thank you, Ms. Champagne," Marc said before returning his attention to Barbeau and LaFleur. "As I figured, the caller used a burner."

"A burner?" LaFleur asked.

"A disposable phone, and if he's smart, that particular phone has already been destroyed," Marc said.

"Any possibility of locating the signal source through the cell towers?" Barbeau asked.

This time, Sylvie answered, "Probably not. It appears the signal strength was weak, and roaming. I think it may have come from somewhere outside the Montreal metropolitan area."

"From outside the area?" Barbeau asked. "I thought you said Karlsson's car was found on Nuns' Island?"

"It was, but that was two days ago. Whoever's kidnapped him has had plenty of time to move him someplace else," Marc said.

Barbeau exhaled deeply. "Fucking great. What are we to do in the meantime, just wait around for these people to call us with further instructions?"

The room became quiet. The only sound filtering through the paneled walls was a distant siren, either the police or an ambulance, Marc figured.

Finally, Barbeau spoke. "Jacques, maybe we should consider calling in the police."

"Out of the question," LaFleur snapped. "The caller said that if we want to see Hugo Karlsson alive again, we are not to call the police. Who knows what kind of people we're dealing with? For all we know, they may be watching us right now. I don't want to be responsible if this thing goes wrong." Marc could feel the apprehension in LaFleur's voice.

Marc paused a moment, "Mr. LaFleur has a point. If the police get involved, they will, of course, be interested in getting Karlsson returned, but their main objective will be to close the case, that is, to make an arrest. If I'm reading you correctly, you're more interested in getting Karlsson safely returned than you are in having his kidnappers arrested. Plus, with an arrest comes a lot of unwanted publicity."

"Precisely," LaFleur said.

"And it appears the kidnappers have chosen Mr. LaFleur to be the company's contact person," Marc said.

Marc noticed a sheen of perspiration had developed on LaFleur's forehead. "Mr. LaRose, why don't I just give you my phone? You know how to handle these people. I don't," he said.

"It may be better for all involved," Marc said.

Barbeau looked at Marc, "But the kidnappers know Jacques' voice. Won't they get suspicious hearing someone else answer when they call?"

"Possibly. I'll simply inform them that I represent Barbeau in any further negotiations. If these people are truly in the kidnapping business, and I suspect they are, they are used to dealing with a third party, someone who is objective and not tied directly to the kidnapped person or his family."

"Makes sense," Barbeau said. "So what's our plan?"

"First, does Barbeau Transport carry any kind of kidnap and ransom insurance on its employees?"

"Of course, but only for overseas travel—South America, Africa and the Middle East. Besides, this is Canada; not exactly a kidnappers' haven," Barbeau said, while drumming in fingers on the long table. "The short answer to your question, Mr. LaRose, is no. We'll have to come up with the money ourselves."

Marc sensed Barbeau's apprehension and tried to put him at ease. "Mr. Barbeau, no one should criticize you for not providing kidnap insurance for Hugo Karlsson. I'd say that was a reasonable business decision that you had to make. But you have to understand kidnapping is simply another form of business, albeit an unsavory one. The professional kidnapper is usually interested in one thing, money. And the people from whom the victim is taken want to make sure the person, in this case, Hugo Karlsson, is returned alive. So the first thing we need to do is to make them prove Karlsson is safe, that is, for the kidnapper to provide us with a proof of life."

"What do you mean? Ask them if Karlsson is still alive?"

"Something like that, but it's a little more complicated. We tell them that before we can meet their demands, they have to prove that Karlsson is still alive. That's a basic requirement before we can move forward. The kidnapper likes to think he or she is in control and may hesitate at first. But, if the victim is still alive, they will eventually comply. Like I said, they are mainly interested in getting the money."

"What do we do, ask to see him? Get a photo of him, or something?" Barbeau asked.

"We could. But how would we know if what they're showing us is a video or photo they took before they killed him. No, we ask for something personal, something that only he and someone else very close to him, his wife perhaps, would know. Something like where did they go on their first date, the name of their first pet, his grandmother's maiden name, something like that."

"We'll have to contact Karlsson's wife and hope she can help us out with this," LaFleur said.

"I'll take care of that," Marc said. "We had a pleasant conversation when I spoke to her a couple days ago. She isn't even aware of the kidnapping yet, so this way, I can gently break the news, and at the same time ask her to assist us in his safe return."

"Sounds like a plan," Barbeau said. "Mr. LaRose, would you like to use one of our offices to work in?"

"Thanks, but I don't think that should be necessary," Marc said, then shifted his gaze toward LaFleur. "Mr. LaFleur, I'm sorry, but I will need to hold onto your cell phone. When the kidnappers call, I want to be able to answer them immediately."

"All right, I guess. But, remember, I use that for personal as well as business calls."

"Give me a number I can route your calls to."

"I do have a company cell number."

LaFleur wrote the number on the back of his business card and handed it to Marc.

"If for some reason, the kidnappers get word to you via another phone number or other means, please contact me right away."

"Anything you need. Just let me know," Barbeau said.

"I just have a couple more questions," Marc said.

"Sure, anything," Barbeau said.

"What is Hugo Karlsson's position in the rollout of the Laser?"

Barbeau looked over at LaFleur, "Jacques, that's your department."

LaFleur hesitated, apparently collecting his thoughts.

"Hugo is not only the head of R&D, but he's also the overall project manager for the Laser. I suppose there are others who could stand in. I suppose, without Hugo, it can be done, but…" LaFleur let his answer trail off.

"Tell me, who do you think would benefit if this rollout was suddenly delayed or cancelled?"

"In the short run, I'm not sure anyone would benefit. I only know that Barbeau Transport would not. Providing the inaugural trip from Montreal to New York City is successful, our contract to build a hundred more Lasers will go into effect, almost immediately."

"And in the long run?" Marc asked.

"Well, we are the low bidder, so perhaps, if we were found to be negligent…If the inaugural run is unsuccessful…the next low bidder could conceivably be awarded the contract. But that would set the project back several years and would cost everyone concerned millions of dollars."

"Who was the next low bidder?"

LaFleur hesitated and glanced toward Barbeau. He cleared his throat before answering, "Canton Jade. They are, as you may logically assume, a Chinese company. They also have contracts in India, Pakistan and Indonesia, and we understand they have plans to expand toward a more global presence. This bid was their first overture in North America. At first, we figured they were just testing the waters, you know, throw a bid against the landscape, and see what emerges. Their bid was not as low as ours, but it was surprisingly lower than we expected."

Marc thought back to his conversation with Jean Pierre St. Onge at Antoine's Restaurant. "Have you ever heard of Canton Jade using underhanded tactics?"

"Underhanded? No, I don't think so. They're known for their aggressiveness, if that's what you mean, but seem to play by the book," LaFleur answered.

Marc glanced at the wall clock. It was almost ten a.m. "I'd like to contact Mrs. Karlsson before the kidnappers get back to us, so if you'll excuse us, gentlemen, we should get started," Marc said as he stood followed by Sylvie.

Barbeau and LaFleur also stood.

"We'll wait here for any word then," Barbeau said.

Marc handed both of them his card.

"Let's keep Mr. LaFleur's main phone line open," Marc said, holding up LaFleur's cell. "If you need to contact me, my cell number is on my card."

"Understood," Barbeau acknowleged.

"I"ll contact you as soon as I hear anything, or by five this afternoon, whichever comes first." Marc said as he and Sylvie started for the door.

"And obviously, if we should hear something, we'll do the same. Let me walk you to the entrance," Barbeau said.

When they reached the front entrance to the building, Barbeau held the door open for them.

"Thank you for your assistance in this matter, and of course, your discretion. But one thing we haven't talked about is your fee," Barbeau said.

Marc glanced at Sylvie, "My standard fee for a kidnapping assignment is two hundred dollars an hour; American, plus expenses."

"Fair enough. I believe this is going to be a long day for all concerned," Barbeau commented as Marc and Sylvie passed through the doorway.

"Let's hope it's not too long," Marc said over his shoulder as they continued toward the Yukon.

As they reached Sylvie's car, Marc asked, "Do you think the kidnapper's cell signal was strong enough to ping?"

"I doubt it. The app I used is pretty accurate. Besides, to run a ping, I'd have to go through our Electronics Tech Division. They'll want a case number, which means I would have to report this as a kidnapping."

"I don't think we want to do that, at least not yet," Marc said.

As Sylvie slid behind the wheel, she asked, "Where to?"

"I'm heading back to Plattsburgh, so if you could drop me off at the parking garage, I'll get my car and be out of your hair."

"What do you mean? I agreed to help you locate Karlsson. Just because he's been kidnapped doesn't change anything."

"The circumstances are different now. There's no sense putting your job at risk."

"Look Marc, we both heard what Barbeau said. He doesn't want the police involved. If something happens to Karlsson, it's on him. I'm on leave and officially off duty. My role in this is simply as an observer, accompanying a friend."

"Oh, we're friends now," Marc said with a grin.

Sylvie ignored Marc's quip and clicked her seat belt. "After we pick up your car at the parking garage, where to?" she said firmly as she put the Yukon in gear.

Marc knew there was no use arguing. "Do you have your passport?"

"We're going to talk to Mrs. Karlsson in person?"

"I'll call her first just to make sure she's in. We could be there by noon."

Chapter Ten

Marc knew Annika Karlsson suspected something was amiss the moment he saw her. He had called earlier and she sounded all right on the phone, but when she answered the door, Marc saw her tired, red eyes. Her cheeks were moist as if she had recently wiped away some tears. Her shaky hands clutched a soggy handkerchief. She was so distraught that she didn't even notice Sylvie, until Marc introduced her. Annika led them to the parlor where she and Marc sat on the couch, Sylvie on the Louis XV Fauteuil armchair.

"Mr. LaRose, when you called, you said you needed to speak to me in person. Hugo is dead, isn't he?" Her face was pained as she waited for the bad news.

"Not unless you know something I don't," Marc replied.

She broke down, sobbing tears of relief that her worst fears were unfounded.

"Then what is it that you wanted talk to me about?" she said between sobs.

"Mrs. Karlsson, we believe Hugo has been kidnapped and is being held for ransom."

"Kidnapped? Who? Why?" she asked, as she slowly regained her composure.

"We're not sure. Someone contacted the president of Barbeau Transport this morning and said they were holding Hugo. They demanded ten million dollars for his return."

"Ten million dollars? Where can I get that kind of money?" she tearfully asked.

"Mrs. Karlsson, they're looking to Barbeau to come up with the money. We believe Hugo is being held because they know he is vital to the impending rollout of the Laser."

"How can I help?"

"I need to establish that they are holding Hugo, and that he's still alive. To do that, I need something, some fact, that only you and Hugo would know the answer to."

"Oh, I see. Let me think." Annika stared off toward one of the tall curtained covered windows and remained silent for a long moment as Marc and Sylvie waited patiently. The only sound came from the large wall clock situated between the two windows on the opposite side of the room, its long pendulum swinging lazily back and forth as its gears clicked off the passing of time. As Marc was about to break her reverie, Annika made a small sniffling sound, wiped her nose, and said, "Well, Hugo and I will be celebrating our thirty-fifth wedding anniversary in September."

Marc paused before answering, "That may help, but it would be better if you could tell us something that only you and Hugo would know. As you may be aware, marriage information is often available through online data searches."

"Oh dear, let me think," she said, perplexed.

"It doesn't have to be a major event…something private…that only the two of you know and haven't shared with anyone."

She hesitated. "There may be this one thing, but I don't know…"

Sylvie looked at Marc. "May I?"

Marc nodded.

"Mrs. Karlsson, we realize how difficult this is for you. We all have our secrets. But if there is something, anything you can think of, it may help."

Annika gripped her hands together and leaned slightly forward, as if by doing so, no one else could overhear her. "It was back in Finland. We hadn't been married long, less than a year, when I discovered I was pregnant. At first, we were very happy. But then, as time passed, I knew something was wrong. I went to a doctor and he told me that I was no longer pregnant."

"That may be a very private piece of information, Mrs. Karlsson, but I'm not sure how we can use it," Sylvie said, but was interrupted as Annika continued.

"The doctor said it was a boy. We were going to name him Matias, after my grandfather. We never told anyone."

Sylvie shot Marc a glance.

"Did you have any other children named Matias?" Marc asked.

"I never got pregnant again."

"I'm very sorry you lost your child," Sylvie said.

"It was a long time ago. But I will never forget it, and I'm certain Hugo hasn't forgotten it either."

The three of them sat in silence as the clock slowly ticked away.

"Was there anything else you needed?" Annika finally asked.

"No, what you've told us should help. But before we leave, is there anything we can do for you? Anything you need?" Marc asked.

"Only one thing. Please bring my Hugo back to me alive." Tears spilled down her still moist cheeks.

"I promise that we'll do all we can," Marc said as he rose from the couch.

"You'll call me then, as soon as you've heard something, anything?" Annika pleaded as the three walked to the front entrance.

"As soon as we hear anything," Marc nodded, assuringly. Then he patted her hand and gave her a light hug.

When Marc and Sylvie reached the car, he turned and saw Annika standing by the open door. He waved, but Annika simply slowly closed the door and disappeared from sight.

As Marc pulled the Civic onto U.S. Avenue, he said, "We're not far from my condo. I need a change of clothes, then I'd like to take care of Rye and Brandy."

"Marc, do you think it's wise to be drinking now? We have a lot to do."

"No, silly. Those are the names of my cats, Brandy and Rye."

"Oh," she said, shaking her head in amusement.

A few minutes later, Marc pulled into his driveway.

"Care to come inside?"

"Sure," she said. A light grin creased her face.

Marc retrieved the newspapers from the paper tube and a couple of flyers from his mailbox.

Brandy and Rye met them at the door, meowing and circling Marc's feet.

Sylvie knelt and made a few kissy sounds. "*Jolis chatons*," pretty kitty, she said while she petted Rye, causing his butt to elevate.

"Traitor," Marc said jokingly. "Come on, Brandy, let's find you some fresh kibble." Then turning his attention back to Sylvie, "When you're through sucking up to my cat, have a seat. I should only be a minute."

"Your daddy is so jealous," Sylvie said as she continued playing with the cat. But at the sound of fresh kibble clinking in a bowl, Rye scurried off to the laundry room to investigate.

A few minutes later, Marc reappeared wearing pressed khakis and a golf shirt. He glanced at the wall clock. It was almost one-thirty.

"What do you think? Time for lunch?" Marc asked, as they headed out to his car.

Jacques LaFleur's cell phone buzzed in Marc's pocket. He noticed the caller ID had the local 518 area code.

"Hello," Marc answered.

There was a pause. Then a mechanical voice said, "Who is this?"

"Where is Hugo Karlsson?" Marc asked.

"Do you have the money?"

"Before we talk money, I need to speak with Mr. Karlsson."

Another pause. "You will talk to him in due time, providing you get us the money."

"You know it's hard enough to scrape up ten million dollars on any given day, but on a weekend, it's virtually impossible."

"That's your problem," the voice responded.

"Regardless, I need to confirm you indeed have Mr. Karlsson, and he is alive."

The mechanical voice paused again. "We're not bargaining. You want Karlsson, get us the ten million dollars."

"You'll get the money, but first, we need proof he's alive. What was the name of Karlsson's child?" Marc asked.

Another pause. "You know Karlsson doesn't have children."

"If you ask him, he'll tell you. What were he and his wife going to name their first child?" Marc insisted.

"For Karlsson's sake, you better not be playing games," the voice said. A beep indicated the connection had been cut.

Marc stared at the cell phone's screen. "I think we threw them a curve. They weren't aware of the child the Karlssons almost had."

"Well, if they can get that answer, Karlsson is still alive, somewhere."

"Yeah, that's the big question. Where the hell are they keeping him?"

"Marc, give me the phone number they called from. I'll see what I can find out."

Marc read off the numbers before putting the car in gear.

After a couple of minutes of research on her smart phone, Sylvie said, "Look's like another burner. Purchased about six months ago from a convenience store."

"Any chance of pinging that number?"

Sylvie seemed to ignore Marc's question as she continued to fiddle with her device. After a few moments, she said, "Can't get a location, but it appears the call was routed through a tower somewhere north of here. There are towers all along the border. It's hard to say which one."

"Canada is just twenty-five miles to the north. Either they're holding Karlsson somewhere just across the border, or they're moving him around, using different locations and different phones," Marc said.

Five minutes later, they were heading north on Margaret Street, through an eclectic cluster of fast food restaurants and cheap motels. Sylvie's gaze drifted toward Lake Champlain off to their right.

"Dawn Motel, thirty-five dollars a night?" Sylvie said, reading one of the motel signs. "What kind of motel has rooms for thirty-five dollars?" She asked.

"You're a cop. What do you think?" Marc said with a mischievous grin.

"Oh," she replied.

As they passed the city limits, Marc asked, "Getting hungry?"

"What do you suggest?"

"McSweeny's Michigan stand is coming up on our left. Are you feeling adventurous?"

"I don't know," she replied, with suppressed enthusiasm.

"You've had them before? Michigan hot dogs, I mean."

"My parents used to take my brother and me to the Plattsburgh beach every summer when we were kids. 'Michigans' were all the rage back then."

When Marc pulled into one of the parking spots facing the front of the restaurant, the door flew open and a teenage girl sprung out at full gallop, her ponytail whipping back and forth with each stride. She slid to a halt at Marc's side window, order pad at the ready.

"Hey guys. What can I get you?" she asked with a perky smile.

"Just one for me, Marc. No onions. Diet Coke," Sylvie said.

"Three Michigans, two with, buried; one order of fries and two diet Cokes."

The girl scribbled on her pad. "Be about five minutes," she said. And as fast as she had appeared, she was back inside the restaurant.

"Buried? I haven't heard that term since my father used it way back when," Sylvie said.

"Best way to keep the onions from falling into your lap," Marc teased.

After a few moments of silence, Sylvie asked, "So Marc, what are the chances? Do you really think Karlsson's alive?"

"We've told the kidnappers to come back with some proof. If they can't come up with the name Annika gave us, that would leave us with one option, contact the police."

"Where does that leave Jimmy Lee and the MC club in all this?" Sylvie asked.

Just as Marc was about to answer, he was distracted by the roar of motorcycles coming off the interstate. Two Harleys heading in their direction. As they passed the restaurant, Sylvie said, "Marc, I think those may be two of the bikes we saw parked at Le Club Erotika last night."

"Looks like your question may have just been answered." Marc started the Civic and put it in reverse.

"Hey, mister, what about your Michigans?" Marc heard the carhop yell.

"Sorry, sweetie, something's come up! Gotta run!" Marc shouted through his open side window.

As Marc swung the car out of the parking lot, he could see the motorcycles a quarter mile ahead, approaching the city limits. The

Civic's four-cylinder engine screamed as he held the accelerator to the floor.

"Marc, you think they're going to Annika Karlsson's to get that name out of her?"

"I can't think of another reason why these goons would be in Plattsburgh at this moment."

Marc retrieved his cell from his shirt pocket and tapped 911.

Almost instantly, a female operator answered.

"Clinton County 911. What is the nature of your emergency?"

"I'd like to report a burglary in progress at the Old Barracks at 942 U.S. Oval. I think someone is trying to break into my house. Please hurry." Without waiting for the operator's reply, Marc ended the call. "We might need a little assistance," he said.

As the Civic crossed the Scomotion Creek Bridge and onto North Margaret Street, Marc eased off on the accelerator. He had closed the gap between him and the Harleys to a couple hundred yards. The helmeted riders seemed to be taking pains to obey the city's 30 MPH speed limit, probably in an effort to stay under the police radar. The slow-moving convoy continued into the downtown section of the city. When the bikes stopped for a red light, Marc pulled into a parking space and waited for the light to turn. As he waited, two other vehicles got between them. When the light changed, Marc continued following as the Harleys slowly popped and kabanged in the direction of Annika Karlsson's residence.

At the intersection of the former Plattsburgh Air Force Base, the Harleys turned onto the Old Base.

"Either these guys have been here before, or they're using a GPS," Marc said.

When the bikes again turned onto US Oval, Marc could see two Plattsburgh PD patrol cars parked in front of Annika Karlsson's residence, their emergency lights flashing. Rather than following, Marc turned away onto the ring road that ran parallel to the Karlsson residence and pulled into a parking space. From this vantage point, across the old parade grounds, he and Sylvie continued watching the bikes, as well as the residence.

"The cops must be inside, talking to a confused Ms. Karlsson," Marc said.

They watched as the Harleys slowed, then continued past the residence.

"Apparently they're not prepared to confront the police," Marc said, as he pulled the Civic back onto the street, keeping the bikes in sight.

"Marc, if these guys are here to confront Annika Karlsson about the name of their child, does that mean Hugo is already dead?"

"I don't know, but I don't think it's a good sign."

They watched as the Harleys made a left turn at the next intersection. Marc sped up to keep them in view. At the next right hand turn, he could see the brake lights of the motorcycles as they waited at another intersection for the light to change, four blocks ahead.

Marc handed his cell phone to Sylvie. "Scroll down, find the number for the Plattsburgh PD, and call it."

As Sylvie worked on the phone, Marc watched the two motorcycles move off as the light turned green. She handed Marc his phone. "It's ringing," she said.

"Police Department, Sergeant Rabideau."

"Dave, this is Marc LaRose. I have…"

"Was that 911 call to the Karlsson residence your idea?" Rabideau shouted. "The responding officers said when Mrs. Karlsson answered the door, she thought the worst, and it took them a full minute to calm her down."

"Shit! Dave, I apologize for that, but give me a minute to explain."

"You've got ten seconds. Better make them count."

"I've tracked Hugo Karlsson's whereabouts to Montreal, but there's been another development."

"Five seconds."

"Karlsson's been kidnapped. Someone called the head offices of Barbeau Transport in Brossard this morning demanding ten million dollars for his safe return. I can't go into all the details right now, but when I made that 911 call, I was tailing a couple guys who may be involved. I think they were going to Karlsson's residence to obtain some 'proof of life' information from Mrs. Karlsson. I admit it was a bit drastic, but it was the best I could come up with at the time to keep her safe."

The line was silent for a moment. "Where are these supposed kidnappers now?" Rabideau asked in a mollified tone.

"Right in front of me, just passing by city hall. They're riding Harleys, heading north on US Avenue and about to turn onto City Hall Place. When they saw the patrol cars parked in front of Karlsson's, they slowed down, but kept going. Apparently, they're not too anxious to get into a fight with the law."

"Look Marc, I only have four patrols on the road. Two are still at Ms. Karlsson's, one is investigating an auto accident, and the other's involved in a neighbor dispute on Bailey Avenue. I could call the State and see if they have a patrol available."

Marc thought quickly. "Dave, if it's all the same, I'd like to tail these guys and see where they're heading. Maybe they'll lead me to where they're keeping Hugo Karlsson."

"Yeah, see what you mean. But be careful. Hey, when this is over, we're going to have a long talk. I need a little more heads up next time you decide to use us for your boogeymen."

"Thanks, Dave." Marc cut the connection.

"Sounds like your friend at the PD's a little miffed," Sylvie said.

"He'll get over it."

As Marc continued to follow the Harleys, it appeared they were retracing their route north out of town, past McSweeny's.

As the bikes approached the Interstate I-87 ramp, Marc was surprised to see that they continued straight, rather than taking the direct route back to Montreal.

"That's interesting. I wonder why they're heading up Route 9," he said.

Sylvie remained silent for a few moments. "Maybe they're not going to Montreal."

"Possibly, but there isn't much between here and the border. Just apple orchards, corn fields and a few villages."

Two other vehicles had gotten between the Harleys and Marc's Civic. On the open road, Marc could see the bikes had opened up some distance between them. Eventually, one of the vehicles ahead pulled off and Marc sped up to keep the bikes in view.

As Marc passed over a rise in the road, he saw the bikes about a quarter mile ahead entering the hamlet of Chazy. Disregarding the posted thirty-five mile an hour speed limit, Marc closed the distance between them. Four miles later, the bikers turned right on a side road, which Marc knew would take them toward the Village of Rouses Point.

A few miles later, the Harleys entered the Village. Off on the right, Marc and Sylvie could see the expanse of Lake Champlain and the bridge that crossed over the narrow end of the lake connecting New York and Vermont at the north end of town.

In the village traffic, the bikes had slowed.

"Either they're going back to Canada through one of the smaller ports, or they'll turn onto Route 2 toward the bridge to Vermont," Marc said.

No sooner had Marc said this, the bikes turned right toward the bridge.

"Vermont it is then," he said.

But a quarter mile later with the bridge looming ahead, the Harleys turned left and maneuvered past a steel gate blocking a dirt road to a field filled with dense underbrush. A rusty sign affixed to the steel barricade read, 'Private Property, No Trespassing.'

"What the hell?" Marc exclaimed.

"Could that be some sort of back road to Canada?" Sylvie asked, aware there were many unguarded dirt roads connecting the two countries.

"No. That's a path that leads to old Fort Montgomery. The Fort's been abandoned since the mid-eighteen hundreds. There's nothing there, except…"

"Except what?" Sylvie asked.

"Access to Lake Champlain, right between the Canadian and U.S. Customs Marine stations."

Marc continued past the entrance the bikers had turned into and crossed over the bridge to a rest area that doubled as a 'scenic view' pull-off on the Vermont side of the lake. He found a parking space facing back toward New York. Less than a quarter mile across the lake and just north of the bridge, the massive stone fortifications of the long-abandoned Fort Montgomery were plainly visible. From their vantage point, they could see the Fort's pair of forty-foot limestone bastions rising out of the lake connected by a long stone curtain. Along the sides of each bastion were a multitude of embrasures through which the Fort's long-ago artillerymen could fire cannon shots at enemy ships seeking to slip by. Although the fort never saw combat and over the years had deteriorated to a skeleton of its former self, it still offered an imposing sight.

"Why do you think the bikers pulled in there?"

"Beats me," he said, as they watched a few powerboats leisurely motor north under the bridge, then pass between the rest area and the old fort as they made their way to Canada.

"So anyone coming from Canada has to stop at the U.S. Customs boat dock, which is just off the bridge, south of the fort, right?"

"That's right. Technically, they're in the U.S. once they get to the Fort. If they choose to stop at the Fort and then elude the Border Patrol, they're in.

"If the kidnappers' call to LaFleur's mobile phone came from near here that could explain the unusual cell signal I saw when I tried to trace its location."

"As well as Karlsson's disappearance from Nuns' Island," Marc added. "They must have a boat stashed somewhere near the fort."

Marc took out his cell and dialed a number.

"Who are you calling?" Sylvie asked.

"I think it's time we get the troopers involved. I'm going to try Tim Golden and see if he's available."

Golden answered on the first ring.

"Tim, Marc LaRose. I have a situation and hoped you'd be available."

"I'm kinda busy. What's up?" Golden answered, impatiently.

"I've been working on a missing person's case and believe I've tracked my guy to old Fort Montgomery in Rouses Point."

"So? That's your shtick, what do you need me for? If it's something serious, you could try the Rouses Point PD," Golden answered testily.

"Earlier this morning, the missing person case turned into a kidnapping and my victim is being held for ransom. You haven't heard about it because most of this has occurred in Montreal. It's a little complicated, but we've been following a couple of members of the Rock'n Rollers motorcycle gang. We believe they are holding my guy on the Fort Montgomery property. I think they used a boat to get him there. If we storm in on them, they may try to escape back up the Richelieu River to Montreal."

There was a pause.

"Marc, where are you now?" Tim asked, his tone subdued.

"In the rest area on the Vermont side of the Rouses Point Bridge," Marc said, glancing at Sylvie. "We'll keep an eye on things, but if you could get a few troopers over here and block the road, I'll call the sheriff's office and see if their boat is nearby."

"Marc, stay where you are. I'll contact the Chazy barracks and see who's available. Then I'll check on a boat. Don't make a move until I get there. If you see anything, call me right away," Golden said and ended the call.

"He wants us to stay put until he arrives," Marc said.

"That sounds sensible," Sylvie replied. "It would be foolish for the two of us to bust in there. No telling what we'd be up against."

"I know. I just hate the thought of sitting here, waiting for something to happen," Marc said, fidgeting with his cell.

"I thought you liked surveillance work," she said, as a smirk curled the corner of her mouth.

"I do, but this is different. Karlsson's life could be hanging in the balance."

Jacques LaFleur's cell phone buzzed in Marc's pocket.

He glanced over at Sylvie as he looked at the screen.

"Hello."

"Are you ready to make the exchange? Ten million for Mr. Karlsson," the modulated voice said.

"Sure, as soon as you prove he's still alive. Did you get the answer we're looking for?"

"Look asshole, we've asked him and he doesn't remember. We're through playing your fucking games. If you want him back alive, get us the money now or his death will be on you."

"Like I told you, we're working on that. What you need to do is prove to us he's still alive. We're not giving you ten million for a dead body."

The connection suddenly went dead.

"Hello," Marc said. No answer.

He looked over at Sylvie. "This doesn't look good. They weren't going to give us 'proof of life,' but they called anyway."

"Sounds like they're getting desperate," Sylvie said, her voice edged with concern.

A long moment of silence passed between them.

Finally, Marc said, "I can't just sit around waiting for Golden to arrive. Drive me to where we saw those Harleys slip past that gate. I'll get out and you come back here and wait for Golden."

"Marc, you think that's wise? Golden said to wait. What are you going to do when you get there? The Rollers are nobody to fool with."

Marc handed Sylvie his cell. "Take my phone. If Golden calls, tell him where I am. If something comes up, you can call me using LaFleur's cell number."

Before getting out of the Civic, Marc retrieved his H&K semi-automatic from under the front seat. Sylvie remained seated, impassively staring across the lake toward the Fort.

"Sylvie, come on, we haven't much time," he urged, as he clipped the automatic to his belt.

Reluctantly, she slid behind the wheel. Marc got in on the passenger side.

As they passed over the bridge, Marc said, "Let me off just past the barrier. When I get out, you circle back to the rest area and wait for Golden. Knowing him, he'll be here with a cavalry of troopers in less than half an hour."

"OK Marc, but be careful. I'm familiar with this gang. They'll shoot first and ask questions later. Usually though, they just shoot and forget the questions."

When Sylvie stopped the car, Marc got out, then quietly pushed the Civic's door shut. As she drove off, he made for the brush that lined the sides of the dirt path. Keeping the path to his left, he stayed low, below the five feet of thick brush. Crouching and holding his

H&K to his side, he carefully picked his way toward a stand of swamp cedars that lined the back of the Fort where he figured the Harleys were holed up a hundred yards away. The traffic from the bridge road helped muffle any sounds he made. When he stepped on a small clump of sedges, however, the snapping noise startled a pair of wild turkeys that had been nesting nearby. The birds made a few clucks as they scampered off, but luckily weren't frightened enough to take flight. After another ten minutes of slow-going, Marc crept to about twenty yards from the Fort's ruins when he heard voices. They were faint at first, but got louder with each step. As he closed in, he began to hear them more clearly. Someone was speaking French, and although he couldn't catch all the words, it sounded like a one-sided conversation, as though someone was talking on a cell phone. Marc thought it seemed more like an argument than a conversation.

Gripping his H&K in his right hand, he edged closer and the voice more became more intense.

Someone's really pissed about something.

Although the unseen person was speaking rapidly, Marc was able to understand some of what was being said, "Fuck…old man…out…what are we…overdose…cat." He tried to make sense of the one-sided argument. Then as suddenly as the argument began, it stopped. Had the call ended?

Then, still in French, but much clearer, Marc heard another voice, "What does he want us to do?"

"Get rid of him," replied the one who had been on the phone.

"Get rid of him? Here, in the U.S.?" Marc heard the second man say.

"Well, we're not taking him back over the border. Poppy wants us to dump him down here. Maybe we could just throw the old bastard in the lake. He's so fucked up he'll probably just drown. No one will know the difference."

Marc quickly thought about what he'd heard. The kidnappers had apparently drugged Karlsson to keep him quiet and in the process he'd been overdosed. Thinking back to the phone conversation, he surmised the 'Cat,' probably stood for Ketamine, an anesthesia commonly used as a date rape drug. An overdose could cause respiratory failure.

"Andre, we should hold off until dark when no one will see us throw him in the water," Marc heard one of the men say.

"You want to explain to our crazy boss why you wanted to wait until dark? He'll have your ass."

Just then, Marc heard the sharp metallic sound of a semi-automatic pistol slide being racked, loading a bullet into its chamber.

Got to act, now.

Holding his H&K in both hands, he rose, bringing his head just above the level of the brush. Thirty feet away, he saw two men wearing black leather vests, their backs toward him. They were looking down at a man on the ground, partially hidden in the shade cast by the limestone wall of the fortress. One of the men held a pistol.

As the man raised his weapon, pointing it toward the man on the ground, Marc called out in French, "Stop right there or I'll blow your fucking head off."

The two men turned.

At first, the men seemed confused, but the man holding the gun made the mistake of pointing it in Marc's direction.

Taking no chances, Marc fired a single shot, hitting him in the arm, causing his pistol to fall to the ground. He yelled, then grabbed his wounded arm with his other hand and moved to retrieve his weapon.

"Touch it and you're dead!" Marc called out in French.

The wounded man complied. The other man, seeing what Marc had done to his comrade, remained motionless.

"Kick the gun toward me," Marc ordered, moving cautiously toward the men.

The biker hesitated at first then, with hate in his eyes, did as he was told.

The pistol bounced in Marc's direction.

Marc slowly made his way out of the brush into the clearing, his firearm pointed in the direction of the kidnappers.

"Face down on the ground, hands out to your sides."

The men hesitated.

"Now," Marc ordered, as he continued forward.

"American asshole! How can I get down with a bullet in my arm?"

"Get down, or the next bullet will take your fucking arm off," Marc shouted as he motioned menacingly with his gun.

Reluctantly, the two complied.

"Don't move," Marc ordered.

Marc retrieved the biker's handgun, then with one eye on the men, he went to where the man lay in the shade.

Apparently overdosed with Ketamine, the old guy looked in bad shape. He was unresponsive, sweating profusely, and pale. He'd obviously been beaten. Both eyes were swollen and his face was badly bruised. His hands and ankles were bound with duct tape.

Keeping his pistol trained on the kidnappers, Marc reached down with his left hand and felt the man's carotid artery. His pulse was weak, but he was alive.

Marc dug LaFleur's cell out of his pants pocket and, for the second time that day, dialed 911.

As Marc finished giving the dispatcher directions for the EMS to find Karlsson, he heard the groaning engines of several vehicles coming through the field toward him. He kept his pistol trained on his captives, but positioned himself behind a tree, fearing these could be more bad guys coming to check on Andre and his buddy.

Suddenly, a State Police SUV broke through the wall of tall grass, its flashing red and blue lights blazing. It slid to a stop not far from where the two men lay. A uniformed trooper exited his vehicle, his weapon at the ready. Marc immediately recognized Trooper Rodney Carron from his previous career in the State Police.

"Rodney, Marc LaRose. I have two kidnappers and their victim on the ground," Marc called out.

"Lower your weapon, Marc. I'll take over from here."

A moment later, an unmarked car pulled up alongside the SUV. Tim Golden was behind the wheel. Golden got out of his car and approached the scene, gun in hand.

"Marc, you alright?"

"I'm fine, but Karlsson's in rough shape. I just called 911. EMT's are on the way." Marc nodded toward the men on the ground.

"I've already retrieved one of their guns, but they still need to be searched."

"I'm shot! I need a fucking doctor," the kidnapper pleaded in French with inflated agitation.

"What'd he just say?" Golden asked.

"I winged him when he pointed his gun at me. He said he needs medical attention," Marc replied unsympathetically.

Golden and the trooper handcuffed Andre and his accomplice.

A moment later, Sylvie arrived in the Civic. She ran to where Marc was standing.

"Are you OK? I heard a gunshot."

"I had to shoot one of the kidnappers. He's fine, but Karlsson's not so good."

Marc and Sylvie carefully removed the old man's bonds and were tending to him when the ambulance arrived. Eventually, more troopers from the Chazy and Plattsburgh stations showed up at the scene.

Marc explained to the EMS personnel about the possible overdose as they were loading Karlsson into the ambulance, along with the wounded kidnapper, his uninjured wrist handcuffed to an adjoining stretcher.

Tim Golden instructed a trooper to ride in the back with them, then ordered a second trooper to follow the ambulance to the hospital. Yellow crime scene tape was strung around the area pending the arrival of the forensics team.

"Marc, I'm going to need you and your girlfriend to meet me at the Plattsburgh barracks for a statement," Golden said, nodding at Sylvie.

"But Tim, Sylvie's a…"

"I don't care who she is, Marc. Just get your butts down to the station. Looks like we're going to need an interpreter as well."

"Tim, Sylvie's a Brossard Police Detective. She's been assisting me in my hunt for Karlsson, and she speaks English as well as I do."

Golden paused, "In that case, maybe we won't need that interpreter. But I still need you both down at the station," Tim said, then turned to instruct another trooper to remain at the scene to await the forensics team.

Chapter Eleven

As Golden was leaving, Marc pulled Sylvie to one side. "If they used a boat to transport Karlsson to the fort, it's still got to be around here somewhere."

Sylvie shrugged. "Well they obviously didn't bring him here on a motorcycle. I suppose a boat could be hidden in the bushes down by the water."

Marc turned to the trooper, "We'd like to take a look around over near the lake, if it's OK with you."

"Go for it. Just don't mess around with the scene," he said motioning to the cordoned off area.

Marc remembered exploring the Fort as a child. As he and Sylvie climbed over its back wall, he could see that not much had changed, except for Mother Nature's reclamation efforts to cover the ruins with brush plus, some additional graffiti that adorned the flat stone surfaces of the once-proud Fort.

Stepping around chunks of broken limestone, they came to the stone curtain that formed the Fort's truncated wall connecting the bastions facing the lake. Marc led Sylvie north along the wall, then down a path toward the water's edge. From that vantage point, they could see across the lake to the rest area where they had parked an hour before. A long stone dock, originally meant to moor barges used to haul the limestone to build the Fort, could be seen sloping up from beneath the water. They walked toward a group of low-lying trees near the water's edge.

"I'll bet that's where they moored the boat," Marc said, continuing toward the trees. "Be careful, those stone slabs look slippery."

Carefully making their way to the end of the stone dock, they found an area where pleasure boats had been landed in the past, but there were none there now. Waves splashed against a long slab of granite that was partially hidden by overhanging birch trees and a cluster of swamp cedars.

"Look," Sylvie said, pointing to a piece of orange mooring line that had been tied around the trunk of a birch tree.

Marc tried to untie the small piece of rope, but it had been tied so tightly, he had to use his pocketknife to work the knot free.

"Looks like whoever tied this wasn't a boy scout, or an avid boater for that matter. That's probably why they decided to cut it."

"Or maybe they were in a hurry," Sylvie said.

"Possibly," Marc said as he shoved the bit of rope in his pocket.

Seeing nothing else of interest, they started back toward the Civic. They walked in silence for a few moments, then Marc asked, "Sylvie, where is the closest marina north of here?"

Sylvie seemed to consider the question, "That would be across the border at Ile Aux Noix, about eight kilometers downriver."

Marc smiled as he mentally interpreted the name of the island to English. "Yeah, Nuts Island, that'd make sense. Let's go."

"Marc, you think it's wise to go there now? I think your friend, Tim Golden, said he wanted us to meet him at the State Police Station in Plattsburgh."

"Let me worry about Tim. First, I want to check out that marina. Somebody had to stay with Karlsson when we saw those bikers in Plattsburgh. Whoever it was probably heard the gunfire and made their getaway. We might find them there."

Sylvie looked at Marc. "I think Golden's going to be, what is it you Americans say? 'Pissed-on?' That we didn't go to the police station."

It's 'pissed-off,' and don't worry, I've pissed him off before," Marc said, grinning. "Besides, he's got his hands full with those two scumbags and Karlsson shot full of dope. I'm sure he won't mind if we're a little late."

After getting back to the Civic, Marc drove to the Village of Rouses Point, then past the U.S. Custom's station as they headed for the Canadian border.

As they approached the Canadian Customs house, Sylvie said, "Let me do the talking. You still have your firearm, and I don't believe you have a Canadian pistol permit."

"Shit, I forgot," Marc said as he shoved the H&K under his seat.

At the border station, Marc handed the guard his Enhanced Driver's License. Sylvie flashed her Police ID and badge.

"We've been working on an investigation in Plattsburgh. We're just heading back to Brossard," she said.

The border guard took his time as he ran Marc's license through the scanner then, after inspecting Sylvie's credentials, he returned their documents and with a wink, said, "Good luck with your 'investigation.'"

Marc returned the wink, and with a smile of his own, pulled out of the inspection lane and continued north.

"If memory serves me, the marina at Ile Aux Noix is only a few miles straight up this road," Sylvie said.

They rode in silence for a couple of miles, then Sylvie continued, "You know, Marc, that marina is pretty big. More than a hundred boats can be berthed there at any one time. What are we looking for?"

"Anything coming from the states within the past half hour would be a good start. I'm thinking a pretty good-sized boat with one or maybe two people on board. The marina owner should be able to help us out."

Canadian Route 223 is a well-paved road, as Quebec country roads go, and Marc was able to make good time, arriving at the Village of Ile Aux Noix in less than ten minutes. With the Richelieu River just off the main street, the marina was easy to locate. He found a parking space and they made their way toward the piers on foot. The remnants of an old fort standing on the island that gave the town its name could be seen in the middle of the River, not far offshore. Marc and Sylvie came to a building at the head of one of the piers with a sign over the door, 'Bureau de la Marina Ile Aux Noix.'

Inside they found a combination dry goods store, grocery store, snack and coffee shop, as well as a place to rent a boat or a berthing space on one of the marina's docks. A large window faced out onto the river and the piers. The docking slips appeared about half full, which did not seem unusual with the weather, perfect for a cruise on the water.

"*Bonjour*," the middle-aged proprietress with graying hair in a bob said as they approached the counter.

"*Bonjour, Madame*," Sylvie replied as she produced her police credentials for the woman to see. "We are looking for a boat that may have arrived here recently from the U.S."

The proprietress looked puzzled.

"*Je regrette*, but we have over ninety boat slips. I cannot keep track of where all my clients go, or where they have been," she said.

"Would you mind if we had a look around your marina?" Marc asked.

"I don't see why not, but as you know, the summers are short, and with such beautiful weather, many of my customers have their boats out on the water now. Some go north to St. Jean, but quite a few go to the States for the weekend. As tomorrow is Monday, I assume most will return later this afternoon."

"*Merci, Madame,*" Sylvie said.

They left the store and walked down the gravel drive toward the piers. There was a pedestrian access to the main pier that ran adjacent to the shoreline about twenty feet from shore. A few handcarts were lined up near the entrance of the main pier for the boat owners to cart supplies from their vehicles to their boats. A sign at the entrance to the pier read in French, "Private, Boat Owner's and Guests Only." About a dozen shorter piers extended from the main pier outward toward the center of the river. Each pier looked to hold six to eight boats on each side. A mixture of sailing and powerboats were tied up on either side of the shorter piers. Several boat owners were casually lounging about their crafts, enjoying the summer weather, while a few others did the odd jobs of boat ownership, washing their topsides, conducting minor repairs or generally preparing for the next adventure.

At the far end of the pier, Marc saw a white powerboat with a partially enclosed cabin parked at the marina's refueling station. The craft was too far away to see who, or, how many people it held. He did notice that although its hull was below the level of the pier, there was something about it that looked out of place.

They continued their stroll in the general direction of the refueling station and as they worked their way to the end of the main pier, Marc saw a young man wearing a polo shirt, the same color that the woman inside the marina had on, operating the gas pump.

"How much gas does that tank hold?" Marc asked, in French, in an attempt to make conversation.

The boy glanced over his shoulder at Marc, then back to the gas pump.

"Not sure, but she's taken on forty liters so far."

Marc looked at the pump meter and saw the numbers ticking upward, then looked down at the boat. He saw that it was actually a type of wave runner with an enclosed hull attached. He was about to ask if the owner was around, when a woman wearing a boater's cap appeared from under the enclosure. The woman concentrated her gaze southward, towards the U.S., apparently unaware of Marc and Sylvie's presence on the pier.

Just then the boy operating the fuel pump snapped the pump handle a few times to top off the tank, and said, "That's all she'll take, forty-five liters."

The red-haired woman turned her attention toward the boy and Marc immediately recognized her as Giselle Montclair, Hugo Karlsson's assistant at Barbeau Transport.

"*Merci*," Giselle said, and handed the boy a credit card.

As the boy took the card, her gaze wandered to where Marc and Sylvie were standing nearby.

"Madame Montclair, I didn't realize you were a boater," Marc said.

At first, Montclair seemed a bit bewildered, apparently trying to place the man who was calling her by name, then a flash of distress crossed her face, quickly replaced by a strained smile.

"Why, Monsieur LaRose. What brings you to Ile Aux Noix?" she said a bit too anxiously.

"The fresh air and the view," he said with a grin.

After an awkward pause, she continued, "Have you made any progress locating Mister Karlsson?"

"Funny you should ask. He was kidnapped and held for ransom. We found him on the grounds of old Fort Montgomery in Rouses Point."

Montclair seemed unfazed by this bit of news, her eyes blinking rapidly. "Oh. That's terrible. Is he all right? Have you spoken to him?" she probed.

"No. He's in the hospital under police protection. He probably won't be saying much until the drugs the kidnappers gave him wear off."

Giselle's gaze strayed toward Sylvie who was piecing together what had transpired.

"Oh, forgive my bad manners. Ms. Montclair, this is Detective Champagne of the Brossard Police Department. Detective, this is Giselle Montclair, a workmate of Hugo Karlsson."

Sylvie, who was almost as surprised as Giselle Montclair at this sudden revelation, returned Giselle's smile, then, as she exposed her police credentials, her face took on a serious pallor. "Ms. Montclair, I have a few questions for you. The boy will tend to your boat. Now, if you would come with me, please."

Giselle remained standing in the back of her boat, holding onto the side of the pier, her facial expression now a mixture of confusion and panic.

"Questions? What kind of questions. There must be some kind of mistake."

"Please, Madame, this should only take a moment. If you refuse, I will hold you here until I procure a warrant."

Giselle glanced southward, then said, "All right. If it won't take long. I just have somewhere to be and…" Giselle let the thought drift off.

Marc extended a hand to help Giselle out of the boat. Reluctantly, she took Marc's hand and was brought up onto the pier.

"We can speak in the car," Sylvie said as she held her hand out to Marc for the keys.

"I'll be along shortly after the boat is secured," Marc said tossing them to Sylvie.

Sylvie took Giselle by the arm and started toward the opposite end of the pier. As they walked off, Marc noticed Giselle glancing back anxiously.

She's hiding something.

The boy who was attending to the fuel pump tapped Marc on the shoulder. "*Monsieur*, I have other customers who want petrol. Could you please move the boat over there?" He pointed to an open berth a few feet away.

As Marc untied the line from the pier's cleat, he noticed it was orange nylon, the same as the one tied to the tree at Fort Montgomery. He retrieved the rope from his pocket and compared the two—an exact match. He guided the boat to the open berth and after securing it, he stepped into the attached hull of the wave runner and took a moment to study the craft. It was actually a jet ski, fitted into a twenty-foot pontoon boat, the bottom of the pontoon section was made of ridged plastic.

Perfect for landing in shallow water, like back at Fort Montgomery.

There was a small covering over the hull, big enough for two people to sleep in. Inside the covered section, he found a blow-up mattress covered with a dirty sheet. In addition to the grime, there appeared to be bloodstains on the sheet. A black canvass bag lay nearby. He opened the bag and dumped the contents onto the sheet. Syringes and a vial of clear liquid fell out onto the mattress. 'Le Ketamine,' was printed on its label.

Marc replaced the contents into the bag and after a last look around, climbed back onto the pier, canvas bag in hand.

He found Sylvie and Giselle sitting in the back seat of the Civic. Giselle appeared stressed. He slid in behind the wheel and laid the canvas bag on the passenger seat.

Sylvie dropped the keys on the seat next to the bag. "We're going to need a little air," she said.

Marc started the Civic's engine and turned the AC on 'High.'

"I've just informed her of her Canadian Charter of Rights to remain silent and that she is being held on suspicion of kidnapping," Sylvie said.

"*Je veux un Avocat.* I want to talk to my lawyer," Giselle blurted. Marc could see tears forming in her eyes.

Sylvie spoke to her with a sympathetic tone, "Look, Giselle, kidnapping is a federal crime. If you are charged with kidnapping, I have to turn you over to the Mounties. Think about it. You could be spending your best years wasting away at the Port Cartier Federal Prison in Laval, or…you can save yourself a lot of anguish by helping us."

"I don't know what you're talking about. I don't know anything about any kidnapping," she said defiantly.

Marc turned in his seat to face Giselle. He held the piece of nylon line in his hand for her to see.

"Do you know where we found this?" Not waiting for an answer, he continued, "Fort Montgomery in Rouses Point about an hour ago. We also found Hugo Karlsson, unconscious, but lucky for you, still alive. This piece of rope matches the line on your boat."

"So what, I took my boat there for a day trip. I don't know anything about Hugo being kidnapped," Giselle said, her voice as convincing as a little girl caught putting on makeup for the first time.

"Then explain this," Marc said as he reached into the canvas bag and produced the bottle of Ketamine. "Since when do people take vials of Ketamine and syringes when they go sailing?"

Giselle said nothing as she sniffled back more tears. Slowly, her expression turned to one of resignation. The look on her face told Marc she knew she'd been caught in a lie.

"What will it be Giselle? You can talk to us…or to the RCMP. The choice is yours," Sylvie said.

Giselle turned her head and stared out the window.

"What you do right now will impact the rest of your life," Sylvie said. "Talk to us, and you have a chance. Play hard ball and your fate will be in the hands of the Mounties and the Federal Prison System."

Giselle sighed and shook her head.

Marc handed her his handkerchief. She wiped her face. "It's not the Mounties, or the Federal Prison I'm afraid of."

"Who then?" Marc asked.

"The mob. You know what they do to people who talk."

"What mob?" Sylvie asked.

Giselle hesitated. "The Rollers. The Rock'n Rollers Motorcycle Gang."

"Go on, I'm sure there's more," Marc said, encouragingly.

"Mr. Karlsson suspected Jimmy Lee had designed the Laser with a secret compartment built into the body of the locomotive."

"Why would Jimmy Lee do that?" Sylvie asked.

"For money, of course. Jimmy Lee was approached by the gang to build the compartment. Lee needs money. He gambles a lot. The gang intends to use the compartment to smuggle drugs and money from the U.S. to Montreal and back. Mr. Karlsson was going to meet with Mr. Barbeau and tell him of his suspicions when he was kidnapped."

"Who is your contact with the MC?" Sylvie asked.

"MC?" Giselle asked.

"*Mon Dieu,*" Sylvie snapped, exasperated. "What is the name of your contact in the Rock'n Rollers Motorcycle Club?" she demanded.

Giselle looked down at her hands holding the sodden handkerchief, and muttered something that sounded like a name.

"What? I didn't hear you," Sylvie asked.

"Maurice," she sniffed. "Maurice Bashaw, but if he knows I told you, he will kill me," Giselle said, her tears were now accompanied by a quiet sob.

"Bullshit," Marc finally said.

"What do you mean bullshit? I'm cooperating with you. Why do you say that?"

"Who kidnapped Hugo Karlsson, and why?"

"I just told you."

Marc stared at Giselle for a long moment.

"Giselle, you're not cooperating."

"I've told you everything I know. It was Bashaw and the Rollers," she sobbed.

"I know what you told me. But look at this from my point of view. What sense does it make for the mob to kidnap Hugo Karlsson and let him live when he knows about the Laser's secret compartment? With Jimmy Lee's expertise, they have the opportunity to smuggle drugs, money, whatever, for years to come. Why would they throw it all away by demanding a few million for Karlsson's ransom? They could easily make that in a year with this kind of smuggling operation."

Giselle continued to stare out her side window, then she looked directly at Sylvie and said something in rapid Quebecois.

Marc grew up speaking French as a child, but had lost some of his fluency from lack of use when he entered the public school system.

He glanced at Sylvie.

"What'd she say?"

"She said, 'she needs to use the toilet.'"

Marc knew Giselle had communicated more than a request to use the bathroom, but figuring Sylvie had an angle, he decided to play along.

"Oh, I see," he said, feigning uneasiness. "Why don't you accompany her to the Marina's rest room?"

Marc pulled the passenger seat forward, allowing the two women to exit the Civic."

All three got out of the car and walked to the *toilette's* entrance located at the rear of the Marina. Giselle and Sylvie went through the door marked, '*Femmes*.' Marc kept a respectable distance, but stayed close enough to assist Sylvie if needed.

Inside the women's rest room, Sylvie found that it had a common sink and two enclosed toilet stalls.

She asked, "OK, what's this all about?"

"If you help me out, I can make you rich," Giselle said, her voice laced with nervous tension.

"I'm a detective with the Brossard Police Department. You were found operating a boat containing evidence implicating you in the kidnapping of your boss, Hugo Karlsson. I don't take bribes."

Giselle remained quiet for a long moment. "You really think that old man back at Fort Montgomery was Hugo Karlsson?"

Somewhat stunned, Sylvie replied, "of course it was. I think you and your two friends overdosed him with Ketamine and were holding him there for ransom."

"You simple fool. You fell for the oldest trick in the book. Like your asshole American friend said, 'why would they let him live?' knowing to do so could jeopardize the whole plan."

"Then, if the old man we found at the Fort was not Hugo Karlsson, where is he, and what is this 'plan' you're talking about?"

Giselle took her time before answering, "what do I get if I tell you?"

"Giselle, you're really in no position to bargain. Like I said before, if you want to avoid a long prison sentence, you'll have to cooperate."

Giselle seemed to give Sylvie's words some thought before answering.

"*D'accord*. I'll do it your way. But first, I really do have to use the toilet. May I please have some privacy?"

Sylvie hesitated, then opened the door to one of the toilet stalls and looked around. She checked to make sure there was no window to the outside.

Satisfied there was no chance of escaping, Sylvie said, "Go ahead, I'll wait right here."

Giselle entered the stall and closed the door.

Sylvie leaned with her back against the lavatory sink and listened as she heard Giselle unbuckle her belt, lower the toilet seat, and slide her pants off. There was the sound of urine splashing in the bowl, accompanied with some coughing, followed by a few moments of silence. Sylvie waited.

"Giselle, everything all right?" she called over the stall.

"*Oui*, I just need another moment. Can't a girl go to the bathroom in private?" She said, testily.

Another minute passed.

Sylvie suspected something was wrong and pulled on the stall door, but to her surprise, she found it was locked from the inside.

"Giselle, unlock the door," she commanded.

"Fuck you, detective. You're too late."

"What do you mean?" Sylvie said, as she frantically pulled on the stall door. Finding it wouldn't budge, she opened the door to the outside and yelled for Marc.

Marc could see the panic on Sylvie's face and hurried inside the toilet.

"What happened?"

"I don't know. She wanted a moment to relieve herself, but she's locked the door and won't come out."

"Giselle, unlock this door," Marc called out.

"Too late," Marc heard her say in a voice just above a whisper.

Just then they heard something drop on the wooden floor.

A vial rolled out from the space beneath the toilette stall door. Marc scooped it up.

"Ketamine," he read on its label.

Marc put his foot against the wall, and pulled the door with everything he had. The latch gave with a splintering sound.

Giselle was slumped on the toilet leaning against the wall, her pants down to her ankles and a hypodermic needle inserted in the vein of her arm.

Marc removed the needle, pulled her hair back to raise her face, and sharply smacked her cheeks in an effort to awaken her.

"Giselle! Giselle!" He yelled.

No response. Her eyes rolled to the back of her head.

"If she's taken the whole vial, she could be going into respiratory arrest. Call 911," he yelled to Sylvie.

Sylvie stepped outside to make the call.

Marc pulled Giselle from the stall, laid her on the bathroom floor and continued his efforts to revive her.

A female patron opened the door to the rest room and saw Marc kneeling over Giselle with her pants down. Thinking the worst, she screamed and slammed the door shut. Sylvie was finishing the 911 call and seeing the woman run from the toilet, returned to help Marc.

"The ambulance is coming from the Ile Aux Noix fire station. They're volunteers, but it shouldn't be long," she said.

"Great, but could you give me a hand with this," he said as he tugged on a corner of Giselle's jeans.

"I assume you're trying to pull them up?" Sylvie said, her tone a bit cheeky.

"Were you able to get any information from her before she went inside to the toilette stall?" Marc asked, as Sylvie secured the snap.

"She said that the old man we saw at the Fort was not Hugo Karlsson. I pressed her for more information, but that's when she went to use the toilet and locked herself inside the stall. I'm sorry, Marc, I really didn't think she was suicidal."

The sound of a siren could be heard getting closer.

"Sylvie, gather up the hypodermic and the empty vial. We need to give those to the EMT's so they know how best to treat her."

Marc opened the door to the rest room. He could see the ambulance pulling into the Marina's parking lot. Someone in the lot was directing the ambulance driver toward the toilets.

Sylvie identified herself to the EMTs and while she explained what had happened, gave them the ketamine vial and the syringe.

"They are taking her to the emergency room in St. Jean Sur Richelieu. It's the closest one in the area, about twelve miles away."

"If she emptied the bottle, it's going to be close," Marc said.

"*Excusez moi, monsieur*," Marc heard a woman say. He saw that it was the Marina proprietress they had spoken to when they first arrived.

"The door to my *toilette* is broken. Who will pay?"

Marc gave her a look of disbelief.

"Hold her boat as payment until she returns." Then, motioning toward Sylvie, he said, "Come on, let's get out of here. We have someplace else to be."

The proprietress continued her protestations even as Giselle was being loaded into the ambulance.

Marc steered the Civic out of the Marina parking lot and headed back toward the U.S. border.

"You going to let me in on where we're going," Sylvie asked over the sound of the Civic's four-cylinder engine screaming at full throttle.

"We need to find out who those two goons we saw back at Fort Montgomery work for. Then, of course, there's the old man. I assumed he was Hugo Karlsson, but maybe he wasn't. "

"And if he wasn't?" asked Sylvie.

"I don't know. This whole thing isn't making any sense."

Chapter Twelve

After passing through the U.S. Customs station in Rouses Point, Marc headed south toward Plattsburgh.

Twenty minutes later, he led the way to the emergency room entrance and identified himself to the admitting nurse. He asked about the elderly man and the shooting victim that had been brought in for treatment.

"The state police are guarding the gunshot victim in one of the rooms, but you can't go in there without their permission. Besides, the doctor is treating him now."

"How about the old man that was with him in the ambulance?"

"He should be in cubicle C4," she said pointing with her pen to a curtained-off section in a corner of the ER. But, of course you can't go in there either, not without the doctor's permission."

Sylvie, having lagged behind, heard what the nurse had said, and, took the opportunity to look in cubicle C4 for herself.

"Miss, excuse me, where do you think you're going?" The nurse called out just as Sylvie pulled the cubicle curtain back.

"Papa!" she called out toward the unconscious man laying on the gurney, now covered with a sheet and blanket. There was a plastic bag containing clear liquid dangling from an IV stand with a tube leading to the man's left arm. Sylvie turned toward the nurse and in her best-accented English said, "He is my papa. I need to be with him."

The sudden news that a relative had come to identify an apparent uninsured client trumped the nurse's desire to control patient visitation.

"All right, but just for a moment. Then I need to speak with you about your father's hospitalization insurance."

Marc saw what Sylvie was up to and decided to divert the nurse's attention back to him and the shooting victim.

"Nurse, can you at least tell me who's treating the shooting victim?"

"What? Oh, him," she said, giving Marc an annoying look. "If you must know, the MD on call is Doctor Racine. I already told you, the police are with him, so you will have to get any further details from them."

Just then, the nurse's desk phone rang, further distracting her. "If you'll just have a seat, I'm sure one of the troopers will be by eventually and maybe they can help you."

"Emergency room, Nurse Hacket speaking," she announced into her phone.

Marc looked toward the cubicle where he'd last seen Sylvie, and saw that the curtain had been pulled shut. He took a seat not far from the nurse's desk in case he'd have to run interference again.

Alone, inside the cubicle, Sylvie looked the man over. His face had been badly beaten. His eyes were swollen shut and he had contusions on both cheeks. His lips and chin were bloody and swollen.

"Mr. Karlsson, can you hear me?" Sylvie said in a soft voice, low enough that it did not carry outside the curtained cubicle.

An almost inaudible moan came from somewhere deep inside the barely conscious figure. Sylvie repeated the question, this time in French, "Mr. Karlsson, can you hear me?"

The man, apparently unable to speak due to the extent of his injuries, again moaned and this time shook his head so slightly that it was barely a quiver.

"What do you mean by shaking your head? No, you can't hear me? Or No, you're name is not Karlsson?"

The man lay motionless for a few moments, moaned again, then struggled as he tried to raise his left arm.

"What are you trying to tell me?" Sylvie asked, again in French, as that seemed the language he was responding to.

Another moan as he pulled at his sleeve.

Sylvie reached over to help him by unbuttoning his sleeve, then slowly pulling it up, exposing his forearm. Tattooed on the back of his forearm was a Fleur-de-Lys symbol and over that was the name "Guillaume."

As Sylvie mouthed the name, the cubicle curtain suddenly slid open, startling her. It was Marc. He pulled the curtain shut behind him.

"The charge nurse stepped away from her desk. Have you been able to get anything from him?" he asked, nodding in the man's direction.

"Look," she said pointing to the man's arm. "Giselle's claim that he is not Hugo Karlsson may be correct. I believe this man is French Canadian and his name is Guillaume."

The man let out another low moan.

Marc retrieved his phone and took a photo of the man and his tattooed arm.

"Did he tell you anything else?"

"No, he's still pretty much out of it. They beat him so badly he can't even talk."

Marc looked down at the man. "There's not much more we can do here." He pulled the curtain back so he could see the front desk where the charge nurse had been sitting.

"She's not back yet. Let's get out of here," he said.

Marc led the way out of the emergency room and across the parking lot to the Civic. Once in the car, he started the engine and turned the A/C to 'MAX.'

"Let's go over what we know so far," Marc said as he clicked into his seat belt. "First, we witnessed an apparently fabricated kidnapping staged by men associated with the Rock'n Rollers motorcycle gang. One of the kidnappers is in the emergency room and the other in custody at the State Police station. Second, we have some poor slob named Guillaume on a cot in the ER, the victim of an assault, as well as a drug OD. Third, Ms. Montclair is at the ER in St. Jean because rather than talk to us or the police about her role in the staged kidnapping, she tried to take her own life. And for all we know, she may have succeeded."

"Besides that, it appears two of Hugo Karlsson's closest associates, Jimmy Lee and Miss Montclair, are connected with Karlsson's actual and/or staged kidnapping. What are we missing?" Marc asked, as he thumped his fingers on the steering wheel.

Marc felt his cell phone buzzing in his pocket. The caller ID read "Tim Golden." Marc let the call go to his in-box.

"Tim's gonna be pissed, but we have to get this sorted out," he muttered as he stuffed the phone back into his pocket.

"Marc, who first notified the police regarding Karlsson's disappearance?"

"His wife. Why?"

"Then she called you, right?"

"Yeah. So, what are you getting at?" Marc asked.

"Well, if Karlsson went missing in the course of his employment, why didn't his employer get more involved? He was traveling on company time in a company car to a company meeting, when mysteriously, he disappears. You'd think his boss would have shown a little more concern."

Marc continued drumming on the steering wheel while he thought about what Sylvie had said.

"You're thinking maybe Karlsson's boss may be involved in his disappearance?"

"I haven't talked to him. You have. What do you think?"

"I hadn't thought about Jean Pierre St. Onge being involved in Karlsson's disappearance. But I suppose, with all that's gone on over the past twenty-four hours, perhaps we should speak to him again. Problem is, it's Saturday. He's probably off work today and he lives somewhere up near Montreal.

Marc stopped his drumming.

"With the rollout of the Laser scheduled for Monday, do you think he'd really be off work today?" Sylvie said.

Marc hesitated, "I guess it wouldn't hurt to make a return visit to the assembly plant and see if he's there. It's only a few minutes away."

Marc put the Civic in gear and headed out of the hospital parking lot.

In less time than it took to place a take-out order at a McDonald's drive through, they were approaching the security gate at Barbeau Transport. The security guard in her booth looked up from the magazine she was reading and slid the window open.

"May I help you?" she asked in a tired voice.

"I'm here to see Jean Pierre St. Onge," Marc replied.

"Well sir, it's Saturday. Mr. St. Onge rarely works on weekends."

"That's funny, he just called and told me to meet him here," Marc lied, raising his cell up for her to see. "Would you mind checking with his office?" Marc asked.

"I suppose," the guard said skeptically. And who should I say is asking?"

"Marc LaRose. He'll know what it's about."

"Hold on," she said sliding her window closed to keep her communication private, as well as to keep the hot afternoon air from invading her air-conditioned space, Marc figured.

While the guard concentrated on her phone, Marc scanned the mostly empty parking lot and spotted St. Onge's silver BMW parked at the far end near the main office entrance. He could also see the guard was speaking to someone.

A moment later, the guard's window slid open.

"Mr. LaRose, it appears that I owe you an apology. Mr. St. Onge apparently arrived before my shift started. He asked me to direct you to the main entrance. He'll meet you there."

"No apology necessary," Marc said, and put the Civic in gear.

After parking the car, the pair approached the main entrance. Marc could see St. Onge standing just inside the main door. When he pushed the door open, Marc could tell something was wrong by the look on his face. In lieu of his usual business tie and jacket he was dressed in a tee shirt and blue jeans.

"Sorry I didn't call ahead. I took a chance that you might be here," Marc said.

"I'm glad you did, Marc." St. Onge said, as he glanced toward Sylvie.

"Jean Pierre St. Onge, I'd like you to meet my, uh, associate, Ms. Sylvie Champagne."

St. Onge gave Sylvie's proffered hand a perfunctory shake.

"Let's go to my office where we can talk," he said, and led the way. Once inside, he closed the door and pointed toward a pair of leather chairs facing his desk, motioning for them to have a seat.

While St. Onge worked his way around to his side of the desk, he said, "You'll have to excuse my appearance, I haven't left the office. I've been preparing for the rollout, and of course, now with Karlsson's disappearance, things are complicated."

"I understand," Marc said.

"I heard through the Brossard office that Hugo's not just missing, but has been kidnapped. I thought about calling you, but figured you had enough on your plate without any pestering from me. Have you made any progress in the investigation?"

"Yes…and no," Marc replied.

"Marc, forgive me, it's been a long night. What do you mean?"

"As you probably heard, there has been a demand of ten million dollars for Karlsson's release. We were able to locate the kidnappers and rescue the victim. We also located an accomplice, your own Ms. Giselle Montclair."

"What? Ms. Montclair was involved in the kidnapping? Why would she kidnap her own boss?"

Marc could see this latest bit of news genuinely stunned St. Onge.

"That's where the 'No' part comes in. Hugo Karlsson wasn't the kidnapped victim."

"Marc, you're not making sense. First I hear Karlsson was kidnapped, and now you're telling me that one of my own employees is involved, but the victim was not Karlsson?"

"It's kind of a long story. I'll try to make it as brief as possible."

Marc related the details of his investigation, including the suspicion he and Sylvie had that the Montreal motorcycle gang were apparently involved, how they had followed the two bikers to Karlsson's residence at the Old Plattsburgh Air Force Base, the shooting at Fort Montgomery, then, finding Giselle Montclair operating the boat that carried someone who they thought was Karlsson.

"What do you mean 'thought' it was Karlsson?"

"The man the kidnappers were holding matched Karlsson's general description. He was so badly beaten, we assumed it was him. However, after looking at a tattoo on his arm, we now believe the victim is some poor old fellow named Guillaume. He had no other identification on him."

"You said Giselle Montclair is involved in this as well? I find that hard to believe. She's always been a devoted, hard working employee."

"I was as shocked as you are. Right now she's in a hospital bed in St. Jean, Quebec, fighting for her life as the result of a self-induced overdose of Ketamine."

"*Mon dieu*," St. Onge managed, obviously stunned by this latest revelation.

"Do you have any idea who this stand-in for Karlsson could be?" Marc asked.

"None at all. Guillaume is a common name in Quebec. It means William in English, as I'm sure you're aware."

"When we left him at the hospital, he was still pretty drugged up on Ketamine, which appears to be the drug of choice for these guys. It looks like he'll live, but it will be at least a day or so before we can get more out of him."

"So that brings us back to Hugo Karlsson. Any idea at all where he could be?" St. Onge asked.

"Good question. According to a witness, we believe he was last seen sitting in a car with Jimmy Lee on Ile de Soeurs, arguing with another man. That was the same day he was supposed to be attending the meeting in Brossard—the meeting he never made."

St. Onge swiveled in his chair as he thought about what Marc had told him.

"You're telling me the mob may, or may not have Karlsson, but knowing how much he meant to us, they substituted this Guillaume in a kidnapping ploy, so they could extort ten million dollars from Barbeau. As insidious as it sounds, it still doesn't make any sense."

All three sat silent for a moment.

"Jean Pierre, I understand the official rollout date is set for Monday."

"Yes, officially you're correct. But with all that's happened I don't know what the company bosses in Brossard will do," he answered.

"It would seem prudent at this point, to consider postponing it," Marc said.

St. Onge answered without hesitation.

"I tend to agree, but I seriously doubt that will happen. This thing has been in the works for over a year. The President of Barbeau Transport, the Premier of Quebec as well as the Mayor of

Montreal are scheduled to be on that train when it arrives here in Plattsburgh. After the usual photo ops, the Mayor of Plattsburgh and the entire high school band will board the Laser, then travel to Albany where the Governor of New York and his entourage will board the train."

"From there, it will continue south to Penn Station to be met by the Mayor of New York City. Amtrak has a huge celebration planned, as this is the first of forty Amtrak routes the Laser is scheduled to run throughout the United States."

"Mr. LaRose, I don't care how you do it, but it is imperative that we find Hugo Karlsson before that train leaves Montreal. As for compensation, I will triple whatever Ms. Karlsson is paying you."

"Thanks, Jean Pierre, but I'm afraid the incentive of more money won't help us locate Mr. Karlsson any faster. What we need are solid leads and maybe a little luck."

St. Onge pushed back from his desk and stood.

"I didn't mean to imply you're working only for the money. I just feel so helpless. If there's anything I can do to help, just ask."

By the way St. Onge reacted to these new revelations, Marc doubted he had anything to do with the kidnapping.

"I'll let you know as soon as I hear anything," Marc said. The three shook hands again, and St. Onge accompanied Marc and Sylvie back to the front door.

As Marc drove out of the parking lot, he glanced at his watch. It was a little after six.

"I don't think there's much more we can do down here. We should get back to Montreal and locate Jimmy Lee. Maybe he will lead us to Karlsson," Marc said. Sylvie agreed.

Marc pulled the Civic out of the Barbeau parking lot and turned right, back toward the center of town.

Sylvie seemed suspiciously silent a long moment as she glanced around the neighborhood.

"Is there something the matter?" he asked.

Another pause.

"Marc, do you know of any public *toilettes* in the area?"

Marc gave her a fiendish smile.

"Oh, no. I can't use your Chi Chi's bottle. Come on Marc, I didn't want to ask St. Onge to use his facility, and now it's becoming an emergency."

"I think McSweeny's Michigan stand has a nice rest room. Besides, we never ate that lunch we ordered and you must be getting hungry."

"I guess I am, but right now, all I can think about is a toilet."

Marc turned down Margaret Street toward the north side of town in the direction of McSweeny's. As he passed Shirley's Flowers he glanced over at the shop. He noticed Shirley's car parked out front along with the same car he had noticed once before.

Strange. Maybe Ann Marie has a new car.

At McSweeny's, the same car-hop recognized them as they drove in.

"You going to stick around for your food this time?" she asked with a half smile.

"Sorry about that. We had a sudden emergency. Something came up that needed our immediate attention. We'll come inside this time and sit at a table." Marc said.

Once inside, Sylvie glanced around, then disappeared through the rest room door.

"No worries. We gave them to another customer who came in right after you left. They were happy with the fast service. So, you want the same, three Michigans, fries and cokes?" she asked.

"Better make that four Michigans," Marc replied.

A few moments later, Sylvie returned.

"Hope you're hungry," Marc said as Sylvie slid into a chair across from him.

She sat quietly for a moment, then said, "Marc, what are we going to do in Montreal? It will be almost dark by the time we get there."

"Been thinking about that. I doubt Jimmy Lee will tell us anything we don't already know. I think I need to revisit Le Club Erotika, and speak with Maurice Bashaw again."

Just then, the waitress delivered the food.

Sylvie squirted a line of mustard along the length of the hot dog, then, while cutting off a section, she paused. "Do you think speaking to Bashaw again is wise, especially on his home turf? That night club gives me the creeps with all those goons standing around watching our every move."

Marc had just crammed a third of a Michigan into his mouth. He wiped his lips with a paper napkin and slowly chewed as he thought about Sylvie's reservations.

"I understand how you feel, but time is of the essence."

"Don't you think they know we've figured out that the old guy in the hospital isn't really Hugo Karlsson by now?" Sylvie said, sprinkling some vinegar on her fries.

"Possibly, but it's a chance I'll have to take," he said, inhaling another bite of his dinner.

Sylvie looked over at Marc, "You say that like you're going to leave me sitting in the car while you're inside the club talking to Bashaw."

"It's too dangerous. No argument this time," he said before taking a long swallow of soda. "I'm depending on you to be my eyes and ears on the street while I'm inside the Club. It's senseless for both of us to go in with no back up. We could be trapped in there with no way out."

Sylvie was quiet as she nibbled on a fry, but Marc could tell she was not happy with his plan.

"There are a couple of things we need to do first; I have to check in with Investigator Golden. No doubt he's pissed that I haven't called him back. While I'm doing that, would you mind contacting the hospital in St. Jean and find out how Giselle Montclair's doing?"

Sylvie took her time before answering.

"I'll do as you ask, Marc, but first let's get something straight. I'm not your girl Friday. I thought I'd made that clear when we first talked. I'm quite capable of taking care of myself when it comes to people like Bashaw or any of his fucking hoods."

Marc looked over at her with a sympathetic smile. He knew he had touched a nerve as Sylvie's face was flushed. "I didn't mean to imply that you weren't capable. I just think we need to work as a team. If we both go inside Bashaw's nightclub together, we're vulnerable. This way if something happens while I'm inside the club, you'll be able to come to my assistance, or, if needed, call in the cavalry."

"Let me think about it," she answered.

As they finished the meal in silence, Marc sensed an uneasy truce had settled between them. He knew if he wanted Sylvie's continued help, he'd have to be respectful of her ability to perform as an equal.

When the waitress dropped the bill in front of Marc, Sylvie quickly scooped it up. "My turn, you bought lunch yesterday," she said.

As they left the restaurant, Marc pulled his cell from his pocket. "I'm going to call Golden. Let me know what you find out about Ms. Montclair's condition."

Without replying, Sylvie got in the Civic and started working on her cell phone.

Marc dialed the number for the Plattsburgh State Police Barracks and asked for Investigator Tim Golden.

A few seconds later, Golden came on the line. "Where the hell have you been, Marc? Don't you ever check your phone? I've left you a dozen messages to call me."

"Tim, I apologize. After you left Fort Montgomery, we got busy following a lead. Are you getting any answers from those two goons you picked up at the Fort?"

"Marc, you're so full of shit. We rescue your pitiful ass and I get stuck with these two scumbags. Then you put me on ignore for three hours. Now you call, pumping me for information. I've got two words for you, old buddy, and they're not 'Happy Birthday,'" Golden said, his voice dripping with sarcasm.

"Tim, I understand you're pissed. Just give me a minute to explain."

Marc could hear Tim exhale into his phone.

"OK, but this better be good."

"After you took those two guys into custody, Sylvie and I headed up to the Marina at Ile aux Noix, Quebec, on the theory that the old guy had probably been transported across the border to the Fort by boat."

“Sounds kind of crazy, but I suppose it’s possible,” Golden responded, his voice less icy. “Go on.”

“When we got to the marina, we spotted a boat coming from the south.”

“Get to the point,” Golden said impatiently.

“The boat was driven by none other than a Barbeau employee who worked for my missing person, Hugo Karlsson, the guy we thought was being held captive at the Fort.”

“Marc, hold on. You mean the old guy at the hospital is not Hugo Karlsson?”

“No, he’s not. We believe it’s some poor schmuck named Guillaume that the mob was trying to pass off as Karlsson to collect the ransom money. We tried talking to him, but, in addition to his injuries, he was pretty doped up.”

“Who was this guy operating the boat?” Golden asked.

“It’s a woman. Her name is Giselle Montclair. I initially interviewed her at Barbeau Transport right after Karlsson’s disappearance. When I searched her boat I found a medical bag with syringes and a vial of Ketamine.”

“Where is Ms. Montclair now? Or should I be afraid to ask?”

“She was taken to the hospital in St. Jean, Quebec. She tried to OD on some of the Ketamine, the same drug she gave this Guillaume guy.”

“Jesus, Marc. This whole thing is turning into a fucking shit storm.”

Marc glanced over at the Civic where Sylvie was still talking on her cell.

“Tim, how’s that guy I shot at the Fort doing?”

“We have him here at the Barracks. His arm is in a sling. Your bullet went right through. They patched him up at the hospital and he’ll be all right. We’re holding him and his buddy on illegal possession of handgun charges until we can get this mess straightened out. The old guy who we thought was Karlsson is still recovering. Guess we’ll have to keep him in custody at the hospital until we can determine just who he really is. In the meantime, I need you and your assistant to come to the barracks for statements.”

Marc knew it was standard procedure. Golden needed written statements from himself and Sylvie about the shooting at the Fort, which could take hours.

"Tim, you're going to have to trust me on this. Those two goons you picked up at the Fort are members of the Rock'n Rollers motorcycle gang. I'm heading to Canada right now to talk to their boss. I'm pretty sure he knows where Karlsson is. As soon as I learn something new, I'll let you know."

"Marc, you're not hearing me, I told you I need your asses down here at the barracks—now!"

"Hello, Tim, what did you say? I can't hear you. I think my battery's low," Marc said.

"Marc, don't you hang up on me," Golden shouted as Marc ended the call.

That will cost me.

When Marc got in behind the wheel of his car, Sylvie was still speaking to someone on her cell in French. He was able to pick up some of the one-sided conversation and knew she was talking to someone at the hospital in Quebec. Finally, she ended the call.

"Sounds like they're not giving you much information," Marc said.

"Not much, but I got enough. Giselle is still there, but while I was talking to the nurse, I overheard someone calling for a doctor, code blue."

"That's not good," Marc muttered.

Sylvie glanced at her watch.

"You got someplace else to be?" Marc asked.

"No. I was just thinking. If you want to catch up with Bashaw, we'd have a better chance to see him before the club opens. The first show starts at nine. If we leave now, we could be there in a little over an hour."

"Sounds like a plan," Marc said as he eased the Civic back onto the main road, then took the entrance ramp for the interstate heading north, back toward Montreal.

Chapter Thirteen

They rode in silence as Marc drove toward the border.

A few miles before crossing back into Canada, Sylvie asked, "Aren't you going to call the Club to make sure he'll be there?"

"No. Let's surprise him."

Sylvie glanced over at Marc. "I thought you wanted to talk to him alone."

"Change of plans. When we were there last night, he knew we were a couple, so to speak. He could see us on his CCTV. I'm thinking we could use the ruse of the 'big deal,' we alluded to."

Sylvie hesitated a moment. "OK, so we talk to him using the angle of your 'big deal,' but what if he wants specifics? What kind of a 'big deal' are you thinking about? More importantly, how do we get him to talk about Karlsson and the kidnapping?"

"I have an angle," Marc said as he reached into the car's center console and retrieved a vial clearly labeled Le Ketamine. "I think this might get his attention," he said as he held the container up for her to see.

"Where'd you get that one? We sent the one Montclair had with her to the hospital."

"Found it in the boat Giselle was operating when she docked at Ile aux Noix. I figured it might come in handy, so I held onto it," he said, shoving the vial into his pocket.

They passed through the Canadian border on Interstate 87 without incident and proceeded toward Montreal. Once they crossed the Champlain Bridge, a fifteen-minute cross-town drive brought them to St. Laurent. As Marc was approaching Rue Pombrio and Le Club Erotika, Sylvie spoke up, "Let's use the laundromat's parking area again."

Marc made the turn. Five minutes later, they approached the front door of the Club. Sylvie pushed the doorbell. No one answered. About a minute later, Sylvie tried the bell button again.

"Maybe they've decided it was time for a summer vacation," Marc said with a smirk.

Just then the door opened. It was Oliver, the hulking Nazi helmet guy they'd encountered before. In the daylight, Marc and Sylvie could clearly see his impressive array of tattoos on his forearms, with barbed wire around his right, and a cobra coiled around his left, the snake's head just visible above the neckline of his black tee shirt.

"What you want? Don't open until nine tonight," he sneered in French, jerking his thumb toward the sign posting the club's hours.

Marc held up the business card Maurice Bashaw had given him the night before. "We're here to see Mr. Bashaw about some business, but if it's not a good time, I suppose we could come back when it's more convenient," he replied in English.

This seemed to throw the hulk off his stride as he stood there, apparently trying to translate what Marc had said.

"Lemme see dat!" Nazi helmet growled, his English drowning in a mixture of second grade education and a thick Quebecois accent.

After scanning the business card, he glared back at Marc and Sylvie for what seemed like a full minute.

Can this ape actually read, or is he pretending?

"Wait here," he finally said, and firmly closed the door, leaving Sylvie and Marc standing on the sidewalk.

Knowing they were probably being monitored on the closed circuit TV, Marc and Sylvie waited patiently in silence for either Oliver the Hulk, or another one of Bashaw's thugs to return. They didn't have to wait long.

When the door to Le Club Erotika opened again, it was Maurice Bashaw who held it open and invited them inside.

Marc noticed he was wearing the same tan jacket as the night before, but today it covered a yellow shirt and a brown leather vest.

"Mr. LaFountain, I'm so pleased to see you again," he said, shaking Marc's hand. "I see you've brought your friend along as well," Bashaw continued, with a quick nod toward Sylvie.

"Pardon the intrusion, but Madame Clair and I have been discussing the offer of assistance you mentioned last night. We thought you might be interested in hearing about our project."

Bashaw glanced at his watch, then looked back to his guests. "I take it that your banker turned you down," he said, studying Marc's face.

This guy can read people, have to be cautious.

Marc paused, trying not to appear too anxious with Nazi helmet lurking just inside the doorway.

"As you're aware, bankers rarely keep Saturday hours, besides, what we have in mind probably wouldn't interest a conventional lender. We thought it would be…perhaps…more discreet to find out what you thought of our venture before looking elsewhere."

"I see," Bashaw said hesitantly, glancing at his watch again, "Why don't we discuss this further in my study?"

He turned to Nazi helmet, "Oliver, would you mind showing these nice people upstairs?" Then turning back to Marc and Sylvie, "If you don't mind, I have another matter to attend to. I'll be with you momentarily, then we can discuss your proposition further, in private."

Without waiting for a reply, Bashaw disappeared inside the entrance. Oliver motioned them to follow, turning left, the same way they had entered the club the night before.

After a short flight of stairs, and a few twists and turns, they found themselves in a large room. It was very different than the one Marc had been taken to the night before. There was a leather corner sofa and several overstuffed chairs at one end of the room facing a TV screen that practically filled the wall. Marc noticed a wet bar along the opposite wall, complete with built-in shelves displaying a colorful array of bottled alcoholic drinks. A stemware holder containing an assortment of wine and drink glasses was suspended over the bar.

"Sit," Oliver said, motioning toward the leather sectional. He took a seat in one of the plush chairs, crossed his massive arms over his chest, and stared at his guests, assisted by the tattooed cobra that seemed to keep watch from its nesting place, peering over the neckline of Oliver's shirt. Somewhere in the background, Marc could hear the thumping of dance music.

Probably the Tangerine Dream practicing tonight's routine.

The three of them sat awkwardly quiet, the only sounds, the muffled thumping and an occasional car horn from the street.

"From the outside, you'd never know this place was so nice," Marc announced, attempting to break the tension.

Oliver remained silent as he continued to stare at his 'guests.' Sylvie made a nervous chuckle.

A minute later, the door suddenly opened and Maurice Bashaw entered the room.

"Sorry for the delay," he said as he ambled in toward the bar. "What can I get you?"

"Molson Export, if you have one," Marc said.

"Of course. And for you, Madame Claire? What would be your pleasure?"

"*Vin blanc, s'il vous plait.*"

Bashaw retrieved a bottle of Molson's from the fridge below the bar along with a bottle of white wine. Marc noticed he also filled a rocks glass with ice and topped it off with a healthy portion of Johnny Walker Blue. Placing the drinks on a tray, he carried them to where Marc and Sylvie were sitting.

"Thank you, and merci," Sylvie said as they took their drinks.

After setting the tray on a table, Bashaw pulled one of the chairs closer to the leather sectional, spilling some of his drink on the plush carpeting as he did so. He raised his glass slightly and said, "To a successful business deal."

Marc and Sylvie raised their glasses in return, and all took a sip of their drinks. Oliver remained impassive, content on staring at his boss's new business prospects, or maybe he was daydreaming about Sylvie.

"So tell me, Mr. Gilles LaFountain, what is your business, and why do you need my help?"

"I'm sure you're familiar with a product known as 'Special K'?" Marc asked.

Bashaw took a leisurely sip of his drink, then slowly set his glass on the table.

"Of course, I have it for breakfast a few times a week. It's loaded with vitamins. At least the box says so," he said with the hint of a smirk.

Marc reached into his trouser pocket.

Reflexively, Oliver whipped his automatic handgun from its ankle holster which was concealed under his trousers and pointed it directly at Marc.

"Easy there, big guy," Marc said.

"Oliver, it's alright. *C'est bon.* Put away the gun," Bashaw said.

Oliver grunted and then did as he was told.

Marc, with one eye on Oliver and using just his fingertips, retrieved the bottle of Ketamine from his pocket, and put it on the table in front of Bashaw.

"You must excuse my assistant. Oliver is a good man, but, as you may suspect, we've had our share of incidents here, and he gets a little, uh, how do you say? 'Overly protective' at times."

"Yes, I see," Marc said.

Bashaw picked up the bottle and examined it closely.

"May I ask where did you get this?" Bashaw asked, rolling the glass vial in his fingers.

"The question you should be asking is, 'How many can you get me, and at what cost?'" Marc said.

"Your business is drugs?"

"We facilitate. People want drugs. People need drugs. Ketamine, or as some like to call it, 'Special K,' is the perfect 'club drug.' Our price is competitive and more importantly, there is no supply problem."

Bashaw sat quietly, then replaced the vial on table, leaned back in his chair, crossed his arms, and exhaled deeply. "Tell me, Mr. Gilles LaFountain, or whatever your name is, why are you really here? I don't believe you are here to sell me drugs. You must be aware that I can get almost any drug, any time I want. So why are we talking?"

"I believe we have a mutual friend, Mr. Jimmy Lee."

Bashaw hesitated a moment as he continued to take in these two strangers sitting in front of him. "I don't believe I know anyone named Jimmy Lee," Bashaw said with practiced certainty.

"That's odd. We talked just a few nights ago while having dinner at the Casino. That's when he mentioned you and your Club.

He said something about doing odd jobs for you at times. Anyway, he thought you might be in the market for a new supplier."

Bashaw did not respond.

Marc started to get up from the chair, "Look, Mr. Bashaw. If what Jimmy Lee said wasn't true, then please accept my apology."

"Sit down," Bashaw ordered, then again glanced at his watch.

Marc slowly resumed his seat.

"You're not from Montreal, are you," Bashaw said, more a statement than a question.

"Is my accent that bad?" Marc asked.

Bashaw simply stared back at him, waiting for an explanation.

"I was born at the Hotel-Dieu Hospital, right here in Montreal. However, when I was four years old, my parents split. My mother was American, so she moved us back to New York, and I grew up there."

Bashaw seemed to think about Marc's explanation, then turned his attention toward Sylvie, "If you don't mind my asking, what is your relationship with this man?" he asked, nodding toward Marc.

"If you must know, we are '*conjointed*.' I'm sure you're familiar with the Quebecois term for shacking-up. Have for three years now. I originally introduced Gilles to Jimmy Lee. I know Jimmy from the time I worked at Barbeau Transport."

"So you just happened to run into Jimmy Lee at the Montreal Casino one evening and decided to strike up a conversation? Sounds unlikely, don't you think?"

"I don't know what you're implying. Jimmy and I had a close relationship at one time, and yes, we did run into each other at the Casino. He had hit it big at the black-jack table and bought us dinner. We mentioned the business we're in, and in passing, he recommended that we talk to you. So here we are."

"How long has it been since you worked for Barbeau Transport?" Bashaw asked.

"Oh, I don't know, six months or so. Why do you ask?" Sylvie inquired.

Bashaw ignored Sylvie's question and turned his attention back to Marc, "So, you've been in the drug business for, what, a few months? That's not much time. What makes you think I'd do business with you? Other than your supposed dinner with Jimmy Lee, I really don't even know who you are. For all I know, you could be a couple of undercover cops."

"We didn't expect you to simply take our word for it. Talk to Jimmy Lee. Call around. We have other customers in the club trade. When you're ready, give us a call. You have our number in your records from our visit last night," Marc said.

Bashaw stood, signaling the meeting was over. "Let me give this some thought, and if you don't mind, I'll hold onto this," he said, pocketing the vial.

"Fair enough," Marc said, as he and Sylvie also rose from the couch.

"Oliver will show you out. Enjoy the rest of your evening."

As they followed the big man down the long corridor toward the front entrance, Marc could still hear the music, a little louder now, as it sent vibrations through the thin walls of the building.

When they reached the main door, Oliver held it open for Marc and Sylvie to exit then, without as much as an '*Adieu,*' he closed the door behind them.

Back on the street, they strolled in the general direction of the laundromat. Marc could see the Harley parking lot was about half full. He also noticed that the club's side of the street was empty, save for a Black Lincoln Navigator parked about fifty feet from the club's entrance. Marc saw it had an Ontario plate and made a mental note of the tag number.

"Rather than return directly to the laundromat, I think we should walk a bit, just to make sure we're not being followed," Sylvie said.

Although there was an hour or so of daylight left, the streetlights were just coming on.

"Did you notice that black SUV parked outside the Club?" Marc asked.

"Yes, I did," she answered.

Marc scribbled down the number on his pocket pad, tore out the page, and handed it to Sylvie.

"Would you mind running that plate number when you can? I'd like to see who it comes back to."

Sylvie put the note in her purse. "OK, but I don't think it will do any good."

"Why's that?" Marc asked.

"I noticed the tags as well. The letters on the plate are typical for those assigned to rental car companies."

The two continued on in silence for a few moments.

"Don't you think Bashaw seemed a little preoccupied when he was talking to us?" Marc asked.

"You mean like when he was glancing at his watch?"

"Yes, that and he all but admitted knowing Jimmy Lee after telling us he didn't. I think there's something else going on, and it may have something to do with whoever arrived in that Navigator."

They continued on in silence for another block before crossing the street at the next intersection, taking a circuitous route back to the laundromat.

As they shut the doors to the Civic, Marc buckled his seat belt, then, drummed his fingers on the wheel, a habit he had formed while trying to decide a matter when there were few alternatives.

Finally, he said, "I think we should find out where that Lincoln is going tonight. I seriously doubt the passengers of that car are casual customers of the club."

"I can't say as I disagree with you. The club doesn't open for another hour or so. But, I'm kind of surprised they'd leave their car out in front, in plain view."

"I was wondering about that as well. Maybe, they just feel comfortable leaving it there, it being a rental."

"But even rentals are traceable, although we'd probably need to get a judge to issue a subpoena to access the rental agreement."

"Yeah and how long do you think that'd take?" Marc asked pessimistically.

"Oh, counting the time I'd probably get suspended for after telling my captain what I'd been up to, we could be looking at a week or so."

"Forget that I asked. Where's a good place to park? I'd like to find out where that SUV goes after it leaves the Club."

Sylvie directed Marc to a side street a few blocks from the Club in the direction the SUV was facing. It was more residential and with the onset of darkness Marc hoped his New York tags wouldn't draw attention to his car.

"I know watching for that SUV may seem like a long shot, but right now, I don't see many options," Marc said as he parked between two other vehicles, leaving the Civic in the shadows. He cracked the side windows, allowing a wisp of evening breeze to blow inside, then reclined his seat back down, "might just as well get comfortable."

Sylvie slid her own seat back, but remained upright. They took turns keeping watch on the intersection for any sign of the black Lincoln. An hour later, Marc was thinking of circling around to see if the SUV had left its parking space in front of Le Club when Sylvie said, "Marc, there it is."

He looked up in time to see the tail end of the car pass through the intersection. He started the Civic's engine, but when he pulled up to the stop sign, he was blocked by a line of six or seven cars following behind the big SUV.

"Come on, come on," Marc said, cursing under his breath.

Finally, there was a small opening in the line of traffic and despite the angry horn from an oncoming car he swung the Civic back into the lane behind a large delivery van. The two lanes of traffic were heavy in both directions leaving Marc with no chance of getting closer to the Lincoln. Around the van he could see a traffic light a block ahead. It was holding green. Marc continued to hug the center line, watching for any sign of the Lincoln making a turn. Ahead, he could see a few cars turn left into a side street, but none of them was the SUV he was looking for. Marc held steady and closely followed the van in front of them.

"I see it. It just made a right turn at the next traffic light," Sylvie said.

Marc's view was still blocked by the van.

As they were approaching the intersection, the van's brake lights flashed red, and it came to a stop.

Marc and Sylvie were close enough to the intersection to see the traffic light over the box van. It had turned red.

"Hold on," Marc yelled.

Laying on the horn and flashing his headlights, Marc swung the Civic into the opposing lane and whipped around the van, then made the hard right hand turn onto the street in pursuit of the Lincoln. This was met with a chorus of horns from several of the cars.

"Crazy American," Marc said, imitating the infuriated drivers around him.

Up ahead, they saw the Lincoln SUV stop at the next light, a block away. He floored the accelerator in an effort keep the pursued car in sight. After passing through the intersection, Marc slowed the Civic to follow at a reasonable distance. A few blocks later, the Lincoln turned onto one of Montreal's main highways, locally known as "autoroutes." A traffic sign ahead reflected in Marc's headlights, 'Pierre Elliot Trudeau Airport, 3 Kilometers.'

"I'm guessing that car was rented at the airport," Sylvie said.

"We'll soon find out," Marc answered.

As the exit for the airport came up, Marc prepared to follow the Lincoln off the autoroute, but, to his surprise, the Navigator continued past the airport.

Marc continued the pursuit, while blending in with the flow of traffic.

"Any idea where they could be going?" Marc asked.

Sylvie considered the question, "We're heading south. Up ahead, this road intersects with the main East-West autoroute in just a couple of miles, not far from the St. Lawrence River.

As Sylvie was speaking, the Lincoln signaled for a right hand turn. The exit sign simply said, "Air/Rail Industrial Park."

"Do you know anything about this place?" Marc asked.

"Not much. It's mostly a bunch of warehouses for small- and medium-sized industries. It's a convenient area to receive materials used in manufacturing, as well as a hub for shipping goods to other locations.

As they continued, the flow of traffic seemed to diminish, allowing the Lincoln to get further ahead. After another quarter mile, they watched the Lincoln turn into a traffic circle. Marc noticed that each exit off the circle led to a different business listed on a signpost. He saw the Lincoln's turn signal light come on as it approached the second exit. There were two businesses listed for that exit: Wheeler Industries and CJ Properties.

Marc slowed then continued past the exit that the Navigator had taken, while at the same time, keeping an eye on where the Lincoln was heading.

"We'll swing back around and see if we can find which way that SUV is going," Marc said.

In the center of the circle was a stand of pine trees, blocking their view. Marc circled back around and turned at the exit the SUV had taken.

Not too far away was an intersection with another set of road signs. One sign indicated Wheeler Industries to the right and the other CJ Enterprises to the left.

"Any ideas?" Marc asked.

"Your guess is as good as mine," Sylvie replied, looking in either direction.

At this time of the evening, the area seemed quite deserted, save for a few moths flitting around the streetlights above them.

Marc turned the Civic left toward Wheeler Industries. He'd driven about 500 yards when he came to a security gate that completely blocked the road. Beyond the gate they could see what appeared to be a warehouse. The outside was brightly lit surrounded by a large parking lot. Except for a few delivery vans lined up along the loading dock, no other vehicles were in the lot.

"Not much going on there. Let's go back and try CJ Enterprises," Marc said.

Although Marc could not recall ever hearing the name, it had a strangely familiar ring to it.

Marc retraced their route passed the intersection and soon came upon a sign, "CJ Enterprises, Restricted Area." Just beyond was another closed gate, this one with a security shack off to one side. Through the cyclone fencing surrounding the property, they could see the entire area was brightly lit. As he was thinking what to do next, Marc saw a flash of red near the far corner of the structure—like a set of brake lights flashing.

Marc cut his headlights and stopped the car.

"No use going any further. We can't get through that gate, and even if we could, we would be alerting whoever is there of our presence."

Marc made a three-point turn and headed back the way they'd come.

"What do you have in mind?" Sylvie asked.

"Not sure, but we can't just hang around here without arousing suspicion," he said, then, turning the Civic's headlights back on, he retraced their route to the main highway.

They had only traveled a few hundred feet on the autoroute when Marc signaled for a right turn into a rest area that included a gas station, a Tim Horton's café, and an all night pizza parlor. There were a few cars in the parking lot along with a pizza delivery truck off to one side. He pulled into a space near Tim Horton's.

"Sylvie, can you get Google Maps on your phone? I'd like to see an overhead view of the CJ Enterprises property."

Sylvie went to work. A few moments later, she announced, "I think I have it," and handed the phone to Marc.

They huddled over the center console studying the phone's screen. It showed the roof of a large commercial building at the end of the road where they'd seen the SUV moments before.

Sylvie tapped the screen a few times to adjust the view.

From the security office, the road led to a parking lot at the front of the main building with a wide paved area around the back, apparently used for loading and unloading. There was an area of cleared land surrounding the building on all four sides. The area beyond appeared to be heavily wooded.

"I'd bet that property is protected by some sort of security fence around its perimeter," Marc said.

Sylvie made a few more taps, zooming in on the area in question.

"If it does, I can't see it. It could be hidden under those trees, or it may be too small for the satellite to pick up."

"Can you zoom back out to the surrounding area?"

When she did, he could see the main autoroute and the rest area where they were parked. CJ Enterprises was on the opposite side of the highway from where they were sitting.

He opened the glove box and retrieved a flexible plastic container and checked to see that his set of lock picks were still inside.

Sylvie gave Marc a concerned look. "So now you're breaking into that building?"

"What? Break in? That's illegal. I just use these in case my key doesn't work," Marc grinned.

"You know I can't be involved in a burglary. It could cost me my job, to say nothing of getting arrested. Besides, like I said, we're not even sure that SUV had anything to do with Karlsson's kidnapping."

"That's why you should go and plant your cute little butt on one of those stools inside Tim Horton's. I'll be back before you finish your second cup."

Even in the dim light from the coffee shop, Marc noticed Sylvie blush.

Could I be the first guy to comment on the shape of her ass?

After a moment, she said, "Alright, but if something goes wrong, don't say I didn't warn you."

Before opening his door, Marc reached under his seat, retrieved his H&K semiautomatic pistol and secured it to his belt, then grabbed a small flashlight he kept in the car's center console. "See you in a half hour," he said.

"Be careful," she managed just before the driver's door slammed shut.

Marc kept to the shadows as he made his way along the edge of the parking lot, and waited for a break in the traffic. When he saw his chance, he scurried across the northbound lanes to the median. Keeping low in the thick grass, he repeated the process over the southbound lanes before disappearing into the woods on the other side of the highway.

It took him about five minutes to make his way through the wooded area he had seen on Sylvie's phone map, then he came up against a chain link fence. Through its crisscrossing wires, he could see the light from the sodium vapor bulbs casting an eerie orange glow on the CJ Enterprises building sitting in the middle of the clearing. Two freight trailers were parked at the rear loading docks.

The trouble was, to get to the building, he had to figure a way to get over the ten-foot steel fence, which happened to be topped with barbed wire. As Marc was about to touch the fence, he noticed a thin wire had been woven through the fencing, running about shoulder high, and immediately backed away.

Some kind of sensing cable, no doubt hooked to an alarm system.

There wasn't enough light to see if cameras were mounted on the building, but given the level of security Marc had seen so far, he had to assume they were there.

He carefully made his way along the fence toward the closed gate. Through the trees, he spotted the security office he had seen the SUV pass by earlier. The perimeter fencing appeared to end at the guard shack. Picking his way through the woods in the direction of the security building, he noticed there were a few lights burning inside the main warehouse. The two trailers parked at the far end of the parking lot were the only vehicles to be seen. As he came even with the corner of the fencing, he could see the security office was actually outside of the fence perimeter. From behind a large oak, he watched for any movement.

Could the guard be sleeping?

As he crept toward the darkened building, he kept an eye out for approaching headlights, then, keeping low, he darted across the roadway to the side door. He silently climbed the two steps and peeked inside the window. Dim light cast by a computer screen partially lit the inside of the security shack's single room.

Marc could see a stool positioned in front of a sliding window where a guard would ordinarily be seated to admit visitors and workers onto the premises, but no guard could be seen. Trying the doorknob, he found it was locked.

"What do you think you're doing?" A voice came from somewhere behind him.

Marc whipped around, dropped to one knee, and reached for his H&K. He froze when he saw Sylvie standing in the shadows on the opposite side of the roadway.

"You trying to get yourself killed?" he said in a forced whisper.

"You trying to get yourself arrested?" she replied and came to where Marc was kneeling.

"Look, if you didn't want to get involved, you should have stayed in the cafe."

She looked around a moment, then gave a long sigh, "*Merde*, we've come this far, we might just as well get on with it. Besides, I'm not a big fan of Tim Horton's," she said, showing the flash of a grin.

Marc shook his head in mock disbelief, then retrieved his lock picks and went to work. A minute later, they were inside the guardhouse. He relocked the door behind them and began inspecting the interior. Except for the computer screen, it seemed surprisingly lacking. No CCTV screens, books, crossword puzzles, girly magazines…nothing one would ordinarily expect to find.

Just then, Marc caught the flash of headlights approaching the guard shack from the direction of the autoroute.

"Someone's coming, keep low!"

When Sylvie hesitated, Marc grabbed her by the arm and pulled her to the floor. They heard the office's computer emit a series of tones similar to a phone being dialed. Marc looked up and saw a phone number with the 514 Montreal area code register on the computer screen. Then there was a buzzing sound as the security gate began to slide open. The vehicle's headlights reflected off the security office window glass as it passed through. Marc peered over the window sill and saw the darkened outline of another SUV heading into the wide parking lot toward the back of the main building. The buzzing sounded again as the security fence started to close.

Seeing their chance, Marc said, "Let's go," and opened the building's side door. Sylvie followed him down the steps and through the gate just before it closed. They watched the taillights of the SUV disappear around the corner of the building in the same direction they had seen the Lincoln go a half-hour before.

Keeping close to the building, Marc led the way as they crept in the direction of the taillights. Except for the scattered chirping of crickets and the constant hum of traffic from the autoroute in the distance, the night was still.

They heard the distant sound of a car door closing, followed by another, then another.

"Sounds like there were at least three people in that SUV," Marc whispered.

They continued to inch their way along the side of the building until they came to a corner. When Marc peeked around, he could see the outline of the two freight trailers he had spotted from the woods across the clearing. As his eyes followed the perimeter of the building, he saw the two SUV's parked near a side entrance door. Light poured through the door's single glass pane.

Slowly, the pair continued along the building's wall toward the door, watchful for any sign that they might have been discovered.

When they reached the door, Marc listened for any sounds coming from inside the building, but, other than the constant hum of tires from the autoroute on the other side of the woods, all was quiet.

Marc took a quick peek through the entry door's window. He could see a lighted hallway with several doors leading off to either side. Expecting to find the door locked, Marc slowly turned the doorknob. To his surprise, however, the door was unlocked. He took another peek through the window. The hallway remained empty. He slowly opened the door and silently slipped through, then motioned for Sylvie to follow. Marc quietly closed the door behind them. Inside the hallway they both stood still for a moment, listening. The only sound was the cool air rushing from the air conditioning vents overhead.

With Marc in the lead, they proceeded down the hallway, then stopped at the first door which was on the left-hand side, away from the direction of the loading dock. Finding it locked, they went to the next door, which was on the right. When Marc pressed his ear close to the door he could hear something, but couldn't tell what it was. He tried the doorknob. It turned. Opening it a crack, he peeked inside. The dimly lit room appeared quite large with a few partitions enclosed with wire mesh. At first glance, Marc thought it looked like some kind of manufacturing warehouse.

As he took in the vast scene before him, the muffled sounds he had heard through the closed door were now a bit louder, but still far away, possibly at the other end of the room. Marc led Sylvie around a large partition, which ran from floor to ceiling and was covered with shelves.

"I hear voices coming from somewhere over there," Marc said, motioning toward the opposite end of the cavernous room.

"I don't like the look of this," Sylvie said.

Even in the dim light, he could see the concern in her face.

"I just need to take a quick look around. If we don't find anything, we'll leave."

She hesitated again. "OK, I guess."

"Stay close," he said. Reluctantly, Sylvie followed. As they entered the darkened football field-sized room, Marc could see more light at the opposite end, the same direction the voices seemed to be coming from. He carefully led the way toward the voices as they passed a few more partitions that Marc suspected were tool and parts cages.

Silently, they passed piles of cartons, mounds of wire, and sheets of metal stacked on shelving that seemed to stretch forever. As they crept closer, Marc suspected that whoever was talking was speaking French. He whispered to Sylvie, "Can you understand what they're saying?"

The voices that echoed off the uneven walls were distorted through the pillars of equipment and material.

"No, we're still too far away. I can hear someone speaking French, but I think there's another language as well. It sounds more Chinese, or something," Sylvie whispered.

Marc guided Sylvie past an aisle of machine parts when he spotted a short flight of steps that lead upward, toward what appeared to be some kind of wire-enclosed storage bin on a catwalk that ran along the outside wall. Sylvie followed as he carefully ascended the steel steps. Once in the elevated bin, they silently continued toward the voices, careful to use the stacks of materials for cover.

Inching closer, Marc could see through the screening, a makeshift table had been set up in the middle of what he figured was some kind of an assembly area. Around the table, there were three people having a heated discussion. Marc immediately recognized the two men facing in his direction: Maurice Bashaw, proprietor of Le Club Erotika, and Oliver, his tattooed bodyguard.

Seated across the table from Oliver, with his back to Marc, was another man who seemed to be interpreting for a fourth man who was hidden from view, save for a pair of hands that remained clasped on the table. Although Marc couldn't tell for sure, he thought the unseen man was speaking an Asian language.

Marc and Sylvie strained to listen to what was being said between Bashaw and the interpreter.

"Mr. Bashaw, part of your contract was simply to apprehend Mr. Karlsson and bring him to us unharmed," the translator said.

Marc heard the unseen man say something, gesturing with his hands and arms as he did so. The tenor of the unseen man's voice was not loud, but confident and firm.

The interpreter said, "Although you were well paid for your services, we now learn you demanded more money, not from us, but from Barbeau Transport, claiming you were holding Karlsson for ransom."

Bashaw replied in French, "Mr. Khan, I'm sorry if you are somehow offended, but this is business. You wanted Karlsson, I delivered him to you. However, our agreement to smuggle items across the border for you did not include a weapon of mass destruction. I intended that the Laser's hidden compartments would be used for my purposes for years to come. But what you propose would end all of that, costing me a fortune. That is why I decided to recoup my losses by demanding money for Karlsson's return, money I could have made without your scheme of using the Laser to blow up Penn Station, greatly hindering my means of earning a living."

The translator related Bashaw's concerns which brought a quick and rather terse retort from the man identified only as Khan.

"Without consulting me, you tried to pass off some imposter as Mr. Karlsson, and in the process you've put our entire plan in jeopardy. That was not only stupid, but totally unacceptable."

With that, Bashaw abruptly stood and said to the unseen man, "Mr. Khan, you've asked me to meet you here tonight to discuss our arrangement and I came in good faith. Let me remind you, you are not in North Korea. You are in Quebec—on my turf. I call the shots here. You can tell that piss-pot boss of yours, Kim Jong what the fuck, to stick this deal up his crazy fat little ass. Space in the Laser's compartment is no longer for sale."

There was another quick translation, followed by a moment of silence. Khan calmly said something in his native language, then rapped on the table three times.

Knock. Knock. Knock. The sound echoed around the warehouse.

This turned out be an apparent predetermined signal, as suddenly, half a dozen men appeared from the shadows carrying nunchucks, pistols and automatic rifles.

Oliver, who had also risen from his chair, made the mistake of reaching inside his jacket in a misguided attempt to protect his boss.

A single shot rang out, and Oliver fell forward onto the table. The bright HID lighting reflected off the stream of blood coursing from the back of his head. Marc and Sylvie watched as his body slid off the table and onto the concrete floor. A pool of blood spread outward around Oliver's head and shoulders like a spilled bottle of Sangria wine.

Too bad he forgot to wear his Nazi helmet.

Bashaw, seemingly unmoved by the loss of his bodyguard, turned his gaze back toward Khan.

Khan arose from his seat and rounded the table to where Bashaw stood, and where, for the first time, Marc could see his face. He appeared relatively short, but quite stocky. He was wearing a snug fitting black sports jacket, slacks, horn-rimmed glasses and a twisted grin. He reminded Marc of a character from an old James Bond movie, but without the steel-rimmed top hat.

"Mr. Khan, I apologize for my employee's foolish conduct. I'm sure we can work something out," Bashaw said, his voice still firm, if a bit less confident.

"I'm sure we can," Khan said as he switched to English. He talked slowly, assuredly, with just a hint of an accent. "Now that we understand each other, this is what you will do. First, we will continue with our prior agreement and arrange for Mr. Jimmy Lee to place four packages into the Laser's hidden compartments, tonight. He will have no trouble gaining access; however, he may need some assistance as the total weight of the items is a little over three hundred kilos."

Khan seemed to give Bashaw time to digest his demand.

"Mr. Khan, I'm sure you are aware that security around the Laser is extremely tight."

"Lee is one of only a handful of people that have access. Anyway, how you accomplish this task is your problem. You figure it out."

Bashaw's look of confidence seemed to fade with each of these pronouncements as he stood, surrounded by the circle of North Korean henchmen.

Khan continued, "Mr. Bashaw, we are not unreasonable. As you previously indicated, we realized that our plans for the Laser would put an end to your personal gravy train, pardon the pun. To help make up for your loss of future revenue, I have been authorized by the Marshal of the Democratic People's Republic of my country, to forward to your Swiss account an additional five million U.S. dollars upon the successful completion of this task."

Bashaw hesitated, as he seemed to digest Khan's offer. "I assume you mean, when Lee has hidden the packages in the Laser?" Bashaw clarified, his voice tinged with concern.

"Hardly. The money will be transferred to your account only after the task is complete. That is to say, when the Laser arrives at its final destination, Penn Station in New York City, and the package has been successfully deployed."

"But what if Lee doesn't want to perform this procedure or, if he should be unsuccessful?"

"Mr. Bashaw, don't be coy. It doesn't suit you. Lee has been in your employ since he started work for Barbeau. We know he built the compartment to your specifications, which just happened to be ours as well."

Upon hearing this, Bashaw's shoulders slumped at the realization he'd been duped into having the Laser's compartment built not for his use, but to further a terrorist plot under the direction of North Korea.

"I'll assist Lee any way I can," Bashaw finally said.

"Good." Khan glanced at his watch. "There is no time to waste."

Khan snapped his fingers and two of his soldiers pulled a plastic tarp that was covering a mounded shape from a nearby pallet. Marc and Sylvie could see the pallet held four long wooden boxes. The top covering each box was removed revealing what appeared to be a metal cylinder inside. Two were silver and two were black in color.

Marc estimated the silver cylinders were three feet in length and about a foot in diameter, whereas the black ones were the same length, but only about six inches in diameter. Then, to Marc's surprise, one of the loading bay doors opened beneath where he and Sylvie were standing. They watched as a black SUV was backed into the room.

"My men will accompany you to your Club where you will make the final arrangements with Mr. Jimmy Lee to conceal the cylinders in the Laser. He is awaiting your arrival there now. Although my men will remain with the canisters, you are ultimately responsible for them. Protect them with your life, and uh, be very careful with them, especially the silver ones."

"I've had experience with explosives. I know them when I see them," Bashaw grumbled.

"Perhaps, but just so there is no confusion, the black ones are filled with semtex. You are probably aware semtex requires an external detonator for it to explode. Without the detonator, it is fairly harmless. Mister Jimmy Lee will take care of that. No, it's the silver containers, the ones containing a highly refined form of ricin that will cause you the biggest problem if, somehow, they are accidently dropped. Ingesting a single molecule will cause a slow and agonizing death. You are looking at two hundred kilos of ricin that will be dispersed by igniting the semtex when the Laser reaches Penn Station."

"So Lee knows what to do with this?" Bashaw asked.

"He does. He will take care of the installation. Your job is to make sure he gets it done on time."

"What about my man there?" Bashaw said, nodding at Oliver's body lying on the floor. The red stain of his blood continued to spread outward on the concrete floor forming an imperfect circle around his body.

"Forget about him. You have more pressing business to contend with without bothering with funeral plans."

Khan snapped his fingers again and his henchmen replaced the lids over the boxes, then loaded the canisters into the back of the SUV before re-covering them with a tarp.

"Providing all goes as planned, I suspect we shall not see each other again, Mr. Bashaw."

"That would be my wish as well, Mr. Khan," Bashaw said with resigned contempt.

Bashaw went to the SUV and got in on the passenger side. One of Khan's henchmen got in behind the wheel and two others climbed into the back of the vehicle with the canisters. Marc watched as the vehicle backed out of the warehouse.

Marc and Sylvie held their positions in the storage bin above the overhead door.

Khan said something in Korean to one of the remaining men, who motioned to another. They lifted Oliver's body and placed it on a tarp. Then one man gathered up what appeared to be machine parts from one of the bins and hastily threw them on top of Oliver's body. Finally, they tightly rolled the tarp up with the body and the machine parts inside, securing both ends with bits of rope.

"I suspect Oliver's taking a dive in the St. Lawrence," Marc whispered.

They continued to watch as another SUV was backed into the room and Oliver's body was unceremoniously loaded inside.

Khan barked something—an order to dispose of the body, Marc assumed, and the two henchmen left in the second SUV.

The overhead door slid shut, leaving Khan alone with Marc and Sylvie still watching from their secluded perch over the door.

Khan looked around the room, as if taking it in for the last time. As he left the area, however, he seemed to glance up to where Marc and Sylvie were hiding.

Does he suspect we're here?

They watched as Khan faded into the darkness, walking toward the door Marc and Sylvie had entered a half hour before.

The sound of the North Korean's shoes scuffing on the concrete floor slowly diminished, then there was the echo of a distant door slamming shut.

Chapter Fourteen

"Sounds like they have Karlsson hidden away somewhere, but I'd say our immediate concern has to be those canisters that are headed for the Laser," Marc said.

Sylvie looked at her cell phone screen. "*Merde*, my phone's almost out of power, and I can't get a signal inside this building. Marc, we've got to get out of here so I can call headquarters. We need to alert the people at Barbeau Transport about what's going on.

Marc felt his pocket for his cell, then remembered he'd left it in the Civic.

"We've got to get out of here and back through the security gate."

Quietly the pair descended the metallic stairs then made their way toward the door from where they had entered. Aware there could be more of Khan's henchmen lurking in the area, they took their time, working their way past the aisles of machine parts and supplies. Eventually, they rounded the last tool cage.

As Marc reached for the doorknob, the loud snap of a switch being thrown echoed throughout the room and the area was suddenly awash in a blaze of overhead HID lighting.

"Not so fast," an unseen voice commanded.

Blinded by the sudden explosion of light coupled with the announcement of their discovery, Marc instinctively dropped to one knee and withdrew his H&K. Sylvie did the same.

"If you want to see tomorrow, drop those guns, now!" The command came from an unseen voice off to one side.

In a determined effort to escape, Marc reached up to turn the doorknob that was just within reach. To his dismay, it had been locked.

A shot rang out, hitting the concrete floor a foot away from where he was crouched.

"Last warning! Drop your guns. Now!"

Marc recognized Khan's voice.

Knowing that Khan was not prone to bluffing, and with no target in sight, Marc slowly set his gun on the floor. Sylvie did the same.

From around one of the bins, Khan slowly approached, holding a pistol pointed in their direction.

"Back away from the door," he ordered, motioning with his pistol.

Marc and Sylvie stood and did as they were commanded.

Khan kicked the handguns away. Marc watched them skitter out of reach under a nearby tool bin.

"It appears we have a couple of trespassers. Who are you and who sent you?"

Marc and Sylvie glanced at each other, but remained silent.

"I see. Get down on your knees, both of you, and put your hands behind your heads."

At first, they hesitated, which brought a sharp retort from Khan. "Now, or I guarantee, the next shot will not be at the floor," he shouted, pointing the gun directly at Marc.

Marc slowly bent down on one knee, then the other. As he laced his fingers behind his head, he continued to keep a close watch on Khan. But, to his surprise, Sylvie remained standing.

"My name is Sylvie Champagne. I am a police detective with the Brossard Quebec Police. My department knows exactly where we are and I expect someone will be here shortly. It would be in your best interest to put down your gun, immediately."

Got to give her credit for trying.

Khan's mouth slowly twisted in a sly grin.

"I assure you, we will get around to proper introductions in due time, meanwhile, get on your knees before I shoot them out from under you."

Sylvie slowly did as Khan had ordered.

Khan raised his left wrist to his mouth and said something Marc assumed was in Korean. Marc noticed, for the first time, Khan was also wearing a discreet flesh colored earpiece.

Khan turned his full attention to his captives. "Good. Remain as you are and you will not be harmed, at least not right away. " He said with a confident sneer.

Khan grabbed a folding chair that was leaning against a sidewall, dragged it toward his captives about ten feet away, opened it, and sat, holding the gun in their direction.

"I have to assume you saw and heard everything that went on during the past half hour, so I'm not going to waste time and lie that everything will be all right. Everything is not all right. You observed a man getting killed, and you probably heard some other things that you shouldn't have. What I need to know from you is who else knows of our plans for the Laser? Talk now!" The force of his voice reverberated around the spacious room.

The brief silence was broken by footsteps coming from the hallway, then the door Marc and Sylvie had tried to escape through burst open. The two henchmen who they had seen carrying Oliver's carpet-wrapped body away had returned.

Khan said something to them in Korean.

One of the men walked over to Marc, and using his foot, pushed him, face forward onto the floor. With his knee pressed into Marc's back, he searched his pockets, retrieved Marc's wallet and car keys and handed them to Khan. The other Korean conducted a similar procedure on Sylvie, finding her police ID and cell phone.

Khan examined the findings.

"So, Ms. Champagne, you really are a police detective. Interesting," Khan said, then returned his attention to Marc.

"And you, Monsieur Gilles LaFountain?" he said, his voice tinged with skepticism as he slid the driver's license out of Marc's wallet and examined it. "Are you a police detective also?"

Marc had forgotten that he still had the bogus license in his wallet. He remained silent, staring back at Khan.

"Something tells me this isn't your license," Khan said as he continued to examine it.

Marc knew Khan was not easily fooled. He had to come up with something plausible… and fast.

"Think what you want, but what detective Champagne told you about the police knowing where we are is true."

Khan glanced down at Sylvie's cell phone in his hand.

Marc continued, "I am a private investigator hired to find Hugo Karlsson. The detective was simply assisting me."

As Marc explained this, Khan was busy scrolling through Sylvie's address book.

"I see her last call was earlier this afternoon. A call to her mother?"

"Yes, her father is not well. She used the police radio in her car to call in our location," he lied. "Whatever arrangement you have with Mr. Bashaw is none of our business. All we were trying to do is locate Karlsson and return him to his home in Plattsburgh."

Khan said something to the man guarding Marc, then threw him Sylvie's phone. The man dropped the phone on the floor, stomped on it and ground the remains into the concrete.

Khan returned his attention to Marc.

"Mr. LaFountain, or whoever you are. Don't take me for a fool. There's no question you both know too much. Simply put, you have become a liability. Just because that fool Bashaw kidnapped Karlsson does not sanction your presence here this evening. There is far too much at stake to allow either of you to live. The one thing I do need, however, is for you to tell me who else knows about this."

I've got to buy some time.

"What you said is true, we witnessed a killing, but we have no idea who the killer was, or even the man who was shot. And true, we did overhear something about a secret compartment, but we have no idea what you were talking about," Marc lied again.

Khan seemed to consider what Marc had said.

"My initial instinct is to kill you now and be rid of you. However, you may still be of some use, especially you, pretty lady," he sneered, motioning toward Sylvie with his pistol.

Khan lifted a roll of duct tape from the tool bin and threw it to one of his men. He again said something to the henchmen, then, returned his attention to Marc and Sylvie, "Put your hands behind your backs, please. If you resist, we will simply break your arms," he said, sounding matter-of-fact, like he was ordering a plate of kimchi.

A minute later, their hands were firmly secured.

Khan gave his men another command and Marc and Sylvie were assisted to their feet and lead back through the doorway they had originally come through, then down the end of the hallway to a storage room. In the small, stuffy room, both were pushed down onto their stomachs. Their ankles were taped together and duct tape wrapped around their heads, covering their eyes and mouths.

Blinded by the tape, Marc heard the muffled sound of a light switch, the door slam shut, and the steps of the men as they retreated back down the hallway.

Marc lay on the floor for a few moments, then rolled onto his side and slowly brought himself up into a sitting position. He attempted to speak, but with the tape covering his mouth, all that came out was a muffled grunt. He sat there for what seemed like ten minutes contemplating his predicament when he thought he heard the shuffling of footsteps.

Shit, don't tell me those goons are back already.

Then he felt a gentle pair of hands holding his face.

"This might hurt just a little," he heard Sylvie say.

A quick pull ripped the tape from his face.

"Ouch! I'd hate to find out what you think a lot of hurt feels like."

"Shhh, keep it down," she whispered.

As Marc's sight began to return, he could see a thread of light from the hallway slither in from under the door.

"How'd you get free?" he whispered.

"Never underestimate the power of a woman, especially one with a set of tweezers in her pocket."

"Tweezers?" he asked, hesitantly.

"Don't ask," she said and continued to remove the tape from his bound up wrists.

After his hands were free, he rubbed his wrists to revive the circulation, then he felt where Sylvie had removed the tape from his face.

"Guess I won't need to shave for a couple of days," Marc said as he began unwinding the tape from his ankles.

Without answering, Sylvie crept to the door. She tried turning the knob.

"It's locked. You still have those picks?"

Marc retrieved the picks from his back pocket.

"They were so concerned about your cell phone, I guess they neglected to do a thorough search," Marc whispered.

He went to work on the lock. Two minutes later, he slowly turned the knob, opened the door, and peeked down the hallway.

They carefully made their way toward the outside door. Through the door's window, he could see the perimeter lights. Looking to his left, Marc could see one of the SUV's still in the parking lot.

The other one must be hauling the bomb to the Laser.

Marc held his breath as he turned the door handle, aware that someone may have armed the alarm system. Thankfully, nothing happened as he slowly pushed the door open. No bells, flashing lights or growling attack dogs…nothing but the hum of traffic coming from beyond the woods.

He motioned for Sylvie to follow and, after closing the door, turned in the direction of the lone SUV.

"Marc, where are you going, the gate we came through is back there," she said, pointing in the opposite direction.

"I know, but we can't climb over that gate, and we don't have a cell phone to call the number to open it."

Marc wasn't sure what he'd do when he got to the SUV, but he couldn't just wait around for Khan to discover they had escaped.

A few minutes later, they made it to the SUV hidden in the shadows of the building. Marc tried the driver's side door. It was locked.

"Shit," he whispered.

He peered through one of the side windows, but its dark tint prevented him from seeing anything inside. He went to the front of the vehicle, and although he couldn't see much because of the darkness, he thought he saw what looked like a bundle in back of the SUV.

Must be Oliver's body, wrapped in the plastic tarp coffin.

Marc looked around for something to use to break the vehicle's rear window. Finding nothing, he started unlacing his shoe.

"Marc, you can't be thinking of breaking out a window. That could set off the car's alarm, Sylvie whispered."

"You have a better idea?"

Sylvie remained quiet.

Marc held his shoe in the center of the vehicle's rear window with his left hand, and struck the shoe hard with the heel of his right hand. The window shattered, and to their relief, no car alarm sounded. He pushed the remaining shards of glass inward, and climbed into the back of the SUV.

"What are you doing Marc? The car is locked, do you think they left the keys in it for us to find?" Sylvie said in a low voice.

"No, probably not, but it's only right to have a last viewing of poor old Oliver here." Marc said as he undid the ropes used to tie Oliver's makeshift coffin and pulled back the tarp. "He looks so peaceful, especially with that cobra head poking out above his tee shirt."

"Come on Marc, we don't have time for this. Besides, it's kind of morbid."

"Just keep out of sight. I'll only be a minute," Marc said.

Marc searched Oliver's pockets and he found his cell phone. Although the holster clipped to his belt was empty, a search of his ankle holster revealed the nine millimeter semi-automatic handgun he had reached for back at Le Club Erotika. Its magazine was fully loaded.

"Sweet dreams, old buddy," Marc whispered as he quickly re-covered the body. He secured the handgun in his belt and shoved the cell phone in his pants pocket, then climbed back out of the SUV.

"Come on, let's get back to the gate," Marc said.

"But how are we going to get out of here? You said yourself that we can't climb that fence."

Marc waved Oliver's cell phone at her.

"Where'd you find that?" Sylvie asked.

"A parting gift from an old friend."

Keeping close to the building, they carefully picked their way to the security gate they had come through an hour before. Using Oliver's cell phone, Marc dialed the number he remembered seeing on the computer screen in the guard shack. They heard an electric motor start, and the gate slowly began to open.

"Bang!" A shot rang out, the bullet hitting the side of the building just over Marc's head. He felt the spray of brick shards on the side of his face. He had no idea where the shot came from, but knew they had to get away, fast.

"Let's go," Marc shouted and the two sprang toward the opening section of the gate.

Another gunshot sounded and a bullet struck a window in the guard shack, shattering it just as Marc pulled Sylvie through the open slit of the gate. A third shot hit the top of the security gate frame. They cleared the perimeter and headed for the wooded section surrounding the warehouse. Keeping low, they scrambled into the woods. As they scurried into the thicket, they heard several more shots, but for the time being, they were shielded by the barrier of trees and brush.

With only the ambient light of the city reflecting overhead and the noise from cars passing on the autoroute to guide them, the pair continued through the brush in the darkness. Marc held his hands in front of him to prevent the tree branches and twigs from stinging his face.

"Ow!" Sylvie yelped.

Marc stopped and grabbed Sylvie's hand.

"You OK?"

"*Oui*. I think so. A branch hit my face, but I'm all right, keep going."

Marc pushed ahead. After another few minutes of thrashing through the thick brush they finally arrived at the roadway. Although it was late evening, they could see the traffic was still heavy.

Beyond the car lights that whizzed by on the four-lane highway, lights from the rest area and Tim Horton's Restaurant were visible on the opposite side of the roadway.

"Do you think it's safe for us to cross? What if they see us?" Sylvie gasped, inhaling gulps of air from the run through the woods.

"We'll watch for a break in the traffic and scoot across the southbound lanes. The grass in the median is pretty tall. We'll hide there until we can safely get to the rest area."

A few minutes later, they made their way across to the median. The grass and weeds hid them as they crawled toward the opposite two lanes. When they reached the opposite side of the median, they could see the Civic where they had left it next to the Tim Horton's Café. They also noticed the dark silhouette of an SUV parked nearby, facing out towards the highway with its high beams illuminated.

"Marc, that looks like one of the SUV's we saw at CJ Enterprises…the one with Oliver's body in the back. They must be looking for us."

"I doubt they're taking a coffee break," Marc said, staring at the vehicle.

As they lay in the grass deciding their next move, Sylvie gave Marc a nudge, "Look, there's an SQ patrol car pulling into the parking area."

Marc recognized the white Ford LTD with its green and gold markings as a Surete du Quebec Police vehicle, better known to Anglo's as the QPP, or Quebec Provincial Police.

They watched as the police vehicle circled around the back of the restaurant, then reappeared in the restaurant's drive-thru lane.

"I've never had a Tim Horton's doughnut," Marc said in an effort to lighten the mood.

Sylvie shook her head, "Anybody ever told you that you have a pathetic sense of humor?"

"Never," Marc said with a wry grin.

The SUV remained at the front of Tim Horton's parking lot, facing away from the restaurant, with its headlights still pointed toward the median where Marc and Sylvie lay.

"I wonder if whoever's in that SUV saw the police car turn into the drive-thru?" Sylvie asked.

"Who knows? They're probably so intent on looking for us, they might have missed it."

Marc had an idea. "Look, the SQ may be our ticket out of here. When the patrol car starts to leave, I'll make a run for the rest area's entrance ramp and try to flag them down. It will be safer if I go alone. You wait here," Marc said.

"All right, but be careful," Sylvie said, reluctantly.

Another minute passed before Marc saw the patrol car start to leave the drive-thru. He rose up from the weeds and started off in the direction of the Tim Horton's on a dead run, but when he got to the edge of the highway, the traffic was heavy, and he couldn't take the chance of crossing the road. He looked in the direction of the SQ patrol car and started raising his hands to attract their attention, but to his surprise, the patrol car stopped alongside the SUV.

Wonder if that smashed out rear window attracted the cop's attention?

When Marc looked back at the line of traffic, he saw a small opening in the line of headlights heading his way. He glanced back over at the patrol car and saw that the cops were apparently talking to someone inside the SUV.

Marc knew timing was everything if he wanted to get across the two lanes alive. As he sprang across the first lane, he was met with the blare from an oncoming driver's horn, then, after sprinting across the second lane, he headed toward the restaurant's parking lot.

With Tim Horton's a hundred feet away, he looked toward the two sets of headlights from the patrol car and the SUV, and was astonished to see the lights of the SUV had started straight toward him. Barely aware of the red and blue flashing lights of the police car, there was only one place for Marc to go…a concrete pylon that acted as the base for one of the parking lot lights. It was his only chance to avoid being run down by the SUV. He dove behind the pylon just as he heard gunfire and the sound of a bullet striking the aluminum light pole. Tires screeched as the black vehicle made a turn around the pole in an effort to get at Marc, but Marc kept the pylon between himself and the SUV.

Then Marc saw the flashing lights of the police car as it pulled between the SUV and the pylon in an apparent attempt to block it, but the SUV continued forward. The SUV rammed into the side of the police car, pushing it against the light pole, its tires smoking as it pinned the police car against the pylon, blocking any attempt by the officers from exiting their car.

Despite the smear of fresh coffee that had been splashed inside the passenger window of the police car, Marc could see the two officers inside the car were desperately trying to escape from their precarious situation. Any attempt by the officers to exit the car through its rear doors was made impossible by the caged partition separating them from the back seat.

Marc retrieved Oliver's semi-automatic pistol from his waistband and stepped from around the pylon, aimed, and fired two shots into the SUV's front driver's side tire.

The driver's side window lowered and Marc recognized one of the Asian men he'd seen in the warehouse—possibly the one who had shot Oliver. The muzzle of a pistol appeared through the window from the SUV's interior darkness. Before Marc could react, a hail of bullets punched spider webs into the windshield of the SUV. The driver of the police vehicle had slid his side window down and opened fire on the occupants of the SUV. Although the bullets seemed to deflect off the windshield, the SUV's driver had apparently had enough and its rear tires suddenly screeched in reverse. The SUV spun out of the parking lot back onto the roadway, creating a cacophony of car horns from the line of cars on the autoroute.

The officer driving the police car yelled to Marc in French, "You OK?"

"*Oui*!" Marc yelled back.

"Remain where you are, we'll be right back," the officer yelled in French, as he reversed the damaged police car from the pylon and took off in pursuit of the SUV, lights flashing and siren wailing."

The SUV's tire shouldn't last long with two bullet holes.

Chapter Fifteen

As Marc watched the flashing lights of the police car disappear among the river of taillights from the other vehicles, he caught a movement off to his left. He looked and saw Sylvie running across the autoroute amid another chorus of car horns. As she reached the parking area where Marc was standing, she asked, "Are you alright?"

"I think so," he said, as he tucked the pistol back into his belt. "This place will be swarming with SQ officers any minute. We should get to Barbeau Transport and warn them about what Khan and the North Koreans are up to."

When he reached in his pocket for his car keys, however, there was nothing but lint. Then, remembering his keys were taken from him back at the warehouse, Marc ran to the front of the Civic and felt behind the bottom of his license plate.

While on a surveillance in the Adirondacks a year before, he had accidently locked his keys inside his car and had to hike five miles before he got a cell signal to call Norm and have him bring another key. Since then, he had fashioned a slotted key holder on the reverse side of his front plate just for this purpose. He had taped his car key, his house key, and a handcuff key held together on a small ring and fitted them inside the holder.

A few patrons from the coffee and pizza shop had ventured outside to find out what had happened.

Sylvie flashed her badge, "It's alright, folks. If you would be so kind, please remain here for a few moments until the SQ detectives arrive. They may want to talk to you about what you saw."

A few of them stood staring, while a few drifted away, apparently reluctant to get involved with a police investigation.

"Come on Sylvie, let's go," Marc said, as he unlocked the car door.

When Marc drove the Civic out of the rest area toward the entrance ramp, he could see a line of glaring red brake lights off in the distance.

"It looks like the SQ's caught up to the Koreans. They probably have the road closed off," Marc said as he thought of what to do.

Seeing a break in the line of slowing traffic, he gunned his engine and headed straight across the median toward the opposite side. The Civic's narrow tires and low wheelbase made for a bumpy ride through the tall grass and weeds, but in a few seconds, they were heading south, away from the fray.

"What's the quickest way back to Brossard?" Marc asked.

"Straight ahead. The Honore-Mercier Bridge is coming up in a few miles. That will take us back across the St. Lawrence to the South Shore. From there, it's about a half hour, depending on the traffic."

Marc handed Sylvie the cell phone he had taken from Oliver's body and gave her the phone number for Barbeau Transport. "Try that number. With luck, someone's still in the office. We have to talk to someone at Barbeau and let them know what's going on."

Sylvie dialed, then said, "*Bonjour, Monsieur LaFleur*? *Un moment, s'il vous plait*," Sylvie said, handing the phone to Marc.

Marc was curious, but relieved that LaFleur would be manning the phones at the office this time of night.

"Mr. LaFleur, this is Marc LaRose." Marc put the phone on speaker mode.

"Mr. LaRose? Uh, we've been expecting your call. Any progress on locating Hugo Karlsson?"

"Actually no, I'm sorry to say. But something else has come up, and I'm afraid it's kind of urgent."

"Oh? What could be more urgent than locating Mr. Karlsson?"

"Are you familiar with Karlsson's protégé at the Plattsburgh plant, Mr. Jimmy Lee?"

"Mr. Lee? Well, yes, of course. What does he have to do with Karlsson's disappearance?"

"I'll explain that when I see you. But right now, I need to know where the Laser is being kept. What is its exact location?"

Silence.

"Hello?" Marc said, thinking the call had been dropped.

"I'm still here," LaFleur said, "I was, uh, just thinking how to answer your question. You must understand, that with the Laser's trip scheduled for tomorrow morning—carrying the Premier of

Quebec and several other important politicians on its maiden trip to New York City—its location has been kept secret."

"Does Jimmy Lee have that information?"

Another pause.

"I believe he does."

"Why would he know where it is?"

LaFleur exhaled heavily. "Mr. LaRose, I think you're straying a little off the reservation with your missing person investigation. But if you really must know, I…we… felt that, with Karlsson gone, we needed someone familiar with the project to take charge of its rollout. Jimmy Lee is not only the most familiar, but next to Karlsson, he's the most qualified."

"I have some bad news for you," Marc said as he glanced over at Sylvie. "We believe that Lee may be behind Karlsson's disappearance."

Another pause, "I don't understand. Are you sure?"

"Right now, I'm not sure about anything, but it would be a big help if I knew the location of the Laser. I understand the need for secrecy, but…"

LaFleur interrupted, "Mr. LaRose, maybe we should discuss this in person. Where are you now?"

"We're crossing the Honore-Mercier Bridge. Is Mr. Barbeau with you?" Marc asked.

"No, and I'm not sure I can reach Mr. Barbeau on such short…"

Marc interrupted. "You need to get in touch with Mr. Barbeau and have him meet us at your office, and while you're at it, call the police department and have them meet us there as well. We have some critical information that they'll want to hear about. We'll be there in fifteen minutes. The future of your company, Mr. Karlsson's life, and possibly the lives of many others depend on it."

Marc cut the connection.

"Asshole," Marc whispered, and handed the phone back to Sylvie.

They rode in silence for a few miles.

"Marc, did you get the impression LaFleur wasn't interested in hearing about Jimmy Lee's apparent role in this matter?"

"Like I said, he's an asshole."

They passed a lighted highway sign indicating the exit to Brossard was coming up in five kilometers.

"Have you given any thought to the idea that Jimmy Lee may not be acting alone in this matter?" Sylvie asked.

"Of course he isn't. He's got that goon, Khan, and his henchmen with the apparent backing of The Supreme Leader of North Korea, the local head of the Rock'n Rollers MC gang, plus at least one of his co-workers, Ms. Montclair. Am I missing anybody?"

"I don't know. Guess I'm just a little confused," she answered.

Marc drummed his fingers on the steering wheel as he sped along.

"You thinking what I'm thinking?" Marc asked.

"I don't know. What are you thinking?"

"I'm wondering, who the hell picked Lee to head up the Laser's rollout?" Marc asked.

"Good point. It would seem a job that important shouldn't be left to a design engineer, unless..." Sylvie left the thought unfinished.

"Unless someone else at Barbeau is connected to this plot and doesn't want their fingerprints all over it."

"I agree, but who?" she answered.

"There's only one way to find out. We need to speak with Jules Barbeau in person. Between him and LaFleur, one of those guys has the answer."

Ten minutes later, Marc turned the Civic into the parking lot of Barbeau Transport's main office. There were only a few cars in the parking lot and most of the building's interior lights were off. A black Mercedes occupied the parking space designated for Jacques LaFleur, but Jules Barbeau's space was empty.

"Looks like Barbeau hasn't shown up yet, and neither have the police," Marc said, glancing at the mostly empty parking lot.

Sylvie simply nodded as Marc parked in the first open space he came to. When they got to the building's front entrance, they could see a maintenance person mopping the main lobby. Marc pulled on the glassed entrance door, but it was locked. Rattling the door a few times, he caught the janitor's attention. He stopped what he was doing and came to the door.

"*Désolé, nous sommes fermé*," he yelled through the closed door, indicating the offices were closed.

Just then LaFleur, apparently having overheard the commotion, appeared from around a corner and instructed the man to open the door.

"Monsieur LaRose, I'm so sorry. I should have left instructions that you were expected," LaFleur said, leading the way toward the conference room where they had met earlier. Marc heard the soft click of the door latch as LaFleur closed the door behind them.

"Can I get you anything? Coffee? Something stronger?" he asked.

Marc ignored the offer. "Where is Mr. Barbeau and the police? I thought I made it clear on the phone that this is an urgent matter, and we need to talk to everyone, tonight."

LaFleur hesitated, "Barbeau called just before you arrived and said he'd be here shortly, as will the police. In the meantime, please have a seat and make yourselves comfortable," he said, gesturing toward the conference table.

Reluctantly, Marc took a seat in one of the chairs facing the doorway. Sylvie sat next to him. LaFleur turned toward a large globe resting on a pedestal at the opposite end of the table and, at about the equator, swung the northern hemisphere over on its hinge, revealing a mini bar inside. "Sure I can't get you something?" he asked as he picked some ice out of a container and dropped a few of the frozen cubes in a rock's glass.

Marc thought it curious that LaFleur seemed to be taking his time as he proceeded to retrieve a bottle Woodford Reserve from the mini bar and pour two fingers of the bourbon into the glass.

"No, thanks," Marc said.

LaFleur sat at the far end of the table.

"On the phone, you mentioned you had information that Jimmy Lee could somehow be responsible for Karlsson's disappearance. If true, this is obviously a very serious matter. What kind of proof do you have?"

"Have you ever heard of the Rock'n Rollers Motorcycle Gang?" Marc asked.

"Of course, who in Montreal hasn't?" LaFleur replied.

"Are you familiar with the head of the gang, Maurice Bashaw?"

"Only what I've read about him in the papers. Drugs, prostitution, loan sharking. He's a typical mobster. Why do you ask?"

"We believe Jimmy Lee is working for him."

LaFleur seemed to take this revelation in stride as he took a deep swallow of the bourbon. Marc and Sylvie waited while LaFleur took his time, crunching on one of the ice cubes before finally setting his glass on the table.

"Mr. LaRose, you mentioned on the phone that you thought Lee was responsible for Karlsson's kidnapping, which, as you might understand, I find incredible enough. Now, you're telling me that he and Maurice Bashaw are working together?"

"I wish it were that simple," Marc said.

"Oh?" LaFleur said, as he swirled the drink in his glass before taking another swallow.

"We also believe Jimmy Lee and Bashaw are, as of this moment, in the process of planting something in the Laser's locomotive compartment."

"What do you mean, planting something? Are you suggesting that Jimmy Lee is aiding a known mob boss to smuggle contraband across the border in the Laser?"

"From what we've learned, it doesn't sound like ordinary contraband."

"Well, what then?" LaFleur asked, almost matter-of-factly.

Marc drummed his fingers on the table as he watched LaFleur finish the last of his drink.

"We're not exactly sure what they plan to do. But we overheard a man by the name of Khan, who we suspect is a North Korean agent, instruct Bashaw to transport four crates to the Laser. He also said that Lee would know how and where they were to be installed."

LaFleur slowly swiveled around in his chair back toward the mini bar to refresh his drink. When he was finished, Marc noticed his drink size had increased to four fingers. "Sure I can't interest you in a drink? This is excellent bourbon, some of the best Kentucky has to offer, I'm told."

"No thanks," Marc said impatiently.

Sylvie looked toward Marc, "May I?" she said, gesturing toward LaFleur.

Marc shrugged his shoulders.

"Monsieur LaFleur, how long has Jimmy Lee worked for Barbeau Transport?"

LaFleur took a sip. "I'm not really sure. A couple of years, I suppose."

"Before he was hired by Barbeau, who did he work for?"

LaFleur bit down on another ice cube, then swirled his drink again. Marc suspected LaFleur was playing for time. "I don't know who he worked for, exactly. But I believe he's been in the locomotive design business for some time."

"You believe, but you're not sure?"

"What are you getting at? Are you accusing me of something? And who the hell do you think you are talking to, you pathetic little Quebecois shit?"

LaFleur casually took another sip of his drink.

"I'll tell you exactly what we're getting at," Sylvie snapped. "You think Jimmy Lee has worked for your company for maybe a couple of years, but you're not sure. You don't know who he worked for before you hired him. Yet you put him in charge of the largest project your company has ever had. It sounds to me like Jimmy Lee isn't the only employee at Barbeau with a gambling problem."

LaFleur stared at Sylvie over his glass. "Madame, you're beginning to get on my nerves." He glanced at the wall clock over the door.

Marc could see that agitating LaFleur was getting them nowhere.

"Mr. LaFleur, I must say that…" Marc began, but was interrupted as the office door was suddenly pushed open. One of the Asian's they'd seen earlier at the warehouse rushed into the room pointing a handgun at Marc and Sylvie.

"Well, it's about time," LaFleur said.

"You can thank these two for that," the Korean said, motioning toward Marc and Sylvie.

"Ahhh, you've been in on this all along," Marc said, looking at LaFleur. "That explains a few things."

Just then, Khan entered the room, also holding a handgun.

"Well, here are my little mischief makers. I hope you enjoyed your little escapade back at the warehouse. I assure you, it will be your last," Khan said.

Marc was surprised to see Khan and wondered how he had escaped the Quebec Provincial Police. He was sure he had put a bullet in the SUV's tire back at the rest area.

"It had better be," LaFleur chimed in. "These two are proving to be quite the nuisance. It's time you did your job, Khan, and put them someplace where they can cause no further trouble."

"Don't worry, I know what to do with them," Khan said. Turning his attention back to Marc and Sylvie, he motioned with his pistol, and said, "One at a time, stand up and put the palms of your hands on the table." Marc did as he was ordered. Khan's goon got behind him and professionally frisked him. He slid Oliver's handgun from Marc's waistband, then pulled the cell phone from his pants pocket.

"Take good care of those, Khan, Mister Bashaw may want them back, a little something to give to Oliver's next of kin."

Ignoring Marc, Khan turned his attention to Sylvie, "OK, missy, you're next. Hands on the table."

After a cursory search, Khan's goon said something in Korean, apparently indicating there was nothing more to find.

LaFleur took another swallow from his glass, then held a couple of the ice cubes in his cheek, like a chipmunk storing nuts in his mouth while looking for a place to bury them. He paused a moment, letting the ice melt. "I never want to see or hear of these two again. Is that understood?"

"Don't worry, you won't. I guarantee it," Khan said.

"I'll hold you to that. Now go," LaFleur said.

As the Korean henchman motioned to Marc and Sylvie with his pistol, Marc gave LaFleur a look, "I don't think Mr. Barbeau will be too pleased when he hears about this."

"Barbeau?" LaFleur chuckled. "Don't concern yourself with him," he said, swallowing the remnants of his drink.

Once they were all in the hallway, Khan stopped and ordered Marc to hold out his right arm and Sylvie her left. Khan retrieved a plumber's zip tie from his pocket and bound their wrists together, very tightly.

Marc looked around for the janitor they had seen when they first arrived, but he was nowhere in sight.

They were taken outside to the black SUV and loaded into the back seat. Marc noticed the rear window was busted out, but there was no sign of Oliver's tarp-wrapped body. The henchman drove and Khan, in the front passenger seat, turned toward Marc and Sylvie, his gun still pointed at them. Khan said something to the driver in Korean, and the SUV moved out of the parking lot onto the street.

"Where are you taking us?" Marc asked.

"You'll find out soon enough," Khan replied.

"Tell me, Khan, what did you do with Oliver?"

"Oliver? Who's Oliver?"

"The man you killed at the warehouse then stuffed into the back of this car."

"Oh, him," Khan laughed. He made a great diversion rolling around in the middle of the road. "I assume the police found him by now, or what was left of him."

When Marc glanced into the back of the SUV, he noticed it was empty, except for an aerosol can of 'Fix a Flat,' that rolled with each turn.

Guess that explains how they fixed the tire.

A few minutes later, Marc could see they were crossing back over the Champlain Bridge toward the City of Montreal. When the SUV turned north after the bridge, Sylvie said, "I think I know where we're going."

"Enough talking," Khan ordered.

Ten minutes later, the SUV turned onto a side street and passed a chain-link fence. Marc noticed a weathered metal sign as they passed, "Montreal Locomotive Works. Private."

When they approached a guarded gate, Marc thought he might have an opportunity to signal the guard, but the SUV was quickly motioned through. The driver seemed to know exactly where to go as Khan gave him no further instructions.

Despite the poor lighting, Marc could see that the Montreal Locomotive Works was one long brick building with railroad tracks coming in one end and out the other. The building was obviously dated, and probably not used for the production of trains any longer, but possibly could still be used to house them for maintenance and repair.

The SUV stopped in front of an overhead door. The driver tapped the horn twice. As the door slowly rose, bright overhead lighting from inside the building crawled toward the SUV, up along its hood, then slammed through the windshield. Marc had to momentarily close his eyes and look away. The SUV was then driven inside the building.

And there it was—right in front of them. The Laser. The engine, just like the prototype Marc had seen at the Plattsburgh plant, looked like a silver rocket on rails. Along its length was printed in steel blue, "Barbeau Transport," with its name, "LASER," underneath. The driver of the SUV turned left, away from the engine toward the rear of the train. The whole assembly appeared to be one long car, but Marc could see there were actually four. Except for the round glass windscreen at the very front of the engine, all the cars appeared at first to be identical. Then Marc noticed three of the cars had side windows, while the last car had no windows at all. The SUV stopped alongside the windowless car at the rear of the train.

Marc's door was opened and Khan, still turned in his seat, motioned with his pistol for him and Sylvie to exit the SUV. "Have a pleasant trip," Khan said with a dead pan smirk. Three more of Khan's henchmen appeared and pulled Marc and Sylvie from the vehicle, then up the short flight of stairs to a door at the rear of the train car.

"Goodbye, Mr. LaFountain, or should I say, Mr. Marc LaRose. May we never see each other again," Khan said, then slid his window closed. Marc and Sylvie were hustled through the train car's rear door.

Inside, as Marc's vision adjusted to the reduced glare of lighting, he could see the interior of the car was divided into open numbered compartments lining both sides that ran the entire length of the car. The vestibule that separated them from the adjoining car was closed off with a solid door. In the few compartments that Marc passed, he saw stacks of boxes and large bags that had "Canada Post, Purolator, Canpar, FedEx and UPS inscribed on them.

Must be some sort of same-day mail delivery car.

One of their captors snipped the plastic plumber's strap that connected Marc's wrist to Sylvie's, while another kept his gun pointed at Marc.

"This way, pretty lady," the henchman said, and led Sylvie into one of the dividers. Another of the captors shoved Marc down the center passageway and brusquely pushed him into an empty compartment on one side of the train. He motioned with his gun for Marc to sit on the floor. Retrieving a set of handcuffs from his pocket, he one-handedly ratcheted one end firmly to Marc's left wrist and the other to a metal cargo ring built in to the side of the compartment. Still covering Marc with his pistol, he repeated this procedure with Marc's right wrist.

Marc leaned back against the wall of the train car, his arms spread, held by the handcuffs to the sides of the compartment. He heard Sylvie yelp in pain. Then, he could hear the metallic ratcheting of another set of handcuffs from the direction of the divider Sylvie was pushed into.

"Ow," not so tight, you freaking goon, you're cutting the circulation to my hand," she protested.

"Never mind, you won't need that hand where you're going, pretty lady," the captor said with a heavy accent.

Then there was the distinctive sound of duct tape being ripped from a roll. "Not that aga…" Sylvie started.

A few moments later, the same goon approached Marc with the roll of duct tape and liberally circled the tape around his head over his mouth and eyes three or four times.

Wonder if these people own shares of 3M stock.

He heard the men speak to each other in their native tongue, which Marc assumed was Korean, then he heard the muffled sound of one of the men walk past him toward the front of the car. A minute or so later, the footsteps returned toward the back of the car and he heard the rear door of the car open. Through a slit in his duct tape mask, he could see that the overhead lights had been turned off.

The rear door slammed shut. The rattling of a key in its lock was followed by the muted sound of his captors descending the rear steps.

Marc remained in his sitting position, now in total darkness, occasionally testing his shackles, giving them a tug, then a shake. Other than sliding the handcuffs along the holding ring, this accomplished nothing except to pinch his wrists even more. He thought he could hear Sylvie rattling hers as well. He tried to stand, but his shackles only allowed him to get just beyond the kneeling position. That was not only quite uncomfortable, but painful, so with his back against the wall, he slid down and remained seated on the floor. The car was eerily silent save for the occasional hint of a dampened sound that managed to seep through from the outside.

I wonder what time it is. Must be somewhere around eight o'clock in the evening.

Thinking back, he remembered the train was due to depart Montreal around eight o'clock the following morning. It would take about a half hour to reach the border, then another twenty minutes to Plattsburgh, he figured.

Not much I can do while I'm shackled with these handcuffs.

Marc decided to relax, save his energy and try to think through his situation. He thought back to the warehouse and the crates that Khan ordered sent to the train so Jimmy Lee could install them in the locomotive's secret compartment. Jacques LaFleur had handed him and Sylvie a one-way ticket out of Montreal south to New York City with a load of semtex and enough weaponized ricin to spread over half of Manhattan. He'd gotten Sylvie involved in this and he had to find a way to get her out.

He tried to relax, but with his arms outstretched and the sharp edges of the handcuffs biting into his wrists, it was difficult to focus on a plan of action. Minutes dragged by. Bound up as he was in complete darkness, time seemed to stand still, and he knew time was of the essence. Every moment that passed was one less moment he had to think about what to do. Mental pictures of his ex, Shirley, and his daughter passed before him. His mind flashed back to the strange way Ann Marie had acted when he last saw her in the flower shop. Was there something she wanted to say, but felt she shouldn't?

Soon, the pain in his wrists seemed to dull. Had his body reached some kind of tolerance point? Had the shackles cut a nerve in his wrists? In any case, he could no longer feel them.

As the evening slipped by in the dark stillness, Marc felt his mind drifting into semi-consciousness. Through the murky haze of pre-slumber, Marc thought of a younger Ann Marie sitting with Sophie Horton in the flower shop. How long had Sophie been back from New Zealand? In his mind's eye, he pictured Sylvie outside the flower shop looking in through the front window. Despite the handcuffs, Marc waved for her to come inside, but she remained on the sidewalk, seemingly content to look in. Shirley was busy at the counter making a flower arrangement with red roses, lots of them. Mixed among the roses were white carnations and baby's breath. She had attached a ribbon to the arrangement. There were words on the ribbon, but Marc couldn't read them. Shirley was crying now, and so were Sophie and Ann Marie. Sylvie began knocking on the door, but Marc wanted to see what was on the ribbon. The closer he got to the door, the louder Sylvie knocked. Ann Marie looked up at Marc and pointed to the ribbon.

"This is for you, Daddy," she said, still pointing.

Marc could just begin to read the ribbon. Sylvie and Sophie were beside him, pulling him back. "Marc, Marc, don't look," they cried.

But Marc had to look. He was finally close enough to smell the roses and he could read the words on the ribbon.

"Father" was all it said. Even in his partly comatose state, it finally struck him. These were his funeral flowers.

Then, still lost in a murky cloud of semi-cognizance, Marc thought he felt something, or someone, touching and probing his face.

As his mind slowly pulled itself back to reality, he thought he faintly heard a voice. "Are you all right?" the voice said.

Was this part of the dream?

Marc tried to say something, but the tape made it impossible for him to speak. All he could manage were a few grunts and a forced whine.

Then, he felt the probing fingers again as they seemed to locate the end to the tape.

Sylvie, is this you again? Do you still have those tweezers?

He felt the tape slowly being peeled from his face.

Marc heard the voice again, but as his awareness of the situation slowly returned, he knew it wasn't Sylvie talking to him; it was a man's voice. "Sorry, but this is going to hurt a little."

Shit. Second time today someone's told me that.

As the man spoke, Marc noticed the voice had a familiar accent, one he thought he'd heard before, but he couldn't remember where.

Layer by layer, Marc could feel the tape being slowly peeled from his face. At times, it felt like his skin was being removed, as well as the hair from his eyebrows. A minute later, the job was apparently finished, but he still couldn't see due to the darkness.

Marc coughed as he tried to clear his throat, "Who are you?" He finally managed.

"I'm a prisoner, just like you."

Marc could feel the man's hands run along one of his arms, then down to his wrists.

"Seems you're in a bit of a pickle. What did you do to deserve this?" the man asked.

Marc ignored the question. "Reach in my pants pocket. You should find a key ring." He turned his body to one side, giving the unseen person easier access to his pocket.

"There are three keys on the ring. A car key, a door key, and a smaller key. The small one is a handcuff key. It's rounded at one end with a key flag at the other. Can you feel which one it is?"

Ever since retiring from the State Police, Marc had kept his old handcuff key, more as a memento, never thinking he'd ever really need it.

Marc listened a few moments as the keys jingled together.

"Yes, I think I have it," the unseen man said.

"Good. The handcuffs have a flat section, between my wrist and the chain."

Again, Marc waited as he felt the stranger's hands slide down his arm to his wrist.

“On the flat section of the handcuff, there is a round keyhole with a notch. It may be hard to find, but it’s there.”

It seemed to take forever, but finally the voice replied, “I believe I’ve found it.”

“Good. Now, put the end of the key into the hole and turn it one way, then the other.”

The stranger had Marc’s wrist in one hand and was feeling around with the end of the key for the hole. Finally he heard a faint click, then, felt the metal strap of the handcuff strand release its hold. The man pulled the handcuff open and Marc’s arm fell to his side. He worked his hand back and forth to get the blood flowing in his wrist again.”

“Thanks. Give me the key and I’ll do the other hand myself,” Marc said.

The man did as he was instructed and a few seconds later, Marc had his other hand free. As he slowly brought himself back to a standing position, he began to feel nauseous, and leaned against the side of his compartment.

“You all right?” the man said.

“I’ll be OK in a minute, thanks,” Marc said.

“You’re not alone, are you?” the man said.

“No. My partner is in another compartment, toward the back of the car.

“Just a moment, there should be a light switch back here somewhere,” the man said.”

Marc heard him retreating as his feet shuffled toward the rear of the railcar.

Suddenly, Marc was blinded as a row of overhead florescent lights buzzed to life. He covered his eyes with his hands as his eyes adjusted to the sudden brightness.

As his sight returned, Marc looked back toward the end of the railcar and saw the stranger who had freed him of his bonds. He looked to be in his late sixties, tall with gray hair. Although there were a few bruises on his cheek, and a small cut on his chin, Marc recognized him from a photo he had seen only a few days before.

Chapter Sixteen

"You're Hugo Karlsson, aren't you?" Marc said, mesmerized.

Karlsson nodded, "Yes, have we met?"

"No, we haven't. My name is Marc LaRose and I'm a private investigator hired by your wife to locate you. She was worried something had happened when you didn't return home from the meeting in Brossard."

He then took a few moments to bring Hugo Karlsson up to speed on what he'd learned so far.

Karlsson sat quietly for a long moment.

"Thank you. That explains a lot, Mr. LaRose."

Marc then said, "I'm curious, if you knew where the light switch was, why didn't you turn it on before?"

"I wasn't sure who you were and I didn't know when the people who put me in here would return and find out that I was conscious."

Marc still couldn't believe that he'd finally located Hugo Karlsson, even though they were both prisoners, locked in a train car. The rattling of Sylvie's handcuffs broke his reverie.

Marc went to her, knelt beside her, and removed the handcuffs from her wrists. He carefully removed the duct tape from around her head. Like Marc, she was also blinded by the light as she blinked her eyes once or twice, but then kept them shut. "Stay where you are and don't try to move until you regain your footing."

Sylvie seemed confused, then blinked her eyes again as they slowly adjusted to the bright lighting.

"They didn't hurt you, did they?" Marc asked.

Sylvie cleared her throat and moistened her lips before she answered, "No, other than a few cuts from the handcuffs, I think I'm fine. I must have fallen asleep. I just need another minute to gather myself."

She slowly looked up at Marc as if seeing him for the first time. "Marc, how did you get out of your handcuffs? And, who turned the lights on?"

Karlsson was slowly making his way to where Sylvie was sitting.

"Sylvie, I'd like you to meet an acquaintance of mine."

“An acquaintance? Marc, what are you talking about?” she asked as she tried to focus on the stranger.

“This is Hugo Karlsson.”

Sylvie looked up at Karlsson, standing in front of her.

“*Mon Dieu*,” she managed.

“Sorry, young lady, I’m not God, but with any luck, I think I can get us out of here,” Karlsson said.

“Mr. Karlsson, why didn’t they tie you up?” Marc asked.

“I suppose they didn’t think they had to. They gave me something, some kind of drug, I think. I was out for at least a day, maybe longer. When I finally came to, I knew they would be back to check on me, so I pretended I was still out. They even kicked me a few times to see if I would respond. I knew if they suspected I was conscious, they would give me more drugs, or worse, so I just held it in.”

“Do you know why we are being held captive here, on the train?” Marc asked.

Karlsson was silent for a moment, as he seemed to think about what Marc said.

“Not really. I think Jimmy Lee is involved in whatever it is, but beyond that, I don’t have a clue.”

“Mr. Karlsson, we believe there is a group of people, North Koreans who plan to do something when this train reaches Penn Station in New York City. I’m not certain, but I think they are going to blow this train sky high along with two containers of weaponized ricin,” Marc said.

Karlsson ran a hand through his thick mane of hair as he stood in the aisle, looking off toward the front of the train car.

“It’s beginning to add up,” he finally said.

“What do you mean?” Marc asked.

“Jimmy Lee, as you may have discovered, was part of my team. He was in charge of the overall physical design. Don’t get me wrong, the Laser’s cutting edge. It has great aerodynamics, sleek, with minimal wind resistance. He’s done a wonderful job and everything about it seemed perfect. But when I ran the numbers for component space allocation against the Laser’s total interior envelope, the figures didn't add up. The locomotive is about four cubic meters larger than it needs to be."

"You discovered this just before it was due to make its maiden trip?" Marc asked.

"It's complicated. You see, originally the locomotive's power train was designed to be a bit larger, but that was five years ago. Since then, with increases in technology, we were able to shrink the dimensions of the traction motors to almost half of the original design. But I discovered that some of this shrinkage never showed up in the final schematics. I asked Jimmy Lee about it, but it felt like he was giving me the run-around. I took my concerns to Jacques LaFleur. He told me he'd gone over the plans thoroughly and assured me that everything checked out and that I should move on to the next project."

"What did you do then?" Marc asked.

"I still felt uncomfortable with the situation, so I decided to talk to the owner of the company, Jules Barbeau. I was set to meet with him, but while I was driving to the meeting, Jimmy Lee called and said he needed to talk to me."

"Was that when you met him on Ile de Soeurs?" Marc asked.

"Yes, how did you know?"

"Long story. What did Jimmy Lee want to talk to you about?"

Karlsson turned away for a moment, "I should have followed my instincts and gone right to Mr. Barbeau's residence. Anyway, while I was making my concerns known to Jimmy Lee, these goons pulled up and took me to a warehouse somewhere on the other side of Montreal. They tied me up and stuck a needle in my arm. I guess I passed out. When I finally came to, I found myself inside this train car. I've continued to play dead, sort of, since then. I figure I've probably been here for well over thirty-six hours."

Marc considered what Karlsson had said.

"We might have six hours or so before they get this thing going. The way I see it, we either have to prevent the train from leaving, or disarm whatever they have set to go off once they reach Penn Station."

Karlsson scratched his head and appeared to be scanning the car's ceiling.

"To do either, we'd have to get to the engine compartment."

"How are we going to do that?"

"Not easily. Besides, getting to the engine is one thing. Stopping the train and disarming whatever it is these guys are planning to blow up is another matter."

"But there is a way to get to the engine, right?" Marc asked.

"Possibly. There is a ventilation channel above those ceiling panels," Karlsson said, pointing up and motioning with his arm along the length of the car. "That's where we install the electronics to control and maintain the doors, brakes, and lighting."

"But, does the channel run between cars?"

"When they are coupled together, as we are now, yes. The channel is sealed when the cars are uncoupled. But there's another problem."

"What's that?" Marc asked apprehensively.

"When we work up there, the ceiling panels are off. With the panels closed, the space is too small for a grown man to crawl through."

Marc considered what Karlsson had said, then glanced down to where Sylvie was sitting.

"Maybe too small for us, but what about Sylvie?" Marc said motioning toward her.

Karlsson looked at Sylvie for a moment, "Are you athletic?" he asked.

Sylvie looked up at Marc, "Thanks for volunteering me to do something you apparently can't." Then returning her gaze toward Karlsson, she said, "Maybe, but unless there is some kind of lighting up there, wouldn't I need a flashlight, or something? And how am I supposed to know what to look for and what to do when I find it?"

"Reasonable questions," Karlsson answered. "Other than a small amount of light coming through the vent slits in the panels, there is no lighting above them. I can tell you what to look for and what to do, as long as you can find it." He reached into his pants pocket, produced a disposable cigarette lighter and flicked it. "Unless one of you can think of something better, this may have to do."

Sylvie stared back at him in disbelief.

"I can see this is not going to end well," she managed.

Karlsson looked over at the mail and packages heaped up in their respective cubicles, "I think the first thing we need to do is sort out some of these larger boxes and mound them high enough to get you up to the ceiling."

"Sounds like a plan, but what if those goons come in and find us?" Marc said.

"They've locked the rear door from the outside. I've locked both doors from the inside. I doubt they counted on us locking ourselves in. Besides, if they're planning to blow this thing up anyway, they probably think this is the best place for us to be."

"Then I guess we should get started," Marc said as he began pulling some of the larger boxes out of their stalls. "Look for boxes that seem full so they won't collapse under her weight."

"Do I look like a plus size to you?" Sylvie said with a grimace.

Ten minutes later, they had arranged a pile of boxes into a series of steps about half way to the ceiling near the front of the car.

"Now we need something to unscrew the ceiling panels," Karlsson said.

"Think this will do?" Sylvie said, producing her tweezers from her shirt pocket."

"That may be difficult, but I suppose it's worth a try," Karlsson said.

"Never underestimate a woman with a set of tweezers," Marc said teasingly.

"What?" Karlsson asked.

"Sorry, inside joke."

Both men steadied the pile of boxes as Sylvie slowly made her way to the top, then using the handle of the tweezers, she tried twisting one of the screws from the panel.

Marc could see she was struggling as the ends of the tweezers kept slipping out of the grooves in the screw.

"That's what I was afraid of. The screw heads have a kind of pentagon configuration meant to make them tamper proof."

"This isn't working," she finally puffed.

Marc looked at the pile of boxes stacked in one of the bins and decided to open a few to see what they contained.

“Isn’t there a law against tampering with the mail?” Sylvie asked, playfully.

Ignoring the quip, Marc spotted a large box with “IKEA” printed in blue across the top. He ripped the box open and began pulling the plastic bubble wrapping that held what appeared to be parts for a small computer desk. A minute later he found what he was looking for.

“Try this,” he said, and handed it up to Sylvie. It was a cheap Allen wrench with three snap-on heads of odd-shaped configurations intended for assembling different parts of the desk.

Sylvie studied the three screw heads.

“I’m not sure about these. They seem a little different than the screws in the panels.”

“Let me take a look,” Karlsson said, and examined the heads, “These two, definitely not,” he said as he discarded them, “but this one has possibilities. It certainly isn’t going to be an exact fit, but it’s worth a try.”

Sylvie fitted the makeshift head into the screw, and pressing upward, turned the wrench. At first, it slipped, but after a few grunts, the screw finally began to turn. A minute later, the first screw dislodged.

“One down, nine to go,” she announced, and immediately went to work on the next screw.

Three screws later, Marc could see Sylvie was tiring, “Mind if I give it a try?”

They exchanged places, and Marc tried his hand.

It took Marc about ten minutes to remove the remaining screws. When he poked his head into the channel, he could see past the vestibule separating the baggage car from the next car. There were dim reflections of light coming through the air slits in the panels of the car up ahead.

He climbed back down the pile of boxes.

“Looks like the way is clear for Sylvie to do what needs to be done."

“Let me take a peek,” Karlsson said, as he climbed up to look for himself. After a few moments he carefully descended back down the box ladder, shaking his head.

“What’s the matter now?” Sylvie asked.

“Disengaging the car we’re in from the rest of the train is possible, but that could also be a problem.”

“What do you mean?” Sylvie asked.

Marc interjected. "I think he means that if we detach and stay here we’d eventually have to deal with those Korean goons and their motorcycle mob cronies. The terrorists would be left to carry out whatever scheme they have planned when they reach Penn Station.”

“Exactly,” Karlsson said.

The three remained silent as they considered their options.

Finally, Sylvie broke the silence, “If I’m hearing you correctly, you can separate the cars from inside the channel?”

“It’s a bit complicated, but yes, we can. Although the system was not built so the cars would detach this way, it is possible.”

“The way I see it, we have to figure out a way to stop these terrorists and elude capture by them or the mob,” Marc said.

Karlsson appeared somewhat detached and looked off toward the back of the train. Then, without saying anything, he stepped around the pile of boxes. He went to the door at the rear of the car and appeared to be checking the door’s locking system. He fiddled with the lock for a few moments, then turned back toward Marc and Sylvie. A strange mixture of contentment and anxiety creased his face.

Marc could tell Karlsson had come to some kind of conclusion as he slowly made his way back to where he and Sylvie were standing near the pile of boxes.

“I may have an idea, but it could be tricky.”

“At this point, I’d guess we’d be open to anything. What do you have in mind?” Marc asked.

“Like I said, it’s complicated, so bear with me. Typically, railroad engines, and for that matter, all rail cars are designed to run with the least amount of drag, or, in railway terms, rolling resistance. OK so far?”

Marc and Sylvie both gave a slight nod.

“The Laser’s overall construction, thanks in part to the work of Mr. Jimmy Lee, was designed with a heightened rolling resistance coefficient, maximizing the velocity threshold. As the power train load or drag is diminished, the rolling coefficient is increased as is the velocity threshold."

Sylvie looked over at Marc. "Is he still speaking English?"

"Look, we're not engineers, just mere detectives," Marc said. "Can you translate this into layman's terms?"

"Sorry. I'll try to keep it simple. The Laser is powered by a hybrid power plant, a jet-fueled engine that turns an electrical turbine. As the drag on the engine increases, the engine accelerates to create more electrical power to keep the velocity threshold in sync with the rolling coefficient. This is controlled with a variety of individual computers that feed information to the main computer located in the engine's operating cubicle."

"Mr. Karlsson, the technical operation of the Laser is something we don't have time to learn. What's your point? How we can separate ourselves from the Laser without falling victim to these thugs and still prevent the Koreans from carrying out their stated intention of blowing this thing once it reaches Penn Station?"

Karlsson's facial expression was serious, but confident. "Have you ever taken the Amtrak train to New York City?" Karlsson asked.

Sylvie shook her head no.

"Once, years ago. Shirley, my ex and I made the trip from Plattsburgh." Marc glanced at Sylvie, then continued, "It was in the dead of the winter, February, I think. There was a florist convention at the Javits center. She wanted to attend and we used the occasion to take in the sights and see a play. We found the ride down to the city quite scenic, travelling along the shores of Lake Champlain, but arduously slow. Lots of twists and turns. Then, of course, there were all the stops along the way. Port Kent, Westport, Port Henry, Ticonderoga, Whitehall. I thought we'd never get there."

Karlsson spoke again. "Except for a brief stop in Plattsburgh and Albany to pick up some political dignitaries, this trip is pretty much straight through. But it's not the stops that I'm interested in. It's the places you mentioned before and the twists, turns, and dips the tracks take as it follows the route along the lake. Although the Laser was built to glide through these turns and dips with little change of speed due its onboard tilt compensation system, it's impossible to maintain full throttle through some of them. The worst ones are located where the tracks were cut through rocky outcrops along the lake. Most of these are between Port Kent and Westport."

"Yeah, I remember. There was a lot of screeching as the train made some of those turns. It practically came to a stop at one of them."

"That's the one I'm thinking of. It's called, 'The Bow.'"

"So what do you have in mind?" Marc asked.

The Laser's computers are 'aware' of the problems with the track and it compensates in a variety of ways to maintain speed at the velocity threshold I spoke of earlier. I'm thinking, if we can decrease the drag sufficiently at the right moment, we might fool the computer into believing it should increase its rolling coefficient."

Marc looked over at Sylvie, "You getting this?"

Before Sylvie could respond, Karlsson interrupted, "All I'm saying is if we can disengage the cars from the engine at just the right moment, the engine's computer will think that it needs more speed."

"Thereby causing the engine to jump the tracks as it goes into 'The Bow,'" Marc finished.

"Yes, exactly. It's kind of a long shot, but right now, I believe it's our only chance."

"But won't the rest of the train crash into the engine when it goes off the tracks?" Sylvie asked.

"It shouldn't. The automatic braking system will engage as soon as the cars separate from the engine," Karlsson said.

"So what you're saying is that I'm going to crawl through the channel, over the heads of dignitaries and who knows who else, and at a precise moment, disengage the engine from the rest of the train, then hold on as the car comes to a screeching halt," Sylvie said with unmasked concern.

"It's a controlled stop, not a screeching halt, but in essence, what you have described is correct."

"How will you tell me what to do while I'm all the way up near the engine and you're back here?" she asked.

"I'll draw you a diagram of what to look for and where to find it. What you'll have to do is disconnect a wire that runs from the main computer to the decoupling system at the exact moment. I'll have to signal you somehow. We'll figure that out later, but first we need to find something to write with so I can draw you a schematic of the wiring configuration."

"Schematic? This already sounds too complicated." Sylvie said doubtfully.

"Sorry, maybe I should have said 'diagram.'"

"Call it anything you want, just keep it simple."

Karlsson tore open a few more boxes until he found one with a supply of Sharpie permanent markers of various colors.

"I have black, sky blue, aqua, lime, mint, marigold, and magenta. Any preference?" Karlsson asked.

"What, no berry, or plum?" she answered with a touch of sarcasm.

Karlsson started toward one of the bins, "Well, I could open a few more of these packages and see if…"

"*Noir*, Black!" Sylvie shouted.

Karlsson stopped and looked back toward Sylvie.

"The rumor that engineers have a limited sense of humor is apparently not just a rumor," Sylvie said, exasperated.

Marc chuckled.

Sylvie and Karlsson glanced over at Marc.

"OK, I'll bite. What's so funny, detective?" Sylvie asked.

"I was just thinking. Here we are prisoners of sorts, locked in a rail car and you two can think of nothing more important to argue about than the color ink to draw a diagram that might stop a train loaded with explosives and enough ricin to kill a million people."

They all stared back at each other.

"Now that I've said it, I guess it really wasn't all that funny," Marc said with a forced grin.

Karlsson cleared his throat. "Actually, we'll need four colors." He ripped a piece of cardboard from one of the boxes and started drawing.

Just then, Marc felt a slight jolt.

The three of them grabbed the side of one of the bins to keep their balance.

"The train is moving," Sylvie said.

The three remained silent for a full minute, listening to the faint tapping sound as the car's wheels slowly passed over the railroad track connections, every thirty-nine feet.

Karlsson stopped drawing and looked toward Marc and Sylvie, "I never asked you where we are right now, where they took you to get here."

"Apparently, we're leaving the old Montreal Locomotive Works. I don't know a lot about the place, but I've heard that even though there's no manufacturing done here anymore, the rail tracks still run through it," Sylvie said.

"A perfect place to secretly imbed their deadly cargo into the engine's compartment," Marc said.

"I suppose," Karlsson said. "Now they'll need to bring the train to Montreal's main rail station. If I remember the schedule correctly, the Premier of Quebec and his entourage will board the train a little after 7:30 a.m. We leave Montreal at eight o'clock for the U.S. border, then on to Plattsburgh for another brief stop before heading on to Albany and New York City."

"We could make it interesting for them when the train stops at the U.S. border crossing in Rouses Point for inspection," Marc said.

Karlsson looked over at Marc and Sylvie, "It could, if the train was to stop there, but it isn't going to," he said, briefly looking up from his schematic.

"What do you mean? All passenger trains have to be cleared by the U.S. Customs and Border Protection in Rouses Point."

"Not this train, they won't. Except for us, the passengers onboard will have been pre-cleared by CBP before the train leaves the Montreal station. There are only three stops planned—Plattsburgh, Albany, and New York City."

Marc could tell the train was picking up speed as the clicking sounds increased in frequency.

As if reading Marc's mind, Karlsson said, "Once we leave Montreal, we won't even have those noises to listen to. All the tracks have been welded together to increase passenger comfort and make for a smoother ride."

Sylvie said, "What if, when we get to the train station, we start banging on the sides of the car and try to attract attention. Surely, someone would hear us. Someone would have to investigate."

Marc and Sylvie looked at Karlsson expectantly.

Karlsson stopped working on the schematic. "You have to know what you're dealing with. If the North Koreans think we're about to ruin their plan, we run the risk of forcing them to do what they plan to do in New York City, just a little sooner. Of course, they wouldn't get the same results, but the headlines would be the same, and for a terrorist, headlines are what they're all about. Besides, these cars are double insulated and were built to withstand noises that are inherent on existing railroad beds. I doubt if anyone would hear us from outside the car."

"Then there's nothing we can do?" Sylvie asked.

"No, not right now. I think our best chance is to wait until the Laser is at its most vulnerable, when we're passing through the Bow."

"When should I start making my way through the channel toward the locomotive?" Sylvie asked.

"The sooner, the better. I just need go over the wiring diagram with you."

Karlsson and Sylvie sat together, and using his hand-drawn schematic as a guide, he explained what needed to be done.

"There are three cars in line behind the locomotive, the last one, the one we're in, then next to our car is the passenger car. Right behind the locomotive is the dining car. You have to go all the way through the dining car to reach the control box. The main panel is about a half-meter tall and a meter in width. It's green. Are you with me so far?"

"Go on," she replied.

When you locate the panel, remove the outside cover; there are two latches. Pull them back then swing the cover out of the way. Inside, you'll see a small connection box. It's located in the upper right-hand corner of the panel," he continued. "Once you've opened the connection box, you'll see a set of four wires."

Karlsson used one of the markers as a pointer. "The four wires are held in place with push and release connectors. When you push in on the connector tab, you release the wire. There is a red wire that I've drawn here in magenta, a black wire that I've drawn in black, an orange, and a white wire. Because I didn't have orange and white markers, the white wire is represented in mint and the orange is represented in marigold. Do you follow me so far?"

"*Oui*, I think so," Sylvie replied, hesitantly.

"As you can see, I've made a legend along the side of the cardboard indicating which color represents which wire," he said pointing again with the Sharpie.

"What you need to do, on my signal, is to detach, or unplug, the red and the white wire, at the same time. All you have to do is push on the tab underneath the connection, then pull the wires upward."

"That will decouple the cars from the locomotive?" Sylvie asked.

"Yes, but only if the red and the white wires are disconnected at the exact same moment."

Sylvie thought about Karlsson's directions.

"What happens if I can't disconnect the wires at the exact same time?"

"Nothing. The cars will stay connected, but a signal will be sent to the main computer indicating that there is a wiring problem. Of course, this would alert the conductor who would have to investigate. I'm not sure if he would know exactly where to look right away, but I've no doubt he would eventually track the problem, which of course, could leave you vulnerable to discovery."

"If I fail the first time, can I reconnect and try disconnecting them again?"

"Yes, but here it gets tricky. The computer will sense there is a problem. You will only have one last chance to disconnect the wires properly. If you fail the second time, the train will then come to a controlled stop and an alarm will sound."

"An alarm? What happens then?"

"Here again, the conductor and possibly others will immediately investigate the cause of the alarm. You would be discovered, probably pretty quickly."

"I see." Then, after a moment, she asked, "You said that timing is important. That the cars must be separated at the precise moment as the train reaches The Bow to fool the engine's computers into thinking it needs more speed. How am I supposed to know when that precise moment is? I'm going to be two full car lengths away."

Karlsson seemed to consider her concern.

"You should be able to see the lights from this car through the channel. The moment I think we're approaching the Bow, I'll turn our compartment lights off. That will be your signal to disconnect the wires."

"And all I'll have is your lighter to see with?"

"Yes. We've been through quite a few of these boxes and unfortunately we haven't found anything better."

Marc sensed the train was slowing as the intervals between the wheels clicking over the track separations grew longer. He looked toward Sylvie, "Sounds like we may be coming to the main Montreal Train Station."

"You should probably start making your way through the channel to the connection box," Karlsson said. "There shouldn't be very many people, if any, in the passenger car now. It would be good to get through there before we stop at the station."

Sylvie folded the schematic and pushed it under her belt.

"Climb up the boxes, I'll hoist you up into the channel," Marc said as he held out his hand.

She took Marc's hand, but before stepping up on the pile of boxes, she turned to Marc. "Wish me luck," she said, then put both her arms around Marc's neck and pulled him close. They held each other for a moment. Before she released him, she gave him a soft, but brief kiss on his lips.

"Don't worry, you'll do fine," Marc said, and with a smile, he helped her up to the open ceiling panel.

"It's kind of tight," she said as she scrunched her shoulders together. Marc held her legs up, then, gave her butt a push.

"Fresh," Marc heard her say through the slots in the panels.

Inside the channel, Sylvie worked toward the front of the car, using her feet to push along the sides of the channel while pulling with her hands and arms.

When she reached the gangway connecting the cars, her advance was slowed somewhat, but from Marc's vantage point he could see that she eventually made it to the passenger car.

Although the air slits in the panels allowed some light to get through, Sylvie couldn't see if anyone was inside the car. Moving as quietly as she could, she carefully continued her way toward the far end of the car, toward the dining car and the engine. About half way, she felt the train stop and heard the doors on one side of the car open. Then there was the muffled sound of voices. She remembered Karlsson saying that the Mayor of Montreal and the Premier of the Province of Quebec would be making the trip to New York. From the sounds below, she suspected that each had an entourage accompanying them.

Back in the baggage car, Marc and Karlsson waited in silence. With no windows, they couldn't see where they were or who, if anyone was boarding the train. Karlsson was familiar with the schedule and told Marc what he figured was happening. Marc occasionally would stand on the boxes and try and check on Sylvie's progress, but the lack of light made it virtually impossible to tell how far along she had gone.

"I wonder if Jules and Jacques are on board," Karlsson said.

Jules and Jacques?" Marc asked.

"Jules Barbeau, owner of the company and Jacques LaFleur, the company president. They were scheduled to accompany the other dignitaries."

Marc hesitated as he thought how to ask the question he was thinking of.

"What's your opinion of Jacques LaFleur?" Marc asked.

Karlsson hesitated before responding, "Why do you ask?"

"Because LaFleur's in with the terrorists working with the North Koreans. He turned us over to Khan at Barbeau's office when we went to tell him that we had learned that the Koreans were going to use the Laser to transport the terrorists' weapon to New York City.

"My God. What about Jules Barbeau?"

"I don't think he has any idea what LaFleur's up to."

Karlsson seemed to lose himself in thought for a few moments. "I thought he sounded kind of funny when I called to tell him we needed to talk before I headed up to Brossard for the meeting. But, I had no idea that it had come to this. I wouldn't think he'd be on the train, knowing what's going to happen when it reaches New York City."

"He's probably made up some kind of excuse not to make the trip," Marc said.

"Possibly. He's quite creative," Karlsson said, obviously surprised by the news.

"Tell me, how will we know when we have reached The Bow?" Marc asked, as he stepped down from the pile of boxes.

Karlsson shook his head, apparently trying to shake the thought of his former boss turned traitor, "Our next stop is Plattsburgh, from there it is about fifteen minutes to Port Kent. The Bow is just another five minutes after that. We can tell we're near when we feel the train slowing. That's when we'll turn off the overhead lighting that will give Sylvie the signal to disconnect the wires to uncouple the train."

Marc stared over at the pile of boxes, "I realize that this plan may be our only hope, but I'm concerned that so much of it depends on theory and assumptions. I appreciate your expertise. I just hope you're right about this."

"Theory, assumptions, and a little luck," Karlsson said his voice ripe with a sobering timbre.

Chapter Seventeen

They sat in silence for a few moments before they felt the train move again. Marc's eyes wandered to the multitude of packages and boxes still stacked in the bins, plus the ones they had used to construct the stairs to get Sylvie into the channel.

"We might as well make the best of the short time we have left. I want to go through as many of these boxes as I can to see if there is anything useful."

"I suppose so," Karlsson said with a sigh. "Ironically, both the package recipients and terrorists will be the ones disappointed if we're successful in foiling this plot."

"Good, let's piss off as many people as we can," Marc said. He started searching through the bin where he had found the Ikea tools. He had no idea what he was looking for. A moment later, Karlsson joined him.

Marc concentrated on opening not the largest boxes, but the ones he thought might contain something useful. After about ten boxes, he came across a hunting knife with a seven-inch blade and a sheath wrapped in plain white paper. A card was attached.

"To Uncle Louie from your favorite niece. Happy Birthday, Kathy." Marc looked at the address on the box. "I wonder what Louie could be hunting for in the Bronx?"

"Depends on the intended prey," Karlsson said, flexing his eyebrows.

Marc hooked the knife sheath to his belt, then, used the knife to open more boxes, slashing the packing tape with its razor-sharp blade. There was a plethora of electronic gadgets, all in need of a charge. There were smart phones, dumb phones, ipads, cameras, GPS devices, X-Boxes, PlayStations, Nintendo's…the list went on. There was even a box of hockey trophies destined for the Hempstead High School on Long Island.

"Too bad we didn't think to put charging ports in the baggage car. We designed the passenger car with a port at every seat. We never thought of installing one in the baggage car in the outside chance there'd be hostages trapped inside," Karlsson said sarcastically.

Marc was busy unrolling a small log of what appeared to be dark green vegetable matter tightly wrapped in plastic, then rolled in newsprint. As he unrolled the newsprint, coffee grounds sprinkled onto the floor.

"Is that what I think it is?" Karlsson asked.

"If it fits, it ships," Marc replied with a cheesy grin. "And if you're thinking marijuana, you're correct. BC bud—at least a kilo."

"Interesting. But why the coffee grounds?"

"Supposedly, it hides the scent from drug sniffing dogs." Marc stuffed the bag and its contents back into its box, glanced at the package addressee, and tossed it in the pile with the other discarded items. "I wonder if 'Mr. Gibbons' bothered to insure his package." Marc added with a chortle as he selected another box.

A few boxes later, Marc finally found a gadget that could be useful, and best of all, it didn't need to be plugged in to work.

"Well, look what 'James' bought on e-bay." He exclaimed examining a small black flashlight. "It's a tactical light with a lifetime warranty, and best of all, it even comes with a supply of 'C' cell batteries."

Marc slipped two of the batteries into the flashlight and turned it on. It had a 'Regular,' 'Bright,' and a 'Strobe' mode." Marc flipped from one mode to the other. He pointed the beam at Karlsson, and when he switched on the 'Strobe mode,' Karlsson put his hands in front of his face.

"Turn that thing off," he yelled as the flashlight's LED bulb emitted pulsating bursts of light. "You trying to blind me?"

"Sorry about that. This might come in handy," Marc said, unapologetically, as he hit the off switch and shoved the light into his pants' pocket.

As Karlsson recovered from the effects of the tactical flashlight's demonstration, the two continued their search for anything else that might be useful.

It wasn't long before the train slowed again.

"This should be the Plattsburgh stop," Karlsson announced. "We shouldn't be here long. I believe the mayor and a representative from the county legislature are the only people boarding."

Marc looked over at Karlsson, "Didn't you know that the Plattsburgh High School band was also scheduled to board?" Marc asked.

"No, I didn't," Karlsson said. He appeared taken aback by this latest revelation. "That must have been LaFleur's idea."

A moment later, the train stopped.

Marc climbed up the staircase of boxes and peered toward the front of the car. Using his newly found gadget, he turned the light on regular beam and scanned the air channel for some sign of Sylvie. In the distance, he saw a dark object, about three quarters of the way to the dining car ahead. Focusing the beam, he could see the bottoms of Sylvie's shoes as she slowly worked her way to the front of the car.

Descending the pile of boxes, Marc heard someone fiddling with the rear door latch.

"Either someone's expecting a package or one of the terrorists is trying to check in on us," Karlsson said.

The latch jiggled a few more times.

"Are you sure they can't get in?" Marc whispered.

"You don't have to whisper. No one can hear us, even if we wanted them to. And no, I'm not sure they can't get in, but I seriously doubt it. They'd have to have a master key, of which there are only two." He produced a key from his pocket.

"Mr. Karlsson, who has the second key?" Marc asked, although he already suspected who it was.

They heard the latch rattle again.

"Jacques LaFleur," Karlsson managed. Just then the door burst open. LaFleur pushed his way into the car, followed by the man Marc recognized as Mr. Khan, holding a semi-automatic handgun. Khan quickly closed the door behind them.

LaFleur looked at Marc and Karlsson standing amid the pile of opened boxes. "So, Mr. LaRose, I see you've solved your missing person case. Congratulations. Too bad you won't live to collect your fee."

Karlsson looked over at LaFleur. “Jacques, what’s this all about? Why are you doing this? The Laser is a state-of-the-art passenger train and you are the president of the company. What do you hope to gain by aligning yourself with terrorists intent on using your train to kill innocent people?”

LaFleur studied Karlsson for a long moment. “My train? True, I am president of the company that developed the Laser, but what makes you think this is ‘my’ train? Who’s name do you see on the sides of the locomotive?”

“Well, of course, Barbeau’s name is on the locomotive, but you’re the key man responsible for making the Laser the success it is. Without your management skills, it could still be on the drawing boards. The Laser represents years of development and a major breakthrough in ground transportation, largely thanks to you.”

LaFleur’s face contorted into a nasty grin. “Let’s just say I’ve had a better offer.”

“A better offer? From whom, and how can you top this?” Karlsson said waving his arms around. “The Laser will go down in history as a major technological achievement. Please, before you go any further, think about what you’re doing.”

“Believe me, there’s nothing that occupies more of my waking hours than planning the future of rail transport—a future without Barbeau. Of course, my next generation of locomotives will use many of the technologies developed in the construction of the Laser, but with one major difference.”

Karlsson hesitated, then meekly asked, “If you don’t mind, just what is this difference you are so intent on employing?”

“It will bear my name, my logo. LaFleur Transport will be emblazoned on its sides. It will be mine.”

Marc remained silent, keenly aware of the gun in the henchman’s hand.

“Barbeau’s name will be poison, as will yours by association. Besides, where would you get the necessary funding for any new train? Without Barbeau’s connections, you will have virtually no monetary backing.” Karlsson said.

Marc could tell Karlsson was stalling for time.

"The funding is already in place. Ordinarily I wouldn't say, but under the circumstances, it soon won't matter what you know. I have worked out a deal with a foreign entity, someone not as intimidated, or threatened with Canada as some might be with the United States."

"I can only think of one country with the means it would take to bankroll such a project, and I certainly don't mean its puppet represented by these thugs," Karlsson said, motioning toward the North Korean. "You're obviously referring to China."

LaFleur's lips twisted into a hideous grin. "You're smarter than I gave you credit for. Before you get anymore wild ideas, you should know the conductor is on my payroll." He glanced at his watch, "But, I've already said more than I wanted to, so if you'll excuse me, I have a pressing engagement elsewhere."

LaFleur turned toward Khan. "Wait until I leave, then kill them," he said, and made his way out the rear door of the car.

Marc heard the lock turn in the door. They were still trapped inside the baggage car, but now with Khan, a North Korean killer.

The henchman spoke English as he leveled his pistol at Marc. "Mr. LaFleur will certainly relish the idea of being rid of you, Mr. LaRose, and so will I. You've been nothing but a nuisance since we first crossed paths back at the warehouse."

Marc gripped the flashlight in his pocket and slipped the switch from 'regular,' to 'tactical' mode.

"Look, Khan, before you pull that trigger, tell me what's in this for you? You must know LaFleur is crazy. He'll never pull this scheme off."

"This 'scheme,' as you refer to it, is not your worry, and if you must know, I take my instructions only from my supreme leader, Kim Jong-un himself."

Marc knew he had to distract Khan, if just for a moment. He glanced up at the missing panel in the ceiling overhead, hoping that Khan would follow his gaze.

"I wonder why Mr. LaFleur didn't bother to ask about the lady police detective who was with us earlier," Marc said.

The revelation that Sylvie was not with them didn't seem to faze Khan at first, as he kept his gaze fixed on Marc. Slowly however,

Marc could detect a slight change in the Korean's demeanor. For an instant, Khan followed Marc's glance upward.

This momentary distraction was what Marc was counting on as he quickly focused the flashlight's LED beam now emitting a dizzying display of staccato flashes, while at the same time he ducked and dove headlong toward the man's knees.

Stunned by the blinding flashes of the strobe, Khan let go with a burst of gun fire…at the same time trying to shield his eyes from the light with his non-shooting hand.

With everything he had, Marc drove his shoulders into Khan's knees. Although Khan was not tall, he was muscular. Khan's legs felt as sturdy as tree trunks, but Marc kept pushing as hard as he could, and in that instant, he remembered how his high school football coach, 'Scotty,' had taught him to push the blocking sled years before…

"Dig, LaRose! What are you? Some kind of pansy? Dig, dig, dig!" He could still hear Scotty scream into his ear as Marc pushed forward with everything he had, until finally, Khan's footing gave way. Somewhere during his assault, he sensed that the firing had stopped, but still, Marc kept digging and pushing forward, until the Korean's body finally toppled and his full weight fell onto Marc's rump.

"Woomph!" The Korean had fallen forward pinning Marc's legs. Marc felt trapped beneath the North Korean and now it was Khan's turn to do some damage. Using his empty pistol as a hammer, he repeatedly slammed the butt of the gun into the backs of Marc's knees and legs. In an attempt to get out from under the muscular Korean, Marc continued to dig and claw forward, but Khan was relentless. Suddenly, Marc heard the sickening crack of something hard coming into contact with bone. The attack stopped.

Unsure what had happened, Marc continued digging until he finally extracted himself from beneath Khan's body. Exhausted from the melee, Marc pulled himself toward the rear of the car, leaned against one of the cubicle's walls and heaved in gulps of air, half expecting to find Khan still coming after him, or reloading his pistol, or both.

But the Korean was still, face down on the floor of the baggage car. Over him stood Hugo Karlsson, holding a hockey trophy, his fingers gripping the statue of the 'Player of the Year,' which was poised to take a slap shot. Then Marc noticed a corner of the trophy's thick white marble base was bloody. As his gaze returned to Khan's body, he saw a deep gash at the base of his skull.

Although Khan's attempts at combat had ceased with the apparent mortal wound, his lower extremities still jerked randomly, as if he was not yet willing to give up the fight. A few seconds later, his lungs emptied with a death rattle and the twitching finally stopped.

Marc remained on the floor as he slowly regained his composure. "Thanks," Marc said, his breath slowly returning.

"I'm afraid I may have struck him a bit too hard," Karlsson said, still holding the bloodied trophy.

The gash at the base of Khan's skull oozed blood mixed with bits of bone and flesh.

"That could get you five minutes in the penalty box for 'unnecessary roughness,'" Marc said with a tired smirk.

A few moments later, Marc reached over and pried the pistol from Khan's hand, the dead man's fingers still tightly wrapped around its grip. He examined the handgun and pointed to the pistol's grip, "this is an older model and the star indicates it's of Chinese manufacture. It's a wonder it didn't jam. He racked the slide a few times, finding the chamber empty of bullets. He rolled Khan on his left side and patted his pockets. Finding nothing, Marc rolled Khan on his right side where he found a key and a single bullet in one of his back pockets.

"That's the master key for the back door, but I wonder why he kept one extra bullet?" Karlsson asked.

"Probably for himself, in case he failed in his mission. You just saved him the trouble."

Marc loaded the bullet in the pistol, and secured it in his waistband along with the hunting knife, then dropped the master key in his pocket.

Suddenly they felt the train begin to move.

"It's only fifteen minutes to Port Kent before we signal your detective friend to begin the decoupling process."

Marc glanced at his watch. It was nine-thirty. Although the train ran very smoothly, Marc could sense it picking up speed.

The two sat in silence as the minutes ticked by.

"Mr. Karlsson, I was thinking. What if, after the train decouples, the locomotive doesn't automatically speed up and jump the tracks like you theorized?"

Karlsson appeared to contemplate the scenario.

"I suppose anything's possible. If that happened, we'd have to warn Albany and hope they can stop the train and somehow disarm the device before it reaches another urban area. The train is scheduled to pass through Glens Falls and Saratoga before it gets to Albany."

"Couldn't someone simply throw a switch that would redirect the Laser either off the track or direct it to a less populated area?"

"You're talking old school. Modern railroad switching is computer driven. Once the switching computer receives its instructions from the engine's computer, a manual override is very difficult, especially on such short notice."

Marc felt the train slowing.

"We have to get word to the police," Marc said.

He ripped off a piece of cardboard from one of the boxes. "Give me the black magic marker, please," Marc asked.

Confused, Karlsson handed him the marker.

Marc quickly scribbled a note on the cardboard. It was brief, but to the point. He stuffed the note into Khan's trousers, then turned toward the door with the master key in his hand.

"Marc, what are you doing? You're not thinking of opening that door now, are you?"

"Yes, unless you can think of a better way of rolling this guy out of here."

"Throw him off the train? That's kind of extreme, don't you think?"

"We're about to go through the hamlet of Port Kent. We could throw all kinds of notes out onto the tracks. To most people, it would just be a spray of litter. But a body, with a note tucked inside his pants, now that would get noticed. The note is a message to call Investigator Golden at the State Police in Plattsburgh and tell him that the Laser Train is heading to New York City on a terrorist mission."

Marc opened the door and looked out the back of the train. Karlsson was right. They were definitely going too fast to exit the train, but only if you were still alive. He recognized the area they were passing through as Wickam's Marsh, which he knew was a mile or so north of the hamlet of Port Kent. For a brief moment he recalled days as a child when his parents took him there for picnics along the shores of Lake Champlain…too many childhood flashbacks in one day.

"Hugo, give me a hand."

Karlsson hesitated.

Marc started pulling Khan's body toward the open door.

After a couple of pulls, Karlsson saw that Marc was struggling with the Korean's bulk and joined in.

"We can do this if we both pull together," Marc said.

"Ready, pull," he yelled over the noise of the train car's metal wheels speeding along the steel rails. Khan's body slid about half way to the door. "Pull," Marc yelled again, and again, and again.

When they finally reached the top step, there wasn't enough room for both men to pull the dead man any further down the stairs. They lifted Khan by the shoulders so that his head was hanging over the step, his neck bent down, as if viewing the blur of railroad ties passing below. Marc picked up the dead man's feet in an effort to push him down the three steps and out of the car, but again, the man was too heavy to move alone. Karlsson joined in, and while he took one leg, Marc took the other.

Marc yelled, "Now," and with a final push Khan's body slid out of the train car and onto the tracks. With the train travelling more than sixty miles an hour, his body bounced when it hit the railroad ties and became airborne, then did a full gainer and bounced again and again, as the limp hulk flailed wildly, almost like it was vainly trying to catch up to the train. Then it twisted and rolled a few times, finally coming to rest in the middle of the intersection of Port Kent's Main Street. Marc could see the crossing gates with their lights flashing and for a brief moment, he heard the receding sound of the crossing's warning bell. Port Kent is a small burg, and Marc could see that there were no cars waiting at the crossing that would have seen the body roll to a halt. Marc pulled the door closed. "I'm sure someone will be along eventually and discover the body," he said.

"That's the most gruesome thing I've ever seen," Karlsson said between gulps of breath as he absentmindedly wiped his hands on his trousers.

"Not as gruesome as what could happen if this thing reaches Penn Station and discharges its payload. Besides, I'm sure Khan didn't feel a thing."

They remained motionless for a few minutes as they recovered from the labor of throwing the Korean's body off the train.

Finally Karlsson said, "Marc, it's time to signal Sylvie to start the decoupling process."

"You kill the overhead lights, and I'll try to get her attention with the flashlight," Marc said.

Karlsson hit the overhead light switch. The cabin went dark.

Marc climbed the mountain of boxes to the vent opening, then pointed the flashlight's beam toward the front of the car where he had last seen Sylvie. But, to his surprise, she was no longer there. Using the powerful beam, he scanned the channel to no avail.

Where the hell could she have gone?

As he was about to give up in his search, he noticed a movement from beyond where he had last seen her. Due to the swaying motion of the coupled cars, it was difficult to tell if it was real or imagined. A few moments later, Marc was relieved as he caught a glimpse of Sylvie's face. She had somehow got herself turned around and was crawling back in his direction, but she was still beyond the end of the passenger car. She gave a quick wave, then turned to her left, toward the panel Karlsson had instructed her to look for the connecting wires. Marc saw a spark of light, as she ignited the lighter Karlsson had given her. Marc kept his beam trained on Sylvie in an effort to help her see the wires. He could see she was looking at Karlsson's wiring diagram, but he couldn't tell if she was succeeding.

"Marc, what's going on? We're getting close to The Bow," Karlsson said anxiously.

"She appears to be working on something," he called back.

Another long minute ticked by as Marc watched. Sylvie hadn't moved since she had started working on the panel.

He then sensed the train slow ever so slightly.

"We're in The Bow. It's now or never," Karlsson called out, his voice ripe with frustration.

Marc watched, straining to catch glimpses of Sylvie as she worked to decouple the cars from the engine.

Come on, Sylvie, you can do this.

The seconds ticked by.

"Is she still working at the panel?" Karlsson called up.

"I believe so, but I can't tell if she's made any progress."

Another minute passed. But there was still no change in the train's speed.

"I think we've passed The Bow. It's been way too long."

Ten more minutes dragged by.

Suddenly, Marc sensed, as much as heard, the faint sound of what he figured must be the train's horn, then he felt it slowing, rapidly.

"She must have finally disconnected the wires. Too bad it took so long. I'm not sure exactly where we are now. Probably somewhere near Essex, I assume." Karlsson said.

But why the horn?

They were both silent for a few moments as they felt the train slowing more and more until there seemed to be no movement. Apparently, the train had come to a halt.

"There's something wrong," Karlsson said.

"I agree. Why did the train's horn sound? You don't think Sylvie had anything to do with that?"

"I doubt it. It doesn't make any sense."

"One thing seems for sure. We're stopped, so the engine must have disconnected and hopefully jumped the tracks," Marc said.

"No, you don't understand. The braking mechanism is controlled by the main computer in the locomotive. The fact that we've stopped so fast means we're still connected."

Marc looked through the channel and saw Sylvie was making her way back toward the baggage car. After a few moments, she finally made it to the open panel. Marc helped her down.

"What happened? Were you able to decouple the cars from the engine?" Marc asked.

"No, I never got close. The panel covering the circuits is secured with a series of tamperproof connecters. I tried the makeshift tools you gave me, but nothing worked. I even found another panel, but both are secured with the same kind of connectors."

"I should have known. Jimmy Lee probably had something to do with that. He was always very security conscious. Now I know why," Karlsson said.

"Question is—why are we stopped?" Marc said as he retrieved the key from his pocket and headed toward the rear door of the car. But when he turned the key in the lock, the door would not open. "I think the door's stuck."

Karlsson reached around him and turned the door lever in the opposite direction. The door opened.

"Another safety feature."

Marc looked out the back door to the tracks below. Indeed, the train had stopped. He descended the steps and cautiously peered around the back of the baggage car toward the front of the train. About a hundred yards ahead, a large farm tractor attached to an oversized bulk tank was stopped in the center of the crossing. The farmer operating the tractor appeared to be feverishly working to get his tractor moving off the crossing, but one of the bulk tank's rear wheels had slid off the crossing's paved portion and seemed to have lodged between the pavement and the railroad tracks. Marc noticed a signpost off to the right of the tracks read "Station Road."

We're just south of Essex.

By this time, Karlsson and Sylvie had joined Marc, taking in the scene in front of the Laser.

"What's happened?" Karlsson asked.

"It appears this state-of-the-art Laser locomotive, loaded with enough chemicals to kill thousands of people is being held up by a tractor pulling a load of liquid cow shit."

"The conductor must have stopped the train, rather than risk pushing the tractor out of the way, probably because we have some political figures on board," Karlsson said as he started toward the locomotive, with Marc and Sylvie following close behind.

As they passed the passenger car, Marc could see the perplexed looks on the faces of the students dressed in their band uniforms, looking down at the three strangers beneath them on the railroad bed. As the trio continued toward the dining car, Marc noticed Jacques LaFleur's face was also starring down at his three former captives. Then, LaFleur's face quickly disappeared from view.

"Whatever you have in mind, we had better make it fast. Jacques LaFleur's spotted us and he's on the move," Marc said.

"First, we need to uncouple the locomotive from the rest of the train." Karlsson said.

"I've already tried that. What makes you think you'll be successful now?" Sylvie asked.

"It's easier from the outside of the train, but we have to hurry," Karlsson called back as he arrived at the flexible accordion-like portal connecting the dining car to the passenger car. He then ducked down and disappeared beneath it.

Marc crouched down to see what Karlsson was up to.

"What can I do to help?" He asked.

Karlsson didn't respond at first. Marc looked under the portal and saw he was trying to pull up on what appeared to be some kind lever attached to the dining car.

"Marc, give me a hand. It must be stuck."

Marc crawled under the vestibule and grabbed hold of the lever Karlsson was pulling on. With both of them pulling, it finally gave way.

"OK, now we have to turn the lever sideways to release the support pin on the Buckeye coupler that will uncouple the two cars," Karlsson said.

"I don't know what a Buckeye coupler is, but if that's what we have to do to get this train separated, I can handle it," Marc said as he began to push on the lever.

"Hold it right there," came a loud voice, coming from the opposite side of the car.

When Marc looked up he could see Jacques LaFleur, crouched down on his haunches, holding a pistol pointed directly at Marc.

"Let go of that lever or you're a dead man, LaRose."

Marc hesitated, "Give it up, LaFleur. This crazy scheme has come to an end. Besides, you wouldn't shoot with all these people around."

Just then, Marc heard a loud 'bang'.

Apparently thinking it was a gunshot, LaFleur glanced toward the front of the train. Marc saw his chance and scooped up a handful of railroad ballast and tossed the stones in LaFleur's face, distracting him.

Marc pushed Karlsson down onto the tracks just as LaFleur's gun went off, the bullet ricocheting off the steel Buckeye coupler that still held the train cars together.

With LaFleur still disoriented, Marc withdrew Khan's pistol from his belt and fired the remaining bullet.

LaFleur yelped as the bullet struck his arm, forcing him to drop his pistol. He recovered quickly, however, and holding his injured arm, took off in the direction of the railroad crossing and the farm tractor with its load still stuck on the tracks.

Marc dropped the empty Chinese pistol and with both arms gave a last pull on the uncoupling lever. The apparatus responded with a metallic 'clunk'.

"You did it, Marc," Karlsson yelled.

Marc scrambled from under the train and immediately looked for LaFleur, but he was nowhere in sight. He located LaFleur's pistol where he'd dropped it and tucked it in his belt.

By this time, Sylvie had made her way around to the side of the train where Marc was standing.

"Marc, you go after him, I can finish what I need to do here myself," Karlsson yelled.

Marc yelled to Sylvie, "Find the conductor and tell him and the passengers that the train is unsafe and everyone is to get off and get away as soon as possible. Then call 911 and have them connect you with Tim Golden. Tell him where we are and what's happened. I'm going to look for LaFleur. Be careful, he may have headed back to the passenger car."

Sylvie nodded, “But Marc, where are we?”

“We’re on the Station Road outside of Essex. He’ll know where it is.”

As Sylvie ran back toward the passenger car, Marc heard the sound of several car horns from the drivers stuck at the crossing.

They’re probably trying to make it to the ferry boat landing, Marc thought, knowing the Champlain Ferry connecting Essex to Charlotte, Vermont, left every half hour.

Chapter Eighteen

As Marc scanned the area for LaFleur, he noted that the farmer was still feverishly working the tractor in an effort to remove the load of manure from the tracks. The tractor's exhaust belched a plume of black diesel smoke as its engine struggled at full throttle.

He headed for the tractor at a dead run in an attempt to signal the farmer to leave the machine on the tracks, thus blocking the Laser from continuing. However, the farmer was apparently too busy to notice Marc and continued his efforts to pull the manure wagon out of the train's path.

As Marc got closer, he could see the John Deere's massive rear wheels begin to spin as the tractor struggled with its heavy load. The farmer rocked his tractor back and forth to free the wheel that was wedged between the pavement and the railroad tracks. Again, the farmer gunned the big tractor's engine, causing its front tires to rise up off the roadway. Finally, the pinned wagon wheel pulled free and the farm tractor with its load continued toward the opposite side of the crossing, slowly clearing the way for the train to pass.

Somewhere in the background, Marc heard the high pitch of the locomotive's turbine winding up. Someone inside the Laser had seen that the track was about to clear and was determined to continue its ill-fated trip.

The Laser's locomotive and dining car started toward the crossing, and, although, the ribbed vestibule was still attached, the weight of the uncoupled cars caused the accordion-like gangway between the dining and passenger cars to tear apart and what remained of the vestibule hung limply behind the dining car as it bounced along the tracks like a broken oversized drainage tube.

The liquid manure spreader had barely cleared the crossing when the front of the Laser struck the bulk tank's rear assembly, ripping away its array of spray nozzles attached to the back of the tank. Liquid manure shot out of the broken piping at full force, spraying the side of the Laser's engine as it passed.

Marc instinctively sprinted toward the remnants of the dining car's sagging vestibule, knowing he had to do something to stop the train. The shrill of the Laser's jet engine throttled up and Marc could see its speed was increasing rapidly. With a lunge, he clutched to the remnants of the vestibule and held on. As he was being pulled along he saw the steps leading up to the dining car were just out of reach, when he spotted two long steel supports, meant to hold the vestibule upright. Marc frantically pulled with all he had until one foot, then the other found purchase on the supports.

Above the noise of the train's engine, Marc could hear, then smell, the liquid manure splattering the side of the vestibule as it cleared the crossing.

So much for that 'new car' smell.

Marc inched his way up along the dangling vestibule as it swayed and bounced along the tracks. The dining car's rear door was almost within his grasp, but the train was accelerating quickly. Pulling with everything he had left, he found a footing on the dining car's landing just below the level of the door, and was able to grab the handrail, slick with the film of manure spray. Despite the noxious odor, he took a moment to catch his breath. Marc then took a quick look behind and caught a glimpse of the tractor tugging its odiferous load. The farmer, still intent on getting away from the crossing was apparently unaware of the damage as the bulk tank continued spraying the line of cars waiting for the train to pass. Ironically, the sounds of car horns from their impatient drivers had suddenly ceased.

Break out those pine-scented air fresheners.

Marc struggled to raise himself to where he could peek through the dining car's rear window. He could see a long stretch of dining tables on each side of the car with rows of swivel seats attached to the floor facing the side windows. But, of course, today there were no diners present, and anyway, the view out the window was not very appetizing.

Although he felt safe for the moment, Marc wondered where LaFleur had gone.

He reached for the door handle to give it a turn, but found it was locked. The train continued to pick up speed as the sound of the steel wheels reverberating up the damaged vestibule intensified.

Clinging to the slime-covered railing with one hand, he retrieved the master key from his pocket with the other, and inserted it in the door's keyhole. It turned. He pulled himself inside the car and shut the door behind him. The quietness inside the dining car was immediate.

Assuming that LaFleur could be anywhere, Marc proceeded slowly. He could see there were two doors on either side of the dining car entrance marked with one identifying word, "Toilet."

That should help eliminate any confusion for those unsure of their sex.

At the opposite end of the car he saw a dividing wall off to the right side that separated the dining area from the kitchen.

Continuing toward the kitchen area, he couldn't help but notice the windows on the car's left side, stained with film and globs of coagulated cow shit that were streaking horizontally as the train sped toward its intended destination.

About half-way to the kitchen area, Marc heard a noise behind him. He turned to see Jacques LaFleur coming out of one of the toilets holding a wad of blood-soaked toilet paper over the wound on his arm.

When LaFleur spotted Marc, his initial surprise was quickly replaced with a sneer.

"Mr. LaRose. How did you…" he stopped in mid-sentence, apparently aware that it no longer made any difference how Marc got on the train. He was here and would be dealt with.

"Sorry to spoil your plans for a weekday blast in the Big Apple, Jacques, but I've had enough of your shit and so has the Laser," Marc said, gesturing toward the windows. "Your counterparts are either dead or on the run. This demented conspiracy you've hatched has been exposed. Your strategy of using the Laser to terrorize New York has been foiled by your greed and a load of liquid manure, which is what this senseless scheme amounted to in the first place."

Jacques LaFleur silently stared back and slowly replaced his grin with a look of apparent surrender.

"What's the matter, Jacques, cow shit got your tongue?"

Marc had the feeling that although LaFleur appeared to have been beaten, he might still have another ace up his bloody sleeve.

"No, Mr. LaRose. I have to admit, I have underestimated you. Your persistence has paid off. When the train arrives at Albany, I plan to surrender to the authorities."

As LaFleur dropped his hand holding the toilet paper over his wound, he reached inside his suit coat.

Marc quickly drew the pistol from his waistband. "I hope you're not so foolish as to pull another gun on me," Marc said, suspicious of LaFleur's admission of defeat.

Jacques hand paused for a moment, hovering near his jacket pocket. "No, you have my only gun. But if you'll be so kind…" he said, still reaching toward his pocket.

"If you have something to show me, use your other hand," Marc ordered, gesturing toward LaFleur's injured arm."

I can't let myself get too close. He's still capable of anything, even with that injury.

LaFleur grimaced as he slowly brought the hand with its bloody sleeve across his body toward his inside suit coat pocket.

"Slowly, just use your thumb and forefinger," Marc instructed.

"Mr. LaRose, I am the beaten one. I'm trying to surrender so we can put an end to this."

"No quick moves, or I swear, the next one's between your eyes," Marc threatened.

Slowly, Jacques LaFleur retrieved what appeared to be something the size and shape of a smart phone from his pocket.

Still leery of his intentions, Marc commanded, "hand that to me."

As LaFleur extended his hand holding the object, Marc noticed him doing something with his thumb on the device.

"It's all yours, detective," LaFleur said, a little too confident for a 'beaten' man, Marc thought.

As he took the device, Marc felt the train's speed suddenly increase. The device's screen and its unusual weight didn't appear to be a standard cell phone after all.

Through the film of shit smeared along the windows, Marc caught a glimpse of the Westport Depot Theater as the train sped by.

We're going well over seventy miles an hour.

Looking at his reflection in the polished face of the device, Marc surprised himself with his own look of desperation. Keeping one eye on LaFleur, he felt around the edges of the device for a button, something that would indicate what this gadget was and how it worked.

"OK wise ass," Marc said as he dropped the implement on the closest table. "Let's see if this thing's bullet proof," he said, raising the pistol, the barrel of his gun grazing its screen.

"I wouldn't do that," Jacques said, with a sudden hint of concern.

"And why not? It's apparently of no use to me," Marc said.

"I wouldn't go so far as to say that. It just doesn't recognize you."

"What do you mean?"

"It's been programmed to only recognize my voice commands."

"Then you have the ability to stop this thing," Marc said, as he retrieved the device.

"Yes, I do. You see, it's a miniaturized conductor. The Laser is fully computerized and this device has the ability to communicate with the Laser's main computer."

"If you mean what you say, you will instruct it to stop the train before we get to Albany," Marc said, holding the device out toward LaFleur.

"Whatever you say, Mr. LaRose. This should only take a moment."

"Remember, I'm listening and watching your every move," Marc said, guardedly.

LaFleur paused before speaking.

Marc noticed LaFleur's facial expression had reverted back to the sinister grin.

"Every plan, no matter how well thought out has to have backups, in this case, a 'Plan S,' if you will."

Marc felt the train sway, then tilt inward on a long turn, the sound of its composite steel wheels screaming through the thick floor insulation as it maneuvered the corner at a speed he suspected was testing the train's limitations.

“Jacques, this doesn’t sound like surrender to me. It’s time to end this charade.”

LaFleur’s grin turned to an almost warm smile of satisfaction.

“You see, that is where ‘Plan S,’ comes into play, Mr. LaRose.”

“Grow up. How did you think you were going to get your ricin loaded bombs to Penn Station? By ‘Sailing’ them down the Hudson River?” Marc accentuated the ‘S.’

“Very funny, detective. Let’s just say it’s time to stop ‘horsing around.’”

‘Horsing around?’ That’s an odd thing for him to say.

LaFleur looked around the inside of the dining car, as if seeing it for the first time. “As you may have suspected, The Laser has exceeded its safe traveling speed, and there are some treacherous portions of track coming up shortly. If you want to live, and if I were a betting man, I’d say you do, now is the time to hand me the controller.”

Horsing around? Betting man? What does this guy have in mind? Marc thought. Then, he remembered what Norm had mentioned about betting on a horse race just two days before. LaFleur had apparently given up on Penn Station and had decided to deploy the train’s cargo somewhere before Albany. August in Saratoga is the height of racing season and the train tracks run right through the city, which would be teeming with people attending the races.

Marc estimated the train was quickly approaching the Village of Ticonderoga only a few minutes away.

“If the Laser’s engine is pre-programmed, then why do you need the controller? Shouldn’t it automatically slow down on the tight turns?” Marc said.

For the first time, he noticed beads of sweat forming on LaFleur’s brow and upper lip. Droplets of blood ran down his wounded arm onto the new dining car carpet.

He needs the controller to change the Laser’s program.

“Look, Mr. LaRose. Maybe we can make a deal. I can make you rich. All you have to do is hand me the controller.”

Marc gripped the controller tightly and leaned against one of the metal dining tables nearby to hold his balance.

“Jacques, you think you’re talking to one of Maurice Bashaw’s stupid goons?” You’re in no position to bribe your way out of this. There is only one thing left for you to do and that is to stop this thing before more people get hurt.”

Jacques let out a long breath and looked down at his wounded arm. Blood was pooling on the carpet.

Wonder if they treated it with Scotch Guard.

LaFleur remained motionless for a long moment, until finally he said, “I suppose you’re right. If you would just hold the device toward me, I can give the Laser the order to stop,” he said as the Ticonderoga Train Depot flashed by.

Marc hesitated, fearing a double cross, but knowing this may be the only way to get the train safely stopped, held the device toward LaFleur.

Jacques cleared his throat, and was about to say something into the device, when, through the dining car’s insulated canopy, Marc heard a loud ‘boom,’ that sounded like a crack of thunder.

At first, this even baffled Marc, as the day was clear and the sun was shining.

LaFleur gave a startled glance toward the clouded window and seeing nothing turned back to Marc. With panic in his eyes, he yelled, “You’ve tricked me. The police think they can stop the Laser.”

“Maximum speed, maximum speed,” he shouted.

Marc felt the train car surge ahead even faster as the Laser’s locomotive obeyed LaFleur’s voice command for even more speed.

Then, remembering where they were, Marc yelled, “No, that’s just the noon cannon demonstration at Fort Ticonderoga.”

But it was too late. The train rounded a slight curve giving LaFleur additional momentum when he swung at Marc with his uninjured arm. The car swayed with the increased speed, and coupled with the force of the blow, Marc fell backwards onto one of the dining tables, then, slid between the tables and onto the floor. The centrifugal force of the car rounding the bend pinned him under the table and against the car’s wall.

Marc last glimpsed LaFleur’s feet heading for the front of the car.

For an instant, the light coming through the side windows went dark, as Marc remembered the short narrow tunnel, a holdover from decades before, that served as a bridge for the Fort's access road. The noise and suction caused by the speeding train as it cleared the short tunnel, invaded the interior of the train car.

The train continued to increase speed as it approached the trestle over the La Chute River connecting Lake George with Lake Champlain. Hitting a small dip in the tracks leading to the causeway, coupled with the increased speed, the locomotive's rear wheels became unseated, and along with the dining car, the speeding two-hundred ton locomotive jumped the tracks, tearing out lengths of rail and parts of the causeway with it. The Laser then became airborne and plunged a hundred feet into the La Chute River Bay, hitting the water at well over a hundred miles an hour.

The crowd of visitors assembled for the cannon demonstration at Fort Ticonderoga stood in horror as they watched the massive locomotive and the dining car with the remnants of its vestibule flagging behind crash through the bridge. It sailed through the air and splashed into the bay, causing a small tidal wave that pushed toward the opposite shore.

With the water depth near the bridge at about thirty feet, the locomotive sank immediately. However, the force of the crash caused the dining car to decouple. Upon hitting the water, with its sealed exterior and lighter weight, it remained partially afloat and upright, in the usually tranquil bay.

When he came to, Marc found himself wrapped around the post of one of the dining room's stools, which probably saved him from being thrown against the car's bulkhead with the force of the crash.

Disoriented, he slowly raised himself off the floor, using one of the tables for balance. He suspected the train had stopped, but was puzzled by the way it bobbed, first one way, then the other. A peek out the side window, now suspiciously almost totally cleared of manure, told him why. The car was floating on the bay. Trouble was he literally had a sinking feeling. The car was beginning to take on water that was already seeping in under the rear door.

Still dazed, he looked around for LaFleur, but he was nowhere in sight.

He knew he had to get out of the car, but he needed to find the Canadian first.

"OK, Jacques, where are you?" he yelled, feeling a sharp pain in his chest.

Might have broken a rib.

Still dazed from the crash, he tried to clear his head.

"LaFleur, are you here?" he called out again.

Clinging onto the backs of the stools for balance, Marc made his way toward the kitchen area, the direction where he last saw LaFleur heading just before the crash. Each time he grabbed onto one of the stools however, he felt a sharp pain in his chest and suspected he had broken a rib or possibly two. But the pain was not the only thing that bothered him. He also noticed his feet were sloshing on the wet carpet, as the water level inside the car rose.

"LaFleur, you asshole, where the hell are you?"

"*Ici*," came the weak, raspy response.

Marc made his way around the partition that separated the dining portion of the car from the kitchen, which he discovered was more of a dispensary for precooked items. A stainless steel counter separated the passengers from refrigerators, freezers, and microwave ovens built into the wall. Several refrigerator and cupboard doors had opened from the impact and much of the packaged food was piled up behind the counter. A colorful menu listing lunch items that previously hung from the ceiling had broken free of its fasteners and hung askew over the counter and along the floor.

As Marc scanned the debris, he saw LaFleur's legs partially hidden behind an opened refrigerator door and held there by a mountain of pre-packaged food items, trays, boxes of condiments, napkins, and utensils that had been shaken from their storage bins and pushed toward the front of the car.

Marc made his way along the counter and through the opening at the front of the car where Jacques was pinned. Through the searing pain in his chest, he began pulling and shoving the pile of debris away from the refrigerator door in an effort to free the door so he could pull it away from LaFleur. The water was rising faster, making the job of clearing the area more difficult.

"Hang on. I'll have you freed in a minute."

LaFeur's only response was a wet grunt.

After clearing away as much of the debris as he could, he again pulled on the door, but it only moved and inch or so. Frustrated, he pulled again and again. The pain in his chest intensified with each pull. He put his foot against the car's front bulkhead for leverage and, struggling through the pain, finally managed to pull the door away from LaFleur's body. To his surprise, Marc saw that LaFleur's body remained pinned against the wall, his arms hanging limp to his sides. It was only when Marc attempted to pull him away from the wall that he found that LaFleur's body was actually attached to the bulkhead.

LaFleur let out another watery moan, weaker than before.

Knowing there was little time to waste, Marc used what strength he had left and lifted LaFleur's body in a final attempt to free him of whatever was holding him there. When he felt the body break free, he pulled him further away. It was then he discovered that a chest-high doorstop equipped with a blunt rubber tip had been installed with the intent of preventing the refrigerator door from banging against the bulkhead. Marc figured that LaFleur might have tried to take refuge inside the kitchen's refrigerator unit when the force of the train car hitting the water had apparently thrown LaFleur's body against the doorstop. He was pinned down by the door and all the loose debris. Marc dragged the now unconscious body over to the serving counter.

Water inside the car had risen to over a foot, and at this rate Marc knew they'd be totally submerged in a matter of minutes. He slid LaFleur's limp body off the counter, then, holding him under his armpits, dragged him back through the dining area toward the car's rear door.

By the time Marc had arrived at the door, the water had risen to more than two-feet deep inside the car. A quick glance toward the side windows showed the car was quickly sinking. The shit-smeared windows were almost clean, as the lake water was splashed against them.

When Marc tried to open the dining car's rear door, it stuck, and only by letting go of LaFleur's body and using both hands to force the door handle downward, was he able to push it open. A surge of water gushed into the car. He felt the back end of the car tilting as the incoming tide began to fill the car.

Marc grabbed LaFleur by his coat collar and pulled him into the vestibule. With the combination of the incoming surge of water and the downward pull of gravity, Marc took a gulp of air and, with everything he had left in him, pulled LaFleur through the vestibule in a last ditch effort to get free of the sinking car.

Holding onto the body with one hand while pulling with the other, Marc kicked his way free of the dining car just as it was settling on the floor of the bay. After a few more kicks that seemed to take an eternity, he made his way to the surface. Looking around him, the closest thing to grab onto was a bale of styrofoam serving trays that had floated out of the dining car. Grabbing onto the bale with one hand, and LaFleur with the other, Marc kicked toward the concrete pylons of the now partially-destroyed bridge, and with a still unconscious LaFleur in tow, headed toward the closest one.

As he struggled with the body's dead weight dragging behind him, Marc became aware of a distant buzzing sound in the water.

Cannot let go. Got to get to that pylon.

With every kick however, the buzzing seemed to get louder. Just a few more feet, he thought as he gasped for air. The buzzing sound persisted.

Could I be slipping into unconsciousness?

Then, he felt something pulling him upward. Glancing back, he saw the hull of a small aluminum boat. Someone inside the boat was talking to him, but he couldn't make out the words. The buzzing sound seemed to have stopped.

Must be the boat's engine.

"Our boat's too small to pull you in, mister. Hang onto the side. We'll get you into shore," the voice said.

"Jimmy, you hold onto this guy. We've got to get 'em back to the dock."

Marc assumed the boy was talking about LaFleur, at least he hoped he was. He could feel the boat change directions. With his arms draped over the boat's hull, he looked up and could see a young boy holding onto LaFleur's body in the water next to him, but his face was barely above water. His head was bent back, his mouth and his eyes were wide open.

A long five minutes later, Marc could feel his feet dragging on the bottom of the bay as the boat got closer to shore.

"Throw me a line," Marc heard a distant voice cry out.

Marc felt the boat bump up against a dock that was attached to the end of the pier. He rested his feet on the bottom of the river, and stood, coming about chest high with the boat.

"Somebody, help me get this guy out of the water," Marc heard one of the boys yell. He could see an older man tugging on LaFleur, attempting to pull him out of the water and into the boat, but he was too heavy, and the boat was beginning to take on water.

"We're gonna need help," Marc heard the older man say.

Marc saw what the volunteer was trying to do, and waded over to where LaFleur's body was.

"Hold onto his arms, I'll lift his legs up," he said.

He reached into the water and brought one leg up so his shoe was wrapped over the edge of the boat. The pain in Marc's chest increased. He repeated the process with LaFleur's other leg, while the man and the boy pulled on LaFleur's body until he was entirely in the boat.

"Jeez, look at that hole in his chest," one of the boys cried.

Still holding onto the side of the boat, Marc made his way around to the dock where he found a set of aluminum stairs. After being helped up onto the dock, he sat there, exhausted, with his feet dangling off the side. He could see LaFleur's body lying motionless in the bottom of the boat atop of what appeared to be some fishing gear. The older man tilted LaFleur's head up against one of the metal seats, his mouth still open. The faint sound of sirens coming from somewhere grew steadily louder.

"You OK, mister?" a voice asked.

Marc looked up and saw a teenage boy kneeling next to him. His eyes were wide with trepidation.

"Not sure. I might have broken a couple of ribs," he said, wincing as he touched his side. "Is this your boat?" he asked the boy.

"My dad's. We were fishing over there, not far from the trestle," he said, pointing to the railway bridge, "just after we heard the Fort's cannon go off, the train came zooming onto the bridge. Then, it just seemed to fly off into the water, and, sploosh. Jeez, the waves must have been ten feet high, weren't they, Tommy?" The boy said as he rolled his arms upward mimicking the waves. "I thought we were going to capsize."

Tommy nodded his head in agreement. "It was the wildest thing I've ever seen. The front of the train sank right away, but the train car stayed afloat for a few minutes before it started to sink, that's when we saw you and that guy there in the water," he said pointing toward the pale body lying in the boat.

"Thanks for pulling us out," Marc managed.

"That's OK mister. The fish weren't biting anyway. I can't wait to tell the kids at school. Jeezum crow, craziest thing I've ever seen."

Marc heard quick footsteps on the pier. When he looked up he saw a man and a woman running toward him wearing orange vests.

"Anybody know anything about a train running off the tracks?" the woman yelled.

"Yeah, this guy knows all about it," The boy said, pointing towards Marc, "and that guy too, maybe," nodding his head towards LaFleur's body.

From the patches on their sleeves Marc could see they were EMT's from the Ticonderoga Volunteer Fire Department."

The female EMT knelt down next to Marc, "Sir, are you OK? Do you want to go to the hospital?" Marc noticed she wore a nametag, "Betsy."

"I'm fine," he lied, "but I think you should take a look at him," Marc motioned towards LaFleur.

The male EMT was already stepping down into the boat. It took him just a few seconds to come up with a diagnosis.

"Bets, we need to call the hospital and let them know what we have. This man's in tough shape. I seriously doubt he's going to make it."

Marc heard more sirens. He watched as 'Betsy' headed back to the ambulance to retrieve a gurney. A fire truck along with a state police cruiser pulled in near the pier's entrance, emergency lights flashing.

Chapter Nineteen

A few minutes later, a burly state trooper approached, took a look at LaFleur lying in the boat and asked, "Anybody see what happened?"

The boy, Jimmy, answered. "Uh, we did sir. The train went right off the bridge and into the water while we were fishing out there," he said, pointing in the direction of what remained of the trestle. "We heard the train coming when all of a sudden it seemed to fly off the tracks and crash right into the lake! But we didn't catch any fish sir, honest." Jimmy said, more concerned about catching an illegal fish than the disaster that had just unfolded before him.

"Anyway, that's when we saw that man swimming towards the shore with the man in the boat," he said, pointing toward Marc. "We went over and helped them and towed them here, to the dock."

The trooper climbed down into the boat, holding onto the pier's pylon for balance. He looked at LaFleur, then, felt around his neck for his carotid artery. When he pulled LaFleur's shirt open Marc could see there was a red stain surrounding what looked like a puncture wound. The trooper looked over toward Marc.

"Any idea how this man got this hole in his chest?"

"Yeah, I think I do. We were both on the train when it went into the lake." Marc hesitated, "You haven't heard from Investigator Tim Golden by any chance, have you?"

"Tim Golden? He works out of the Plattsburgh Barracks. What's he got to do with this?"

"He's familiar with the case, or at least, he should be by now."

"What's your name?" the trooper asked as he retrieved his notebook.

"Marc LaRose." Marc eyed the trooper's nameplate, 'Lawliss.'

The trooper hesitated.

"Are you the Marc LaRose that was involved in the incident in Lake Placid last winter? The former State Police Investigator?"

Marc nodded, "Fraid so."

Lawliss hesitated. “I see. So tell me, was this that new train that was supposed to be going to New York City? The one they called the Laser?”

Marc glanced around him, “Trooper Lawliss, if it’s all the same with you, I think we should discuss this someplace private.”

Lawliss hesitated again, then nodded in the direction of his troop car. “OK, we can talk on the way. But first, where are all the passengers? I thought there were supposed to be dignitaries and school kids on the train as well.”

“They’re back in Essex. Part of the train got separated from the engine.”

By this time, Marc could see a group of onlookers beginning to venture out onto the pier, apparently curious to find out what had happened.

Lawliss motioned for the curiosity seekers to remain where they were. He then retrieved his cell phone and snapped a couple of photos of LaFleur and the boat, as well as the two teenage witnesses. He activated his hand-held radio and began speaking into it. Although Marc couldn’t hear everything, he was sure Lawliss was calling his zone headquarters advising them of the apparent train crash and the possibility of fatalities. After a moment, Marc heard the response from Ray Brook, “Secure the scene. The Zone Commander is enroute to your location.”

Lawliss responded with his shield number.

After getting the boys’ names and addresses, he said, “Fellas, I have to ask you to hang around for a while, and I might have to call your parents.”

“We’re not in any trouble, are we, sir?”

“No, you helped save a man’s life. You’re actually a couple of heroes.”

The boys looked at each other in amazement. “Heroes. Wow, wait until the kids in school hear about this,” Tommy said.

Lawliss said, "Please come with me, Mr. LaRose."

Marc winced as he struggled to get up off the dock. The pain in his chest had renewed its intensity.

“You all right?” Lawliss asked.

"I'm fine. But I need you to do me a favor," Marc said as the two walked down the pier toward the shoreline.

"What do you need?"

"I've been working with Investigator Golden on something connected with this incident. Could you ask headquarters to advise him where we are?"

"Sure," he said, then looked at the gathered crowd approaching them, "Give me a minute to get these people off the pier first."

As they walked toward the shoreline, the trooper motioned the onlookers back off the pier.

Hesitantly, they complied, with several hanging around the end of the pier, some taking photos of the trooper, Marc, the pier, the lake, anything they figured could possibly be sensational enough to post with their mobile devices.

EMT Betsy approached the trooper. "You know the man in the boat has expired."

"I know. Do you have something to cover him with? I'll call for the coroner."

"Sure thing," she said, and left in the direction of the ambulance.

When Marc and the trooper arrived at the patrol car, Lawliss said, "Have a seat up front."

Marc eased into the car's front seat, wincing with the pain in his chest as he did so.

The trooper saw Marc's face grimace. "Sure you don't want to go to the hospital to get that checked out?"

"Eventually, but there's still a few things that need to get done first."

Lawliss situated his patrol car to block the entrance to the pier.

Marc listened as Lawliss explained the situation to Zone Headquarters, requested some help at the scene, and asked that the county coroner be advised of the apparent death of Jacques LaFleur.

After verifying Marc's identification, Lawliss asked to briefly describe what happened, his pen and pad at the ready.

Marc looked out over the now still water, "The train jumped the tracks as it was approaching the trestle and went into the water."

Lawliss stared at him.

"Mr. LaRose, can you be a little less brief?"

"Sorry, it's been a long thirty-six hours with no sleep. You've probably heard that the Laser was making its maiden voyage from Montreal to New York City today."

"We got the message, but it was only for informational purposes. We were to take no action, at least until now," Lawliss said.

"Well, now the engine and the dining car are at the bottom of the lake."

"How many people were on the train?"

"Not sure, maybe a couple dozen when it left Plattsburgh. But when it went into the water there were only two, as far as I know—myself and the guy in the bottom of that fishing boat," Marc said, motioning toward the dock at end of the pier.

"Wasn't there supposed to be someone from the Quebec government and the Plattsburgh Mayor, plus some school kids on the train as well? Where are they?"

"Far's I know, they're still in Essex. That's where two of the train cars separated from the locomotive and the dining car."

A few more patrol cars arrived. After a brief conversation with Trooper Lawliss, two of the troopers began taking statements from the boys and other witnesses.

Just then, Marc heard the police radio dispatcher; "Be advised, Investigator Golden is enroute and needs your exact location."

"I'm at the end of the Fort Ticonderoga Road at the old fishing pier parking lot, just across from the train trestle. He'll see all the fire trucks and people. Advise the zone commander we're going to need the diving detail.

"Investigator Golden wants to know if you have a Mr. Marc LaRose with you," Marc heard the radio dispatcher say.

"That's affirmative," Lawliss answered.

There was a momentary pause as the dispatcher relayed Lawliss's information to Golden.

"Investigator Golden advises to secure Mr. LaRose in your troop car and not let him out of your sight until he gets to your location. 'Handcuff him to your steering wheel if you have to,' his words."

“Message received,” Lawliss answered.

He glanced over at Marc, “What did you do to piss Golden off?”

“Just a little misunderstanding. I’ll get it ironed out, and don’t worry, I’m in no shape to run off, even if I wanted to.”

“So Mr. LaRose, what were you doing on the train in the first place?”

Fifteen minutes later, Marc finished relating the pertinent facts of the case when they saw Tim Golden’s car coming from the direction of the Fort, a cloud of dust trailing behind. As Golden’s car screeched to a stop, Marc saw Sylvie in the front passenger seat and Karlsson in the back. When Golden stepped out of the car, Marc could see his facial expression was somewhat less than pleasant.

“I don’t know Investigator Golden that well, but I’d say you may be in for a tough interview,” Lawliss said as he slid his side window down.

Skipping the introductions, Golden announced, “Good work, trooper. We’ve called for the divers. I want you to wait here and direct them to where they’ll need to start looking for any survivors. In the meantime, I’ll take it from here.” Turning his attention to the passenger seat he jerked his thumb in the direction of his car, “My car, Marc. Now.”

Lawliss watched as Marc carefully eased himself out of the troop car, “I think he sustained an injury when the train went into the lake.”

With no compassion, Golden replied, “Too bad.” Then he motioned for Marc to join him.

Marc said, “Tim, before you get started, you should know there was another person on the train when it went into the water.”

“Who was it, the engineer?” he asked, maintaining his agitated tone.

“Jacques LaFleur, President, or I should say, former President of Barbeau Transport. He’s down there in that fishing boat,” Marc said, pointing toward the end of the pier.”

“Why was he operating the train?” Golden asked with a confused tone.

"This is where it gets complicated. LaFleur was in cahoots with North Korean terrorists, intent on blowing the Laser up when it got to Penn Station."

"Terrorists? Are you on drugs? You're not making any sense. Why would the president of the company be working with terrorists? And who was driving the train?"

Marc ignored Golden's questions and continued, "The train was apparently preprogrammed and ran mostly by itself, sorta like an Uber train. But LaFleur could override the train's program with a specialized wireless device."

Tim hesitated. "Wait. The guy we found on the tracks in Port Kent was a terrorist?"

"Correct. As far as I know, he was a North Korean agent and his name was Khan."

Tim hesitated as he processed this latest revelation.

"Did you have something to do with this Khan ending up on the tracks with a note stuffed in his pants?"

"It was the only way we had of warning someone that the train was under the control of the terrorists."

"*Excusez-moi, Monsieur* Tim," Sylvie interrupted. The man you found on the train tracks up in Port Kent…he was going to kill us, but Marc, with the help of Mr. Karlsson, was able to disarm him. It was too bad he had to die, but we were locked in the baggage car with no way of communicating our circumstance other than to throw him off the train with the note that Marc left on his body.

Tim looked in his rear view mirror at Sylvie, then made a few notes on his pad.

"Mr. Karlsson, can you corroborate this story?"

"Yes, that's about what happened. I cracked the Korean on the head with a hockey trophy, then helped Mr. LaRose throw the body off the train."

"A hockey trophy?" Tim asked.

"That's another part of the story. We can fill in the blanks when we have more time," Marc said.

Tim paused as he thought about their stories.

"I take it then LaFleur's the one they've called the coroner for?"

"Yes," Marc replied.

Tim tapped his pen on his notepad, "Well, let's have a look," he said, he voice less stern. He again looked into his rear view mirror at Sylvie, "Detective Champagne, you want to come along or, would you prefer to remain in the car."

"I think I should see this as well," she said.

Before heading out to the boat, Tim retrieved a camera from the trunk of his car. As the three walked down the wooden pier their steps echoed off the lake just a few feet beneath them. At the dock, they could see a white sheet had been placed over the body and the two EMT's stood next to an empty gurney, its wheels locked in place.

Tim climbed into the boat and pulled the sheet back.

LaFleur's lips had turned purple, which contrasted with his pale skin. What blood that was left in his body was sinking into his torso. His mouth was gaped open and his unblinking eyes stared across the bay, toward Fort Ticonderoga. The open hole in his chest seemed more obvious than before.

"Besides being the President of Barbeau Transport, what can you tell me about him?" Tim asked.

Marc paused. "This may take a few minutes." He then went on to relate how LaFleur had conspired with a Barbeau employee, Jimmy Lee and the North Korean government to design the Laser with secret compartments and how Karlsson had learned of the compartments and then been kidnapped, which got Marc involved in the case.

"Secret compartments? I don't understand."

With the pain in Marc's chest getting worse, he briefly went over the pertinent facts of the case involving Karlsson, Jimmy Lee, the Rock'n Rollers Motorcycle gang, Giselle Montclair, then his being held captive by Khan and LaFleur on the train.

Tim scratched his head and glanced down at his notepad, then at the growing mob of people gathered around near the entrance to the pier. "You know, we're going to need full written statements from all of you. There's not much more we can do here, let's head back to my car."

By the time they got to shore, the Troop Commander had arrived along with a cadre of troopers including the forensics and dive teams. Tim motioned for Marc, Sylvie and Karlsson to continue to his car while he conferred with the Commander.

"Looks like I'm going to be turning this over to my Lieutenant when he gets here, but I have to ask you, how did LaFleur get that injury to his chest?"

"After the dining car crashed into the water, I found him in back of the open freezer door. He was pinned against the wall by the door and a small mountain of loose debris. I think LaFleur probably opened the freezer door just before the car hit the water. The force of the crash would have pushed his body against the door stopper, and then the door slammed against him and was held there by all the debris pushing against it. I suppose either of those actions could have carried enough force to pierce his chest. The stopper had a round blunt rubber tip which could account for the size of the wound."

"Wonder what he was going to do in the freezer?" Golden asked.

Marc reflectively shrugged his shoulders, wincing as he did so, "Beats me, maybe he had a sudden craving for an Eskimo Pie, or possibly, knowing the ricin bombs were going to explode when the train arrived in Saratoga, felt he could escape its deadly effects if he locked himself inside the freezer. I guess he didn't count on the train derailing after it hit the trestle and crashing into the bay."

By this time, several more police cars had arrived. The place was looking like a parking lot for a police convention. Within a minute, they were joined by three state police plain-clothed investigators. Having worked with many of them in his past career, he recognized all, except one, the shortest of the group, the one the others deferred to as 'The Lieutenant.'

Tim said, "Hold on. I'll be right back."

Marc watched as the Zone Commander and the Lieutenant conferred with Golden. Marc surmised that Golden was bringing them up to speed on what he knew. As they talked they occasionally glanced toward the body then over to where Marc, Sylvie and Karlsson were standing.

A few moments later, a woman in a white lab coat arrived. She briefly conferred with the Lieutenant and Tim. Marc recognized her as the coroner's physician, apparently sent to officially pronounce LaFleur dead.

"I wonder where they'll take the body?" Sylvie whispered.

"Probably to the local hospital for a post mortem. They'll need to do an autopsy to confirm the cause of death."

As the EMT's were loading LaFleur's body onto the waiting gurney, the Lieutenant made his way to where Marc and Sylvie were standing.

"So, you're the famous Marc LaRose," he said, more as a statement than an inquiry as he extended a hand.

Through the Lieutenant's practiced grin Marc could see a row of sculptured teeth that seemed too perfect, save for the quarter inch gap between his front incisors. Marc also felt his handshake was a little too firm, like he needed to make a point.

"I am Marc LaRose, but I wouldn't say I was famous," Marc responded, then nodding toward Sylvie, "this is Brossard, Quebec Detective, Sylvie Champagne."

"I am Lieutenant John Bucholt, acting head of the Bureau of Criminal Investigation for Troop B," he said with a voice Marc thought had an annoyingly reedy sound.

Marc saw Sylvie wince slightly as Bucholt gripped her hand with a shake.

"It is my understanding that you were both involved in this, eh, accident," Bucholt said, retaining his split-toothed grin.

Marc answered, "Well, I was on the train when it crashed into the water, but Sylvie, er, Detective Champagne was not. She got off the train in Essex when the passenger car separated from the locomotive and dining car."

Bucholt's gaze turned toward the remains of the train trestle for a moment, then he slowly turned back toward Marc. "So, I understand the Laser's engine and dining car are at the bottom of the bay, but somehow, the last two cars became separated back in Essex," he said, motioning toward the damaged train trestle. The American flag was visible with Fort Ticonderoga in the background.

"They became separated, but the separation of the cars was intentional."

"What do you mean?" Bucholt asked.

“We, Detective Champagne, Hugo Karlsson and myself, knew what Jacques LaFleur and Khan, the North Korean agent, were up to. When the train was forced to stop in Essex by a liquid manure wagon that got stuck on the tracks, Mr. Karlsson and I separated the train cars so at least the people in the passenger car would be safe.”

“So, what you’re saying is that Mr. Karlsson, the detective and you, are heroes in all this,” Bucholt said, his upper lip pulled even with his nostrils, exposing the gap in his teeth for a full examination.

“I wouldn’t exactly say that,” Marc said. “We saw what needed to be done. I just assisted Mr. Karlsson the best I could. There were a lot of innocent people on that train.”

“I see,” Bucholt said, somewhat reluctantly. “How many people do you think are still in the water?”

“To the best of my knowledge, the deceased and I were the only ones left on the train when it jumped the tracks. But I never made it inside the locomotive, so I couldn’t say with a hundred-percent certainty.”

“You’re aware that the governor’s office was expecting the train to arrive in Albany where he and others were to board it for the final leg to Penn Station?”

“Yes, that was my understanding. Lucky for them and for everyone around Penn Station, as well as the City of Saratoga, the Laser’s maiden voyage ended right there,” Marc said nodding toward the bay.

Bucholt paused, “What do you mean, lucky for them?”

“The Laser was fitted with a pair of bombs packed with enough weaponized ricin to kill hundreds, if not thousands of people upon reaching its originally-intended destination.”

“I’m sorry. What do you mean original destination? Was there an alternate target in mind?” Bucholt asked, the tip of his tongue flicking through the gap in his teeth.

Marc briefly related the facts and his actions as he had previously told them to Tim Golden.

As Marc finished, Bucholt made a few notes, then continued to stare off at the ruined train trestle. By now, Mark’s rib cage was beginning to throb. He pulled his arms across the sides of his chest in an effort to ease the pain.

"Look, Lieutenant, I've already related most of what I know. I'd be happy to continue this conversation, but, right now, I need to see a doctor."

"Just a few more questions," he said, his tongue flicking with anticipation. "Tell me about the other people with Investigator Golden.

Marc glanced toward Golden's car. "The woman is a City of Brossard, Quebec Detective, Sylvie Champagne. She was assisting me in locating the target of a missing person assignment I was working on."

"And the man?"

"He's the subject of my missing person case, Hugo Karlsson." They were both locked in the baggage car with me when the train left Montreal this morning."

Bucholt's brow furrowed. "What was Karlsson's role in this matter? How did he get involved with you and Detective Champagne on a terror train bound for New York?"

"He works for Barbeau Transport as the lead engineer for the Laser project," Marc said as he felt another sharp spasm of pain in his chest.

Just then he heard the back doors of the ambulance close. LaFleur's body had been loaded in for the trip to the hospital morgue and it appeared the EMT's were getting ready to leave.

"Lieutenant, as much as I want to cooperate, I think I may have broken a couple of ribs when the dining car hit the water. I'm sure you have many more questions. You can either accompany me in the ambulance, or drive me to the hospital. I really need to see a doctor."

Marc could tell that Bucholt was a man used to getting his way, as he gave Marc a disapproving look, hesitated a moment, then motioned toward Tim Golden to come where he and Marc were standing. "Mr. LaRose says he needs medical attention. I want you to take him to the Moses-Ludington Hospital emergency room in Ticonderoga for an examination. When you're through there, I want you to personally transport him to the Plattsburgh barracks."

The three waited as the ambulance pulled away, its emergency lights flashing, but without activating its siren en route to the hospital's morgue.

“Yes sir,” Golden said, returning his attention to his boss. He then glanced to where Karlsson and Sylvie were standing, “How about the Canadian detective and Mr. Karlsson?”

“I’ll take care of them. You just make sure LaRose gets back to the Plattsburgh station as soon as the doc’s finished,” Bucholt said as his lips pulled back in a natural sneer.

Marc thought the gap in Bucholt’s front teeth seemed to have grown a little wider.

“One other thing, Investigator Golden.”

“Sir?” Golden responded.

“Under no conditions are you to let LaRose out of your sight. Is that understood?”

“Yes, sir.”

As they walked toward Golden’s car, Marc asked, “Does that mean I’m under arrest?”

“Marc, do yourself and me a favor,” Golden said in a hushed tone.

“What’s that?”

“Keep your mouth shut and get into the fucking car.”

When the two had closed their doors, Golden asked, somewhat sympathetically, “Need help with your seatbelt?”

“I can manage,” Marc replied as he struggled through the pain to secure his shoulder harness. When he looked back toward Karlsson and Sylvie, he saw they were being escorted to another unmarked police car.

Golden made the turn onto the Fort Ticonderoga road in the direction of the hospital and for the first mile, they continued in silence.

“Look Tim, I get that you’re pissed that I didn’t get back to you after we last spoke, but believe me, things were happening pretty fast.”

Tim gave Marc another sideways glance.

“You ignore my calls and leave me in the dark, then whenever something happens, you come crying for help. It’s a pattern you seem to have developed lately.”

“You have to understand, Tim, I don’t live in the same structured world you do. With you, it’s a matter of receiving an assignment, developing a plan of action, gathering the resources, then, after receiving the OK from someone higher up like your friend with the Howdy Doody smile, you and your cadre proceed at a cautious pace. With me, it's usually, move now, or get hurt."

They rode in silence for a few moments.

"So Marc, do you really need to see a doctor, or do you have something else in mind that could cost me my job?"

"Relax. I'd like a doctor to examine me to make sure there's nothing else wrong. I took a pretty bad jolt when that train car hit the water. I just need some meds to help with the pain before I have to face that boss of yours again."

Two hours later, the pair had left the hospital and were heading north on I-87 to Plattsburgh. X-rays had shown Marc had two cracked ribs. The oxycodone the doctor prescribed was beginning to kick in and Marc was beginning to feel more comfortable.

"So Marc, what the hell happened up at Fort Montgomery? We still have those two Canadian hit men locked up on gun charges, but we can't keep them there forever. And what was up with the old guy? A toxicology report showed he was pretty doped up on Ketamine. When we interviewed him he seemed confused. He didn't know anything about his captors or even how he got to the Fort."

"Believe it or not, that was an internal problem between the Montreal mob, LaFleur and the North Korean agent, which served as a diversion with the Laser being used as a weapon of mass destruction."

"That's the kind of diversion that could have gotten someone killed," Tim said.

"Those guys play for keeps, and for big bucks. Maurice Bashaw is a Montreal crime boss who felt he was getting screwed by LaFleur. He and his gang will do just about anything for five-million bucks."

"Well, the old guy, Guillaume, or whatever his name is, is still in the hospital. We've sent his fingerprints to the Quebec Provincial Police to confirm his ID, but we haven't heard back from them yet. He's probably a derelict they picked off the street."

Marc went on to fill Tim in on the rest of the case during the hour-long trip to the Plattsburgh State Police substation. As they pulled into the station's parking lot, Marc spotted Lieutenant Bucholt's unmarked car parked behind the station.

"Oh goody, it's Howdy Doody time," Marc said, mimicking the first verse of the 50's children show as he nodded toward the sedan.

"Easy, Marc. Remember your episode with Captain Amos Welch after your escapade up in Lake Placid? Be careful with this guy. Bucholt is as hard as nails and if he finds a crack in your story, he'll make your life miserable and won't think twice about hanging a criminal charge over your head."

As they approached the rear door of the station, Marc noted the sign above the door, "Authorized Personnel Only," Tim waved a proximity card over a reader.

"That's new," Marc said.

"Lots of things have changed since you left the job."

Bucholt had apparently seen Tim's car drive into the lot and met the two as they entered the building.

"Take him to the back interview room," Bucholt said, motioning toward Marc with a nod. "I'll join you in a few minutes."

Marc and Tim walked down a corridor with several office doors on either side. Bucholt followed a short distance behind, then opened a door Marc and Tim had passed and entered, closing it behind him.

Continuing toward the end of the hallway, Marc thought the air felt a little stuffy.

"You guys on an austerity budget or is your AC busted?"

"The AC's fine. It's probably the meds the doc gave you."

Marc grunted in response.

As they came to the last door, Tim held it open for Marc to enter.

The walls of the room were wood paneled with one window that overlooked the rear parking lot. There were two desks, one in each of the opposite corners of the room, each with a chair behind and two in front.

"Some things have changed, but this room looks about the same as it did when I left here almost six years ago, except for that air vent. What's up with that?" Marc said, pointing toward a grill along an outer wall.

“Better that you don’t know. Let’s say it was the result of a little misunderstanding.”

“A misunderstanding?” Marc said, suspiciously noting the two-foot square vent that was about shoulder high. “You mean the kind where someone misunderstood a question and had his head shoved through the paneling? I know it’s hard to patch wood paneling, but an air vent?”

Tim rolled his eyes. “Remember what I said about asking too many questions.” Then after a pause, he continued, “might just as well have a seat. No telling how long he’ll be,” he said, ignoring Marc’s quip about the oddly-placed air vent.

Marc gave a knowing smile, then slowly eased himself into one of the chairs facing the end desk. The top of the desk was clear except for an old ashtray that now served as a paperclip container. The oxy dulled the pain, but his ribs still hurt. Tim took the chair next to him.

“You still have a coffee pot around here somewhere, or have you gone over to using a health conscious juice bar these days?”

“Always the comedian. Cream and sugar?” Tim asked.

Whatever you have that passes for cream. No sugar, please.”

“Pot’s in the patrol room. I’ll be right back. Just don’t go running off,” Tim said as he slid out of the chair and headed for the door.

As Marc waited in the relative silence of the room, listening to the rush of air from a legitimate air vent overhead, he could hear the murmur of voices coming from somewhere else in the building.

A minute later, Tim returned with a single cup of brew and a packet of powdered cream. A wooden stir stick poked above the rim of the cup.

As Marc stirred the coffee, he asked, “Any word on where Sylvie and Mr. Karlsson are?”

“Haven’t seen them,” Tim said without conviction.

Marc gave him a suspicious look as he sipped his coffee.

“Marc, when I passed by the Lieutenant’s office to fetch your coffee, I overheard him on the phone. Sounds like the Troop Commander is up to his neck trying to explain to the Superintendant and the Governor’s office what happened. The parents of the kids in the high school band have been calling, all in different stages of panic."

"Anybody else get hurt?"

"Just a few egos. The Quebec Premier is upset that his own security didn't catch on to what was happening and Customs and Border Protection are questioning their pre-clearance procedure of the train before it left Montreal. Other than that, a couple of buses are transporting everyone back to Plattsburgh. Of course, the National Transportation Safety Board and the FBI have been contacted and will be looking into this mess. In the meantime, I've been charged with babysitting your sad ass, as you are, apparently, the star witness."

Just then, the office door suddenly burst open. Lieutenant Bucholt strode into the room, his jaw set and his lips tightly clamped. Marc noted a throbbing pulse in the vein on his forehead that he hadn't noticed before. Bucholt took the chair behind the desk, facing Marc and Tim, and simply stared at Marc for what seemed like a long minute. Marc remained silent and returned his stare with just a hint of a grin.

"Who the fuck are you?" Bucholt finally asked.

"Marc LaRose, Lieutenant. But I think you already know that," he said, slowly increasing the width of his grin.

Bucholt exhaled loudly through his nose "Do you have any idea of the size of the shit storm you're involved in?" he finally asked.

"I know I barely escaped getting killed in a train car accident, but as far as the 'shit storm' your referring to, that farmer down in Essex did his best to clear the railroad tracks, but the locomotive hit his manure tank and…"

Bucholt exploded, "That's not what I'm referring to, LaRose, and you damned well know it."

"Have we arrived at the point where I need to ask for my attorney to be present before I answer any more questions?" Marc asked, allowing his grin to fade.

Bucholt's lips pulled back, exposing his toothy gap. He closed his eyes and remained still as if he were going into a mini-trance. "You know exactly what I'm talking about, LaRose. Besides talking with the Superintendent, the Governor's office and various federal agencies for the past hour, I've also had the pleasure of speaking with retired Captain Amos Welch. Remember him?"

"I believe so, Lieutenant. How's Amos enjoying retirement?"

"Captain Welch filled me in on your little escapade up in Lake Placid last year. From what he told me, there are still a few unanswered questions regarding your involvement in that little debacle. That investigation remains open."

"Oh? I figured that was settled when they found the bus and its occupants at the bottom of Cascade Lake," Marc replied calmly.

"You know what I mean, LaRose. The radioactive material that was supposedly on that bus was never recovered."

"That's a pretty deep lake, and as you may know, the mud at the bottom is practically bottomless. My guess is the canisters containing the material are probably still buried somewhere in the mud. But, I'm confused. What's that got to do with what happened today?"

"More loose ends, LaRose. That's what that debacle's got to do with this. This is the same fucking thing. Loose ends, and guess what?"

"Uh…" Marc started to answer, but was immediately cut off.

"There will be no more fucking loose ends. Not with this investigation. Not as long as I am in charge and not as long as you are breathing North Country air." Is that understood?"

Marc paused to collect his thoughts. "Lieutenant, I cooperated fully with Captain Welch as well as the Feds. I gave them all the information I had, as did my associate, Ms. Sophie Horton. If there are still loose ends, it isn't because we didn't cooperate. We did. And I am fully prepared to cooperate with you in this matter. But I expect one thing."

"You are hardly in a position to demand anything."

Ignoring Buckholt's statement, Marc said, "I expect to be treated like any other civilian witness. Yes, I retired from this job because of fucking dinosaurs like Amos Welch, who had no compunction against putting the heads of uncooperative suspects through a wall to get them to talk, and who should have probably retired long before he did."

Nodding briefly toward the faux vent to make his point, Marc continued, "None of that justifies treating me like a criminal. I am prepared to cooperate, and I will. But if you think I'm guilty of something, charge me now. Some very scary and well-prepared terrorists intended to murder countless innocent people today. But thanks to the actions of two very heroic people Hugo Karlsson and Detective Sylvie Champagne, a catastrophic tragedy was thankfully avoided."

Bucholt sat silently as he worked the end of his tongue through the gap in his teeth while he seemed to mull over what Marc had just said.

"It appears that we may have gotten off on the wrong foot, Mr. LaRose. If I have given you the impression that our, um, my trust in your judgment and experience in either of these episodes is in doubt, please accept my apology. Up to this point, at least, there are no plans to charge you with any criminal act. You are free to leave anytime you want. But I'm asking for your cooperation as you are a star witness in this matter and your cooperation is, and will be, a key component in the successful completion of this investigation. I'm aware you have suffered a painful injury as a result of the train accident and are presently taking medication. If you feel you cannot continue with this interview, I will have Investigator Golden transport you to your home or anyplace else of your choosing, within reason. I would greatly appreciate it, however, if you would provide us with your accounting of the events leading up to the derailment at this time while the events are still fresh in your mind. We can get into a more detailed written statement at another time when you feel up to it."

Marc sat quietly as he considered Bucholt's request. After watching the Lieutenant's nervous tongue perform a few more dental calisthenics, he asked, "Where are Detective Champagne and Mr. Karlsson?"

Bucholt's tongue suddenly disappeared from between his dental chasm like a night crawler slipping back into its hole and his lips tightened. He paused before answering. "They're here in the station."

"I want to talk to them."

Again, he hesitated, "Mr. LaRose..." he started, but Marc quickly cut him off.

"Lieutenant, don't patronize me. I've no doubt they're in this building in separate rooms, each being interrogated by teams of detectives who will later compare notes. If I were in charge, that's what I would be doing."

Bucholt exhaled. "You're right. They're both here in the station, as you said, undergoing separate interviews, and as of a few minutes ago, they were giving us written statements. If you're still up to it, now would be a good time to tell us what happened as you saw it, and as soon as we're finished, you can see them both."

Marc looked over at Tim Golden, then returned his gaze toward Bucholt. "If you haven't already, I'd like to call Karlsson's wife and give her the news that her husband is safe."

Bucholt slid the desk phone toward Marc. "Go ahead. Just be sure to tell her he's still talking to the police. He will be transported home as soon as we're finished."

"Fair enough. My phone's probably at the bottom of the St. Lawrence River. I'll need to use your phone book as well."

Bucholt opened his desk drawer, retrieved a phone directory and pushed it in Marc's direction.

"Thanks," Marc said as he opened the book and located Karlsson's home phone number.

A minute later, a sobbing, but elated, Annika Karlsson was thanking Marc for the wonderful news and looking forward to her husband's return home.

As Marc set the receiver back into its cradle, he said, "OK Lieutenant, where do you want me to start."

Bucholt retrieved a portable voice recorder from his desk drawer.

"You know the drill, Mr. LaRose. Start at the beginning with your name, the date, time and location. I'll have the recording transcribed for your signature in a day or two. Are you good with that?"

Marc hesitated. "Sure, let's get this done."

Bucholt slid the device toward Marc and pushed the 'Record' button.

It took Marc over an hour and a half to relay the details of his investigation, intentionally excluding a few instances such as sleeping over at Sylvie's apartment and picking the locks to the security shed at CJ Enterprises. During the recording, Golden was summoned out of the room, but returned shortly afterward. When he was through, Bucholt pushed the 'Stop' button, ending the recording.

Although Marc was finished, Bucholt continued to stare at Marc as though he were in a trance.

A minute later, Marc asked, "Lieutenant, was there something else?"

"Huh? Oh, no, of course not. It's just that, well, that's the wildest story I've ever heard."

Marc pushed back from the desk, "If there's nothing else, I'd like to wait for Detective Champagne and Mr. Karlsson in the lobby."

"We've already transported Mr. Karlsson to his residence," Tim said.

"Oh, OK. How about Detective Champagne?" Marc asked.

"We offered to take her back to Brossard, but she said she wanted to see you first. She's waiting in the lobby."

Bucholt rose from his chair and extended his hand. I'd just like to thank you for your cooperation, Mr. LaRose. As you can imagine, this place is going to be a zoo for the next few days until we can get this sorted out. Again, I'll let you know when your recording has been transcribed and is ready for your signature."

Marc took Bucholt's hand and after a firm shake, he left the office.

Sylvie was sitting in the lobby near a window, staring out onto the parking lot. She turned when she heard the interior door open.

"Ready to go home?" Marc asked as he approached her.

She stood. Marc could see tears welling up in her eyes.

"Marc, thank God you're alright, she said, putting her arms around him.

"Careful, doc says I cracked a couple of ribs."

"Oh, *Je regrette,* I didn't know," she said, releasing her embrace.

"No, don't let go," Marc said. "Just don't squeeze so hard."

"Marc, when I saw you trying to climb back onto the train, I really didn't think you were going to make it. I was so afraid I would never see you again."

Tim came out to the lobby. He hesitated a moment when he saw the two clinging to each other. "When you're ready, the Lieutenant has given me instructions to take you wherever you want to go."

Marc turned, surprised to see Tim standing behind him. "I guess I'm going to need to rent a car, so why don't you take us to my condo. I'll arrange transportation to Canada. My Civic is in a parking garage in Brossard, and Sylvie has to get back home.

"But Marc, the Lieutenant said that…"

"I don't care what the Lieutenant said, Tim. If you don't mind, just take us to my condo."

A corner of Tim's mouth turned up in a perceptive smile. "Sure thing. Whenever you're ready."

Ten minutes later, Sylvie was playing with Rye and Brandy in Marc's kitchen as he went to fetch more kibble.

"Poor babies. Daddy's been away and your bowls are empty. You must be starving."

Marc returned with the cat food, "Speaking of starving, according to the old clock on the wall, it's almost seven-thirty, are you up to having something to eat before we head back to Brossard?"

"Food. Is that all you think about?"

"No, but it has been over twenty-four hours since we last ate anything, and you passed up Tim Horton's when you had the chance."

Sylvie nodded, then gave Marc a guilty smile.

"I'll call Enterprise and see if they're still open," Marc said.

Sylvie remained quiet as she petted Brandy.

"Marc, I called my parents while you were being interviewed today. I've also contacted my detective supervisor. After I explained where I've been, he said to take few days off. How about we order out and head back up to Brossard tomorrow?"

"You mean, stay here for the night? Sure. I'll get started making up the spare bed."

"Marc?" She said, more softly.

"What?"

"Can't we just forget about the spare bed?"

Marc hesitated, "Uh, sure. But I probably should change the sheets on my…"

"Marc? She said, in little more than a whisper."

"What?"

"I think dinner can wait."

"Uh, sure. But, my ribs…"

"Marc?"

Chapter Twenty

The following morning, while Marc was showering, Sylvie found eggs in the refrigerator and scrambled them for breakfast.

As he walked into the kitchen clad in a bathrobe, with his hair still wet from the shower, the toaster popped.

"Hmm, something smells good."

"Great timing," Sylvie said, portioning out the eggs on the plates she'd found in a cupboard. Brandy and Rye played around Marc's bare feet, licking the shower residuals from his ankles. "Sit down before the eggs get cold. Hope you don't mind that I raided your larder for a *petit dejeuner*.

"Not at all. Seems nice to have breakfast without opening a bag and finding a soggy hash brown," Marc said, buttering his toast.

"How do your ribs feel this morning?"

He glanced at her over the rim of his coffee mug. "They're sore, but I'll live."

They sat in silence. Marc felt there was something more to discuss, but he didn't want to, not right yet anyway.

"I guess I should call Enterprise, see what they have for rentals and when they can pick us up," Marc said as he put his empty plate in the dishwasher.

"Go ahead. I'll finish picking up here."

While she was putting things way, Sylvie overheard Marc's end of the conversation. Someone would be around in a half an hour to transport them to the Enterprise car rental.

"Guess I'd better get dressed," Marc said as he hung the receiver back on its hook."

Sylvie looked up at him, "We still have a few minutes. Think you might need some help getting dressed?" she asked with a sly grin.

Marc turned back toward the bedroom, "If you think we have time," he said, letting the robe slip to the floor. Rye immediately saw his chance and crawled under the robe, anxious to play.

As Sylvie closed the dishwasher door, she announced, "nice buns."

On the way to the rental car agency, they passed by Shirley's Flower Shop. Marc looked for her delivery van that was usually parked there. Today it wasn't, even though he could see the 'OPEN' sign hanging in the doorway.

Maybe she's got an early delivery?

As luck would have it, they got the last rental car in the lot, a late model Nissan subcompact with a faulty air conditioner. Marc asked Sylvie to drive, hoping she could explain their situation to the Canadian Customs. The day was promising to be another hot one, and even with the windows open, a sheen of perspiration showed on their faces. That, combined with the fact that Marc only had his retired state police ID and Sylvie had virtually no ID at all immediately caught the Canadian Customs officer's attention as they attempted to cross back into Canada. As Marc expected, they were referred to a secondary inspection, where Sylvie explained what had happened, and how they had ended up in the U.S. without their ID's.

"You were involved in that hijacked train incident with the Quebec Premier on board?" the Canadian Customs supervisor asked.

Sylvie explained in French their predicament to the supervisor that her Detective credentials were taken from her by the terrorist Khan, and they were returning to Quebec for the purpose of recovering Marc's vehicle. After a few phone calls to the Brossard PD and the New York State Police, two hours later, they were finally allowed to continue.

Back in the rental car, Sylvie explained to Marc that the Montreal Police, RCMP and the Quebec Surete all were on the lookout for Khan's gang of thugs. Additionally, the Montreal PD had rounded up Maurice Bashaw and much of his gang and were holding them on aiding terrorism.

"Any word on Giselle Montclair?" Marc asked.

"She's alive and recovering at the hospital in St. Jean, under the watchful eye of the Quebec Provincial Police."

Marc thought for a moment. "Wonder what happened to Jules Barbeau and Jimmy Lee?"

"The detectives interviewed Barbeau's wife, and she hasn't heard from him, but the Montreal Police do have someone fitting his description they found wandering around near the waterfront. He was beaten up pretty bad and had no ID. He's in the hospital recovering from an overdose. Pretty sure it's Jules Barbeau, but they won't know for certain until he's recovered. As for Jimmy Lee, the police suspect the mob got to him right after they discovered he'd double crossed them. The Tesla was located at the old port of Montreal ready to be loaded on a ship bound for South America. There was nothing inside his apartment except some expensive jewelry, a stack of gambling IOUs and his Singapore passport. They think he's probably somewhere at the bottom of the St. Lawrence River keeping Oliver company.

"How do your supervisors feel about your involvement in all this?" Marc asked.

"OK, for the most part. Overall, I think they're pretty satisfied that our department had a part in solving this mess."

Marc looked over at Sylvie, "I can see a promotion for a certain Brossard detective in the near future."

She glanced over at him while she held the car's speed steady at one hundred kilometers an hour. "Possibly. That depends," she replied. The hint of a smile curled the corners of her mouth.

"What do you mean? You were instrumental in preventing a disastrous terror attack."

"Yes, while using an undercover vehicle without proper authorization, entering a building without a warrant, not reporting a kidnapping, plus the loss of a service weapon. And that's just a start. I'll be happy just to keep my job."

"I'm sure you can explain your actions to each of those possible charges, especially in light of the consequences had you not taken the actions you did."

"Hope you're right," Sylvie said without conviction.

The pair continued on in relative silence. A half-hour later, Montreal's skyline appeared in the distance.

"Why don't you drive directly to your condo? I'll take care of the rental. I just hope my Civic's still in the parking garage."

"It should be. You still have a key?"

"Yeah, I brought another spare."

A short while later, Sylvie stopped the Nissan in front of her apartment building. She turned toward Marc and said, "when will I see you again?"

"Hopefully, before the next terrorist decides to cross the border," he said trying to keep their imminent parting as light as he could. "Besides, I'm sure there are going to be a few more interviews, inquiries, and investigations followed by who knows how many court appearances."

She extended her hand, "Well, until then, it's been nice working with you, Mr. LaRose."

Marc glanced down at her hand, took it and drew himself nearer to her and put both arms around her. "Whatever happens, let's promise to stay in touch," he said then kissed her gently. He could see tears welling up in her eyes.

He released her and opened his side door. She got out and met him at the back of the car. They hugged again.

"Goodbye Marc. Give my regards to your partner, Norm," she said as she turned and started up the stairs to her apartment.

"Goodbye Sylvie, and thanks for everything," Marc said as he watched her slip inside the apartment door.

Marc stood, watching the door close. A few moments later, he got back into the car and left for the rental car agency.

Chapter 21

Later that afternoon, and after explaining to the U.S. Customs and Border Protection officers why he was without the proper ID, Marc arrived in Plattsburgh. He decided to stop by the flower shop to check in on Shirley. He had a feeling something was different when he last talked to Ann Marie. He felt she knew something, but wasn't in the telling mood. He noticed the delivery van parked alongside the shop.

When the door chimes announced his entry, Shirley glanced up from the vase of flowers she was working on, then just as quickly returned her attention to the flowers. "What's new, stranger?" she said.

Marc noticed she looked a bit different, but couldn't immediately put his finger on it. "I stopped in a couple days ago, but you weren't around. Ann Marie said you were out on a delivery."

"Yeah, she mentioned you stopped by."

Marc noticed her tone seemed distant.

Although the shop's air conditioner ran a lot in the summer to help keep the flowers fresh, Marc thought it seemed cooler than normal, or was it an attitude that he sensed?

"So, how's everything? Staying busy?" he asked, hoping to warm the chill.

She snipped a stem of baby's breath, then worked it into the vase of white carnations. "Matter of fact, business has been great. It's so good I'm thinking of hiring another designer to help out part-time."

"That's wonderful. I didn't realize the shop was doing so well," Marc said.

"You're so busy with your investigative business, how would you know?"

Marc didn't answer.

"Ann Marie won't be with me forever, and I feel the need to get away from here once in a while."

Then he realized it was her hair that was different. Shirley had always worn it down, the ends of her light brown hair just grazing her shoulders, but today it was pulled back in a sort of a casual up-do, barely covering her ears. Not mentioning it, he continued to watch as she snipped the rubber band holding a bunch of leather leaf fern, then, one by one, began shoving the stems around the base of the arrangement.

Marc could sense there was something else. She was holding something back. “Shirley, is there something I should know?”

She laid the remains of the leather leaf on the counter, exhaled deeply, and looked up at Marc. “I’ve met someone.”

“OK. We both meet people from time to time. I thought that was what we agreed. That we’d see other people, but we’d also look out for each other.”

Shirley hesitated, “Marc, this time it’s different. I know you care but I mean, I’ve met someone who cares about me more than his work, someone with a normal life.”

Although he suspected their ‘arrangement’ wouldn’t last forever, Shirley’s announcement hit him like a sucker-punch, taking his breath away.

Without looking back at Marc, Shirley continued to work on the flower arrangement in what he felt was a way of trying to put an end to the conversation. Marc noticed she had suddenly developed a case of the sniffles.

Marc watched her in silence as he tried to recover from the news.

“I, I’m happy for you. You probably don’t think I am, but really, I am. You deserved better than a part-time husband, and I take the blame for that, but I’ve never abandoned you. I guess I thought maybe someday, we would…” He let his thought trail off.

Shirley reached for a box of tissues, pulled a few out of the container, and gently blew her nose. “I know we both thought that, but deep inside, I knew that could never happen. A part of me still loves you Marc, always will. I just think the time has come for us to move on with our lives,” she said, tears spilling down her cheeks.

“Can I ask, how long have you known him?”

“What difference does that make?” she said. Then before Marc could say anything more, she went on, “almost as long as we’ve known each other.”

“Do I know him?”

"I'm sure you do."

"Has Ann Marie met him?"

"Yes, of course." Shirley exhaled deeply. "I might just as well tell you. You'll find out soon enough, and I think it's better you hear it from me. It's Dave, Dave Fish."

Marc was momentarily taken aback at the news. He remembered working with Dave Fish when they were both uniformed state troopers, but the two had never been close. Marc had gone on to the detective Bureau and Dave had risen to the rank of uniform sergeant. Dave had retired a year or two after Marc. He remembered Dave had lost his wife to cancer just after he retired and to the best of his knowledge, he had since remained jobless, living off his police pension.

"Any chance he'll be helping out in the shop?" Marc asked, curious to know what his former wife had taken on.

"That's up to him, and frankly, Marc, I don't think that's any of your business," she said.

"Sorry, I didn't mean to pry," he said without conviction.

An uncomfortable silence fell between them.

"Look Shirley, if there's anything I can do to help, you know how to get hold of me."

Shirley was wiping her face with a tissue. "Don't worry about me. Just concentrate on helping out with Ann Marie. We both owe it to her to see that she gets through college," she said and started wrapping the vase of flowers in cellophane for delivery.

"I guess this is goodbye then," Marc said.

"Yes, Marc. Goodbye, and good luck," Shirley said, her voice beginning to crack.

Marc felt he was in a trance as he walked back out of the flower shop towards his Civic.

Second time today that a woman has told me 'goodbye'.

He got in, turned the ignition, and sat there for a minute before he put the car in reverse and backed into the street. A honk from an oncoming car he hadn't noticed brought him out of his thoughts. The driver gave him the finger and pulled around him, then, disappeared into traffic.

A few minutes later, Marc slowly climbed the stairs to his office, still somewhat shaken. Thankfully, Norm was out, but he could see there were several messages on his answering machine. The air conditioner was struggling to keep the office at just under eighty degrees.

"Shit, I'll have to get a new cell phone," he whispered to the empty room. He found an opened half-empty can of Coke in the little frig under the coffee machine. The soda was flat, but at least it was cold. He sat in his chair. The answering machine had a blinking '5'. He exhaled, and punched the machine's 'play' button.

The first message was from an ecstatic Annika Karlsson. Hugo had told her how Marc had found him and about the escape from the baggage car. She also stated that a bill for his services wasn't necessary as she was sending him a check that included a nice bonus.

Nice to know not everyone's pissed at me.

The next message was from Tim Golden advising him that his written statement was ready for his notarized signature and that Lieutenant Bucholt had a few more questions for him.

Tim must be in line to make Senior Investigator. About time they promoted someone who deserved it.

Another message was someone from the local paper, the Plattsburgh Standard, wanting to conduct an interview.

I better check with that asshole Bucholt. He might want to keep a few of the details out of the news.

The following one was someone who identified himself as an agent from the local FBI office. He left a callback number stating he wanted to talk as soon as possible.

"What, and waste the remains of this refreshingly flat cola to talk to another suit. Get in line, buster," Marc mumbled as a boyish grin creased his face.

The last call was from someone identifying herself as being from the state governor's office. The caller said that the governor had learned of Marc's actions from the State Police Superintendent that may have saved the lives of countless New Yorkers and wanted to thank him personally. She asked Marc to call her back with a convenient time and place for the Governor to meet with him.

Oh brother, what a photo op that would be with an election coming up. I'd do it only if Sylvie and Mr. Karlsson can be there as well.

As he was finishing the remains of the cola, the desk phone rang.

Shit, probably another request for an interview, he thought. He let the machine pick up the call.

The ringing stopped and after Marc's recorded message, there was empty silence. Marc figured the caller had hung up, then he heard a woman's voice, "Marc, are you there? Please pick up. I have to speak with you." Marc immediately recognized the accent, and the voice. It was Sophie Horton.

I sincerely hope you enjoyed reading *Southbound Terror*, my second in the Marc LaRose Mystery Series.

As an independent author, I depend on you, the reader, to spread the word about my books, which can be done through social media and word of mouth. I publish my books through Amazon.com's 'Create Space' and 'Kindle Direct Publishing'.

Amazon offers the reader the opportunity to 'Review' my books. Book reviews are important for readers and authors alike, whether the author is an indie, like myself, or, an established published author using one of the big publishing houses.

I invite you to review my book by going to Amazon.com and typing *'Southbound Terror'*. Click on the book title, then the 'Reviews' tab. This will bring you to the page where you can 'Write a Review'.

Thanks again,
R. George Clark

ACKNOWLEDGEMENTS

First, I thank God for bestowing me with a full life, one that has allowed me to meet so many wonderful people, endowed me with a loving family and has provided me with a multitude of diverse experiences that have helped formulate the stories for the 'Marc LaRose Mystery Series.'

Early on in my writing career, I was fortunate to associate myself with the Aiken, South Carolina Writer's Association, a special group of talented, patient, and knowledgeable people who freely share their time and expertise to help others meet their writing aspirations.

I will always be indebted to my daughters, Elaine and Lori, for their trust and faith that I could see this project through to completion.

I owe a debt of gratitude to my editor: Ms. Carolee Smith, my readers: Mr. Walter Church, Ms. Carol Morenc, Ms. Lise Heroux and Ms. Rita Malloy. Over the course of writing my books, I received words of encouragement from a list of friends, much too long to mention on this page. You know who you are. Thank You.

Lastly, I am most grateful to have been assisted by my best friend and wife for over fifty years, my lovely Delena, who, without her unrelenting encouragement and reassurance, this story would have been impossible for me to write.